Praise for *Atoning for Ashes*

Atoning for Ashes has it all—sweet romance, brow-raising suspense, and enduring spiritual truths crafted into a multi-faceted gem of a story. A welcome new historical fiction voice sure to win reading hearts!

—Laura Frantz,
Christy Award winning author of *The Lacemaker*

Navigating the shoals of marriage to a volatile stranger tests Josie's love, identity, and even her life. Fans of Victoria Holt will revel in the Cornwall setting, complete with smuggler's tunnels, legendary ghosts, deaths, and disappearances. *Atoning for Ashes* had me shivering in delight!

—Catherine Richmond,
author of *Spring for Susannah*

A gem of a novel, *Atoning for Ashes* is historical fiction at its best. The detailed setting is richly written, and the [illegible]table characters draw you right into a story full of he[illegible]nd redemption. Kaitlin Covel is one to watch[illegible]

aut[illegible]ries

Atoning for Ashes

A NOVEL

KAITLIN COVEL

Dedication

I want to dedicate this novel to my amazing family, who believed in me and my dream. Your loving support made this novel possible. Mom and Dad, thank you for inspiring me to give the gift of words to the world and encouraging me to reflect the light of Jesus Christ in all that I do. Josh and Jon, thank you for your patience, grace, and love as I devoted long hours to the keyboard. I am eternally grateful, and I love you all!

Above all, I wish to dedicate this novel to my Savior, Jesus Christ, who loved me and gave Himself for me. He birthed in me the dream and enabled me to make it a reality. To Him be all the glory both now and forever!

Chapter One

*J*osie had always detested black. As she watched the carriage struggle up the winding drive, the familiar sense of dread seeped into her bones in a damp echo of the rain against the window pane. Father's creditors were after them again like a pack of foxhounds baying at their heels. The black flanks of the carriage glistened, and every stride of the horses shook away moisture as they approached. The aura of impending doom borne upon those wheels reminded her of another carriage, decked in black crepe and bearing the ruthless knowledge that her life would never be the same. Mother was never coming back. Even after a full year of mourning she had never gotten over her revulsion to the deathly color. Her soul still wore the stain.

"Josie."

The breathless voice pulled her back to the present. As she turned from the window, her sister's dark, wide-eyed gaze collided with her own.

"Father's creditors are here," Delia gasped, plunking herself down on Josie's bed. If not for the gravity of the situation, Josie would have smiled as she envisioned Delia tearing up both flights of stairs.

"I know, Delie," she said, slathering the calm on thick to hide her own angst. Though older than Josie's sixteen years,

Delia had always needed mothering. Josie regarded her beautiful sister's rather unladylike appearance with fond amusement. Delia's damp, ebony hair tumbled in wavy disarray around her shoulders, unbound by hairpins or combs. Her breast heaved under the square décolletage of her brown day gown, displaying more than was appropriate at this hour without a lace fichu.

Delia smirked at Josie's bold assessment, clearly not caring whether she met with her approval or not. Her full lips appeared even poutier than usual . . . Josie frowned. They were swollen, as though they had been kneaded by the mouth of a lover.

"Where have you been?" Josie asked as her gaze strayed to Delia's muddied hem. "Father has been fretting."

Delia's nostrils flared. "Merely taking my daily constitutional, little sister."

"In the rain? With whom?" Josie asked. Delia's eyes darted over to the window again.

"With my James," she admitted.

Josie's heart sank. "Oh Delie . . . you promised Father you would not have any more clandestine meetings with him."

Delia tossed her head, pelting Josie's cheek with water droplets. "Really, Josephine," she huffed, eyes flashing. "You can't expect me to abide all of Father's unreasonable demands."

Josie's eyebrows rose in silent exclamation. "I've never expected more of you than I do of myself."

For once in her life, Delia had the grace to look ashamed. She broke Josie's gaze to pick at a stray thread on her lap.

"I tried, you know," she murmured after a moment's contemplation. "But I love him, Josie, and he loves me. Wait until you meet the man who makes your own heart skip a beat."

Josie sighed, outwitted by Delia's worldly wisdom. "Go change into something dry before you catch your death of cold."

"You're not going to tell Father?" Delia demanded.

"Not if you promise me that you won't confess your feelings to him tonight. He has enough on his mind as it is."

"Oh, bless you, Josie," Delia exclaimed, bolting from the bed and kissing her cheek.

Josie shook her head as her sister trotted out of the room. Delia had never walked anywhere in her life at the sedate, lady-like pace their governess had tried to teach them.

Josie tried to absorb herself in a novel until the carriage left, but it failed to distract her from the flutter deep in the pit of her stomach. Her eyes darted toward the window more times than she cared to count.

Finally the carriage turned in retreat, and she exhaled a pent-up breath as it passed through the gate. The book slipped from her hands onto the settee as she ventured out to comfort Father. Only silence met her straining ears as she descended the sweeping curve of the staircase. Her fingers tightened around the polished wood of the balustrade as the doctor's words echoed through her mind. *His heart isn't very strong, and he mustn't get overly excited.* She sent a prayer heavenward.

Another flight of stairs carried her to the foyer, where the head butler met her concerned gaze as he shut the library door behind him.

"Graham, where is Father?"

The butler nodded his gray head toward the door, but as Josie went to open it he raised a gloved hand in warning.

"He doesn't want to be disturbed, Miss Josephine. He is quite upset."

Josie nodded in understanding.

"Thank you, Graham, but I have to go to him."

"Very well, Mistress. God knows you are the one who can do him the most good." Graham swung open the door with a sad smile.

"Miss Josephine to see you, sir," he announced.

Josie stepped over the threshold and inhaled the lingering scents of leather, musty pages, and pipe tobacco. Father stood at his desk pouring a glass of port, and the lip of the decanter clanked as his hands shook. He took a deep swig, draining the burgundy liquid with an alacrity that made Josie wince. She intercepted his hand as he went to pour a second, or perhaps it was his third.

"Oh, Father," she murmured. "Come, come sit down now. You are unwell."

He did not protest as she led him to his favorite chair by the fireplace, and he collapsed with a heavy sigh. Josie sank to her knees on the Turkish carpet and rested her arms across his knees as she had once done as a girl. She reached for his hand, squeezing some warmth into the cold fingers once so strong and sure. Her heart twisted as she gazed up into the beloved face ravaged by worry and defeat, aware that the Randolph Chadwick she had always known was slipping away from her.

She pressed her lips against the cool flesh and prominent bone of her father's hand. His distant gaze was fixed upon the window as though he were mesmerized by the rain pecking against the glass. Just when it seemed he was unaware of her presence, his hand reached out and smoothed the hair away from her brow.

"Ah, Josie," he murmured as his mild blue eyes locked with hers at last. Josie summoned a smile for him, but she sensed it falter even as she tried to be strong.

"Is it very bad, Father?"

He raked fingers through dark hair heavily peppered with gray.

"It's bad, Josie my girl," he admitted after a moment's hesitation. "I won't try to hide it from you any longer. The mine is not as profitable as it used to be, while it seems our debts continue to increase. I was desperate, but I see now that I was a fool to invest in such a risky venture as Harrison's mills. The price of cotton is going down, not up, since that blasted tariff." He cleared his throat, and when he spoke again his voice sounded drained of life's vital force. "Harrison was forced to declare bankruptcy. I was counting on those profits to pull us through, but now it seems our only hope lies in Delia capturing the heart of some wealthy nobleman's son at her coming out as heiress of Chadwick Park."

Josie fought against it—the sickening, drowning feeling of knowing beyond all doubt that her father placed all hope upon his undependable eldest.

His gaze grew perplexed, and she bit out the lie.

"Of course, Father. Some rich, handsome heir will come and sweep her off her feet."

The fairy-tale nonsense struck her like a slap in the face. She just couldn't bring herself to kill the fragile hope she saw breathing life back into him. *After all, this is Delia's life, and I can't do everything for her. It is her responsibility to explain her heart to Father.*

Father smiled as he squeezed her hand. "I want to contact my solicitors in London and make it plain that Delia must inherit the estate upon her twenty-first birthday and not upon my death. We have already closed off the west wing due to disrepair, but this neglect cannot continue. George just recently informed me of his concerns that if the roof continues to buckle, it will damage the servants' quarters."

Josie bit her lip as the knowledge that she knew nothing of such matters prevailed over her instincts to warn him against making a decision that would enable Delia's future husband to uproot them from their own home. She had seen this happen before when a financial decline forced the hand of a reputable family. Just last month the Harrisons had been forced to sell their country estate and move to their townhouse in London.

Her own future had always been as clear as muddied waters, overshadowed by the favor shown to her beautiful older sister. Even as Father spoke of Delia's coming out in society, the blank of her own existence gaped. Her fate had always been uncertain. Doubtless after Delia became the heiress of Chadwick Park, no dowry would remain to tempt a suitor of means. The thought did not bother her half as much as the result. She had always cherished the secretive dream of marrying for love, but penniless daughters often attracted only the interest of widowers or the pity of bachelors.

In her heart another thought warred. She refused to become a spinster, living off her family like the leeches that had sucked the life from her mother's body when Josie was eight. The alternative, seeking employment, did not seem much better—but she was confident that the name of Chadwick would bear her in good stead. She was a lady of education and refinement, with an ample grasp of French, music, and needlework. Surely some reputable family would be in need of a governess or lady's companion—but even as she tried to ignore the twinge of doubt that arose at the thought, she knew that her mind would dig it up later to worry over the way a dog worries a bone.

The door swung open, and Josie shot to her feet. A calm, wise gray gaze met hers in a gentle air of inquiry.

"Esther," she said.

Esther's soulful strength emanated from her as she approached father and daughter, her dress flowing around her like an ebbing tide. Father attempted to rise, but the woman's slender fingers brushed his shoulder in protest.

"Please remain seated, Mr. Chadwick." Esther's familiar Scottish brogue steadied Josie's heart as her governess reached for her hand. "Sorry if I startled ye, luve. Och, yer fingers are frozen."

Esther tugged the plaid shawl from her shoulders and wrapped it around Josie with a soothing touch. Her full lips curved in satisfaction as she chucked Josie's chin. Then her expression sobered as she probed Josie's, voicing a silent question.

Josie shook her head slightly, and as Esther turned away, her slender shoulders slumped. "What a dreich day it is, and the fire barely lit," she lamented as she gave the dying coals a reproving nudge with the poker. Only as the rosy light slanted across her stunning features did Josie read the fear written there. Father gave a dismissive wave of his hand.

"Let the servants worry about such things, Esther," he muttered. Esther straightened with the poker still clasped in her slim hand, composure regained once more.

"I ken ye cannae afford to heat all of these rooms, but I cannae bear the thought of my wee bairns being cold neither," she stated.

Father's lined features softened with the warmth of admiration as they always did when he beheld the face of Esther McAllister.

"Delia and Josie are no longer children," he began, but then the corners of his eyes crinkled and took years off him. "But they always will be to you, will they not?"

A smile lit Esther's face and filled the dim room with sunshine.

"Aye."

Father cleared his throat as the worry clouded over again. "Josie and I were just discussing the details of Delia's coming out. But the money I had set aside must go to satisfy my debt to Mr. Creighton now that Harrison's mill has gone bankrupt. I should pay a visit to Mr. Radcliffe and see if he is still interested in purchasing the back pasture."

Josie tensed at the mention of their neighbor, a former captain in Her Majesty's Royal Navy who resided in the pretentious estate of Treathston Heights just up the road. Sebastian Radcliffe had drawn the envy of many gentlemen in Cornwall for the sound business sense that had elevated him to the position of a gentleman—one whose vast wealth and property contended with that of the born bluebloods. He was also Father's gambling partner, and Josie suspected that his luck at the dice box had only plunged them deeper into debt.

Father creaked to his feet, and the poker clanked to the flagstones as Esther stepped forward with an air of iron resolve.

"Ye'll do nothing of the sort in this downpour. I'll have Eliza fix ye a hot toddy, and then it's off to bed with ye. All this excitement cannae be good for yer heart. Remember what the doctor said. Ye can visit him in the morning."

"You are right of course, Esther," Father admitted, and Josie was relieved that he was too exhausted to protest.

Josie watched as Esther went to call Eliza, and even in her exhaustion she found herself smiling. Though she was far past needing the services of a governess, she couldn't imagine life without Esther. She was more of a mother to her than Josie's own had ever been. Whatever social conventions they might be defying, the Scottish governess had become family the day she entered their lives and won their hearts. No doubt Father was just as reluctant to part with the woman who had become so much more to his motherless girls once Delia was wed.

Chapter Two

Charles Radcliffe leaned across the gray stallion's neck as the rosy brilliance of the sunrise began to fade. His breath blew wisps of the silken black mane into the briny air as he murmured, "Stalwart, give me your all."

The stallion's velvet ear swiveled to catch his words above the roar of the crashing waves. Stalwart's nostrils flared with an expulsion of steamy breath as his curved ribs swelled and released. Charles inhaled along with the stallion, closing his eyes as the sea air filled his lungs and salty spray kissed his cheeks. Stalwart broke into his powerful gallop as Charles reined him away from the endless blue of the cliff's edge and into the sloping green expanse of the estate. The wind cleansed his mind and freed him. It was only in times like this, as he thundered along at breakneck speed astride Stalwart, that he ever found peace—as though the ghosts of the memories that haunted his past couldn't catch him.

His greatcoat snapped behind him in billowing folds of wool as he exulted in the stallion's roiling muscles beneath him. At last, he swung Stalwart's magnificent head around with a sense of regret. The rising sun had long since melted the dew that clung to every tuft of early spring grass. Stalwart snorted and hesitated as though echoing his master's sentiments, but

Charles didn't waver from his course as he dug his heels into the stallion's ribs.

No doubt another load of responsibility awaited him in the hours ahead.

Just over the rise, the forbidding outline of Treathston Heights rose to pierce the sky. It was an ominous affair of dark turrets and windswept stone that clung to the steep cliffside with a tenacity that had defied the ocean storms since the Dark Ages. The fortress had resisted all human attempts to tame or civilize it since.

A warm rush of pride surged through Charles's chest as his gaze rested on the modernized stables in the distance. Under his direction, the stables that had fallen into disrepair had been expanded and renovated with the hopes of one day fulfilling his dream to breed a line of strong, pure-blooded thoroughbreds. Stalwart was only the beginning.

Charles patted his mount's neck with fondness as he thought of the foals he would sire. Surely they would possess the same fine carriage of head, the same depth of withers for endurance and speed. Stalwart's hooves crunched over the drive and sent a spray of gravel flying. Charles drew rein until the stallion slowed to a trot. He frowned as he approached the sprawling brick structure, recognizing the bay gelding of Mr. Chadwick in one of the guest stalls, where Alfie the stableboy fed him a carrot from his outstretched palm. Charles dismounted and tossed the reins to Alfie, raking his fingers through his windswept blond hair.

"Has Mr. Chadwick been here long?"

"He arrived shortly after breakfast, sir," Alfie replied, controlling the spirited stallion's head with some difficulty. Charles nodded and clapped the boy on the shoulder. "See that you give Stalwart a good rubdown, you hear?"

"Yes sir," Alfie exclaimed, beaming with pride.

Charles strode across the yard, swinging his crop like a pendulum as his anxiety mounted. Something didn't feel right to him about this visit. The broad oak door swung open, and the butler gave him a starched bow.

"Good morning, Master Charles."

"Craven, where is Father?" Charles demanded.

"He has received Mr. Chadwick in the drawing room, sir," Craven replied, his tone implying the audacity of such an early morning visit. "May I take your greatcoat, sir?"

Charles ignored the butler's efforts to assist him and shrugged off his coat, muttering what a cumbersome garment it was. He flung it without ceremony in Craven's general direction before making his way to the drawing room. All the while, the ridiculous sum that Mr. Chadwick owed his father in the form of a gambling debt danced before his eyes as though the page in the ledger was directly before him. He alone knew how much his father coveted the land that comprised the impressive estate of Chadwick Park. He suspected the gullible Mr. Chadwick was unaware that he played with fire.

He paused just outside of the cracked drawing room door, and the voices carried to his straining ear.

"It's official then?" Mr. Chadwick inquired.

"Perfectly legal and aboveboard, Randolph," Charles's father assured him with the suave smoothness his son despised. His gut clenched with dread as his father continued, "I have forgiven a generous portion of your debt and agreed to pay the aforementioned amount in exchange for the north pasture. The ink is drying as we speak."

Paper shuffled in the background. "As for the other matter we discussed, I shall have to speak with Charles before we can proceed any further, but I have no doubt he shall see the merit of such an arrangement. He has a good, reasonable head on his shoulders. I've taught him well."

Sebastian laughed, but Charles's ear detected the subtle undercurrent of mockery. He stomped to mark his approach before shoving the door open the rest of the way. He would risk his father's ire before listening to such insinuations a moment longer.

"Ah, here he is now," Sebastian Radcliffe said, and Charles recognized the shrewd gleam in his eyes. "We were just talking about you, my boy."

Charles's words dripped with contempt. "Were you indeed?"

He bowed slightly to Mr. Chadwick as etiquette demanded before his gaze strayed to the document on the table.

"Your father has generously agreed to purchase the north pasture from me, Charles. Perhaps you will put it to good use for those fine horses of yours, eh?"

Charles glanced up as his brows knit in concern. Father had wanted that pasture for years, but Chadwick had always resisted.

"Perhaps. It is indeed a fine piece of land, sir," Charles allowed. He disliked the familiar way the man regarded him.

Mr. Chadwick waved his hand. "Well, I'm sure you will be able to put it to better use than I. When I was a lad like yourself I could ride, but now these old bones creak a bit more than I'm apt to admit."

He chuckled and rose with hobbled, painful movements. Pity stabbed Charles's heart. Living beyond his means had aged Mr. Chadwick beyond his years.

"I'll show myself out, Sebastian. No doubt you will want to have a chat with young Master Charles here," Mr. Chadwick said with a wink.

Sebastian laughed at the private joke, setting Charles's nerves on edge as the men shook hands and Mr. Chadwick departed. Charles gritted his teeth as he turned to face his sire.

"Well, Father?" he prompted.

Sebastian Radcliffe fixed his son with an intense look that Charles knew all too well. His blue-eyed gaze was as sharp as tempered steel.

"You expressed admiration for the eldest Chadwick girl, did you not?"

A vision of the dark beauty with spirit to match her coloring arose in Charles's mind. "Yes, what of it?" Charles demanded, his temples beginning to throb.

"Her father just sold me the north pasture in hopes of giving her a suitable coming out in London this next season. Given her beauty and considering that she will become the heiress to Chadwick Park as soon as she comes of age, she shouldn't have any difficulty in winning the hand of a worthy suitor."

Charles inspected the tip of his riding crop with a critical eye, feigning disinterest. "Well, it won't be me. As I recall, Miss Delia Chadwick is an untamed beauty. I could liken her to a wild rose . . . her thorns are as sharp as her petals are soft."

Father did not flicker an eyelid, and Charles knew he was stubborn as a bulldog when he had sunk his teeth into a juicy arrangement.

"A very apt and cunning description, my boy, but it is high time I taught you a thing or two about women. A beautiful woman and spirited horseflesh have a lot in common. Both can be tamed or broken by one who knows how to handle them."

Charles tightened his jaw. "But that is just it, isn't it, Father? Mother broke you. She took your heart in her dainty fingers and crushed it under her slippered heel. You could never tame her. She ran off with another man as wild as ever."

Father's eyes flashed blue sparks. "Then don't make the same mistake I made."

"Oh, come now, Father," Charles protested. "Surely there are plenty of other beautiful women who could be had for only half the trouble."

"None of whom are the heiress of Chadwick Park. Miss Delia Chadwick inherits the estate in its entirety at the age of twenty-one. Son, the name of Radcliffe possesses wealth in abundance. What we lack is the land. Chadwick Park has hundreds of acres that adjoin perfectly with those of Treathston Heights. Consider how vast a property she will inherit! Think of all the assets you would own should you combine them and reflect carefully before you decide. You have a good, sensible head on your shoulders, unlike the rest—foppish society dandies who have nothing better to do with their time than to party, chase skirts, and gamble their fathers' hard-earned fortunes away. Don't throw away this chance, my boy. I promise you, you will never see one like it again."

Charles struck the crop's handle against his leg. "Dash it, what do I know about courting?"

Sebastian laid a hand on his son's broad shoulder, their stocky frames alike though Charles was a good head taller.

"Miss Delia Chadwick is no fool, son. She isn't going to find a better match than you unless she aspires to royalty. I have made Mr. Chadwick an offer he can't refuse."

Charles's eyebrows rose at this new piece of information. "What offer?"

"I have offered to pay off the rest of his debts upon the event of your marriage to Delia."

Charles sighed, oppressed by the fire in his sire's eyes. It would never cease until he gave in. It had always been that way, even if Charles didn't wish to risk a woman's betrayal again.

"All right, Father, all right," he ground out between clenched teeth. "I'll give it a go."

Father's teeth flashed white as a broad smile split his tan face.

"That's my boy," he exclaimed as he slapped him on the back.

Charles grimaced under the approval, withering under the strain of trying to please a man whose ambitions stretched as broad and endless as the distant horizon. One day his father's approval would come at too high a cost, and the grim foreboding rippled through the lining of his gut as he faced the question. How high a price was he willing to pay to atone for his mother's sins?

Chapter Three

"Do you remember when you glued the handle back onto the imported French chocolate pot just in time for mother's guests to be served?" Josie asked her sister, inhaling the fragrant steam wafting from her teacup.

Delia snorted around her lemon biscuit. "How could I ever forget poor Agnes's face when she was left holding just the handle and standing in a puddle of steaming chocolate?"

Josie choked and sputtered on her tea in a most unladylike manner. A mischievous light crept into Delia's eyes as she squinted through imaginary pince-nez and mimicked in a squeaky voice, "Now isn't that just like the hot-blooded Frenchmen? Blowing up without the least provocation."

Josie's gut seized with a spasm of silent laughter so strong she held her side as tears squeezed from her eyes. "Stop, please stop," she gasped out as Delia's lips curved in amusement.

"I'll stop tormenting you," Delia conceded with a sigh. "But it was delightful to make you laugh again. With your face all crumpled and your nose all scrunched up." Delia did a perfect imitation, wiggling her pert nose and scrunching her eyes. "You look like a wabbit."

Josie thrust a warning finger in her sister's direction, determined not to give Delia the satisfaction. A smile tugged at lips that she struggled to fix in a frown of stone.

"Beware or your face will freeze that way," Josie cautioned with mock sternness. Delia giggled, and Josie smiled at the sweet, girlish innocence of the sound as she poured her sister's second cup, still holding back her laughter. She missed the Delia of yesterday . . . the sister who never withheld a single secret or went anywhere without dragging her along.

Setting the teapot back down, she contemplated Delia's ravishing features across the rim of her teacup. How Josie hated change . . . how she wanted to hold on to everyone she loved and keep them safe and sound forever. Her fingernail traced the crackling glaze over the roses on mother's teapot as the tea slid soothing and strong down her throat.

Delia opened her mouth to fire a fitting retort, but the dining room door swung open behind her before she got the chance.

Josie glanced up and met Father's amused grin.

"I know you both will forgive my rude intrusion upon your tea when I tell you that Delia has a gentleman caller awaiting her in the drawing room."

Delia squealed as her cheeks flushed pink with pleasure, no doubt expecting James. But unease rippled through Josie's gut, erasing all traces of amusement. Father was much too pleased with himself for it to be James. Delia pinched more color into her blooming cheeks and bit her lips for the maximum effect of heightened feminine charm before rushing from the room. Josie knew the looking glass in the hall would halt her along the way. She turned sober eyes upon her father.

"Who is the gentleman in question?"

Father beamed as he took a seat beside her.

"Guess," he exclaimed, chucking her beneath the chin.

"Well, really I, I—" Josie sucked in a trembling breath, willing herself to sit straight and level her gaze. "I really couldn't begin to guess. Suppose you tell me."

"Charles Radcliffe has come courting," Father announced with a broad grin. "I gave him my heartfelt permission."

Josie hesitated, but her heart would not allow her to remain silent. "Well, that is wonderful news, of course. Indeed, Father, I think Mr. Radcliffe a very honorable gentleman, but —" Josie faltered, gnawing at her bottom lip.

"But what, my dear?"

"But perhaps you ought to have first asked Delia whether her affections were already engaged elsewhere," Josie blurted.

"That commoner James?" Father scoffed. "You know I would never allow it, Josie. That's calf love. Delia's future, nay your future and the very future of Chadwick Park, rests upon her making just such a wealthy match as Charles Radcliffe. Of course every young woman will have her girlish fancies and fairy tales, but to allow her to act upon them at such a tender age would be foolish indeed. No doubt she will come around, especially when she knows that Mr. Radcliffe has agreed to pay off our debt in its entirety upon the marriage. He will be able to provide for her every need—unlike a dirt-poor miner from the village."

Josie's mouth dropped open as she stared at him, and it was quite some moments before she remembered to close it again.

"But, but why should he be so generous?" she stammered.

"I own I was astonished myself, but I think he found the notion of joining the estate of Treathston Heights with that of Chadwick Park too enticing a prospect to resist. Doubtless he possesses the means. Do you do such a discredit to

Delia's beauty, Josie, that you would consider Charles's interest improbable?"

"Of course not, Father," Josie protested. "Delia possesses a charm coupled with such a face and form that no doubt most men would consider her bewitching indeed. My doubt lies in Delia's . . . maturity in such matters."

Father's mild blue eyes hardened. "Her decision has already been made for her. If she dares to defy me in this matter, I will not hesitate to threaten disinheritance, nay, disownment!"

All of the blood drained from Josie's face. He had never raised his voice to her in such a manner before, but she sensed that his threat was not an idle one.

"Father, pray do not upset yourself so," she murmured as she wrung her hands in her lap, unable to meet his gaze. There was a terrible silence, and when Josie dared to look at him again his features had softened once more.

"Dearest Josie, do not distress yourself, my child," he said in a tone tinged with regret. "Delia is of a romantic temperament, and I am certain she will find Charles a very attentive and passionate suitor. How could she possibly resist his efforts to win her heart?"

Josie pasted a smile onto her face that wobbled in spite of herself. "Indeed," she managed. Could it be true that her father did not really know the depths of his impulsive older daughter's independence and fierce loyalty? She prayed that her sister had exaggerated her feelings for the humble miner— that Delia would think of the welfare of others before herself for once.

But that thought led to another disturbing possibility. "Father . . . where will you and I go upon Delia's twenty-first birthday if we are no longer welcome at Chadwick Park?"

"Nonsense, Josie. When would we cease to be welcome in our own home? Delia's own family, no less?"

"Sometimes that is not the wife's decision. Remember what happened to the Suttons last winter."

Father's brow creased. "I own property in Redruth. If such an unthinkable thing should happen, we could go there until other arrangements could be made. The point is, Josie, that our debt will be gone—in which case I may be able to afford to hold on to some of our land and build us a modest home with the profits from the mine."

Josie hated the look of bewildered vulnerability etched into Father's eyes, knowing she had put it there. She rose and kissed his dear bristled jaw, and her hand lingered on the back of his neck as she wondered how many years with him she had left. She was gratified to see a smile ease the lines between his brows as she excused herself.

Josie blinked away tears as she drifted down the servant's stairs, past the cold rooms guarded by sheet-covered furniture. She knew it was unlikely that she would run across anyone. Their staff had dwindled until only the most loyal remained to share in the family's fall from the wealth to which they had always been so accustomed.

She slipped through the back door unnoticed and reveled in the delicious sense of freedom as the April breeze teased a brunette strand of hair out of her twist and into her eyes. A longing for coarse manes and sun-warmed straw called, and her heart answered. Her step echoed on the cobblestones as she stepped into the building intended to shelter horses—yet somehow a refuge for her as well.

Soft, luminous eyes regarded her through the stalls. Then the most beloved gaze of all eagerly sought hers as a jet-black head thrust itself out as her familiar footfalls carried to swiveling ears.

"Oh Ebony," Josie murmured, stroking the dark muzzle that had become peppered with white hairs of late. Why did every living creature dear to her have to grow old and prove itself mortal and fragile?

She unbarred the gate and slipped into the stall, grasping for the peace that was ever elusive as change rocked her world. She threw her arms around the mare's neck and leaned her forehead against the broad, velvet cheek.

Ebony's warm, comforting breath whooshed against her shoulder. A nicker sounded from deep in the mare's chest, and Josie knew the animal sensed her inner turmoil. Josie allowed the tears to well up in her eyes. She was tired of fighting them— of fighting to keep her loved ones safe and secure, of fighting to remain strong as her efforts were misunderstood. Now she just wanted to feel safe herself. Dear Ebony nibbled at her sleeve as though coaxing her to come out of her dark mood. Josie tugged her arm free, marveling at the effectiveness of animal communication.

Then a different kind of voice, the human kind, called her name. Bitterness surged in her throat, and she did not bother to hide her irritation as she turned to answer. She had wanted, no, *needed* to be invisible, but she wasn't granted privacy. She didn't know how much longer she could be there for everyone without falling apart herself.

Bertram Chatham swept his hat from his dark, curly head as his coffee-brewed gaze locked with hers. His eyes were steeped with an intensity as strong as the beverage they brought to mind. Josie regarded him with teary eyes as her cheek rested in the hollow of Ebony's jaw.

"Miss Josie, may I be of service?"

Josie blinked at him, and he blurted, "With your horse, of course? I did not see anyone else about just now when I was inspecting the tack room. I assumed you wished to go riding?"

Josie doubted their stableman had gone far, but she willed her voice not to quaver as the kindness in his voice threatened to undo her. "Yes, thank you, Mr. Chatham. That would be most kind of you."

"Mr. Chatham?" he echoed in mock offense. "Miss Josie, knowing each other as well as we do, such formality of address is altogether unnecessary. I would count it a great honor if you would call me by my Christian name."

Josie faltered at the fervent hope in his gaze, almost painful in its intensity. She couldn't hurt the childhood friend who had always been like a brother to her, though it was most improper to address their steward in such a familiar manner.

"That would be most kind . . . Bertram."

"That's better," he said with a measure of tenderness. Admiration flared to life in his gaze, and it was much too intimate for her liking. As if he owned her, heart, body, and soul.

He leaned closer, and the back of her head pressed against Ebony's neck.

"Forgive me for saying so, but you appear distressed."

His tone was possessive beneath the guise of concern. She hesitated and flinched as he demanded, "If anyone has dared to insult you, so help me I'll—"

"No one has insulted me, and while your concern is admirable, it really is none of your concern."

He stiffened as though she had slapped him. Josie softened her voice with some difficulty. "Now if you would please help me with Ebony, I would be most grateful."

"I am your slave to command," he murmured, drinking in every line of her face in a way that unnerved her. "Always have been. You know that."

He raised his arm, revealing Ebony's bridle held in brown, calloused fingers. She stepped to the side as he slipped the reins over Ebony's ears. Josie reached out to untangle the mare's forelock from the leather strap. Bertram's hand slid across hers and lingered, infusing warmth and a silent message as his fingers tightened around hers. The heat of his touch scorched her skin, and she withdrew her arm. His sensual mouth tightened in a hard line as he finished saddling Ebony with her cross-saddle. He knew her penchant for riding astride when alone. She didn't blush at the thought. After having been thrown, she was willing to sacrifice propriety for comfort and safety. She blocked out the memory of that day before the sensation of being dragged could resurface.

Bertram led Ebony out into the stable courtyard, where he knelt at Josie's feet and laced his fingers together. She placed her left foot in his hands and swung up. Ebony responded to her prodding and trotted toward the back pasture. His eyes burned through her, and she risked a backward glance to see him standing there as though lost without her at his side.

As she turned Ebony's head toward the sea, the myriad of fears she faced caused an echoing nausea in her stomach. Her tears flowed unchecked. Perhaps she was making a mistake by discouraging Bertram's obvious interest. He had always loved her, and it was true that she had always known it. Could time stir her brotherly fondness for him into something more? She felt trapped by the slimness of the options her future offered . . . caring for Father as a spinster or marrying Bertram.

Bertram's father, their old steward, had passed away last year, leaving his son to serve in his stead and live in the modest cottage on their estate. Bertram had always hung back from Josie as though understanding the invisible barrier of rank between them, but lately he had begun to show his devotion with alarming insistence. For a moment she allowed herself to consider it. As his wife, she would never have to part with her beloved childhood home. Why did her heart harbor stubborn dreams of marrying for love when in reality her prospects were so bleak?

Unlike the heroines of novels who were swept off their feet by the men of their dreams, Josie could boast neither beauty nor wealth. Her features were too soft for beauty, with her ordinary brown hair and eyes that shifted from hazel to green according to her mood. Being loved by a faithful man was better than suffering the fate of an old maid, and he wasn't bad to look at. Perhaps it was not the match Father would have wished for her, but she would be comfortable and provided for by a good man. What more had she ever really wanted than to be a wife and a mother?

Her heart told her the answer as Ebony carried her over the rise and the sea stretched before her as wide as the eye could see. She wanted to love and be loved unconditionally. It was her nature to love in such a way, but her affection had never been returned in the same manner. A deep-rooted doubt whispered that Bertram was incapable of giving. He had always been the one to take what he wanted when he wanted it.

In all her life, only God's love had never disappointed. His love was without condition, constant and faithful as the sunrise.

As she rode, the restless cadence of the waves matched her ruffled spirit and the pounding of her heart. *Oh God, help me to be still and know that you are God.* Her looming fears became a towering wave, threatening to crash over her head and dash her against the rocks of reality even as her heart cried out. With trembling hands, she withdrew the Bible from her pocket. As it fell open, the breeze rustled the pages like an unseen hand. They stilled, and the words gripped her with sharp clarity.

If any of you lack wisdom, let him ask of God, that giveth to all men liberally, and upbraideth not; and it shall be given him. But let him ask in faith, nothing wavering. For he that wavereth is like a wave of the sea driven with the wind and tossed.

The pages fluttered again, taking her to the Psalms.

I waited patiently for the Lord; and he inclined unto me, and heard my cry. He brought me up also out of an horrible pit, out of the miry clay, and set my feet upon a rock, and established my goings. And he hath put a new song in my mouth, even praise unto our God: many shall see it, and fear, and shall trust in the Lord.

Josie raised her fisted hands and released every care that wanted to pound across her heart's shores.

"I don't want to be driven and tossed by doubt like these waves!" she screamed above the gushing roar. *Peace be still,* the tender voice whispered as her Lord calmed the storm within as He had the raging seas.

She closed her eyes as the salty breeze snatched each word from her lips and carried them straight to the heart of God.

"I will wait patiently upon You, Lord, to reveal Your plan for my life and give me Your wisdom. I know You have heard my cry. I believe that You will bring me out of this miry clay and establish my goings. I believe that You will put a new song in my mouth that will bring glory to Your name, because You are all I need . . . and all I have ever needed."

Chapter Four

hwack! The riding crop stripped the branch of its tender leaves as it arced in a whoosh of fury. Charles's features twisted at the hurt that had gripped his scarred heart once again. A year had passed since the beginning of his ill-fated courtship . . . if only he had heeded the instincts that had forewarned him of the impending disaster. How dare that chit Delia refuse him! The flaxen-haired child had vowed that his heart would never bleed so again, and yet here stood a man who had been wounded afresh.

Rejection . . . it bit deeply, and he had never known a sharper pain. His innermost soul winced at the sting as his crippling conclusion seared his being: He was unworthy. He must be unworthy of love, for what other reason could there be for this humiliating pattern?

He had known it was a mistake from the first to lower his guard in pursuit of Miss Delia Chadwick, but he had been torn between fear of her rejection and fear of displeasing his father. Though the greater fear had won out, he wondered if his hunger for Sebastian's favor would prove to be the appetite that mangled him. He never had been able to disappoint his father after that nightmarish day when they had both discovered that his mother was never coming back.

The festering hurt had birthed a resolve in him that was fatalistic in its intensity. He would never bare his heart to the fairer sex again. Women could not be trusted, and he would not allow another the satisfaction of twisting the dagger in his flesh.

The vision of Delia's exquisite face still haunted him from when he had knelt, vulnerable and fragile, before her. He had offered himself body and soul, consumed by the lie that such a goddess could not be heartless. But those dewy lashes had veiled a serpent's hooded stare, those ripe lips had barred a forked tongue, and that honeyed voice had disguised the venom lurking beneath.

How she had despised him. The contempt with which she had uttered the words echoed through his memory. "*You Radcliffes strut around as though you own the world, but I wouldn't have you if you were the last man on earth!*"

His jaw clenched as he drew the crop up and snapped it over his knee. He cried out, flinging the pieces into the brush with the violence with which he wished he could hurl away the memory.

He veered off the path and stood inhaling the spicy forest. He needed to escape. The urgent business in Truro had come at a convenient time. It would give both he and his father time to cool off from their disappointment.

Josie nibbled her lower lip as she drew the scarlet thread through the white cambric in her embroidery hoop and began to shape the next intricate petal. Before she could finish another stitch, Delia burst through the drawing room door, and pain jabbed Josie's finger. The air pulsed with excitement in Delia's wake, blending with the throbbing as Josie glanced up. Her question died on her lips as Delia's gaze gouged her own, raw as a gaping wound. Josie bolted to her feet.

"Delia, what in heaven's name is the matter?"

"Oh Josie, I have sinned—"

Delia's voice shuddered to a halt, and Josie leaped forward to steady her as she swayed. Anxiety constricted Josie's throat. She dragged her sister over to a chair, and Delia slumped into it.

"Delia, what have you done?"

The demand came out sharper than Josie had intended, as fear honed her tone. Delia's dilated eyes pleaded with Josie in mute entreaty, bleeding a numbing horror that seeped into Josie's veins and chilled her to the very marrow. Her wild sister was trapped in a noose of her own making, and it tightened before her very eyes with strangling effect.

"There is no sin too great for forgiveness, Delie. Speak to me, for you are coming undone."

Delia licked her bloodless lips. The seconds ticked into an eternity.

"Did Mr. Radcliffe propose?" Josie prompted as she attempted to rub some warmth into Delia's icy fingers.

"Yes—"

The hesitation ebbed and flowed like a tide as Delia weighed her words.

"And I refused him."

Josie sucked in a shuddering breath as a flicker of her former defiance burned in Delia's gaze.

A thousand protests bubbled in Josie's throat, but they died on her lips as she realized the utter futility of trying to change Delia's mind. She collapsed into her chair. "It would be a sin to marry someone you didn't love, Delia," she managed at last.

Delia burst into tears and sank into Josie's lap. As Josie stroked the tumbling waves of raven hair, she willed her own heart to send healing into the dear frame wracked with sobs as she rocked her sister back and forth.

"You are so good to me, Josie," Delia gasped. "But Father will kill me."

"No, darling," Josie murmured against her hair. "He will be disappointed, yes, but I know you better than anyone. If you had married Mr. Radcliffe, you wouldn't have made him a good wife, because your heart belonged to another. That would have caused a far greater scandal in the end."

"I . . . love my James. I tried to give Charles a chance these past few weeks, but in the end I couldn't betray my James. Ooooh, he was so angry, Josie. He wouldn't listen to me seriously. It was as though he thought I was playing some sort of game with him. Then I got angry and told him I wouldn't marry him if he was the last man on earth."

"Oh Delie, you needn't have been cruel about it," Josie remonstrated.

The words bubbled up in her sister's throat like blood from a mortal wound as she choked out, "If only that was all . . ."

Dread welled in Josie's chest. What could be worse than failing to pay off Father's debts through the match with Charles?

Their father's familiar step sounded in the hall. Delia jerked and shot to her feet. The full weight of Delia's refusal pressed with suffocating weight on Josie's heart as she met their father's hopeful gaze. This stress could kill him.

Oh dear God, have mercy on us. Josie seized her sister's hand in a silent warning to break it to him with gentleness.

"Has Charles gone already?" Father asked.

"Yes, I believe he had some pressing business for the company," Josie said and gnawed her lip.

"Such a responsible young man," Father said. He hesitated, and Josie's breath hitched as his gaze shifted to Delia.

"Come now, Delia, don't keep me in suspense. A young man who is courting does not knock on my door with a bouquet of flowers in his hand and ask to speak privately with my daughter for no reason."

Delia yanked her hand out of Josie's grasp, tensing for battle. "Forgive me, Father, but I could not accept his proposal when my heart belongs to another."

Father's face went ashen in shock, but then his features hardened to stone. "Make no mistake, Delia. You are in no position to refuse Charles Radcliffe, and I will not allow you to entertain such a preposterous notion a moment longer."

Desperation brimmed in Delia's eyes. Her breast heaved. Something elusive lurked there just beneath the surface, seething and writhing. Any untamed creature attacked when cornered. An instinct warned Josie that Delia was about to shatter both their dreams—that her words would break more hearts than one.

"I am in no position to accept him, Father. Not now and not ever. James is the man I love, and—"

"Enough!" Randolph Chadwick's outraged roar quivered on the air. He gripped Delia's wrist, and she grimaced as he bit out the words. "If you do not break this outrageous engagement with James then I will, and you will never see his face again, so help me. Everything, everything rests upon your marrying Charles Radcliffe, daughter. Do you want to see the name of Chadwick ruined? Your father thrown into debtor's prison and your dear sister cast upon the mercy of the poorhouse or God knows who? Is that what you want? For you seem determined to destroy us all!"

"No!" Delia's screech pierced Josie's heart as she shook from head to toe. "That is not what I want, but it is too late, Father. I am with child by James, and I ask you . . . what other man but he will have me now?"

Delia staggered back as the sound of Father's slap resounded through the room, mingling with Josie's cry. Delia clutched the red imprint on her cheek, eyes glazing over in shock as the tears raked her cheeks. She shrank back as their father gripped her shoulders and shook her.

"You're lying," he said. "You know I can't force you to marry Charles if you tell me you carry another man's child."

Rage distended Delia's nostrils. "I may be many things, but I am not a liar, Father. I carry his child in my womb now, and nothing you say can change that."

The searing denial snuffed out Father's expression. His shoulders slumped in defeat even as he demanded, "You still dare to call me father? Don't ever let that word cross your lips again, for you are no longer a daughter of mine."

"Don't judge me!" Delia cried. This time, Josie heard a rippling panic joining the anger and defiance in her sister's tone. "I am not the only sinner to blame for this family's misfortune. I did not gamble away our every farthing until I was so desperate to get out of debt that I was willing to break both of my daughters' hearts!"

Father snarled. "You miserable, selfish whore! I will cure you of your rebellion once and for all." He cursed and drew back his hand.

Josie could bear the scene no longer and leaped to her feet. "Stop it!" she shrieked, seizing Father's wrist. "Stop it, both of you. I will not stand by and watch my family fall apart before my very eyes. Please, Father," she begged. Her gut twisted with each wrenching sob as he jerked out of her grip. The frigidity in Father's eyes chilled Josie to the marrow.

"All hell has broken loose in this house, Josephine, and as for your God, He forsook us long ago. You have been too tenderhearted with your sister, and now I must put my foot down. I will not relent."

Josie gaped as he dragged Delia away. *So now it is all my fault?*

The door slammed in punctuation. As Josie wrenched it open and watched her father hauling Delia up the stairs, the pain in her heart drove sharp. She moved to go after them— but a gentle touch landed on her arm, preventing her. Fear had stirred the fight in her. She flung a desperate look over her shoulder into gray depths of shimmering compassion.

"Let me go, Esther," she insisted, willing her voice not to quaver. "I must go to them."

"Josie."

At the sound of her name spoken with such infinite love, Josie pried her gaze away. Such tenderness would undo her now, and she couldn't take the chance of fracturing while reaching out to catch the broken pieces. Alas, she was fighting the woman whose inner strength had pieced her back together too many times.

"There is naught ye can do now to help them, luve. Time alone is the healer of all wounds. Ye'll only hurt yerself."

Josie's shoulders slumped as the fight drained out of her. She yielded to Esther's coaxing as her old governess tugged her back into the parlor, where she collapsed onto the settee. Esther knelt to retrieve her embroidery hoop.

"Tell me what happened, luve. Dinna let it fester inside ye," Esther prompted as she sank down beside her.

Josie took a shuddering breath and let the words bleed from her wounds. In Esther's soulful gray eyes, every pang of Josie's heart was mirrored until at last Esther opened her arms in a humble offering of embrace. Josie pillowed her head against the openness of that tender heart whose warmth always held healing.

The words resonated from deep within Esther's chest and stilled Josie's being. "Dear Lord Jesus, this did not take Ye by surprise, and though we cannae see where this will lead, that doesna mean that Ye do not have a plan. So we choose to trust Ye in this trial, precious Lord Jesus, for Ye are all powerful. We ken that Ye will work all things together for our good. I ask that Ye will draw Delia to Yerself. She has been running away from Ye a long time, but Ye loved the adulterous woman. Thank Ye for softening her father's heart. Comfort Josie now, for Ye have given her the gift of loving deeply. In Jesus's name, we cast all of these cares upon Ye. Amen."

Josie snuffled and accepted Esther's cambric handkerchief. She blew her nose with an unladylike snort.

"Do ye ken how much I love ye, sweet Josie?" Esther murmured as unshed tears glistened in her own eyes.

The doubt in Esther's eyes pierced Josie's innermost soul. She leaned forward and kissed the lined brow.

"I have always known it, dearest Esther. Don't doubt it for a moment. Your love has healed this heart countless times, and you led me to the One who could heal me when you could not. I owe my soul to you."

Josie hesitated as she kissed Esther's hand, but bravery bubbled to her lips. "And I love you as much as though you were the woman who bore me."

Esther sobbed, and Josie wiped away the scalding tear. "I thank ye for that, luve."

Esther chose to swallow the words Josie glimpsed brimming there. Her hands twisted the excess fabric, and as she glanced down she smoothed the half-finished rose where a heel had marred the unfinished handkerchief. "Ye always did have a way with a needle."

"How symbolic," Josie snorted with rising bitterness. "A trampled wild rose."

Esther squeezed her shoulder as she stood.

"Forgive Delia, luve. She needs ye most now."

"She betrayed us all," Josie flung out. "Can't you see that, Esther?"

"Aye, that she did, luve," Esther answered. "But if ye dinna forgive her, then bitterness is a rust that will eat away at ye. I'm going to yer father now, lass."

Josie bit her lip as she regarded the rose once again. A tear blotched the crimson petal like a drop of dew.

Chapter Five

*J*osie regarded the stone hall's sinister shadows with bile rising in her throat and tightened her grip on the candlestick. Though the servants believed these walls to be haunted, the west wing built by her ancestors had held a mysterious pull for her as a child with its chapel, tapestries, and armor. Her former fascination had become lurid with Delia imprisoned within its tower by their own father several hours ago. The rest of their manor house was massive, as though trying to overshadow the Chadwicks' humble origins, but the modernized addition could never swallow the past. Originally intended to defend against invaders, the tower's sheltering walls had been repurposed as a prison for the Chadwicks' own tonight. Surely their ancestors were turning in their graves.

Josie's heart plunged as she tried the locked tower door, and it didn't budge. The stout hinges dared her to pry apart iron bolts that had withstood the test of centuries. She pounded, and Delia's muffled voice reached her ears. Josie strained to make sense of her tear-clogged words. She thumped on the door until Delia's wails hushed to a whimper.

"Listen, I promise I will get you out. Just trust me, Delie," she yelled. The silence that followed weighed heavy on her spirit. She feared giving Delia false hope.

Josie turned to leave before father caught her here, but she paused in front of a dusty tapestry depicting the St. Bartholomew's Day massacre. Her mouth went dry as a dormant memory stirred . . .

Eleven-year-old Josie snuck down the hall leading to the forbidden west wing. She had tried to obey, but the rainy day was driving her mad with boredom. Surely no one would ever know.

She inhaled the familiar musty air with delight. Today she was eager to play the part of poor Joan of Arc, whom she had just learned about in her history lessons with Esther. She set the guttering candle on a dusty table and knelt on the cold stone, imploring the king to spare her life. "I'm innocent, sire!" she cried, the plea echoing eerily through the hall. With a flourish, she drew her stick sword from her waist as the king commanded his soldiers to seize her. She backed away, but midstep she tripped and fell against the tapestried wall.

A soft click penetrated her dazed senses, and she was falling again. The wall was swallowing her alive. She shrieked as she tumbled onto hard-packed dirt. It was so dark.

Josie fought back against the clawing panic and scrambled for the gleam of candlelight she could see around the edge of the tapestry. After she had darted through and retrieved the candle, her curiosity overwhelmed her fear. She had read about secret panels built during the reigns of Queen Elizabeth and King Charles the Second to hide enemies of the crown.

She tugged the tapestry back. There was a grinding whir, and she stumbled into the tunnel as the panel closed. She forced herself to take a deep breath as she pounded against the wood. Finally she resigned herself to finding another way out. She wouldn't be afraid as long as she had the candle.

Josie ventured through the narrow tunnel, guarding the wavering flame with her hand. It was the only thing standing between her and panic. Cobwebs overran the passageway, and the dirt floor was moist in places. The encroaching walls threatened to suffocate her, and there was still no end in sight. Then the tunnel forked. In the cold, shadowed stillness, her heart pounded in claps of thunder. Which way now? She was being punished for her disobedience.

Then she froze as her eyes fastened on the footprint in the mud. All of the servants' fearful mutterings about Lady Chadwick's ghost suddenly gripped her in icy terror. Then a draft, like an ominous breath, snuffed out the flame. She screamed as the darkness descended, and the twisted echo chased her as she tore into the dark bowels of the underworld. She was going to rot here, and her bones would join those of whatever spectral presence haunted this tunnel. The seconds stretched into an eternity. Then her outstretched hands slammed into solid wood. She flung herself against it, pounding until she thought her fists would become a bloody pulp.

The panel clicked open. Blessed light flooded her as she entered . . . the tower staircase.

Josie shuddered. The memory told her exactly what to do, and much as she dreaded it, she knew it was the only way to rescue Delia. The panel was still there, covered with mortar and thin slabs of stone to appear solid. As she wandered out of the west wing she knew she couldn't rescue Delia until she discovered a solution to pacify their father.

Alarm broke through her musings as she heard Father's raised voice in the library. She knelt down in front of the door without shame, for she alone could protect Delia now. The next voice she heard was Sebastian Radcliffe's as his words carried through the keyhole.

"Charles has gone to the bank in Truro, but I expect him to arrive this evening any time now. I have no doubt I can convince him to marry Delia in spite of this. He will claim the child as his own, and scandal is a small price to pay for the union we both want. He won't dare to defy me in this."

Josie fisted her hands. Such presumption sickened her. How dare those men discuss Delia and Charles as though they were nothing but chattel? She refused to stand by and watch this insanity one moment longer. Unlike the scheming fathers who thought they could jerk their children's heartstrings and make them dance like puppets, she knew Charles would never marry Delia now. His pride had already taken enough blows from her unruly sister.

Recurring nightmares from her childhood were responsible for Josie's deep-rooted fear of the dark, but the night gave her pause for only a heartbeat as she stole toward the kitchen where Eliza kept the door unlocked. Josie blew out her candle, placed the candlestick above the kitchen fireplace, and pocketed the tinderbox kept there. It would provide an emergency source of light if her courage failed. Ironically, her father and Mr. Radcliffe had given her the solution for which she had prayed. Now she just needed to persuade Charles Radcliffe—a task which she suspected would require a miracle in and of itself.

Resolve steeled every nerve in her being and cauterized her heart as she slipped into the crisp night air. She hoped the cost would not be higher than she could bear to pay as she sacrificed her dream on the altar to atone for something much more sacred to her.

Chapter Six

Stalwart's hoofbeats rolled on, pounding in the same endless monotony as the beating of his heart. Charles lost himself in the sound, deliberately blocking out the voices, knowing all the while that the rhythm was only hastening the arrival he dreaded. Home . . . he envied those to whom the word conjured visions of peace. To him it meant only renewed conflict and endless, distasteful duty. His identity had been forged by his father's ambition, and even as a boy he had never been allowed to forget it. He often wondered why being the Radcliffe heir felt more like an obligation than a privilege.

Shadowy wisps of cloud drifted across the creamy orb of the moon, but he was blinded to its beauty. Mental and physical exhaustion punctuated every breath, but he knew better then to expect that he would soon sleep. No doubt Father would wish to renew their argument. Charles groaned and tried to rub the grit out of his eyes. It seemed he had yet to convince his father that Miss Delia Chadwick had been dead serious in rejecting him.

Stalwart snorted and broke the gallop, prancing sideways as though shying away from something in the trees. Charles reined him in and frowned. Shivering shadows blotched the seemingly innocent road. It was unlike Stalwart to be spooked—the stallion was worthy of his name.

Charles scanned the trees, but they betrayed no movement save the occasional tremor as the wind whispered through the branches. He nudged his mount forward with more roughness than he was wont to show as exasperation seethed through him. It was all he could do to stay awake at such an hour without worrying about being ambushed by highwaymen.

The tension in his shoulders eased as Stalwart cantered around the bend without faltering. Then a white form floated into the center of the road.

Charles shuddered as rumors of Lady Chadwick's ghost stirred in his memory. He had always discredited such superstitious nonsense, but the lateness of the hour caused him to question—and if not a ghost, just what *was* he seeing?

Stalwart shuddered as though echoing his misgivings and then, without warning, reared. Charles groped for control with a curse before he fell.

Josie gasped as she watched Charles Radcliffe tumble from the back of the rearing horse. The gray stallion stole the breath from her lungs as his coat gleamed in the moonlight like molten lead. She knew the stallion would bolt the second his thrashing hooves bit the dust. Dashing forward, she seized the reins the instant before he came back down. The stallion could drag her if he chose—but her strength of will had a calming effect on the animal. She ran a quieting hand over the chiseled head as her eyes strayed toward his master.

Charles Radcliffe staggered to his feet. If the muffled curses that proceeded to stream from beneath his greatcoat were any indication, he was not injured. He made quite the picture, greatcoat falling over his face and dust swirling from his stomping boots as he regained his balance. His powerful arms whipped back the folds of wool with an indignant snap, revealing the dull gleam of a pistol.

Josie flinched, causing the stallion to snort. She willed her voice not to quaver.

"Forgive me, Mr. Radcliffe. I didn't intend to spook your horse."

The hair sweeping across Charles's brow gleamed almost white in the moonlight as he tossed his head with affronted dignity and thrust his pistol back into his waistband. His eyes drilled through her until the silence grew unbearable.

"Sir, are you hurt?"

His brows rose incredulously, and his voice thrust through her with the coldness of a blade as he spoke. "It is indeed fortunate that I am not, no thanks to you! I am not accustomed to being thrown from my horse and tossed upon my head just before midnight!"

His stance seemed to bely his words as he winced and reached out to steady himself upon his mount's saddle. "What were you thinking, woman?" he demanded. "Darting across the road in the middle of the night? I could very easily have mistaken you for a highwayman and fired!"

Josie stifled a groan at the absurdity of her situation. "The answer is even more complicated than it appears, Mr. Radcliffe."

"You know who I am, do you? Well, pray tell me who you are. Or are you a ghost like I first imagined?"

Josie grimaced. This meeting was not at all like she had planned.

"I am Josephine Chadwick," she murmured.

Mr. Radcliffe rolled his eyes. "Not a ghost, just a relative of the ghost. Lately I don't know who I would rather deal with more when it concerns your family, Miss Chadwick. Flesh and blood can be even worse than spirits."

He jerked the reins away from her, causing both her and the stallion to flinch afresh. "Considering that I am in no condition to ride until my head clears, why don't you come and explain yourself? I presume you have some blasted important reason for seeking me out at this ungodly hour."

Josie followed him as her stomach tied itself in knots. He led his horse to the shadows beneath the trees and collapsed on the grass, propping his forearms across his knees. Josie went to grasp the reins as they trailed unguarded across the ground, but he waved his hand at her in a dismissive gesture.

"Never mind that. Stalwart won't go anywhere if he hasn't already. It is beyond me why he didn't bolt from here to London by now."

Josie was tempted to ignore the question in his tone, but the extent of her unladylike behavior had already breached the confines of etiquette. "I seized his reins before he could run off, sir."

The man's face was veiled in shadow, but the intensity of his gaze made Josie squirm. She reached out and stroked Stalwart's velvety muzzle. The stallion's luminous eyes held hers with the comforting frankness she found lacking in human companions. His warm breath whooshed onto her hand.

"Stalwart is a fitting name for such a prime bit of blood."

Charles watched her closely. "He doesn't let just anyone handle him that way."

"Oh, he knows he is a handsome fellow, make no mistake," she said with a grin.

Mr. Radcliffe cleared his throat. "He could have trampled you back there you know, Miss Chadwick."

"He knew I wasn't afraid of him. Horses can sense that, just like people." Josie blushed in the moonlight at her own boldness.

"You certainly have a way with horses," he muttered, but his tone communicated that he agreed with her self-assessment—she had a lot of nerve, probably too much.

Josie knelt beside him, taking care to arrange her skirts. She had already broken all the rules of propriety by meeting this man alone in the dark, but at least she could maintain a semblance of modesty in the face of such disgrace.

"It was the least I could do after causing you to be thrown from your horse, Mr. Radcliffe. I assure you I did not intend for our conversation to begin this way."

"Back to that now, are we?" he said as though suddenly amused. "Suppose you tell me why you arranged this midnight rendezvous in the first place, Miss Chadwick. I fear you have yet to make that plain to me."

Josie gnawed at her lip, vowing that he would not have the satisfaction of making her flustered. It was bad enough that he already thought she was a widgeon.

"Mr. Radcliffe, please bear with me. This matter is delicate in nature," she began, hating the vulnerable quaver in her voice. "I would not be speaking to you if I had any other alternative. Father locked Delia in our tower after she refused to retract her rejection of your marriage proposal. My sister has confessed that she is with child by a miner she claims to love. Thus, you see, she really never was in a position to accept your hand. But this evening I overheard a conversation between your father and mine. They are still determined that you and Delia should marry. Your father wants you to claim the child as your own, thinking the marriage will wipe away all scandal in time—"

"No!"

Josie shrank away as Charles sprang to his feet, his features ravaged by an anger unlike anything she had ever witnessed. His body shook as he declared, "Father has finally gone too far!"

In the intense silence that hung between them, the only sound was his ragged breathing. Josie bolted upright as his fist slammed into a nearby tree, and he doubled over in evident pain.

"Please, Mr. Radcliffe!" she cried out, but the plea died in her throat with a choked gurgle of fear as he turned and caught her by the shoulders. His grip was like iron, almost diabolic in the fierceness of his rage. He towered above her as an unnatural light flared in his eyes. His breath fanned her cheek as he ground out the words.

"Know this, Miss Chadwick. Nothing on this earth, not even my father's disownment, could induce me to marry your sister after she rejected me with such scorn. Not ever."

A crazed defiance that Josie suspected was born of vulnerability wavered in Charles's eyes as her gaze swept his like soft rain across raging flames. She grasped the straining, corded muscles beneath his shirtsleeves.

"I know, Mr. Radcliffe. Believe me when I tell you I understand. I know my sister better than anyone. Even if by some miracle you still wanted her, she would throw herself from that tower before consenting. That is why I had to see you tonight. I believe I have the solution to all of our difficulties."

Josie hesitated as the gravity of what she was about to do penetrated her heart. There would be no turning back once she took this step.

Before she could speak the fatal words, Charles frowned. "I fear you are catching a chill. You are shaking."

"Am I?" Josie asked. He nodded, and his expression softened a fraction.

"You were saying, Miss Chadwick?" As he spoke, he unfastened his greatcoat from around his neck and rested its folds around her own shoulders.

"Suddenly it seems foolish of me to even hope that you would consider it," Josie confessed as she tugged the greatcoat closer and willed her limbs to cease trembling.

"I assure you I am willing to consider anything you have to say."

Josie cocked her head at him and offered a sad smile. "You say that now," she whispered.

"What are you afraid of, Miss Josephine?"

Josie squared her shoulders and held her chin steady. It was now or never.

"My father's heart isn't strong. The doctor warned him not to get overly excited or upset, but I was afraid when Delia defied him that he might have an attack. His debt has distressed him enough, and I've watched it age him beyond his years. I think the hope of Delia making a wealthy match has been the only thing keeping him alive. I fear this disappointment will kill him. I couldn't stand by and watch the hearts of both my father and my sister be broken knowing there was a chance I could do something to prevent it. My father will disown and disinherit Delia if she runs away with her lover, which she will surely do the moment I help her escape. Tomorrow his solicitor is coming to disinherit her."

She took a deep breath and then let the plan out in a rush. "If you and I married, it would satisfy both of our fathers. My father would be quick to make me heiress of Chadwick Park."

Charles's expression hardened, and he released her as though the contact with her had burned him.

"I see how it is," he said with sudden coldness. "This is a most convenient turn of events for you, is it not?"

"What are you accusing me of?" Josie cried out.

"Don't act innocent with me. You know full well," Charles sneered. "All women are alike . . . selfish, conniving creatures who care for naught other than their own ends."

Josie blinked as the words seared hot as a branding iron. She wished he had slapped her instead, for a blow would have hurt less.

"Do you find me as repulsive and distasteful as all that?" she blurted.

"I did not court Delia of my own accord," Charles bit out. "My father put me up to it, and I agreed—"

"—because Delia was a beautiful young heiress, and what could you stand to lose?" Josie finished with icy disdain.

"My heart, as it turns out," Charles snapped. "I genuinely cared for your sister and was not pursuing her merely for her inheritance unlike some fortune hunters."

Josie's face flushed in the darkness, and she forced herself to take a deep breath. Everything rested on her calmness at this moment.

"I'm sorry Delia hurt you, but I resent your implication that I am a vulture swooping over you to seize your purse strings. I know I cannot hold a candle to Delia's beauty, but I refuse to stand by and watch my family fall apart when it is within my power to do something about it. I don't think you realize, sir, just what a sacrifice it is for me to give up my own dreams for the sake of my family's happiness. And then to be unjustly sub-jected to your abominable accusations is really more than I can bear. I regret having ever made such a suggestion to you, for I am sure a blinder, more unreasonable man never lived. I bid you good night, Mr. Radcliffe."

Josie wheeled away from him.

"Don't turn your back on me, woman," he snapped as his rough hand grasped her arm.

"Let go of me," Josie hissed, and he obliged even as he held up a reconciliatory hand.

"Now wait and hear me out, Miss Chadwick. I beg your pardon for being unreasonable, but I am not blind to the fact that your proposal is the only amicable resolution for both parties."

Josie's eyebrows rose. "You should have taken a moment to realize that before thoroughly offending me, Mr. Radcliffe. Now that I have seen the disagreeable side of your disposition, I doubt my wisdom in presenting such a suggestion in the first place."

Charles raked a hand through his hair with a heavy sigh. If Josie had not been so angry with him, she doubted she would have been able to restrain the impulse to smooth his tousled, flaxen strands back into place.

"I am no fool, Miss Chadwick, in spite of your less than subtle intimations. I will not pretend to harbor any pleasure at the thought of such a union between us, except for the mutual satisfaction of both of our fathers. As for Delia, I wash my hands of her. I count myself fortunate to escape, as she has proven to be a woman of easy virtue. She may go to the devil for all I care."

He laughed, and Josie winced as she again glimpsed a broken part of him that he was trying to conceal. A part of her cringed in horror at the thought of yoking herself to him. But nor could she bear for Father's blood to be upon her head.

"I am grateful that you are not a man of pretense, Mr. Radcliffe, for I cannot bear to be lied to. But in speaking of Delia in the future, I beg you to remember that God alone is her judge. And forgive me if, in a moment of anger, I have given you reason to believe that I think you a fool, for I do not for one moment. I can assure you of that most sincerely. Indeed, Mr. Radcliffe, I think it unfortunate that circumstances have driven you to such an unflattering opinion of my sex. I swear to you now, by all that is holy and sacred to me, that I will do all that is within my power to be a good and faithful wife to you if that is indeed your wish."

More words bubbled up in Josie's throat, so many of them— a wellspring of dreams and hopes that refused to die. But she could see how futile it would be to reveal herself to him now. The decision and her fate now rested in the strong hands that had covered her when she was cold and seized her in the heat of anger.

"Fair enough," Mr. Radcliffe said as he reached for her hand. His fingers, warm and steady, closed around hers with a gentleness that sought the very trust he seemed incapable of giving.

Josie held her breath as his other hand joined the first and carried hers to rest against his broad chest. The solid thud of his beating heart tingled and resonated through her flesh as he whispered, "Will you marry me, Miss Josephine Chadwick?"

"Yes, Charles, I will."

The wind riffled through his hair, and Josie reached up to stroke the pale strands back into submission. He was hers now, and she resolved to care for him as well as she was able. His shadowed eyes were inscrutable, but as she began to pull away, her fingers lingered against his jaw. His voice rumbled through her fingers still clasped at his chest.

"You said you cannot abide pretense, Miss Chadwick, so I will give you none. I lack many husbandly qualities, but I am not without loyalties of my own. I will be a true and faithful husband to you regardless of the circumstances of our union. That much I promise you this night, Josephine."

Josie seized the precious promise and planted it deep in her heart. It was a pledge of loyalty instead of love, but it was more than she had expected from him. For that she would be grateful. Charles whistled to Stalwart.

"Allow me to escort you home," he said, releasing her hand and mounting. He reached down and grasped her wrist to help her swing up behind him.

Josie leaned forward and rested her cheek against his shoulder, weak with relief. Now if she could only get the next part to go according to plan. Her sacrifice would not be in vain.

"Please give me until tomorrow at teatime before you explain to both your father and mine. If anything goes wrong, I will send our head stableman with a message asking if he can borrow some liniment."

His broad shoulder tensed beneath her cheek.

"Is this secrecy really necessary?"

"I'm afraid it is. As long as Delia is in Father's grasp, he will never consent to her marrying a miner. He would insist you had fathered the child rather than swallow his pride and cause a scandal that would force you to marry her. No, it is better for me to spirit her away. Then Father will have no other choice but to give our betrothal his blessing."

They rode through the moonlit back pasture in silence. Josie suspected his thoughts were much like her own—neither of their lives would ever be the same after tonight.

When they reached the kitchen door that Josie had left unlocked, she slipped from Stalwart's back and stood with the wobbliness of a newborn foal.

"Good night Charles," she whispered.

He nodded before swinging Stalwart's head around. It was only as Josie watched the gray stallion bearing away a prince that was far from charming did she realize that she still wore his greatcoat around her shoulders. The rough wool comforted her as she slipped inside, reminding her of the promise he had whispered with his fingers wrapped around hers. Her heart resolved to cling to the memory of that goodness hiding beneath her betrothed's rough exterior.

Chapter Seven

*J*osie paused in the servant's hall, peering into the kitchen to ensure the banked coals still glowed crimson in the hearth before she shut out the moonlight. Starry pinpricks of red winked through the curfew hood that guarded the coals from the night's spring chill as she eased the door shut.

She knelt on the hearth flagstones and dug the tinderbox out of her pocket. As she raised the curfew's metal hood and rested it against the brick, the dim ruby light enveloped her in the darkness. She retrieved a wood spunk from the tinderbox and lowered the sulfur encrusted tip into the coals. A blue flame flared to life, and she cupped her hand around it as she guided it to the wick in the tinderbox lid. The spark hesitated as she blew, but at last the flame caught.

Josie slipped the base of the tinderbox back into her pocket. She wasn't braving that tunnel without the flint and steel it contained. Weariness weighed heavy on her, but tonight was only just beginning. She would sleep like the dead until the worst of the chaos had subsided on the morrow.

She pulled Charles's greatcoat a little tighter as she approached the west wing. The scratchy wool swallowed her, edges curling as though his presence unfolded around her. Courage mustn't desert her now. Her fear flirted with resolve like the wavering flame beneath her breath.

Shadows chased Josie down the narrow hallway. She reverted to her eleven-year-old self as indecision sent fresh tendrils of fear down her spine. Had it been this tapestry with the tattered horses? No, perhaps it was that one, with the mildewed patches defiling King Arthur's knights. The tapestries' hues were subdued, faded just like the era to which they had belonged. Were the fingers that had once worked them buried in the Chadwick cemetery? Perhaps her grandmother had stitched some of them. Josie shivered, recalling the servants' whispers that Lady Chadwick's ghost wandered here. She had never been superstitious, but now the tragic details of her grandmother's death gripped her and preyed on her vulnerable mind.

Josie paused in front of a grotesque tapestry depicting the St. Bartholomew's Day massacre. A chord of memory stirred. Yes, this was the table where she'd laid her candle.

"Lord, please grant me strength," Josie whispered as every instinct screamed and sent tremors skittering through her limbs. She poked and prodded the panel to no avail. Frustration eclipsed her anxiety as she scowled. Perhaps she had the wrong tapestry after all. She replayed the memory in her mind, and realization dawned. The eleven-year-old girl had increased in stature since then.

Josie prodded the lower half of the tapestry and gave it a hard shove. A faint click echoed as the sinister space greeted her. She stepped into the tunnel, taking care not to nudge the tapestry. The black space gaped as though it were eager to swallow her whole.

Josie steeled her nerve. *For God hath not given me the spirit of fear, but of power, and of love, and of a sound mind!*

Guarding the guttering flame with all she was worth, Josie penetrated the darkness a step at a time. This was what the Israelites must have experienced as they walked through the parted waters—fear and awe intertwined. The shadows retreated from the flickering candlelight, only to surround her from both sides and tiptoe behind her.

None of the cobwebs had been disturbed since her last time here. No footprints leered from the mud. Perhaps she had only imagined it?

Josie almost jumped out of her skin as a cold drop struck her skin, and she stood rooted to the ground as she caught an unnatural sound. A ragged wheeze as her gaze gouged the lurid shadows . . . the sound of her own breathing.

She snorted, and the tunnel growled back. *Get a hold of yourself, Josie.*

She reached the fork in the tunnel, and fresh panic washed over her in the moment of indecision. Footprints in the mud had caused her to flee before. Josie chose the dry path and veered to the right. She almost kissed the wood when the flame illuminated the panel. She gave it a shove but misjudged her own strength, crashing through and scraping flesh against rough stone.

Josie froze, but only silence met her straining ears. She took the stairs two at a time. No form darkened the cot in the corner. Josie's gaze flew to the window. *Surely you wouldn't, Delia!*

The candle sputtered in warning as she whirled. A silhouette darkened the wall. Josie approached the slumped form. Her raised candle illuminated Delia's exhausted features, which still bore the traces of tearstains. Josie committed the beloved features to memory one by one . . . sooty lashes sweeping high cheekbones, tilted nose, sensual lips. Her gaze lingered on Delia's girlish figure, but the flat stomach betrayed no inkling of the babe's presence yet. She was an aunt, but she would never know Delia's child. Father's accusation sliced her wide open again.

"Have I been too soft and tenderhearted with you, Delie? Oh, but how I love you. All I've ever wanted is to keep you safe."

Delia moaned, and the sound roused Josie as she knelt beside her. Her lips pressed against the sweet brow, tremulous with the weight of unspoken worlds.

"Wake up, darling."

Delia stirred and brushed her away. "Go back to bed, Josie. It's not nearly dawn yet."

Tears welled in Josie's eyes as her heart broke. *Oh Delie, why couldn't we have stayed just as we were?*

"But Delie," she whispered in spite of herself, "I can smell popovers, and my tummy is so hungry. Can't you taste them buttered and with Eliza's strawberry preserves?" Josie broke off with a sob.

Delia groaned as she sat up. "All right, Josephine, stop blubbering."

Her eyelids pried open as she squinted up at Josie. Then her pupils darkened in alarm. "Josephine, you know you aren't allowed to light—"

Her voice trailed off as awareness dawned. "I must have been dreaming," she murmured. Her gaze wandered for a moment, and the last shred of oblivion was swept away by hurt. Bitterness dripped from her words. "Did the old tyrant let you in?"

"You've played the part of Rapunzel long enough. Follow me now."

Delia grinned as she uncurled herself. "I knew you'd come to my rescue, Josie. Oooh, I've got an awful crick in my neck."

"You're welcome. Now hush," Josie hissed as they neared the edge of the staircase. "Whatever you do, don't scream—and make sure *I* don't if the flame dies. There is a tinderbox in my pocket."

The firelight slanted across the secret panel as they descended the stairs. Josie ignored Delia's gasp as she shoved her through the door and swung the panel closed by hooking her finger in the wooden niche.

"I must still be dreaming," Delia muttered. The tunnel rasped back, *Dreaming, dreaming* . . . Delia's fingernails dug into Josie's arm. It comforted her to know she wasn't the only one frightened out of her wits.

As they passed the fork in the tunnel, the flame shuddered, plunging the world into a black void. Delia's fingers clamped over her mouth, but Josie couldn't find the strength to scream anyway. Her heart bruised her ribs as the pulsing roar of blood filled her ears, but her limbs were paralyzed.

Fingers rummaged in her pocket. A moment later, a fleeting spark winked and glimmered to life. Delia blew onto it, and a tiny flame leaped. Her fingers encircled it until the light glowed blood red through flesh.

Josie let her take the candle and relight it, and Delia dragged her along until they glimpsed an outline of gray light. Delia thrust through the tapestry, activating the mechanism. A rush of adrenaline sent Josie flying through the shrinking space. The panel clicked like sharp teeth behind her. Her knees jellied, but Delia jerked her upright before she could buckle.

"You can faint after we have put as much distance as is humanly possible between us and that death trap," she hissed.

Delia hauled her along with a grip of steel until the open air kissed their faces. Josie slumped to the dewy grass, and Delia seized her face between her hands.

"Oh Josie, you were so brave, so magnificent, darling," she sobbed, planting moist kisses on both cheeks. "How did you ever manage to get through that horrible tunnel all by yourself?"

"I couldn't bear the thought of you caged like some wild animal in that tower a moment longer."

"How did you know about the tunnel?"

"I found it by accident when I disobeyed Father and played in the west wing as a girl."

"I have never been so terrified in all my life. I would face Father all over again before having to set one more foot in that tunnel."

"Well, now you are out, and that's all that matters."

"Josie, darling, you are shaking so that you frighten me," Delia murmured as she rubbed some warmth into her sister's icy fingers. "You'll catch your death of cold."

"Don't . . . worry . . . about me," Josie managed. She nodded to the oak tree where a neglected swing still hung—a remnant of a childhood that felt further away all the time.

"Your valise is all packed and waiting in the fairy's hut. I stuffed what I could into it, but I'm afraid George will have to bring your trunk later when you're all settled."

Delia smiled at the reference to the hollow in the tree. "Dearest Josie, you are too good to me, but don't bother to pack my gowns. I want you to have them. It's the least I can do, and I won't shame my James by wearing finery. He can't provide for me in the manner to which I've always been accustomed, but he's a good man. I love him with all my heart. He is worth even more to me than Chadwick Park! Please try to understand that, Josie. Don't judge me too harshly for it."

"If you are asking for my forgiveness, you already have it."

A frown creased Delia's forehead as she blurted, "But what are you going to tell Father when he finds out I'm gone?"

"The truth. He'll be pacified when he finds out that Charles and I are engaged to be married."

Delia's eyes glazed in shock. "You . . . betrothed to Charles Radcliffe?"

"Is it really so hard to believe, Delia? There was no other way for this mess to be settled. Now that I am to be heiress of Chadwick Park, both parents will be satisfied. You are free to marry James, and our father can live to a ripe old age without having to worry about debt ever again."

"But Josie. . . you told me yourself it is a sin to marry a man you don't love," Delia choked.

"I loved you and Father more, Delia. One can't have everything the way they want it in this life. Charles Radcliffe is a good man."

Delia's features crumpled in the moonlight. A tear glittered on her cheek. "You promise me you won't hate me for this? Promise that you'll visit me when my babe comes and even before then?"

Josie smiled thinly. "I can hardly hate you for a choice I made, Delia. I'm a grown woman, and don't you consider for a moment that I would even think of not visiting."

Delia flung her arms around her. Their breasts heaved with bittersweet sobs as they acknowledged the crossroad where their lives were forever taking separate paths.

"I love you, Delia. Always remember that," Josie murmured against her sister's hair.

"I love you too."

Josie forced herself to let go, but as they pulled apart she thought it would tear her in two. She brushed a curl out of Delia's eyes.

"Go with God, Delia," she pleaded. "He wants to be your dearest, closest friend always."

"It's not too late, Josie?" Delia whispered.

"Never. He is waiting for you, chasing you with open arms if you can stop running away," Josie promised, squeezing her sister's hand tightly. "He wants to forgive you and cast your sin as far as the east is from the west."

Delia smiled as though the words fanned hope into her lost soul. "I know. I'm forever in your debt, Josie. Thank you . . . for everything."

"Your shoes," Josie said, glancing down at Delia's slippered feet. She feared melting into a blubbering puddle at any moment.

"I don't have far to go. Just into Portreath."

Josie nodded and rooted her feet to the ground as Delia walked out of her life.

Delia pulled the valise from the oak and paused to wave farewell. Josie waved back as though her arm belonged to someone else.

"Good-bye, Delie," she whispered as a lump formed in her throat and threatened to choke her. "Good-bye."

Chapter Eight

*C*harles winced as the razor scraped across his chin. He scowled at his valet.

"Don't be in such a blasted hurry, Thomas."

"Forgive me, sir, but you always seem to be—if you'll pardon my saying so," Thomas said with a boyish grin.

Charles regarded his impertinent valet. If Thomas hadn't been a childhood friend, he wouldn't have let the familiar remark slip—but he knew he deserved the jab. Thomas had always been more than patient with his often unreasonable expectations.

"Are you quite finished?"

Thomas handed him the towel, and as Charles patted his cheeks dry, his mind reverted to the thought that plagued him. He was betrothed to a stranger. Her features had been so elusive in the shadows he probably wouldn't recognize Josephine outside of her voice. Her words mocked him: *I know I cannot hold a candle to Delia.* Was she quite plain . . . or downright homely? In the moonlight he'd been unable to tell.

"Will it be the barrel or the mail-coach knot today, sir?"

"The barrel," Charles answered, ignoring the quirk of his valet's left brow. No doubt Thomas had suggested the dandyish knot just to vex him, but today Charles wanted to delay the inevitable. If that meant wearing his cravat in a terribly fastidious manner, so be it.

As Thomas fussed with the linen folds at his throat, Charles marveled that his path had never crossed with Josephine's before. No doubt it was because he had been sent away to school as a boy, and she had stayed indoors in favor of more feminine pursuits since his return. Delia was the wild one whose daily romps around the countryside had given him his first glimpse of her. Charles recalled Josie's skillful handling of Stalwart, and the realization struck. She was the elusive horsewoman he had seen riding astride at breakneck speed as if all the demons of hell were chasing her. He had admired her ability from a distance and assumed she was one of the miner's daughters to flaunt convention in such a flagrant manner. At least they shared one passion in common. A restrictive sensation broke his thoughts.

"Not too tight," he murmured. Thomas duly loosened the knot and smirked as he caught Charles's eye.

"Miss Josephine Chadwick must be a prime article."

Charles didn't know what he winced at more—the crudeness of the vulgar term or the intimation that he was trying to impress her.

"It is no jesting matter, Thomas," he snapped. "I barely escaped her older sister, and now that Josephine will inherit the estate it is my duty to marry the Chadwick heiress as I first intended."

Charles flinched as Thomas clasped his shoulder. He had never seen his valet wear such a sober expression.

"Yes, but what is she like?" Thomas insisted. "Forgive me for addressing you so informally, Charles, but you are like a brother to me. I'm fond of you, and I wish you happiness. You act as though you do not find the prospect of being leg-shackled to this woman a pleasant one."

"Shackled is a term I never fully understood until now," Charles grumbled. "I could not begin to tell you what she is like, for the woman is a stranger to me. The fact that she appears to be virtuous and kindhearted will have to suffice for now."

Thomas fussed with Charles's cravat in silence.

Charles stood and thrust his arms through the tailcoat that Thomas held out. His heart was already warning him that he had made a mistake, and Thomas's concern only deepened his anxiety. The fact remained as irrevocable as it had the night before: he had already gone too far to in search of his father's favor. He couldn't risk losing it now.

"Well, you will certainly shine down every other man of her acquaintance," Thomas rallied. "She ought to be right proud to be the lady on your arm, sir."

"Convinced as I am of your impeccable taste, if I meet with your approval, I'm sure she shall," Charles said with a smile, returning the shoulder pat. He accepted his top hat and crushed the brim as he slipped out.

Craven bowed and opened the door, but he wasn't quick enough.

"Son."

Charles turned. "Yes, Father?"

"You're certain the solicitor was arriving today?"

"Josephine assured me of it."

"Very well then. Randolph will be as delighted as I am with your betrothal. Josephine is a good girl. And if I have not told you before, you have acted with great delicacy and wisdom in this matter of securing your future. I'm proud of you, son. Proud to call you my partner in business, and proud to call you my heir—for you are deserving on both accounts."

Charles's guard cracked for a moment as he grinned.

"Thank you, Father."

"Now go give your future father-in-law the good news, my boy."

Charles wished that obliging didn't give him such a bad taste in his mouth as he stepped outside. The deep blue of the April sky seemed irreverent when only one day stood darker in his memory . . . the day the most important woman in his life had abandoned him. The knowledge that he was risking a repeat performance shook him to the marrow.

Charles strode through the nodding heads of bluebells and violets, no longer caring if he crushed them beneath his boots. Once he had been foolish enough to craft a nosegay for a fair lady, only for his efforts to be despised. He should have known that such a shallow soul would only find beauty in the petals of a cultivated rose as pampered as herself.

The shadow of Chadwick Park dwarfed him, screaming that he didn't belong as he rapped on the door. It swung open with surprising acquiescence, revealing the stodgy butler.

"Is Mr. Chadwick at home?" Charles asked.

The butler hesitated as though mulling over his options. "Mr. Chadwick is indisposed at the moment."

Charles was already regretting the barrel knot as the starched folds scratched his tensing jaw. No doubt he was to blame for the indisposition—but then a feminine voice spoke. It was sweeter than he remembered.

"It's all right, Graham. Father will see him. Please show him into the library."

The butler grimaced but swung the door wider.

"As you wish, mistress. Allow me to take your hat, sir."

Charles swept his hat from his head as he stepped forward and locked eyes with the face to whom the voice belonged. Hers were a striking pair of eyes. Large and deep-set, shaded by thick lashes, their hazel depths arrested his with a directness he found reassuring. She seemed to have nothing to hide. He followed the cresting slope of her nose, dusted with freckles, down to the rosebud mouth. Her lips curved with tentative warmth, revealing submerged sea greens in her gaze. A fine-boned hand reached up to tuck a stray brunette strand back into place. His scrutiny was disconcerting her.

The butler harrumphed, and Charles bowed in Josephine's direction.

"Miss Chadwick."

Josephine lowered herself in a curtsy, but the technical motion meant nothing to him. He derived more reassurance from feeling the gentle warmth of her gaze rest upon his person like a drop of sunshine as he followed the butler.

"Mr. Charles Radcliffe to see you, sir," the butler said, shoving the paneled mahogany open with a gloved hand. A strained murmur of assent sounded from within, and Charles's knotted gut echoed the dread mirrored there as he stepped across the threshold.

Bookshelves surrounded him, filled from floor to ceiling with books in leather binding. Flames leaped in the stone fireplace, permeating the air with crackling warmth.

Mr. Chadwick rose from a leather chair by the hearth.

"No doubt you wish to talk, Mr. Radcliffe," he said, motioning to the chair's twin. "Do sit down."

Charles perched himself on the edge of the comfortable chair, and Mr. Chadwick eyed him with cold appraisal like a stag sizing up his rival for battle. Charles recalled Josephine's concern as he studied the older man's drawn features and ashen pallor.

"Care to wet your gullet before we begin our discussion?" Mr. Chadwick asked as he helped himself to the depleted decanter residing on the table between them. If his bleary eyes were any indication, he had already been at it for quite some time.

The amber fluid called Charles's name, but he shook his head. He couldn't afford for his wits to desert him now. He would use liquor to dull the pain of the future after this ghastly business was settled.

"I regret to inform you that Delia is no longer in residence if you wished to give her a piece of your mind," Mr. Chadwick slurred. "I had locked her away in the tower to think about the consequences of her disgrace, but unfortunately, my younger daughter has also proven to be deceitful. I found Delia missing just before noon."

"Mr. Chadwick, I beg you not to rake Miss Josephine over the coals on my account. I have washed my hands of Delia. I wish nothing more than to forget the whole matter. I can see now that it was all a mistake." Charles paused to take a cleansing breath as the old man's eyes glittered with suspicion. He could have sworn this room was suffocating him.

"What do you want then, Mr. Radcliffe? What that ungrateful wench did was abominable. I suppose your father has told you that she is with child by that peasant, with whom she has no doubt run off by now. I confess that both your father and I had hoped for reconciliation between you, as I'm sure he has informed you, but now all is lost. I summoned my solicitor this morning, and Delia is a Chadwick no longer."

The veins bulged in the older man's temples until Charles feared for the man's heart.

"Please do not distress yourself unduly, Mr. Chadwick. You and my father are old friends, and I have no wish to drive a wedge between you. I believe I have come to the only reasonable compromise. I have come seeking your permission to marry Miss Josephine."

Randolph Chadwick sobered as the full import of Charles's words struck him like cold water. He grasped Charles's hand. "Then your father has still agreed to settle the debt upon your marriage to my Josie?"

Charles gave the frail, trembling fingers a squeeze. "Yes, sir. For Miss Josephine will inherit now upon her twenty-first birthday, will she not?"

A flicker of something, perhaps comprehension, filtered through the bloodshot blue eyes. Chadwick's clammy fingers twitched in Charles's own.

"Well, my solicitors advised me not to have, er, Josie, inherit until after my death—but yes, she is now the heiress of Chadwick Park."

Charles nodded, wondering why Randolph should be afraid he would change his mind over such a trifle as the time when Josie would inherit.

"I'm sure that is most wise, sir."

The grip around his hand tightened. Tears welled in the rheumy blue eyes as the old man rasped, "You and your father have been most kind and most Christian to me, Charles. I am most grateful, and I am honored to give you my daughter Josie's hand in marriage. I confess I have always been most concerned for the future of my dear Josie. She has always been my favorite, with her gentle, loving ways, and yet I was afraid I wouldn't be able to give her a sufficient dowry. Now I'm sure you will make her very happy indeed. Never touch a dice box, son. It proved to be my father's undoing and almost mine as well."

Charles nodded, surprised the old man would confess to such folly.

Mr. Chadwick yanked a tasseled cord hanging beside the window. Within several moments a maid appeared and looked askance at the drained tumbler.

"Lizzy, fetch your mistress and tell her she has a caller waiting in the library."

Randolph winked at Charles before rising. "I'll leave you two alone."

The old man floated from the room. Charles watched him go almost wistfully. If only his own heart felt so light.

A soft step fell just outside the doorway, and Charles bolted to his feet as Josie walked in. She appeared a trifle uneasy herself. Charles's chest tightened as their eyes met.

"Would you care to show me your garden, Miss Chadwick?" he asked.

"I would like that very much, Charles."

Why did she have to say his name with such blasted familiarity? She wasn't making this easy on him.

Charles pleaded with himself to be strong as he offered her his arm. She slipped her arm through his, fitting nicely against him. Her dark head barely reached his shoulder. Unlike the rest of the women of his acquaintance, Josie had not dressed to impress. Her high-waisted, gray gown was simple, and yet there was an elegance in the way it flowed down her petite frame. Its subdued hue brought out the feathery gold slivers in her irises.

As they strolled together, he found himself comparing her to Delia. It seemed ludicrous that they were sisters. Josie was curves to Delia's bones, the moth alongside the butterfly, content to be a more subtle definition of beauty. She couldn't hold a candle to Delia; she lacked her sister's dazzling brilliance. Yet she was comfortable in her own skin and far from unattractive.

In fact, Charles decided, there was something distinctly different about Josie Chadwick. Her very presence calmed him, and she wasn't noisy to look at.

She did not seem to mind his silence as he stole his surreptitious glance, and the quiet had not yet grown awkward. He was grateful that she gave him a chance to collect his thoughts—to see more than he had seen earlier. His troubles had so preoccupied him that he had failed to notice hers. There were smudges of exhaustion beneath her eyes, accentuating the paleness of her cheeks as sorrow seeped through a strong exterior. How well Charles knew it.

He cleared his throat as the starched folds of the cravat rubbed against his neck.

"Your father thinks I am proposing to you. I did not think it prudent to mention our, ahem, clandestine meeting last night."

"Most discreet of you."

Charles jerked the ends of the cravat free. "My valet never could tie a barrel knot properly anyway."

Her laughter was soft and there, peeking around the corner of her smile, was an adorable dimple in her right cheek. Even her laugh soothed him. The muscles in his back began to unknot.

"I apologize for my father's liberality with spirits."

Charles winced before he could remaster his composure. If only she knew just how much he could relate.

"You have made your father a very happy man, Jo—sephine." He caught himself in time. *Josie is much too intimate.*

A tremor coursed through her. His arm tightened around hers. Had he only imagined it, or did she press into him as into a shelter—perhaps from a storm raging within?

"Are you well?" he asked, steering her toward a stone bench.

"Quite well," she gasped, but chalky lips belied the statement.

Charles sank onto the mossy stone of the bench, forcing her to sit as well. She refused to relinquish his arm, clinging to it as though it were her lifeline. He reined in the amusement tugging at his lips. It was beyond him how she could derive comfort from bodily contact with him. Surely she could see that his touch afforded nothing more than a gentleman's courtesy?

A tear dangled from her bottom lashes, and Charles could not bear for it to defile those eyes. Even as his finger itched to catch it, she swiped it away.

"Forgive me," she said, sucking in a shuddering breath. "No doubt you think me overwrought and foolish."

"There is naught to forgive. I think it has been a great deal more difficult for you with your father than it was for me."

Charles didn't recognize the gentleness in his own tone, but he roused himself from analyzing it further.

"I am just so relieved," Josie burst out, releasing him. "I feared Father would never forgive me for helping Delia escape last night. It was difficult for me . . . to say good-bye. No matter what she did, she is my sister, and I will always love her. I have wondered if what happened was in some way . . . my fault."

All of Charles's former pity toward Randolph Chadwick evaporated in an instant. How dare the man resent his saint of a daughter for saving his unworthy hide!

"Your fault? Now, don't ever let me hear your lips form those words again. I heard your father speak of you before I asked for your hand in a manner that was utterly unworthy of your love for him. If he dared to put such a vulgar notion in your mind, just to lay his own blame on your shoulders, then so help me he doesn't deserve you!"

"But Charles, I have been like a mother to Delia! Maybe if I had watched out for her more, or—"

"No, no guilt. Your father could have made her mind after your mother died. It was his responsibility, for he was her parent, not you. Any parent who makes his child feel guilty for his own sin no longer deserves to be one."

As Josie's tearful eyes studied him, Charles clenched his jaw. It had been unwise to reveal his bitterness toward his own father in such a way. He prayed she hadn't understood him.

"I think for both of our sakes, the wedding should be sooner than later. I'll let you settle upon a date with your father before you notify me. I'm certain I shall be able to concur so long as business doesn't intervene—"

Charles's voice trailed off as something cool and moist nudged his hand. A slobbery tongue peeled across the back of his wrist. He scowled down at the setter, who rested his chin upon Charles's knee with an apologetic half-wag. Soulful brown eyes implored for forgiveness, and a piteous whine sent vibrations skittering up his thigh.

"Byron, you rascal," he muttered as he reached out and fondled the setter's mottled gray and white ears. "How did you get out of your kennel? And to come all the way here, no less."

Byron yawned, entirely confident of his canine charms.

"Are you going to introduce me to your friend who had the gall to interrupt our wedding planning?" There was no mockery in Josie's gaze, only playful light dancing upon the sea green depths.

"Josephine, meet Byron," Charles drawled, grinning as Byron reared back and offered his paw on cue.

"Charmed to meet you, I'm sure," Josie responded, reaching out and grasping the snowy paw. Byron sealed his pledge of undying loyalty with a slobbery kiss.

"Byron," Charles groaned as the setter planted both paws in Josie's lap, and she pushed against the setter's chest to escape further canine worship. Byron rested his panting cheek against Josie's and stared back at Charles with feigned innocence.

"Down, Byron," Charles demanded as Josie beamed at him in delight. Both Stalwart and Byron had fallen victim to her fatal charm, and if animals weren't true judges of character, Charles didn't know what were. *Fiend seize that dimple!*

"I see we are both admirers of Lord Byron's poetry."

"He is usually well behaved."

Josie laughed again, that adorable feather soft sound. "If that is your definition of good behavior, sir, I fear I prefer him naughty."

"Indeed, that does not surprise me, considering your penchant for runaway stallions."

Josie sobered, and Charles wished he could take back the words that had killed the sparkling light in her eyes.

He cleared his throat. "I'll take my leave, for I'm sure you have better things to do with your time than to flap gums with me."

Something hopeful and defiant flared to life in her expression as he stood. "On the contrary, Mr. Radcliffe. I enjoyed our little chat immensely."

"Touché," Charles parried. Nevertheless, the thrust of formality had gone home, leaving him hungry to hear his name on her lips again. Dash her. She already possessed the power to hurt him.

Chapter Nine

Josie stared at the gate from her bedchamber window, picturing the way Charles had strode through it with those powerful, long legs of his and failed to glance back as she waved. Daylight had portrayed him in such a different light . . . leaving her distracted as a schoolgirl. A man whose hair the sun turned to gold really shouldn't hug the blue sky with shoulders quite as broad as Charles Radcliffe's. Blue . . . his eyes were the bluest she had ever seen. Her cheeks flushed as she remembered what it was to lean against the squared muscle and bone of her betrothed—the manly swell beneath her fingertips when his arm flexed.

The words haunted her . . . he had said their wedding day should arrive sooner than later. To think that scarcely a year had passed since she had watched the dreaded carriage arrive bearing their doom through that gate from this very window. It seemed like yesterday, but how her life had changed since that day. Her mouth went dry. *I'm not ready to marry any man, least of all Charles Radcliffe. I'm not certain what is worse in that Nordic temper of his—frosty blue eyes or flying sparks.*

She sighed. Even in the heat of temper, Charles was beautiful the same way a streak of lightning thrilled her as it pierced the clouds. *Whatever could possess him to marry a plain woman like me when he could have any woman he wanted?*

The irony of the truth penetrated thorn sharp. "Because I am the heiress of Chadwick Park," Josie admitted to herself barely above a whisper. The words branded her soul. *Unwanted. Unloved. Unworthy.*

A knock sent Josie's heart thumping. She whirled, knocking a vase from her whatnot and sending it crashing to the floor. Crystal shards and petals scattered into the farthest corners of her bedchamber.

"Josie?" The door shuddered open as Esther peered in. "Mollie said ye needed me. Are ye all right?"

Josie shook her head and covered her mouth.

"Och, luve," Esther murmured, brows drawing together in sympathy. "'Tis not a sin to cry, ye ken."

"I don't think I can do this," Josie sobbed between her fingers.

Loving arms pulled her home against a shoulder scented with sunshine. Healing hands stroked her back and knitted her broken pieces back together.

"I'm so afraid."

"What are ye afraid of, luve?"

"Of sharing his bed, bearing his children, and carrying his name all for the sake of my inheritance. He doesn't want plain little old me, and everyone will see it. I'll have to sit there beside him, enduring the stares and whispers all through the dinner party."

"Who said ye were plain?" Esther's voice was fierce as she gripped Josie's shoulders.

Josie looked at her governess askance. "Delia is the beautiful one."

"Ye and Delia are beautiful in different ways." Esther lowered her voice to a whisper. "Ye are a braw lass with a beautiful heart. When Charles looks at ye, no doubt that's what he sees. Charles is a man, luve. He'd not be marrying ye if he found ye unattractive."

"Not even for Chadwick Park?"

"It's the man, and not the thought of marriage itself that's troubling ye, isn't it? Matches like this are made all the time for money rather than love. Tongues won't wag about the both of ye any more than usual."

"There's something about Charles. I can't understand him, though I've tried."

"Aye, there is. I've sensed it too. But I dinna ken anyone better to draw out his heart than ye."

The persistent doubt still gnawed at Josie. The man remained a mystery and presented a paradox of the heart, alternating between fiercely harsh and fiercely gentle.

"Should I not have done this in such a foolhardy fashion?"

"Ye alone ken the answer to that question, luve. I think ye did a braw, braw thing out of all the love in yer heart. Ye paid a price, ye did, but God alone sees the silent tears my heart has cried for ye, wishing I could do aught to heal yer broken dreams—and yet I cannae. God sees yer sacrifice, luve. I have had to ask myself the question, and then trust ye to Jesus knowing Him as I do. Will not the Judge of all the earth do right by ye?"

"Why is it I cannot feel Him anymore, Esther? I prayed for wisdom and thought He had given me the answer, but now I have so many doubts and fears gnawing at me, and He seems far off."

Esther chuckled as she wiped the tears from Josie's cheeks.

"Aye, doubt does that. It gnaws and nibbles at yer innards like disease. The only cure for it is trust, luve. When we cast all our cares upon Him, kenning He alone is strong enough to carry them, He is free to move. Sometimes we fight God every step of the way. Unbelief quenches the Holy Spirit, so cast those cares, luve. We want the waters to part in our timing, but God makes everything beautiful in His time. Ye have entered a season of waiting upon God to unfold His plan for your life . . . so trust Him, Josie. Just trust Him, kenning it's as the Good Book says: He is a rewarder of them that diligently seek Him."

Josie smiled and cupped Esther's hand against her cheek, overawed by grace. "I'll trust Him and move on one condition. You've always been there for me, Esther. I'm asking you to be my lady's maid as I begin my new life. I just dismissed Mollie to go tend her ailing mother with excellent references and ample funds to cushion her lack of employment until they are back on their feet. Please don't leave me now. I need you."

The plea sounded childish even to her own ears, but she couldn't let Esther walk out of her life now. She couldn't identify the emotion that filtered through the gray depths of Esther's gaze like a plummeting stone as her governess blinked back tears.

"I would cheerfully be a scullery maid for the rest of my life to stay with ye, luve. I will always be here for ye if that is what ye want. Delia never needed me the way ye do, and it would rip my heart out to leave ye now."

The relief left Josie weak. She had survived another wave of the change overwhelming her heart's shore.

"Thank you, Esther."

Questions hung thick on the tip of her tongue. Such a beautiful woman could surely have married and had children of her own to love by now. Yet Esther stood at the end of her calling as a governess, her beauty fading with the passing years. Time had been kind thus far, but Josie feared what would have become of Esther without family or prospects. Governess positions were in high demand among respectable, unmarried women, and Josie wasn't leaving her beloved Esther's future to chance. The title of lady's maid was a flimsy excuse, but it served its purpose. Charles would expect her to bring one into the marriage, after all.

"Enough fretting, Miss Josie. It's time to get Cinderella ready for her betrothal ball, and though I am no fairy godmother, I won't rest until ye feel like the most beautiful woman there."

For hours Josie sat at her dressing table as Esther painstakingly prepared her toilette. At last, she stepped back and beamed with pride. Her voice caught with the words. "Ye are beautiful, Josephine Marie Chadwick, and dinna ye ever forget it. Close yer eyes now."

Josie stumbled as Esther steered her forward in the direction of her full-length mirror.

"Open, luve."

Josie blinked at the apparition in the mirror before her. Surely it was too lovely to be real. Her claret dress kindled a rich warmth against the paleness of her skin and brought a glow to the depths of her eyes. Her porcelain skin was the feminine ideal, freckles hidden beneath the subtle application of powder and rouge. Her dark curls were piled high in the latest style, but Esther had left a few free to brush her right shoulder. She gasped as Esther lowered a glittering strand of heirloom rubies and diamonds to nestle at the hollow of her throat.

"Yer father told me he wanted ye to wear these as befitting the heiress of Chadwick Park. If that is not a beautiful sight, I dinna ken what is. Charles will hardly be able to believe his good fortune," Esther praised as she fastened the last ruby marquise earring.

Josie blinked away the fresh, threatening moisture in her eyes. The romantic dreams her heart had nurtured since girlhood still refused to die.

Chapter Ten

The night air blew cool against Josie's skin as the footman swung the barouche around. Father turned, and his smile of greeting broadened with admiration. She grasped his hand as he helped her into the barouche. He seated himself across from her with a tender light playing in his eyes.

"My dearest Josie, you look so much like your mother tonight."

"Thank you, Father," she acknowledged, shocked that he would say so—and uncertain she agreed. She recalled her mother's brown eyes, black tresses, and vivid coloring unaided by rouge.

The candlelight spilling from within their home shimmered off his gaze as the barouche lurched into motion.

"I'm going to miss you, my dear, more than I care to admit."

Josie mustered a smile, forgetting the flutter in her stomach for the first time. "I know it won't be the same, Father, but I'm only going to the neighboring estate. I'll visit you often, I promise."

"You're a good girl," Father said, patting her cheek. "You've made me proud by redeeming the Chadwick name, and I look forward to the grandchildren you and Charles will give me."

Josie blushed, and her father chuckled as he pressed a kiss against her glove.

"Forgive me for my indelicacy, daughter. I promise to repair the west wing in time for them to romp there as much as they like. How I hated forbidding you to play there as a child. You dearly loved exploring there, didn't you?"

"Yes, I did . . . and you needn't apologize. You know I would do anything in the world to make you happy. I am still unaccustomed to the idea of marriage, that is all."

"Of course you are. Charles is a good man, Josie. I have no doubt you will be happy with him, though it all seems very sudden I know. You should have seen how protective he was when I spoke disparagingly of you letting Delia out of the tower. I fear I was rather harsh on you about that dashed affair. You didn't deserve it. Will you forgive this foolish old man?"

Tears pricked Josie's eyes afresh. The Lord had known how much she needed healing of that wound.

"Certainly, Father. You know how dearly I love you."

Father blinked and tugged at his cravat as though it was too tight, but Josie knew better. "And I love you, dear girl. You get that from your mother too. Always loving this old fool with your longsuffering ways."

Josie glanced out the window as the barouche ground to a halt. The woman her father remembered with such fondness was not the woman she had known. She wondered about it. It was unlike him to forget an injustice or a slight, both of which her mother had administered as faithfully as her complexion cream.

Josie's slippers crunched over the pea gravel drive as she grasped the footman's proffered hand and clung to the love shining in her father's eyes. Never had she needed his support more than in this moment.

A tall, broad-shouldered silhouette strode toward them. The light caught the gold threads in his hair, flirting with his square forehead, sharp nostrils, and sensual lips pressed tight. His deep-set eyes remained hooded in shadow as Charles bowed.

"Welcome to Treathston Heights, Mr. Chadwick, Miss Chadwick."

Josie dipped in what she hoped was a graceful curtsy, but Charles's gaze chilled her through the shadows. As she slid her arm through the proffered crook of his elbow, he was stiff as a wooden soldier. She wondered what inner battle he was waging. Tilting her head, Josie stole a glance at his profile. He didn't twitch an eyelid.

A firm footfall drew her attention forward, her eyes colliding with a gaze of blue steel. A man who could only be her future father-in-law stood before her, eyes boring through her with the intensity of twin pistol barrels, but in a contradiction of nature also offering her inviting warmth. He was scarcely an inch taller than she, yet his presence was commanding.

As though reading her thoughts, Charles's voice broke the suspense. "Josephine, this is my father, Mr. Sebastian Radcliffe. Father, meet my betrothed, Miss Josephine Chadwick."

The stocky man bowed. Apparently, Charles had only inherited the breadth of his shoulders.

"I am so pleased to make your acquaintance, my dear." Mr. Radcliffe took her fingers in a gentle grasp and raised them to his lips.

Josie scrutinized him in turn. He rather resembled a hawk. His longish hair was as black as her father's had once been, threaded with silver at the temples and combed back from his leathery, lined skin. Dark, craggy brows hooded his expression. A hooked nose leered above his lean mouth, which was surrounded by a shadow of stubble.

"I am honored to meet you, sir," Josie said as she dropped a curtsy.

"You may call me Sebastian if you are so inclined, Miss Chadwick. I never cared for such a formal title of address as 'sir.' It makes me feel ancient somehow."

"Most people call me Josie, and I would be pleased to address you by your Christian name in private company, Mr. Radcliffe."

"Josie, eh? I would be delighted to do so. It suits her, wouldn't you say, Charles? Josephine is much too long and stern sounding to be of practical use now, isn't it?"

Josie smiled at his frankness and hoped Charles would take the bait. "Those have always been my sentiments exactly," she agreed.

Sebastian's mouth twitched at her enthusiasm. "I am glad to see you find a crusty curmudgeon like me amusing, Josie. Egad, the light of your smile could charm a fly off a plate. That is what's been missing in this house, son, all these years. The light of a woman's smile."

Charles stiffened beside her, but Father's entrance spared him from replying.

"Ah, welcome, Randolph," Sebastian said. "After meeting your charming daughter, I must confess I feel that I am getting the better end of this bargain."

"I will sorely miss her, but alas, all children grow up and lead lives of their own. Thank God ours will both be close by in our old age, eh Sebastian?"

"Indeed we are fortunate," Sebastian drawled.

Sorrow pierced Josie's heart as she realized that anyone who didn't know better would assume her father was the eldest of the two men. Suffering had aged him indeed.

"Charles, it is early yet before the rest of the guests arrive. What do you say to giving Josie a tour?"

Charles's jaw locked in response, and to Josie's surprise, his words were tinged with sarcasm. "Capital idea, Father. I'm sure that will go a long way toward cozying her up to the notion."

Josie squeezed his arm in sympathy, recognizing his resentment toward his father for forcing them into their hasty betrothal. Apparently, he blamed both of their paternal parents for his unhappiness. He caught her eye and cocked an ironical brow.

"I for one would thoroughly enjoy a tour," Father piped up. "I have yet to see the interior improvements you have made. The grounds are certainly expansive."

Josie cringed at the thoughtless comment. Though his tactlessness usually endeared him to her, in this instance she couldn't forgive him for it.

"It is dwarfed by Chadwick Park, but your modesty is refreshing, Mr. Chadwick. We will try not to bore you with unnecessary detail."

Father and son eyed each other as a tangible current of tension flowed between them. Charles exaggerated his deferent bow. "Lead the way by all means, Father."

Had it always been this way between them? Josie swallowed the bitter pill. Her future home would only bring fresh familial strife.

"Treathston Heights dates back to the Norman conquest," Sebastian began. "The estate fell into the hands of a Roundhead after his uncle, the original heir, was condemned as a traitor to the crown and executed during the civil war. It passed down through his family for several generations. I acquired it after they fell upon hard times."

Sebastian paused in the hallway and gestured to the collection of paintings hemming the stairwell.

"I have always believed that an old house should boast a fine collection of art work, and I continue to collect when I can. Do you recognize that one, Josie?"

Josie's gaze followed his pointing finger to the gilded frame at eye level.

"It is the view of Treathston from the sea."

"Yes, done by a local artist. Good perspective, wouldn't you say?"

Josie studied it and murmured her approval—though she didn't entirely feel it. Did her heart prejudice her against the painting, or was there something ominous lurking in the harsh oil strokes? Boiling waves churned with exaggerated ferocity before dashing against the dark gashes that comprised the cliffs. Sharp parapets gouged the leaden sky, and as the observer's eye naturally followed the right wing, the shore dropped away, plunging steeply to the lean stretch of sand below.

"Treathston Heights was named for that beach you see in the right-hand corner."

As Sebastian moved on, Josie dragged her gaze away from the artist's initials with a prickle of foreboding. She knew those initials—they belonged to the artist she loved like a grandmother. But the painting did not look like one of hers. It was not Suzanne's habit to begrudge the light.

Unlike Chadwick Park, the doors of Treathston Heights were all open as Sebastian pointed out the rooms, allowing the heat to flow in and out as it chose. They followed him into the ballroom. Josie could almost make out her features in the gleaming waxed floor. A life-sized portrait of a little boy caught her eye, commanding attention from the mantle. Her gaze caressed his stiff posture, his flaxen hair almost white in the sunlight as he sat astride a dappled gray pony. His blue eyes tugged at her heart, for the artist had captured a rawness in the expression. Pain, fresh and defiant, cried from a wound that had scarred the man Charles had become.

Sebastian's smooth voice broke into her thoughts. "That portrait of Charles was done when he was ten, shortly after we moved here."

"Pardon my asking, Sebastian, but why did you choose Cornwall? Had you no family elsewhere?" Father asked.

"Sadly, no. My parents were killed in a tragic accident when I was a boy. I entered the navy as a powder monkey and gradually worked my way up to captain. The profession was good to me, and I suppose that's why I couldn't bear to leave the sea after I sold my commission."

Josie tried to hide a frown. The world of things he had left unsaid haunted her. She swallowed her questions for the time being.

Throughout the tour, Charles remained silent. As Sebastian pointed out the servants' quarters, Josie drew the courage to look up at him.

"You've always loved horses, haven't you?" she asked.

Charles flinched as her voice seemed to bring him back to the present.

"Yes."

"I heard you renovated your stables. Would you show them to me sometime?" It encouraged her that he hadn't shied away, though she wondered where he had been when she first spoke.

"If it would amuse you."

"Do you have any available stalls?"

What was close to a smile touched his mouth.

"Always."

"Ebony will be relieved to hear it."

"Your horse, I presume?"

"She's an old mare, but I've had her for as long as I can remember. I could not bear to be parted from her."

"In that case, rest assured there will be a fresh stall waiting for her. Stalwart has been pining for a new lady friend of late."

Josie squeezed his arm with a rush of warmth. *You are as unpredictable as the sea, Charles Radcliffe.* "Thank you."

Charles averted his eyes. The sound of voices drifted to them from down the hall—guests arriving for the celebration of their betrothal.

"Come and greet our guests, you two," Sebastian urged. "We can end our tour here. The upstairs is of little consequence, although I'm sure you will find your suite fascinating."

Charles cursed under his breath.

"It's all right," Josie murmured.

"No, it isn't. He doesn't deserve your grace, Josephine. He enjoys making us squirm."

"Excuse us for a private moment, Father, Mr. Chadwick," he called after their retreating backs. His arm tightened around her gloved elbow as he steered her around the corner and down another hallway.

"Where are you taking me?"

Charles didn't answer as he reached behind her head and leaned against the wall. Concentration thawed his glacial stare as a familiar click rang in her ear. Air gaped behind her, and Josie smothered a scream as Charles whisked her through the panel. Her hands flew against his chest as the inky darkness eclipsed the light. Her ragged breathing filled the narrow space, heart fluttering against her ribs.

"Don't be afraid. It is just an old priest's hole."

Josie gasped for breath as gentle hands cupped her jaw, thumbs traveling to her ears. Silence descended as her pulse thundered against his skin. *Surely he can hear my heart pounding.*

"Listen to me. Tell me where you want to go for the honeymoon, and I'll take you there. I have to get away from Father for a while, and it's not as though I can't afford it. Just tell me."

"Anywhere?" Josie squeaked.

"Yes, isn't there somewhere you have dreamed of going your whole life?"

"Venice."

"Well then," he whispered, warm breath rushing against her forehead. "I'll take you there."

"Thank you, Charles."

"Don't thank me. I am doing it for myself as much as for you."

His fingers left her face. A sliver of light slanted across the intensity of his eyes, crackling with electric blue light, as he opened the panel again. She brushed by him into the open air with a shiver and struggled to remaster her composure. He offered his arm once more, and Josie accepted it as they went to greet their guests like the happy couple they weren't.

By the time dinner was announced, Josie's face hurt from smiling through the charade. Charles pulled out her chair with a discordant scrape. She doubted she would be able to hold down a single bite.

"Where are the two of you planning on honeymooning?" Mrs. Irving inquired.

"In Venice."

"Ah, Italy is where all the young couples go nowadays. Enjoy yourself, my dear."

Charles raised his wineglass to his lips as a flood of claret drowned his smirk.

Cousin Mabel leaned across the table, and Josie took a bite, hoping the mouthful of food would spare her any more prying questions from the infamous Chadwick gossip.

It didn't work. "When your handsome Charles proposed, I trust it was very romantic?"

Josie's eyes watered as the food lodged in her throat. Charles raised his glass with a flourish.

"On the contrary, she proposed to me."

Josie gagged, gulping down her claret as Cousin Mabel exploded in her characteristic cackle.

"Oh, my dear boy, you amuse me. I'm sure you would have me believe you are as desirous as all that, but you will be good for our Josie. She has always been far too straitlaced for her own good—pardon the expression, dearie."

Josie froze her smile in place and kicked Charles under the table. His lips curled as he drained another glass. Was that contempt she saw hidden beneath his amusement? Was that his second or his third glass? *I've already lost count, and that's not all I've lost. Perhaps he was never on my side.*

Snatches of conversation filtered to her ears.

"Pleasant match after her sister's scandalous elopement, to be sure."

"The Chadwicks will be sitting pretty with Charles's living. They say he has nine thousand pounds a year."

Charles's warm breath rushed against Josie's ear, and she almost dropped her fork. "Pay no attention. You don't want them gossiping that you didn't touch your food on top of everything else."

You should pay more attention to your fork rather than your glass.

Sebastian scraped his chair back and raised his glass. "I want to propose a toast on behalf of my son and his betrothal to the charming Josephine Chadwick. May their days be long and their love fruitful."

"Hear, hear!"

Josie held her glass in a daze, and Charles clanked his glass against hers with a maddening grin.

"I'll risk drinking to that."

His burst of laughter raked the heat in her cheeks as she drained her glass, but she couldn't disguise the tremor in her fingers. *I'll not survive another course, and neither will this betrothal.*

Dessert arrived none too soon, but the tart landed tasteless on her tongue. As the chairs scraped back, Charles took her arm and led the way into the ballroom. Josie squelched her child-ish urge to stomp on his foot, detecting the wine on his breath and the shine in his eyes. She prayed he would be steady on his feet as they faced off and bowed. Trilling notes flowed from the orchestra box as she reached for his hand.

"Enjoying yourself yet?" he asked.

Josie's smile wobbled, and she silently dared him to humiliate her as their dance opened the ball. Though he faltered at points and crushed her hand, they managed to get through without disaster. Polite applause rippled as attention slid off them onto the other couples who began dancing, and she could breathe again.

"Pray, excuse me for a moment," Josie gasped.

The flicker of icy relief in Charles's gaze did not escape her, nor did it surprise her when he made a beeline for the punch table.

Josie made her way to the lady's powder room, exhaling with relief when she found it empty. The evening was young yet. She pressed a damp towel to her throbbing temples, longing for Esther's soothing touch. Even the mirror mocked her as she adjusted a stray curl. Stormy gray eyes flashed back at her, belonging to a flushed woman she didn't recognize as herself, taut mouth maintaining the barest semblance of control. Josie wheeled away, vowing Charles would not humiliate her further.

As she scanned the colorful throng, she found Charles, clutching a willowy blonde against his body with far more enthusiasm than he had shown her. He flung his head back in ribald laughter, and the Jezebel regarded him as though he were something to eat. Josie stood frozen in place, anger and surprise vying for position. She wouldn't have expected this of him, even drunk as he was.

The blonde tilted her head, and a fresh wave of shock rolled over her as she recognized her cousin Aurelia. Apparently, she still thought she was entitled to the best the world had to offer, including Josie's betrothed.

A tap on Josie's shoulder cooled her boiling blood as a dashing naval officer bowed. What was his name? She couldn't remember. "May I have this dance, Miss Chadwick?" he inquired.

"You may indeed," Josie purred. Two could play at this game.

As she danced, she caught Charles's gaze landing on them often. Delia had always been the girl highly sought after, but Josie had to give herself some credit. She had never looked more alive or more beautiful, and she knew it.

Minutes lapsed into hours, and Josie never suffered once for a dance partner. While she pretended to be flattered, her heart refused to be fooled. Charles had flung her away like an ill-fitting shoe. Her anger mounted after a glance found Aurelia in his arms yet again. The inevitable question nagged like rain pecking against glass . . . would Charles be as faithful and true to her as he had promised to be, when he clearly resented the circumstances of their betrothal? They weren't even married yet, and he was already favoring the company of other women over her.

It was late in the evening when Charles tapped her partner's shoulder.

"Mind if I cut in with my betrothed?"

A twinkle lit the depths of her partner's dark eyes, and he bowed. "Thank you for the pleasure of such charming company, Miss Josephine."

"The pleasure was all mine."

Charles jerked her into his arms, casting a glare after the officer. "Thought I'd better remind him of what's mine. That cheeky fellow has danced the last three with you."

Josie glared up at him. "Clearly you did not care to remind cousin Aurelia."

Charles scowled, crushing her fingers in his. "It was just to be for one dance, but then you made it perfectly clear that you were happy elsewhere."

"Not here, Charles," Josie hissed. "Take me outside. I need a breath of fresh air."

Charles dragged her out to the balcony. The steps descended into the garden. Josie wrenched her arm away, satisfied that no lovers lurked in the shadows.

"What were you thinking? Getting yourself drunk while you danced and flirted with any woman other than your betrothed? I have never been so humiliated in all my life!"

Charles glared at her like a petulant child. "You can hardly blame a bachelor for enjoying his last taste of freedom before being shackled to a complete stranger."

"I can and I do! Freedom from me—is that what you want? I haven't particularly relished the thought of being shackled to you either, and yet you seem determined to make me despise you before we even begin."

"This wasn't my idea."

Josie's eyebrows soared along with her tone. "I didn't propose for you, Mr. Radcliffe. You made your choice. I can't imagine why you bothered if I am such a thorn in your side that you must endeavor to forget my existence altogether—on a night meant to celebrate our betrothal, no less!"

Charles leaned against the stone wall of the balcony. The moonlight glittered in his eyes with icy radiance.

She hadn't expected repentance from him, yet his silence hurt worse than if he had confirmed that he hated her. "Of course you do not deny it. I must have been mad to think you cared enough to take me wherever my heart desired. If I died tomorrow, you would be glad to be free of me."

"Josephine."

The sharpness of Charles's tone cut her, and she shivered in the night air as the breeze carried through the tear in her soul. *He knows I detest my full name, yet he mocks me. Just like my mother. But if she was the Ice Queen, he is the King.*

A numbing chill drained her fear as he staggered closer. She would welcome a blow. Any reason to end this masquerade would suffice.

But instead he choked out, "It isn't you. Know that for your own sake . . ." His shoulders slumped, voice trailing away like smoke in the night.

Josie's throat burned as he turned his back on her and fled back to the ballroom. The sudden wistfulness in his voice had held her captive, but the words hovering on his tongue to release her had never come. Hot disappointment flooded her eyes as she collapsed on the steps.

"Josie."

The whisper sighed through the branches. A prickle skittered down her spine as she darted to her feet.

Josie stiffened and clenched the iron railing as a silhouette separated itself through the shadows. "Who is it?"

A familiar gaze seared through the night. "It's me, Bertram."

Alarm filled her. "What are you doing here?"

"I have to talk to you."

"I am expected inside," Josie said, mounting a step.

"Please! It will only take a moment."

His desperate cry stopped her. She sighed but found herself descending. "Please state your peace quickly. This isn't fitting, the two of us alone in the dark. I am betrothed to be married."

"He doesn't deserve you."

Something raw and wounded grated in Bertram's voice, resonating with the wound Charles had inflicted. Her thoughts blurred as warm fingers swallowed her hand. "You are so cold—"

She pulled her hand away. "Bertram, I have no choice. I can't stand by and watch my family be ruined after Delia's disgrace. When my chance came to save our good name, I took it."

"Do you love him?"

"No, but—"

"Then listen to me. I love you, Josie. Always have . . . don't go and throw yourself away on him now when I can give you so much more. I may not have a mansion, but at least I have a heart. I know you. You're a warmhearted creature who needs a lover's flame to stay alive, and you'll freeze to death with that man. Come away with me now, my love."

Josie blinked back tears as the trap she had been courting sprang shut. Temptation hovered, but it was too late to turn back now. "Bertram, I'm honored truly. I have always known how much you care, but it's too late for that now. The disappointment would kill Father."

"Josie, you have always put them—your family—before your own happiness. Don't sacrifice yourself when they aren't worth it. No life is worth living without love."

Josie tried to turn, but he grabbed her arms and held her fast. She looked at the ground at her feet. "I'm afraid I don't love you half as much as you love me. You should marry a girl who will adore you equally."

"You will in time," Bertram breathed as he stepped closer. Josie's life flew by as she envisioned a different life and searched his eyes in the darkness. Charles had left her cold . . . and empty. Perhaps Bertram was right that she was too warm-blooded to yoke herself to a heart of ice.

"I love you, Josie. You're the only woman I'll ever love."

She shivered, but she was far from chilled as his trembling hands seized her face. Her paralyzed heart beat fast as his mouth seared her flesh. Her strength came at last. She refused to let him possess her. She would not be owned.

"Stop," she gasped, shoving him away. "For the love of heaven, please stop."

"My love, did I hurt you? I'm sorry—"

"No, you are too good to me, but you must endeavor to forget me now. I have made my bed, and I must lie in it. Forgive me, oh forgive me if you can."

His haunted voice followed her as her feet hammered against the stairs. "You're wrong, Josie. One day you will long for me when you are cold, and I'll be here waiting."

Chapter Eleven

The footman held out the silver tray to her at breakfast. "A letter for you, Mistress."

Josie reached for her serviette and patted her mouth to delay the inevitable. The bold, slanting strokes struck her as masculine, but the hand was too elegant to be Bertram's. His penmanship resembled hen scratches. It bore no seal. She grasped the paperknife and slit it open with a shaky breath.

Dear Josephine,

It is well after midnight, and still sleep eludes me as your lovely, wounded eyes haunt me. My head splits something fierce, but that is what I justly deserve after behaving so abominably toward you. I can honestly say that I would thrash any man who dared to hurt you thus, but I realize that I, the very man who has sworn to protect you and pledged his heart to you in marriage, have betrayed your trust. I have wounded you more than any man with my selfishness and my blind conceit. I am a fool who does not deserve you.

If you wish to sever your attachment to me, then just say the word. My father can survive a little disappointment for once, and as for yours, I am prepared and willing to write him a cheque that will go a long way toward settling his debts, though not in their entirety. It is the least I can do to make amends to you, whose reputation would suffer doubly from our broken engagement and your sister's elopement. Please write and tell me what you desire most.

I remain yours very sincerely,

Charles Radcliffe

Josie read the letter a second, and then a third time. She stared unseeing across the table as her mind weighed the consequences of such a choice. Her beloved Chadwick Park could very well crumble beneath a second scandal. Father would look at her as though she had willfully torn it down brick by brick, for broken engagements were not looked kindly upon in their circles. Potential suitors would look upon her as tainted. What other man would have her after she spurned Charles Radcliffe?

His words echoed through her heart as she asked herself the question. What did she desire? *The impossible,* she scoffed. To be loved by the very man so desperate to be rid of her. A man who would no doubt despise her even more for not letting both of them escape when given the chance. It was just like him to leave the choice and its consequences all in her hands. But—*was* he trying to get rid of her? Or was his remorse sincere?

Her chair scraped back, and Father glanced up in concern. "Was that from Charles?"

"Yes. I confess I will be glad when all of the wedding details have been settled."

She thrust the letter inside her chemise, and as the creased folds rubbed against her skin, she hoped the words would seep through so that her heart could discern the truth. Torn as she was, it certainly wasn't wise to respond just yet.

Suzanne's mysterious painting had prompted questions. Perhaps a brisk walk to visit her friend would clear her head.

She prayed she wouldn't run into Bertram completing one of his many duties on the estate and determined to cut across the north pasture that now belonged to the Radcliffes.

The lulling whisper of the sea breeze caressed Josie's skin. She drank in the elusive sunlight as it peeked through a cloud, chasing away the gloom.

Lord, I've prayed for wisdom more times than I care to remember. Is Charles your answer, or is he the biggest mistake I could ever make?

What a world of difference two words could make. *Dear Charles . . .*

Suzanne's cottage beckoned like a haven. She spotted the old woman sitting there abreast of her easel, paintbrush aloft as though holding the rest of the world at arm's length.

"Suzanne," she called.

A sparkle brightened the squinting depths of the old woman's rheumy blue eyes. "I saw you coming, Josie child. Bounding through the grass jest as graceful as them deer you scairt away jest now."

Josie peered at the canvas, where a half-painted mother doe and fawn nibbled on tender blades of grass. It had all the peace and sunshine of the old woman's usual style.

She bent and kissed Suzanne's creased forehead.

"I'm sorry."

"Don't be. 'Tain't every day I have the pleasure of yer company. Now what's this I hear of yer marrying the Radcliffe boy?"

Josie straightened, heaving a mounting sigh. "You don't miss a thing even way out here, do you?"

Suzanne paused to shadow the grass beneath the doe's underbelly. "Shameful how yer father's drowning in debt. Jest like yer Grandfather Chadwick, living far beyond his means. Old sins have long shadows. 'Tain't right, 'tain't fitting. I had a sneaking 'spicion the ol' Radcliffe devil would send his spawn up here to evict me now that yer father's done sold the north pasture, but to the boy's credit, he paid me a kindly visit and told me not to worry none. He was downright neighborly 'bout it and chopped me some wood. The ol' devil 'tain't poisoned him yet."

Josie gnawed at her lip as Suzanne began to paint the sky with a sweeping brushstroke. The piece fit into the complex puzzle her betrothed was proving to be.

"I'm glad to hear that Charles was kind to you. Our marriage will resolve my father's debt. I came up to ask you about one of your paintings. I saw hanging it at Treathston Heights. It wasn't done in your usual style, Suzanne."

"Aye, the devil's lair," Suzanne quipped. "Apparently he took a liking to it. I sent it into Portreath to sell along with the rest of 'em. Perhaps your light will soften Treathston some, child, but beware of the ol' devil. He's got yer father right where he wants 'im. I don't like it; I don't like it none at all."

Josie patted the hunched shoulder. "You've always told me to have faith, Suzanne. Charles is a good man, like you said. Everything will turn out all right."

Suzanne's watery eyes grew distant as she stared past the canvas into the quivering blades of grass. "I pray 'twill. The seed of evil walks to and fro jest like his father the devil. The father's sins will be visited on the children, jest like the Good Book says: 'Jacob have I loved, Esau have I hated.'"

Her voice trailed off, leaving a frisson of unease in its wake.

"Good-bye, Suzanne," Josie murmured, but the old woman didn't acknowledge her presence in her trancelike state. Josie knew from experience that Suzanne would come out of it and return to her simple, childlike appreciation for beauty. Yet the wise artist's eyes possessed the ability to detect darkness as well as the light. Perhaps her seasoned years had given her the gift of seeing deeper than most.

The Lord had answered nonetheless. Josie flew through the sun-drenched grass back to the exposed paper and freshly sharpened quill that called her name.

"Master Radcliffe, a letter for you, sir!"

Leather groaned as Charles reined Stalwart in from his enthusiastic trot and turned in his saddle. The stableboy's legs churned as he tore down the hill that sloped away from the Treathston stables.

"Craven bade me to run like the wind and deliver it," Alfie panted as he remembered to walk the last several steps at a sedate pace when approaching Stalwart as Charles had instructed him dozens of times.

Dread writhed in Charles's gut as he slid his hunting rifle into its holster and accepted the letter from the stableboy. Alfie's earnest gaze tugged his attention back from studying the feminine penmanship. Charles reached for the cool metal in his waistcoat pocket and tossed the shilling to Alfie. The boy caught it deftly, and his eyes widened at the sight of the silver in his palm.

"Well done, lad. I have indeed been awaiting this correspondence."

Alfie beamed, and Charles swung Stalwart's head toward the sea. Alfie's idolizing expression branded his heart with guilt nearly as much as the paper crushed between his fingers.

Charles gave Stalwart his head, and the stallion broke into his restless stride, carrying him to their favorite cliffside haunt several miles down the rugged Cornish coastline. Stalwart drew up of his own accord and lowered his head to munch on the bluebells of which he was so fond.

Charles willed his hands to stop shaking as he tore into the letter. Josephine's writing struck him as tight, and he could picture her as she formed each word with a frown gouging the milky smoothness of her brow.

My Dear Charles,

My wishes have not changed, but if you wish to sever our betrothal I pray you do so before our first banns are read in church on the morrow. I forgive you with all my heart. When I look at you, Charles, I do not despise you. I see a man torn between duty and scars. While I cannot see them, I have witnessed firsthand their crippling effect on your heart and life. More than anything, I do not want to become another scar in your past. I meant it then, and I mean it now, that I truly want to be a good and faithful wife to you. God requires me to love you as He Himself loves, and I will endeavor to do so. Your promise to me that night was and is enough, for it planted hope and the belief that our union yet bears the prospect of happiness. I know you did not wish to hurt me last night, and while your offer to my father is very generous and noble-hearted of you, I cannot risk the consequences of a broken betrothal. If I do not hear from you before Sunday, I trust that our betrothal will go on as planned.

I remain yours faithfully,

Josie

The breath in Charles's lungs hitched. Stalwart's ears swiveled toward him as the horse nervously tossed his head. Josie's unconditional grace diffused through the hard shell around Charles's heart, filtering through every jagged layer like a stubborn shaft of sunlight. Its warmth probed each tender, swollen portal with a throbbing pang as her words touched his innermost being. He felt rekindled, pulsing and ebbing with the surging rush of the waves below as he fingered the blot that blurred her name.

Her mention of God brought the memories rushing back. He had believed on the Lord Jesus Christ and accepted Him as his personal savior at his mother's knee just before they had both forsaken him. Warmth ran down his jaw—the first tears he had shed in years as the ice thawed from his heart and dripped down his cheeks.

He crumpled the letter in his fist, grieved that she wouldn't let him escape. To accept her forgiveness would mean baring his heart and courting disaster.

He raised his arm to drown the letter, the token of her forgiveness, in the sea—but something wouldn't let him. Instead he smoothed the crinkles out across his thigh and pressed his lips to the tearstain. Somehow he would strive to be worthy of her forgiveness. Surely it would not hurt him to try, and loneliness was a bitter price to pay for stubbornly remaining closed. The demon of his past whispered with poisonous breath that one more betrayal would destroy him, but only time could tell if his yearnings would prove stronger than the fear that paralyzed his heart.

Chapter Twelve

*J*osie's breath caught as Esther handed her the bouquet. Nestled amongst the white roses were wildflowers, and their humble beauty made her think of their bravery, their willingness to grow amidst the wind and rocks. She unpinned the note.

I would be honored for you to carry these and know that I thought of your kindness when I selected them. Your Charles

A lump formed in Josie's throat, and she fingered his name while Esther fussed with a wayward curl. Was the bouquet an omen of their marriage? Did the wildflowers symbolize a beauty born of adversity? Was that what he had meant to convey?

May sunlight broke free from the clouds and gushed through the window, bathing her in blessing. Tradition had it that the sun favored a bride with a fortuitous future. She buried her nose amongst the velvety rose petals, and their wafting fragrance infused her with hope. For the first time that morning, she felt like a bride.

"Let me look at ye," Esther said softly. Her eyes shimmered with pride as Josie obliged her and twirled with bouquet in hand.

Esther settled the matching bonnet atop Josie's curls. "That blush in yer cheeks becomes ye. Ye make a beautiful bride, luve. Charles won't be able to take his eyes off ye."

"If that is indeed so, it will be all your fault, Esther."

Josie smoothed her silk skirt, a pale green echoing the tender buds of spring. Apprehension reared its ugly head again as Esther declared her ready. She wanted this moment to last forever, without the dilution of doubt that was sure to come in the face of Charles's unpredictability.

Sensing her waver, Esther gripped her shoulders and held her steady with a soulful gaze. "What is it, luve?"

"Delie should be here to attend me and take my bouquet at the altar."

"I ken, luve. I ken."

Esther's tremulous lips fastened on Josie's cheek. "Remember that God goes with ye, luve. He holds your right hand and yer future. His grace is sufficient."

Josie nodded, forcing a smile. No doubt Esther sensed her misgivings, but only grace warmed the answering curve of Esther's lips. Her governess was the only person in the world who had ever understood her. It was so cruel that her kindred spirit couldn't also be her flesh and blood.

Josie's gloved hand skimmed the curving sweep of the balustrade as they descended. Father waited for them at the end. She paused, and tears glimmered in his pale blue eyes even as the corners crinkled at the sight of her.

"My sweet Josie," he whispered. "I always knew you would be a lovely bride."

Josie darted down and flung her arms around him, desperate to chase away the haunting sadness.

"No," Father muttered as their embrace broke. "This will never do, child. Tears are unlucky on your wedding day."

They wiped each other's tears away, striving to be strong for the other and failing. Josie turned to Esther, but her features had also crumpled. They all shared a weak laugh, and Father offered his free arm. Esther accepted it as he glanced from her to Josie.

"How am I going to bear it? Losing you both on the same day?" he asked.

"We must not think of it," Esther said while Josie struggled to bury the sob in her throat. "We aren't moving further than next door."

Josie kissed his wan cheek, and to her surprise, Esther followed.

"Well, I can hardly be sad now, can I?" Father joked. "Maybe we should all say good-bye more often."

Josie swatted him as Graham opened the door with raised brows. *There are times, Graham, when a little less decorum would do your humanity credit.*

Josie glided down the aisle, gripping Father's arm tightly, flanked by a smattering of friends and relatives in the pews. A reverent hush fell, but this union would be holy in God's sight alone, because their wedding was nothing more than a splendid act in which no depth of true emotion played a part. Josie tried and failed to draw a complete breath. Even the air in her lungs felt trapped.

Charles's eyes consumed her, but not with smoldering passion. Instead she drowned in a cold blue abyss devoid of light and barren of warmth. Her fingers crushed the stems of the bouquet, not caring if green juice stained her glove. It had been cruel of him to give her fragile hope through that note when she was utterly alone.

They paused just abreast of Charles, and he turned beside her to face Vicar Nance, who opened the Book of Common Prayer.

"Dearly beloved, we are gathered together here in the sight of God, and in the face of this congregation, to join together this man and this woman in holy matrimony; which is an honorable estate . . ."

The drone of the vicar's voice dimmed to a distant echo as Josie fought a spell of lightheadedness. She willed herself not to faint and leaned against her father's frail strength.

"First it was ordained for the procreation of children, to be brought up in the fear and nurture of the Lord . . ."

Josie glimpsed a muscle working in the hard line of Charles's jaw. The thought of children, their children at least, was abhorrent to him.

"Thirdly, it was ordained for the mutual society, help, and comfort, that the one ought to have of the other, both in prosperity and adversity. Into which holy estate these two persons present come now to be joined. Therefore, if any man can show any just cause, why they may not lawfully be joined together, let him now speak or else hereafter forever hold his peace."

Josie measured the heavy silence one painful heartbeat at a time as the abundance of whys in her mind were eclipsed forever. She steeled herself and resolved not to let them pass her lips as Vicar Nance's brown eyes fastened on her.

"I require and charge you both, as ye will answer at the dreadful day of judgment when the secrets of all hearts shall be disclosed, that if either of you know any impediment, why ye may not be lawfully joined together in matrimony, ye do now confess it."

The vicar paused, but Josie remained silent by some miracle of will. His words grated on her as he warned of the consequences of immoral allegations. Finally Vicar Nance cleared his throat and turned to Charles, who regarded him as though he were his executioner.

"Charles Percival Radcliffe, wilt thou have this woman to be thy wedded wife, to live together after God's ordinance in the holy state of matrimony? Wilt thou love her, comfort her, honor and keep her in sickness and in health; and, forsaking all other, keep thee only unto her, so long as ye both shall live?"

Much to her surprise, Charles glanced down at her. His gaze reproached her. *Of course you blame me for not letting you escape.*

His eyes ripped away as he forced the lie between his lips. "I will."

"Josephine Marie Chadwick, wilt thou have this man to be thy wedded husband, to live together after God's ordinance in the holy estate of matrimony? Wilt thou obey him, and serve him, love, honor, and keep him in sickness and in health; and, forsaking all other, keep thee only unto him, so long as ye both shall live?"

"I will," Josie said quickly without looking at Charles. The vicar blinked.

"Who giveth this woman to be married to this man?"

Father tensed at her side. "I do."

The vicar took her hand from Father's, and Charles's clammy fingers swallowed it as he repeated after the vicar. His flat tone betrayed his dutiful motives.

"I, Charles Percival Radcliffe, take thee Josephine Marie Chadwick to be my wedded wife, to have and to hold from this day forward, for better for worse, for richer for poorer, in sickness and in health, to love and to cherish, till death do us part, according to God's holy ordinance; and thereto I plight thee my troth."

Josie likewise repeated after the vicar, finding it within herself to meet Charles's eyes for the first time that day and hold his gaze with all the sincerity her heart bore as she uttered the sacred vow.

"I, Josephine Marie Chadwick, take thee Charles Percival Radcliffe to be my wedded husband, to have and to hold from this day forward, for better for worse, for richer for poorer, in sickness and in health, to love, cherish, and to obey, till death us do part, according to God's holy ordinance; and thereto I give thee my troth."

Charles dragged his eyes away as though her gaze held him spellbound. He laid a gold wedding band on the prayer book's open pages. Vicar Nance placed the ring in his open palm, and Charles reached for her left hand. His fingers shook, but he managed to slide the ring onto her fourth finger. His gaze wavered, but his voice remained steady.

"With this ring I thee wed, with my body I thee worship, and with all my worldly goods I thee endow: in the name of the Father, and of the Son, and of the Holy Ghost. Amen."

They knelt on the floorboards as the vicar began to pray, and Josie steadied herself against Charles's broad shoulder. His muscles knotted at her touch, and her roaring pulse drowned out the vicar's words of blessing.

Vicar Nance joined their right hands together with an air of finality. Charles's fingers held hers in a grasp as cold as the grave.

"Those whom God hath joined together let no man put asunder. Forasmuch as Charles Percival Radcliffe and Josephine

Marie Chadwick have consented together in holy wedlock and have witnessed the same before God and this company, and thereto have given and pledged their troth either to other and have declared the same by giving and receiving of a ring, and by joining of hands I pronounce that they be man and wife together, in the name of the Father, and of the Son, and of the Holy Ghost. Amen."

A tremor passed through their hands at those fateful words, but Josie could not tell from whose hand it came. The consummation was approaching when they would indeed become one flesh.

She shoved the thought out of her mind. It was all she could do to endure one heartbeat at a time.

The blessing, communion, and additional blessings from the Bible followed before they went to sign the parish register. The ordeal was finally over—or was it only just beginning?

Josie signed her married name for the first time. Mrs. Charles Radcliffe. To think that once she had expected to call Delia by that name. Father and Sebastian added their signatures as the two witnesses.

"My best wishes to you both," Vicar Nance congratulated them as Josie accepted Charles's arm. "May you both have every felicitation that matrimony can bring."

"Thank you for everything, Vicar Nance. We will miss worshiping with you during our travels."

His brown eyes twinkled.

"Godspeed then. My prayers go with you."

"See you at the house for the wedding breakfast, my dear," Father said, patting her arm.

Sebastian slapped Charles on the shoulder. "Mr. and Mrs. Charles Radcliffe. It has a pleasant ring to it, eh, Randolph?"

"It does indeed. The two of you make a fine-looking couple."

Josie trotted to match Charles's stride as he steered her out of the church as though it had just caught fire. She squinted in the sunshine as cheers pummeled her eardrums. Rice stung her skin as Charles broke into a run. He half-dragged her through the crowd as Josie flung her bouquet before some single woman could snag a piece from it or her gown for marital luck.

A scream of delight pierced her ears as Charles swept her into his arms and charged into the waiting carriage. She thought she recognized the shrill tones of Cousin Mabel. She bounced off the seat without ceremony as Charles cranked up the hatch like a man possessed. The hood's shadow unfurled, blocking out the blinding light of day.

Charles rapped on the hood with such vehemence that his knuckles threatened to crash through. The carriage lurched forward. Josie slid to the floor before she could regain her balance. She tugged at her tangled skirts and righted her bonnet, but her uncooperative hands shook too much to tie the strings in a suitable bow. She jerked it off and laid it in the seat with the veil still attached.

Charles leaned out the carriage window. "Driver, take the scenic route, and don't turn back until I tell you," he bellowed.

Josie winced, smoothing her curls down and shoving a few wayward pins against her scalp. Her hair was certainly mussed beyond repair now.

Charles collapsed back in the seat, breathing hard and further jostling her. Josie caught his arm and steadied herself as the carriage hurtled down the road. She opened her mouth to ask him to slow the carriage down but thought better of it. Her eardrums were throbbing enough.

Charles leaned back, loosening his impeccable cravat as his broad chest strained against his waistcoat. Blood rushed to Josie's cheeks, and she glanced out the opposite side at the blurred green beyond the carriage.

Charles spoke first. "Listen to that, will you? The quiet, the stillness, no voices."

"It's nice," Josie ventured.

"Oh, how my head pounds," he groaned. "And I swear I haven't touched a drop of spirits since the banquet."

"I wouldn't have thought that you had," she whispered. He didn't know her. She reached out with a tentative hand and smoothed the wave of golden hair back from his brow. When he didn't flinch, she pressed her lips against his pulsing temple. His eyes flew open, and she darted back.

But instead of objecting, he said, "Thank you. I didn't deserve that."

His voice trailed away as the submerged vulnerability and pain surfaced. Her heart broke as she read the question there.

"I meant it, you know," she declared, and the intensity of her tone stunned her. "I meant it when I vowed to have and hold you, to love you, and cherish you, and obey you in sickness and in health forever."

Something she couldn't define flared to life in his eyes. "I know you did."

"Do you?" Josie demanded. "Will you also believe me when I tell you that in my heart, all I desire when I look at you is to do you good and not evil all the days of your life?"

"I want to. Believe me when I tell you that I want to."

"Then what is stopping you? I'm not your enemy, Charles. I'm your wife."

Charles blinked as though her words struggled to penetrate. He leaned out again and shouted with the full capacity of his powerful lungs, "Turn back to Chadwick Park!"

Leaden seconds ticked by as the carriage turned. Then he whispered as though his words were too fragile to be uttered at a louder pitch.

"You're going to have to be patient with me. You'll have to teach me how to trust again. My heart was broken once by my own flesh and blood."

"All I'm asking you to do is try."

That same elusive light glimmered in his eyes again as though she had breathed life into a dying ember.

"Then I'll begin by worshiping you with my body, Mrs. Radcliffe," he said with that mysterious quality akin to tenderness. Josie tingled all over as he reached out and seized her face in his hands, as though seeing her for the very first time. Glacial blue melted into swollen spring sky as his gaze caressed her. His eyes darted back and forth, absorbing her until his gaze birthed awareness in her. *He finds me desirable. He just isn't willing to admit he wants me.*

Josie's lips parted as the once inscrutable windows of his soul unshuttered. His mouth captured hers, and Josie exulted in the sweet strength she tasted there. She wanted more—but then the motion ceased. Their lips broke apart, and as she moaned in protest as his thumb stroked her mouth.

"After the wedding breakfast, we'll stay at Treathston tonight. That will give us this afternoon to refresh ourselves, and it will be better to get an early start in the morning."

"That sounds best," she agreed. "It's my home now, and I want to make it familiar as soon as possible."

The footman opened the carriage door, and Charles leaped down to assist her. Josie clamped her bonnet down, hiding her flyaway strands for the time being. She hoped he couldn't see her heart galloping.

"I am ready to do full justice to our wedding breakfast. I don't know if I've ever been this famished."

Josie smiled. She had an appetite, but food couldn't be further from her mind. She spotted Graham's face in the window, and the next instant the door swung open for them. His lips parted in a very non-stoic grin as he bowed at the waist.

"Welcome, Mr. and Mrs. Radcliffe," he said. "I wish you both the utmost happiness. Pardon my saying so, sir, but we have been rather loath to accept the fact that you are taking the sunshine out of this house with our Miss Josie."

"That is understandable. I'm afraid I need her rather badly at Treathston to brighten up the gloomy old place and cheer up this short-tempered bachelor."

"I see you fully value her inestimable worth, in which case we will forgive you for it."

"You are too kind."

Josie took full advantage of the hall mirror and was gratified to discover that by adjusting a few misdirected pins, she was able to redeem her curls from disgrace. She handed her bonnet off to Graham and tidied her husband's misshapen cravat as he glanced down at her, unamused. Her hand fell away at the echo of a familiar footfall.

"Ah, there are the newlyweds at last," Father announced. "Eliza has outdone herself, and I thought the aromas would drive me mad before you arrived."

Sebastian followed closely on his heels, looking as though he would burst with pride. "Knowing my son, he had the audacity to take a detour while his poor father starved."

Charles's arm descended around Josie's shoulders with gentle possession. "You forget gentlemen that man does not live by bread alone."

Heat bloomed in Josie's cheeks as their fathers roared, but she couldn't stop smiling. *He's proud to have me as his wife. He must not think me very plain.*

In the dining room, the table well nigh groaned beneath the weight of dishes as they entered. Nor was her father jesting about the aromas. Their intimate circle of family and friends surrounded them in a wreath of smiles as they entered.

"Honored guests, it is my privilege to present to you Mr. and Mrs. Charles Radcliffe," Father announced.

Soft applause met their ears as they seated themselves at the head of the table. Father had certainly spared no expense. There was the normal breakfast fare of rolls, toast, jellies, compotes, quiche, ham, bacon, garnished tongue, tea and chocolate, but further down the table, Josie glimpsed other dishes, including mayonnaise of trout, larded capon, pigeon pie, and cheesecake. The wedding cake, a magnificent confection decorated with dainty slices of candied orange peel and walnuts, towered on the sideboard nearby. Of course the definition of "Radcliffe" was money—but it would take a while for old instincts to die.

Josie dropped her head as Father began to say the blessing. "Almighty God, we thank you for this bountiful table that you have blessed us with, and we humbly ask your abundant blessings upon the union of Charles and Josephine. May their days together be long and fruitful. Amen."

Josie hid a smile behind her glass as her husband's hand shot out for the nearest dish. She reached for a platter of rolls and buttered one. The moment her teeth sank into it, her appetite returned. She studied the perfect yellow roses of the epergne that graced their end of the table. Father had remembered they were her favorite.

Charles's breath tickled her ear. "Open your mouth," he whispered.

Josie swallowed her half-chewed roll and obeyed. He placed an orange section between her parted lips, and the exotic citrus juices exploded on her taste buds.

"The last time you sat next to me, you didn't eat enough to keep a bird alive. I won't let that happen again," he said just loud enough that she could hear. She grinned, and juice dribbled out of the corner of her mouth. He brushed his thumb against her lip. "Delicious."

Josie kissed the pad of his thumb before he could draw it away. The tingle on her lips remained long after the last drop of juice had disappeared. She ate until she was afraid she might blow a seam.

As the meal wound to a close, her father stood and raised a glass. "I would like to propose a toast. To my lovely daughter Josie and her husband Charles. May they find a love that grows sweeter with each passing day and never cools."

"To the Radcliffes," their guests echoed.

The resounding clink of glass filled the room. Josie clanked her glass against Charles's. As their eyes fused, he took a drink of the ruby fluid. Steel touched his eyes again.

"To us," she murmured. He nodded as he patted his mouth with the serviette, leaving a red smear. The shadows still lurked, waiting to prey upon her dreams for a second chance at love.

The kiss had been a mistake. Never had he dreamed that a woman could taste so sweet and fit against him so perfectly as the sweep of his jaws met hers. Now it would exact a cost higher than his heart was willing to pay.

Her doe-like eyes searched his with a knowing sheen. He had succeeded in nursing the one glass for the entire meal, but that one perceptive glance drove him to guzzling again. No woman had ever been given the chance to read his soul. Alas, he was flesh and blood. One taste of that intimacy had given him an appetite for the world he had shut out.

Ceremony saved the day—for the moment—as his father summoned him to cut the cake. He stood and pulled Josie's chair back as they rose together. Her green skirts clung to the chair, and he brushed them off as he took her hand. Charles's eyes lingered on the cresting slope of her shoulder. The swirls of frosting on the cake did nothing to distract him.

Josie grasped the knife and plunged it through the molded confection. Her dainty fingers pried a bite-sized wedge from the cake, and as she raised it to his lips, he nibbled her finger-tips along with it. She wrinkled the freckled bridge of her nose at him, and frosting dusted her upper lip when he placed the square in her mouth. Her eyes widened as he bent and kissed it away. She wagged the encrusted knife at him. Perhaps he had underestimated his prim and proper little bride. As he raised his hands in mock surrender, she smeared his nose from bridge to nostril. He captured her hand and kissed it.

"Touché, Mrs. Radcliffe."

His grin broadened as she tossed a serviette against his chest, flashing that adorable dimple with the playful quirk of her mouth. *Steady, Charles . . .*

The guests lingered until well past noon, sluggish from good food and loath to leave such pleasant company—pleasant to them, at least. Charles reined in his fraying nerves with some effort. If he listened to another minute of idle gossip, his head was sure to split. He waited for Josie to finish her conversation with Mrs. Nance before approaching her.

"Let's take our leave now, Josephine."

Stormy gray roiled in her expression. "Let me just bid Father good-bye."

"I'll be waiting in the carriage."

He shifted his weight beneath her scrutiny.

"Is your head pounding again?"

"Just take what time you need," he said and spun on his heel. At last he had escaped. Outside, the tang of the sea massaged his temples as he cranked the carriage hood back down and inhaled the moment of privacy.

His skull began to itch with niggling insistence—a prickling sensation like someone was watching him. It deepened until Charles craned his neck to see to the edge of the woods— and found himself looking into eyes filled with hatred, glaring black as bullets in a stranger's face. Charles's lips parted, but the young man faded into the trees as a motion caught the corner of Charles's eye. Josie was coming. Their guests followed her like a flock of seagulls, squawking and flapping as they wielded the customary shoes to pelt at the carriage as they drove away.

Charles took Josie's hand and barked for the footman to drive on as soon as she had plunked herself beside him. He mustered a half-hearted wave as they lurched into motion, but Josie couldn't seem to stop waving. One by one, shoes pelted the gravel drive for luck. A shoe thrown with unaccustomed enthusiasm landed with a clunk on the carriage floor after just missing Josie's head. With a hiss Charles lunged forward, seized the shoe, and flung it back over his shoulder as he unleashed all the tension coiling inside. Josie regarded him with amusement.

"All's well that ends well, Charles."

"Mrs. Radcliffe, you will rarely find me in the mood for Shakespeare, and I don't care what tradition says. Nearly braining the bride with a heeled shoe like that isn't lucky."

Josie tugged at his cravat until it unknotted, smoothing a cool palm over his aching forehead.

"Well, it's all over now."

Charles grimaced as he leaned back. "Yes, we did it, Josephine. I'm afraid you're shackled to me now whether you like it or not."

A tentative silence fell, but then she leaned her head against his shoulder in a gesture of trust of which he was utterly unworthy. The horse's hooves pounded dull against dirt as the salty breeze wafted through his bruised senses. *Oh Josie, if I had to marry a Chadwick, I'm glad it was you. Delia would have badgered me to death. You're such a gentle beauty. I only pray I don't break your heart.*

On an impulse, he turned his head and pressed his lips against her forehead. "You are too good to me. I don't deserve you."

"You should let me be the judge of that, Mr. Radcliffe," she whispered as their fingers laced. "I believe our prospects for happiness are very great."

The words seemed incredible to him. *Sweet Josie, what I wouldn't give for one ounce of your peace.*

"When we get to Treathston, what do you say to a tour of the estate's grounds? I have a mare for you that isn't too spirited until the footman brings Ebony over."

"Oh, I don't know. I like the spirited ones best," Josie teased.

Charles chuckled. "Now why doesn't that surprise me, considering your fondness for Stalwart?"

"I would enjoy that immensely. Perhaps your cook could pack us a picnic lunch."

"You're hungry already? I can barely stomach the thought of dinner."

"I'm hungry for some time alone with you. A picnic would grant us the perfect opportunity."

He smiled. "That can be arranged then."

"After all, you haven't courted me properly yet, Charles Radcliffe."

His heart ached at the twinkle in her eyes, dreading the moment when she saw through the facade into the man he really was. But he could no more grant her wish for marital bliss than he could pluck the moon from the sky.

Chapter Thirteen

*J*osie blew onto the dim coals in the fireplace as her chest tightened. They mustn't die tonight and plunge her unfamiliar bedchamber into darkness. Her own spirit was reflected there in the ashes, shivering and vulnerable.

The leaping flame of hope had faded to a spark. Now a gentle waft or harsh puff would determine whether her light lived or died. She coaxed a flickering glimmer and then a wavering pulse into the coals. Their ruby glow quickened and waxed stronger.

She could only hope her heart would do the same. She had never dreamed that she would be chilled down to the marrow on her wedding night. Fresh horror stirred as she recalled the sensations . . . being crushed in the darkness amongst soft sheets as his sweet lips grew bitter and bruised her own. He had remained just long enough to consummate their marriage. Then the door had slammed shut to his adjoining bedchamber, sounding the death knell to her dreams of ever finding love with her husband as the bolt clicked. She was being punished for another woman's sins. Some other woman had broken his ability to love her before they had even met.

Josie clutched a hand against her mouth. *Oh God in heaven, what have I done? I've sentenced myself to a fate worse than death.*

The log crunched as she settled it upon the coals. Josie eyed the site of her heart's defilement and stripped off the coverlet, taking it back with her to the fire. She couldn't return to the bed. The folds provided a cocoon of comfort for her shoulders, but she wished she could shield her soul from this existence of sharp edges and raw ache.

Josie collapsed into the chair beside the hearth. *I'm broken, God. The sacrifices I've made have left me broken. How can this possibly be Your plan?*

Silence met her ears. Scalding tears seared paths of fire down her cheeks, burning through her numbness. She didn't know if feeling was a blessing or a curse anymore.

An elusive sensation pried Charles's gritty eyelids apart to the gray light of dawn—the sensation of guilt-ridden shame crushing his chest. He bolted upright as his heart lurched into a breathless staccato. *Surely last night was a nightmare. I can still call off the wedding.*

He unwound his legs from the twisted sheets and eased the deadbolt back with a faint rasp. *Please let it be a dream.*

Charles shoved open the door. Pale light fell upon Josie's wan, tearstained cheeks. Her dark tresses tumbled over the coverlet wrapped around her shoulders. Charles closed his eyes to block out the sight and leaned against the doorway as it all came flooding back.

He clenched his fists. It had begun so sweetly as the darkness fell around them. Then the woman who had penned the letter had reached out and touched his innermost heart. He had endured the bittersweet pain until the woman in his arms ceased to be Josie, and the feminine form represented only the pain he had suffered. He hadn't meant to hurt her, but when she whimpered, he fled like the wretched coward he was.

And she did not pursue him. Of course she didn't. As if his sweet little bride would have followed him after the humiliation she had just suffered at his hands.

The broken way she had said his name haunted him still. He blinked away the moisture. He needed to be near her and watch her sleep. As he took the first tentative step, his eyes savored every line of her glorious features. Her bosom rose and fell in the deep sleep of a child. He choked back a sob. He whispered, "I'm sorry, sweet Josie. I'm so sorry."

He had failed her the moment he had looked at her as a woman instead of his woman. She had trusted him, and he had broken her, betrayed her just as he had been betrayed.

She stirred with a faint little moan that gripped his heart. Her eyes fluttered open and widened, overcast in prelude to a storm. Recognition hardened them as impenetrably as castle walls.

"It wasn't my intention to wake you."

She blinked, pulling the blanket tighter. Her shoulders slumped as defeat sharpened her tone. "It's of no consequence."

As if she'd decided that curling into a wounded ball only made matters worse, she bolted to her feet without warning and let the blanket slip from her shoulders. She began to make the bed as though her very life depended on it, but it was a ludicrous action. Treathston Heights already had more servants than it knew what to do with.

"I know we discussed getting an early start. Breakfast should be ready by the time you finish your toilette. I, ah, will ensure that our trunks have been properly packed before joining you downstairs."

Josie fluffed a pillow and punched it down. "Don't go through undue trouble to join me, Mr. Radcliffe. No doubt if my presence disturbs your sleep, your appetite will suffer from it as well."

Charles was forced to admit that cowardice had its virtues as he retreated from battle.

Chapter Fourteen

he door slammed shut—again—and Josie buried her face in the pillow to muffle her sobs. His heart was forever closed to her. She'd been a fool to hope for anything more than his name.

A strangely joyful melody echoed through the wall—someone was singing. She swiped away her tears, following the sound until she found herself outside of Esther's door.

"When faith is failing me, dark doubts assailing me, be thou my hiding place, my safe abiding place. When griefs are numberless, when cares are slumberless, grant me tranquillity, faith and humility. When joys are leaving me, and deaths bereaving me, my foolish fears allay, wipe all my tears away from doubt's obscurity, from sin's impurity. Oh, set me free by grace so I shall see Thy face."

The note died at her knock. Josie shoved open the door as the voice bade her to enter.

"Oh, good morning, luve," Esther said. "Ye should have rung."

"You are not a servant, and I refuse to treat you like one," Josie snapped.

A faint smile lifted the corners of Esther's mouth. "Yer husband better not hear ye talking like that."

Josie ignored her attempt to broach the infamous subject. "I trust you slept well."

"Aye, that I did," Esther affirmed. "I'll not ask the same of ye."

"I'm hardly the blushing bride this morning, am I?"

Esther curled up onto the settee and settled her Bible onto her lap.

"To what do I owe the honor of yer visit, luve?"

"What were you singing?"

"'Tis an old Scottish hymn, luve. I dinna ken the name."

"It is beautiful."

"Aye," Esther murmured. "It echoes the heart, doesna it?"

Josie sank onto the settee and crossed her arms.

"Did I wake ye, luve?"

"No, Esther, I fear I am rather peckish this morning. Forgive me."

Esther shifted on the settee.

"I woke early and couldna sleep a wink more. I read about Joseph. God gave Joseph the very dreams that caused him to be sold into slavery. After a few years in a strange land, Joseph was accused unjustly and thrown into prison for a crime he didna commit. I'm sure he felt forsaken, but in the darkest moment of his life God was working out the greatest victory of his life. Joseph couldna see the future, but he chose to trust in the goodness of His faithful God. Joseph got out of prison through his gift of dreams and became one of the highest leaders in the land, second only to Pharaoh himself. God used him to rescue his family from famine and bring his people into Egypt in preparation for the day when He would guide them into the Promised Land. Without faith, it is impossible to please God. Something tells me that if Joseph had lost his faith, God wouldna have been able to use him as such a mighty instrument of His will. Just because we cannae see God working doesna mean He isn't. Faith is blind, but His ways are perfect even if they aren't our ways."

"Oh Esther, how did you know what I needed to hear?" Josie burst out.

"God did, luve. I'm only sharing what He taught me."

"I woke up angry with God because my life is falling apart. I'm just like Joseph. I've only tried to do right, but I'm being punished for the sin of others. I feared God had forsaken me."

"Och luve," Esther said brokenly. "It hurts me to see ye go through this trial, and I dinna have all the answers to why just breathing has to hurt so much at times. But I do ken my God, and I ken that I can trust my God. My God makes my brokenness beautiful, because His light shines through the cracks into the lives of others. He brings beauty out of ashes. He is near to the brokenhearted and bindeth up their wounds. Joseph was in that prison for two years, but God was with him until the victory came. Yer victory is coming, sweet Josie. Can ye trust yer God to be faithful even in the midnight hour when yer faith is tested?"

"Yes," Josie sobbed as Esther pulled her close.

"God has given ye a gift, Josie. The gift of a nurturing spirit with a heart that has a greater capacity to love than most. Ye must let Him use that gift to fulfill the purpose He intends. To every season there is a purpose."

"Oh, Esther, I'm so ashamed for doubting Him."

"Think of Him as the heavenly Father that He is, Josie. If yer child came running to yer open arms with tears streaming down their face, ye would be more brokenhearted by the realization that they thought ye incapable of forgiving them than by their sin."

Josie nodded as she buried her face in Esther's shoulder. *Oh God, forgive me for doubting You just because I can't see Your hand. I do trust that You will bring beauty from the ashes of my dreams in time.*

Josie leaned out the post chaise window and sucked in a lungful of the Dover harbor air. Every bone in her body ached from being jostled around on the hard seat for the past week. Her very lips tasted chalky from dust. She had expressed her preference to travel to Falmouth Harbor to obtain a ship for their passage to France, a destination their personal carriage could have reached in mere hours. However, Charles had ignored her request with characteristic disregard for her comfort and insisted upon riding in a hired post chaise all the way to Dover, a difference of over three hundred miles and a week's worth of travel. Perhaps the only benefit of their appalling travel arrangements was that somewhere between the hours of sharing the post chaise by day and still more hours of sharing cramped tavern rooms by night, she and Charles had been forced to come to a civil understanding. They spoke to each other when spoken to, shared their meals, and slept in separate beds. It was far from wedded bliss, but at least it was bearable. Through it all, Esther had endured the physical and emotional discomfort of the trip with the patience of a saint.

Charles wrenched open the door and leaped down with flying coattails. Josie rose to follow, and his gentle fingers gripped her waist as he swung her to the ground. A gust of wind whipped her skirts and billowed through the ship's sails. She only hoped her legs wouldn't prove unseaworthy as her fingers tightened around her parasol.

Charles's hands lingered around her waist. Josie glanced up, and his touch fell away as though the contact had burned him. Charles's valet, Thomas, gave Esther a hand down, and their age gap far from dampened his boyish admiration. Esther caught Josie's eye with long-suffering amusement as Thomas insisted upon taking her arm.

The gangplank wobbled under the bag boy's feet, and Josie's stomach rocked with it as Charles took her arm. She hesitated to follow as he mounted the gangplank. Warmth breath rushed against her ear. "Allow me, Mrs. Radcliffe."

Josie gasped as he swung her up into his arms, and she clung to him for dear life as blue sky and waves tilted along with her vision. The ship's rigging swayed overhead as her feet kissed the swaying deck. His strong hand steadied her as she squinted into her husband's hooded gaze.

"Thank you," she breathed.

His iron jaw relented a fraction with his nod.

"Welcome aboard the *Poseidon*."

Josie smiled and linked her arm through his.

"Enchanting," she murmured.

They were one with the blue expanse of sea as the wind snapped through canvas like the sails were another cloud in the sky. The brisk footfalls of the sailors mingled with the strolling couples on deck as Josie snapped open her parasol. The nod of the waves became pleasant as her feet absorbed the rhythmic dance.

"I cannot help but observe that my wife is at home on a ship's deck, whereas most women of her age and station find the thought of any sea voyage utterly abhorrent."

"I have always loved the sea. My only fear is that my stomach may not be as favorably inclined, as I have neither slept nor eaten upon her before."

"My stomach was never allowed to consider the possibility of squeamishness with my father being a retired captain in Her Majesty's Royal Navy, but I have every confidence that yours will handle the sea with the same nerve with which you jumped that fence astride my mare Dandy the afternoon of our picnic."

"I take it then that you were not thoroughly scandalized by your wife's performance?"

"It had the thoroughly opposite effect on me, I assure you . . . just so long as you don't make a habit of showing off your horsemanship around my gentleman friends. They don't take kindly to being bested by a woman, especially if that woman happens to be my wife."

Warmth flooded Josie's chest at the unexpected fondness of his response. "Somehow I get the impression there are certain gentlemen you wouldn't mind humiliating if given the opportunity."

"Certain young coxcombs could afford to be brought down a peg or two," Charles allowed as they continued to follow the sailor hefting their trunk up the flight of stairs that led to the higher deck.

"Your feminine ears must pardon the expression, but this is the poop deck," Charles explained.

"Ah, so ships have a detailed anatomy too?"

"Quite an elaborate one," Charles agreed. "That is the crow's nest up there."

Her husband gave her a brief tour worthy of a navy captain's son, and Josie reveled in the sense of normalcy until the sailor kicked open the door to cabin number 14. Their trunk thudded to the floor, and Josie's lips pursed as Charles tipped him anyway. She surveyed the small cabin, thankful the voyage would be short.

Thomas grunted as he lowered her trunk to the floor beside it.

"I'm sure you are grateful that I was able to guard your trunk and its contents against such blatant disrespect, Mrs. Radcliffe."

"Most grateful indeed. Thank you, Thomas."

"What? No tip to honor my gallant efforts?" Thomas teased. "If I may be so bold, my lady, a kiss on the jaw would be most—"

"You may not be so bold," Charles cut in. "Mrs. Radcliffe's lips are devoted entirely to her husband's pleasure, if you would be so kind as to remember that in the future."

"As you wish, sir."

"Meanwhile, kind sir, another fair lady and her bags are entirely dependent upon yer most capable assistance," Esther said, softening the atmosphere as only she could.

"Pray forgive me, my dear Miss MacAllister. I am your slave to command." He winked as Esther shooed him out of the cabin.

Charles collapsed on the bunk and tugged a dusty boot off his foot with a groan. He looked genuinely annoyed.

"Charles, I did not take offence. He is just a boy—"

"A boy who is only two years your husband's junior and who is in desperate need of becoming a man so that someday a woman will take his attentions seriously. I have to nip such indelicate behavior to you in the bud now before he makes himself a nuisance. After all, you are his master's wife, not his mistress. He is a good fellow who would never harm a hair of your head, but I will not condone such disrespect toward you."

"Do I sense an underlying current of jealousy beneath your words?"

"I have every right to be possessive of you. You are my wife, and you look utterly exhausted. Can I get you something to eat, something to drink?"

His words hung in the air along with the touching sense of tentativeness so tangible between them.

"I am rather thirsty."

Charles tugged his boot back on. "Lock the door behind me. I'll be right back. You sure you don't want anything to eat?"

"No, thank you."

Josie bolted the door behind him and wrestled the strap off her trunk. Just as she pulled her nightshirt over her head, his stout knock sounded.

"It's Charles."

She unbolted the door, and he handed her a glass bottle of water. It slid cool down her throat, and she wiped her mouth before offering it to him. He perched himself on the edge of the bunk again, and as he drank she eased his boots off his feet and massaged the stiff muscles beneath the clammy socks. He wrinkled his nose at her.

"Surely you don't want to touch my perspiring feet."

"Your feet are my feet, and they look pinched."

His face softened as he stood up, locked the door, and then pulled down the coverlet on the bottom bunk.

"Get some rest, Josephine. Tomorrow we can enjoy the sea together."

Josie breathed easier when he climbed up into his own bunk without touching her.

The sensation of soft warmth flooded her senses. Candlelight pooled in a golden halo as its rays stretched into the corners of the room and chased away the lurking shadows. Her surroundings comforted her—from the blue patchwork quilt on the bed to the worn books on the shelf and the picture of plump puppies romping on the wall.

Loving arms held her close against the curving softness of a heaving bosom, and she heard the rhythmic cadence of a heartbeat that she had always known. She closed her eyes and drank in the nearness of the one who loved her, because the essence of that love was her world. A curling strand of hair tickled her forehead as she breathed a sweet, subtle scent. A honeyed voice she knew well sang a lilting lullaby in low, crooning tones that resonated through her own chest . . . then a nose nuzzled hers. Lips soft as flower petals brushed against her skin, and the voice murmured something as she laid her in a soft place.

Then the first harsh note shattered the peace. An unfamiliar voice. She yearned for the security of the presence she had known before. The voice rose in a note she had never heard before. The unfamiliar seized her in foreign arms. She arched in protest, writhing as something rough scratched against her face. This voice hurt her ears, and then the voice that had always hushed her own cries began to scream.

Her throat vibrated with a screech of protest. She struggled in vain as the presence grew blurred through tears. The black absence of light engulfed her, smothering her, and she could no longer see the presence. Terror suffocated her as for the first time she knew nothing but the roughness of the unfamiliar carrying her further and further away from the presence into the black unknown.

Josie's eyes flew open to darkness as her body impacted something hard. Something coarse grazed her cheek. Terror mounted in cold ripples until it matched the cadence of her racing heart. Fear choked her until a scream ripped from her throat.

There was a muffled cry, and her body pitched sideways as though some mysterious force had gripped her in its power. A thunderous crash shook the floorboards as she fought the folds that pinioned her limbs. A man's hands pawed at her, fingers digging into her shoulders. She fought for the strength to scream again.

"Josie."

She stilled at the sound of her name, familiar and fond. The man's grasp gentled, and her trembling limbs were too weak to resist as he pulled her against his chest. Warm, steadying arms surrounded her as she detected the sound of ragged breathing. Her own chest shuddered with the effort.

"Help me," she gasped out. "Help—"

"It's all right. You're going to be all right," a tender voice murmured. It sounded familiar, but at the same time she had never heard it before. A rough jaw slid up against her skin, and wandering fingers buried themselves in her hair.

"I won't let anything hurt you. You're safe now."

It hurt to breathe in the inky black oppression. The very air was poisoned.

"Light," she pleaded against the man's cheek. "Oh, for the love of all that is sacred, bring me light."

Strong arms lifted her off the hard floor. She gripped the hard shoulder. His voice resonated within her soul.

"Please God, let there be a moon for her sake."

A latch clicked, bathing her in silvery light. The stiff breeze revived her paralyzed senses with a rushing chill. Slowly, she realized where she was as she stared out at the moonlit sea through the cabin's porthole with her husband.

Charles's eyes caressed her in the cold light, warmth bleeding through the shadows that played across the sharp lines of his face.

"You must have had a nightmare."

Josie's face twisted as he clutched her closer against the warmth of his chest.

"I dreamed it again," Josie whispered. "The nightmare. . . comes in night's utter darkness."

The tears stung, and she hated herself for it. "You must think me terribly silly. Forgive me for waking you. It . . . I've had the nightmare since I was a child. Firelight is the only way to keep it away, and even then it often returns."

"No, there is nothing to forgive. You are brave not to let real fear keep you from living."

Josie blinked away the tears. Her blurred vision had not been responsible for his softened features. "I don't understand."

"The darkness is your greatest fear, yet you did not let it stop you that night when you sought me out on the road. You knew the moon could go behind a cloud at any moment, but you didn't let that stop you."

"Then you don't hold it against me?"

"If there is any blame, it lies only with me."

Relief flooded Josie's eyes afresh.

"No, no more tears."

His gaze wavered, but then he bent and kissed her tears away. As his lips found her mouth, Josie flinched at the wound his taste reopened. He broke away, pain shimmering in his moonlit eyes. "I know I have no right, but I had to try to distract you some way."

Josie couldn't hurt him afresh as she reached out and held his face with all the yearning stirring within her. The knowledge that she craved intimacy with him dawned with startling clarity. "No more tears," she echoed and pressed her mouth to his. Healing came with the tenderness she tasted there, mingling with the saltiness of her own tears. Their lips released softly.

"You are as cold as ice."

Carrying her away from the porthole, he laid her on the bunk and wrapped the blanket around her shoulders. "Tell me more about the dream."

"It is always the same. I am in a cozy room filled with candlelight. A woman is holding me, and I feel loved with every fiber of my being. Everything is safe and familiar as she lays me down to sleep. Then rough arms seize me. I hear weeping and screams as I am carried out into the darkness of night. A terrible knowledge fills my heart that I will never see her again, and I wake up. I notice something new each time. Tonight I smelled lavender when she held me."

For a moment Charles was silent while his arms tightened protectively around her. "Who is she?"

"I don't know. That is what haunts me. I can never see her face, although I come so close each time. My tears always blur her features. My heart tells me she is my mother, but how can that be? I wasn't separated from my mother until she died when I was eight. I doubt the woman in the dream is her. The room is so familiar I feel that it is a real place . . . that I would recognize it if I saw it."

Charles shifted on the bunk. Fear clawed Josie's throat. He mustn't leave her now. She couldn't be alone in the darkness tonight.

But he didn't go. The rope springs of her bed groaned as he reclined, hands rubbing soothing circles of warmth into her back. They slipped away, leaving her craving his touch. The soft rise and fall of his breathing eased tense muscles in her back. Her lips curved with newfound tenderness. He was willing to sacrifice his own comfort, squeezing into the tiny bunk just to be with her.

Josie stretched her body across his, resting her head against his broad chest. Her cheek absorbed the steady thump of his heart until her own slowed to meet it. His arms pulled her against him until their bodies molded into one, his hollows and ridges filled by the softness of her curves. Josie sighed, experiencing the belonging she had dreamed of but never known. And she hadn't missed it, when he woke her—he had called her Josie.

"Charles, thank you ever so much."

His lips fastened upon her hair.

"Sleep well," he murmured.

Josie closed her eyes, stunned that this could feel so right. Tonight, the nightmare would not deprive her of sleep.

Chapter Fifteen

harles stirred, and alarm quickened his blood. Soft breaths tickled the hairs on his chest. He craned his neck and froze as Josie's head rose and fell with each breath. Her fingertips tightened around his shoulder as her sooty lashes fluttered. He had married an actress, and a good one at that. In repose her features were relaxed, not fixed in an illusion of calm.

Remorse cut him with a sharp stab. He was so unworthy of her beautiful heart.

Charles drank in her nearness, the softness of her hair and the curved warmth of her body. She stirred a desire in him he knew he could never satisfy, yet someday she would realize her mistake. Some morning he would wake to find her gone too.

Josie purred and nestled closer as though eager to prove him wrong. Her lips curved in a half-smile. Surely her dreams, whether in a real or figurative sense, didn't include him. Last night she had aroused instincts he didn't know still breathed in him. He had shielded her from terror, but he feared being her worst nightmare of all. Her heart stared back whenever he looked at her, vulnerable and exposed to the very hand that could inflict the fatal wound. Both of their hearts wielded the power to heal or destroy. They were one indeed.

Her eyes drifted open, and her gaze melted into his. She kissed his jaw, then slid up closer so she could reach his mouth. She cupped his face in her hands and kissed him with an abandon that sent his heart galloping in his chest. She stole his breath; her caresses rendered him weak as the taste of her intoxicated him more than any alcohol.

"You chased it away, Charles. I've never fallen back asleep after the nightmare, but I did."

"I would forever if I could."

The trusting belief in her eyes unraveled the threads of his very being.

"Maybe you can," she breathed.

He couldn't form a coherent thought. He gripped her shoulders as he sat up, and the top bunk grazed his hair.

"I've got to use the necessary," he mumbled, sliding out of the bunk.

The full force of her disappointment slammed him hard, bruising his heart as he escaped the unrealistic expectations of the woman he was doomed to fail.

Charles staggered from the room as though his shoulders bore a weight too heavy to bear. *My poor darling.* Josie had almost swooned when she had opened her eyes to a gaze as soft and vibrant as bluebells. Last night he had revealed the tender heart beating behind that cold wall of stone. The lurking helplessness in his gaze had beseeched her in a way she could not define. Someone had hurt her man, and his ability to love had frozen over for a time. Josie vowed to heal those scars as the cries of gulls and crashing surf drifted through the open porthole.

A soft knock sounded.

"Enter."

Esther staggered into the cabin. Alarm spurred Josie into action as Esther lurched forward, her lovely face blanched as a corpse. Josie eased her onto the bunk as she brushed a black strand out of Esther's dark eyes. She didn't know this Esther as words formed on her governess's chalky lips.

"Och, the sea doesna agree with me, luve."

Josie moaned in sympathy and grasped Esther's clammy fingers in hers. "Oh, what can I do?"

Esther grimaced as she mopped the sweat from her forehead with a limp handkerchief. "Ye can do naught for me but pray, luve."

"Yes, but surely the ship's doctor would have something?"

"Let's get ye decently dressed first."

Josie barred the door and jerked her nightshirt off with simmering impatience.

"You should have said something, Esther. I wouldn't have brought you if I knew the voyage would affect you this adversely."

"I've never been on the sea. I didna ken what seasickness was, but when I visit those places I've always longed to see it will all be worth it, luve."

Josie rummaged through her trunk and selected a serviceable gray wool dress that the ocean's chill couldn't nip through. She put on her petticoat and tugged a corset over her head before inhaling so that Esther could tighten her stays from where she sat on the bunk. Then Josie got into the dove gray dress without Esther's assistance.

"Oh, where is Charles?" Josie fretted as Esther finished fastening her chestnut locks in place.

"We'll wait right here for yer husband."

Josie gnawed at her lip. After a moment's hesitation she moved to unbar the door.

"Josie, the ship's deck is no place for ye to wander alone."

"Clearly he isn't coming back anytime soon, and you are in no condition to accompany me."

Josie wrenched the door open, walking straight into a gaze blue as the sky above. Charles's eyebrows rose.

"Ready for breakfast?"

"I can't stomach a bite of food until Esther gets something to alleviate her seasickness. Please take me to see the ship's doctor, Charles."

Charles's eyes widened as Esther flew by them and retched over the deck railing. Josie laid an arm around her governess's heaving shoulders and offered a handkerchief. Esther wiped her mouth.

"Allow me, Miss McAllister," Charles murmured as he knelt and lifted her into his arms. Josie's lips curved at the sight. Only a man of good caliber cared for a lady's maid with the same gentleness he did his wife.

As Josie shoved open Esther's cabin door, the stale air smacked her senses, soured by vomit and sweat. No doubt the chamber pot was the culprit. She struggled to unbolt the porthole as Charles laid Esther on the bunk. By the time she reached for the chamber pot, Charles had already beaten her there.

"Tell Esther that weather permitting, we should be landing in Calais before nightfall. I'll go to the ship's doctor to get something for her now."

"Thank you, Charles."

Josie perched herself on the edge of the bunk and stroked back the ebony strands plastered against Esther's forehead.

"Charles says our feet will be on solid ground by nightfall." Esther mustered a weak smile and closed her eyes.

Oh Esther . . . you've always been the strong one. God tossed you into my life as an anchor, knowing how much I needed to be grounded, and now your life will always ripple into mine. I don't know what I'd do if anything ever happened to you.

A heavy step sounded outside on the deck.

"Is that Charles?" Esther mumbled drowsily.

"I believe so."

"I ken how ye love the sea. I'll be all right if I just rest awhile. Go with yer husband now, luve. It is yer honeymoon, and I'll not be the one to spoil it."

"Esther, you aren't spoiling it."

"Och, go on with ye now. I just need to rest awhile, luve."

"I'll be back soon."

A change of scenery wouldn't be unwelcome. Josie planted a kiss on Esther's clammy skin and slipped out.

Charles leaned against the railing as the wind played with his greatcoat. As Josie's shadow darkened the wood, he tucked a red leather volume back into his waistcoat pocket.

"The ship's doctor is attending another patient, but he has promised to bring her a remedy shortly. Allow me to escort you to breakfast."

"I fear my appetite has deserted me."

"I suffer from the same malady."

Charles pulled something from his greatcoat pocket. "But you must keep your strength up, Mrs. Radcliffe."

"My, you are most proficient," Josie praised him as she accepted the roll.

"Thomas assured me they are decent. He handed them off to me earlier. Said he feared I would starve to death before the ladies ever finished their toilettes, but he was in much greater danger of that than I."

Josie smiled as she took it. Whether he cared out of duty or otherwise, she chose to recognize that he cared. She offered half of the roll to him, but he produced another.

"Thank you for being so kind to Esther just now."

"She means a lot to you, doesn't she?"

"She has been more of a mother to me than my own ever was."

Charles ripped a hunk off his roll, and the muscles in his jaw ground as he chewed. There was a restlessness about him. Something dark and relentless coursed beneath the surface, and the facade wore thin.

"I owe you an apology for being miffed the past two weeks over traveling by post chaise. Esther never could have made a sea voyage that long. Your insistence that traveling by land was safer until we reached the nearest port to Calais was wise."

"Think nothing of it."

Josie gnawed her lip as Charles's gaze continued to seek the rumpled expanse of blue. She had married a living contradiction. A sigh escaped her as she dug her New Testament out of her pocket.

He turned to her unexpectedly. "Would you read to me?"

Josie almost dropped the book over the railing. There was no semblance of mockery in his expression. Deep, blue sincerity glistened back at her.

"What would you like to hear?"

He shrugged. "I won't pretend to know much about the Good Book, but I know I shall enjoy listening to whatever you fancy. I like the sound of your voice."

Josie began thumbing pages. *Dear Lord, show me.*

"Go ahead and ask me. I know you're dying to."

"Ask you what?" Josie asked, bewildered.

"Ask me why I never darkened the door of a church until the Sunday our banns were read."

"I think you'll find once we've become better acquainted that your wife is not one to pry, but if you want to tell me why, I won't offer any judgment."

Charles's gaze shifted toward the sea. "It's not because I don't believe. Even at seven years old I understood the difference between heaven and hell."

"Oh Charles, then why have you kept Jesus locked inside a church building? Or did you not understand fully what it meant to receive Him?"

"I understood perfectly at the time, and I've never had a doubt about my soul's salvation."

"But?" Josie prodded.

A vein throbbed in his throat, and compassion swelled in her breast.

"But then God forsook me, along with the person who should have loved me most."

"Mr. Radcliffe?" a voice boomed.

Josie jumped, and Charles scowled as he turned. The doctor waved a small bottle as Charles strode down the deck toward him. Josie hoped the remedy consisted of more than alcohol as she turned back to the pages snapping in the wind.

The men conversed until she grew impatient, but she didn't dare to rouse Charles's ire by interrupting them. At last the doctor resumed his morning constitutional.

"He told me to tell you he has experienced success with this. The dosage is on the label," Charles explained as he handed her the brown glass bottle. Josie perused the faded label.

"Murray's Fluid Magnesia," she read aloud. She glanced up, but Charles's frown mirrored the darkness smudging the horizon.

"What is wrong, darling?" she asked and touched his shoulder. His muscles knotted beneath her palm, and he snatched his arm away as blue sparks rained from his eyes. *Surely he wouldn't strike me.*

"Why do you have to be so blasted observant, woman? Did it ever occur to you that life might be infinitely more pleasant if you were spared some of the ugly details? If you insist upon knowing, there is a storm chasing after us. We may reach the French coast before it hits, and we may not. This would be a fine time to pray to your God if you think He will listen now that you are married to me."

His curling lips blurred in her sight as Josie spun on her heel, chased away by her own tears. She eased her grip on the bottle as she stomped into Esther's cabin lest she shatter it. *How dare he mock me. We're an illusion. That's all we've ever been. Perhaps I should be glad that he has shattered my rose-colored lenses.*

The fluid magnesia worked its magic, lulling Esther into merciful sleep. Josie stayed in the stifling confines of the cramped cabin for as long as she could bear. At last she confessed herself willing to pay the price of facing Charles again for a lungful of fresh air.

Josie stepped onto the deck and heaved a sigh of relief to find him nowhere in sight.

The dim shore of France called in the dusky twilight as she seized the railing. Black clouds boiled in the background, but apparently the very wind the storm had summoned was blowing them to safety.

The deck pitched, plunging over a rebellious wave. Her stomach dipped with it, and Josie closed her eyes as she fought the rolling nausea. Needles of spray stung her cheeks. A presence loomed beside her as though the storm had embodied itself in human form.

"I want you to come inside now."

Josie gritted her teeth.

"Don't make me, Charles. I'll suffocate without the fresh air."

"Are you cold?"

She shook her head. He muttered something under his breath.

"While green becomes you, that particular shade is unflattering. Open your mouth."

Josie opened her eyes to see him holding the magnesia. She obliged and gagged as the magnesia slid down her throat. Charles took off his greatcoat and began to wrap it around her shoulders. Josie stiffened at his touch. The rough wool of the coat scratched her throat, reminding her of the strange arms that had surrounded her in her nightmare. She wrenched it off and flung it against him. His eyes widened as the coat slid from his chest to the deck.

"Stop lying to me and yourself," Josie blurted. "Stop playing the part of the dutiful husband when I already know the truth. It's obvious you wish you had never laid eyes on me, so don't disguise your true feelings with sweet little gestures that mean nothing. I wanted to know you, Charles."

Charles's eyes hardened, though she would hardly have thought it possible for them to become any stonier. "Biblically speaking, we know each other very well."

"That isn't what I meant. You needn't be so hateful about it. What have I done to make you despise me so?"

"I don't despise you, Josephine. I despise myself for letting fear of my father force me into a marriage with a woman who deserves better. I didn't have the nerve to go against his wishes, and now your happiness is forfeit. As for myself, I would have been content to remain a bachelor. I don't deceive myself that I could ever find happiness with any Judas of a woman."

Josie staggered away from him as the scalding tears blinded her.

"I swear to God that one day I will prove to you that your wife is not a Judas."

Charles laughed, and the broken sound mangled her heart.

"I am relieved to see that you have finally realized that I am not your knight in shining armor. It was becoming a bit of a strain."

Josie fled, choking on her sobs. Her hunger for his affection had only bared her heart to his cruelty. He was incapable of loving her.

Chapter Sixteen

*A*we pierced through the numbness that characterized her every waking moment since their fight on the ship: she was in Paris. The scenery was a welcome distraction from the last few days of travel, punctuated by aches and dirt. The beds they had been fortunate enough to get at roadside taverns had boasted lumpy straw tick mattresses and insufficient width to accommodate a sleeping couple. With the rigid form of her husband beside her, she hadn't been revisited by the night-mare—but it was worse to live a conscious one. While other passengers had chatted and laughed, the Radcliffe party had remained silent as the coaches changed every ten miles without fail. No doubt Esther and Thomas had sensed the potent animosity that hung between them like drapes. As her eyes savored the steeples and gilded architecture, Josie hoped that this city steeped in romance had some to spare.

"Conducteur, 223 Rue Saint-Honore," Charles bellowed.

"Oui, Monsieur, l'Hotel Meurice."

Josie could picture the smirk of irony lifting the corners of the driver's mustache as he conveyed his foreign passengers to the French hotel that possessed an untarnished reputation for catering to travelers of British nationality.

Their coach clattered along the cobblestones, and Josie ignored Charles's frown as she threw dignity to the wind and leaned out the window. She was determined not to let a single detail escape her attention. Ladies strolled by wearing exquisite gowns of every description, punctuated by the renowned Paris green. Esther followed her gaze and patted Josie's knee.

"We'll have to get ye one of those, Josie. The green will do wonders for yer eyes."

"Only if you allow me to get you one of those lavender gowns," Josie parried with a faint smile.

"Och, what do I need with another dress?" Esther scoffed, but her eyes twinkled. Josie had never been so thankful to have her Esther back in good health.

The coach shuddered to a halt, and Josie couldn't wait to escape the rolling prison. Charles alighted and reached for her. Josie grasped his hand, and her limbs thrilled as her heart touched the heart of Paris. Her parasol bloomed as Charles tipped the two bag boys.

"Shall we secure our lodgings, Mrs. Radcliffe?"

Josie cast him a tight-lipped nod, and he led her through the mahogany-paneled doors. The lobby of the Hotel Meurice threatened to steal her breath away. Gold and crystal accents caught the light in a display of resplendence. The people scattered throughout consisted mostly of their own countrymen as they approached the gilt desk. Apparently the hotel lived up to its reputation.

Charles signed the guest book with an impatient flourish and requested a large suite and two separate bedrooms on the same floor. The condescending clerk replied in perfect English, "I regret to inform you, Monsieur Radcliffe, that we will not have a suite vacancy until tomorrow evening. At present all I can offer you is one of our finest master bedrooms. There are two more available just down the hall."

Charles's jaw clenched. Josie groaned inwardly. She couldn't take a display of temper right now.

"Please, Charles, that will suffice. I am weary."

Charles flung a glance at the ornate gold wall clock that ticked behind the clerk's balding head. "I will take them," he growled and thrust their bank's letter of credit across the counter. The clerk's lips curved pleasantly, but his cool eyes expressed something entirely different.

"Very good, Monsieur Radcliffe."

The insufferable clerk derived acute pleasure from copying the information down in as slow a fashion as possible. Finally he straightened, pushed the letter across the marble counter to Charles, and held out a gold key.

"Andre will show you to room 24A. I have no doubt that you will find your stay at Hotel Meurice most enjoyable indeed."

Charles snatched up his letter and took the key as though the clerk were a poisonous serpent whose fangs could sink into his hand at any moment.

Andre appeared from where he had been shuffling papers around the corner and led them toward a grand marble staircase. Thomas, Esther, and the two bag boys brought up the rear as they climbed two flights of stairs. Andre paused in front of a mahogany door labeled "24" and bowed before showing Thomas and Esther to their rooms farther down the hallway. It was just as well the young Frenchman seemed averse to conversation after the mood the clerk had put Charles into. The bag boys set their trunks on the Persian rug and scuttled back out the door.

Charles kicked off his boots and collapsed onto a feather bed that appeared to swallow even his six-foot-two frame. All Josie wanted was a hot bath and to breathe air untainted by her husband's presence. She discovered an adjoining powder room and shut the door, convinced that Charles couldn't have cared less if she drowned in the deep copper tub.

Josie eyed the gleaming faucets labeled hot and cold and decided she was not pulling off one article of clothing until the fancy plumbing proved itself. With a faint squeak, she twisted the "hot" knob and fingered the grudging trickle of water. It was icy cold. A frown furrowed her brow. Nevertheless, she let it run, plunking herself down in the velvet chair and watching the trickle deepen to a stream. She refused to wait for a maid to draw her bath the old-fashioned way. Distaste at the thought of joining her husband kept her right where she was as she weighed the virtues of an ice-cold sponge bath.

But then a mysterious element fogged the gleaming copper. Had the water turned hot? Josie fingered the stream again and jerked back from the scalding gush. She reached for the cold knob. In spite of almost boiling herself alive, it was the easiest bath she had ever drawn.

Steam clouded the mirror as she hung her dress and unmentionables on the gold hook and grasped the bar of English soap. A shiver of pleasure absorbed her as she sank beneath the steaming surface and proceeded to scrub up a generous lather of suds that frosted the water like clotted cream. Josie leaned back against the rim of the tub and closed her eyes. Tension and stress melted away along with the roadside dust, until warm, limpid contentment embraced her.

"Josephine . . . Josie, wake up. Please."

Josie's eyes flew open, and she stared up at the green-eyed mermaid painted on the ceiling. Water lapped at her throat. *Where on earth am I?*

A human gaze begged her attention as she raised her head. Concern muted Charles's piercing blue eyes. Josie's heart leaped into her throat. With a splash, she sent the curtain whizzing between them until the billowing white cloth blocked him from view.

"Are you all right?" His voice was muffled through the cloth and steam.

"Other than the fact that my husband caught me looking like a boiled currant?"

"I'm . . . sorry. It was not my intention to frighten you. I fell asleep, and after I woke up I knocked but you didn't answer. So I went to Esther, but she hadn't seen you. Then I got worried, but I decided I had better look in here one last time before I panicked."

Josie's irritation evaporated at the note of genuine worry in his voice. It did not make sense.

He added, "If it's any consolation, I'd rather find a boiled currant than no one at all."

Josie winced as she recalled her earlier thought. Apparently he *did* care.

"Charles, I'm sorry I gave you cause for alarm. I was just so tired I fell asleep and didn't hear your knock."

"You would never leave me?"

The voice was lost and forlorn . . . the voice of the boy in the portrait at Treathston Heights. Josie tugged back the curtain.

"I will never leave you, Charles Radcliffe, unless you ask me to."

His gaze wavered, and then he cleared his throat.

"I'll have dinner sent up . . . unless you prefer for me to take you out?"

Josie grinned as she wriggled her shriveled toes. "I don't think Paris would approve. A private dinner sounds heavenly."

Charles nodded and shut the door with a click. He left her wrestling with a tangle of emotions. The numbness was gone— hope stirring in a reawakened yet fragile flutter.

One of these days, that door to your heart will stay open long enough to let me in, Charles Radcliffe.

Josie stepped out of the lukewarm tub and grabbed a monogrammed towel from the washstand. Then she struggled into her chemise, stays, and dress, wishing that Esther would appear through the woodwork to assist her. She left her damp tresses down and eyed the French perfume on the dressing table as she flung them over her shoulder. She shrugged and dabbed a little behind each ear. It couldn't hurt, even if it failed to put Charles into a romantic mood.

Charles sat at the table by the window overlooking the lights of Paris. Absorbed by the glowing moon that hung above the city, he did not seem to notice her slipping into her seat. Her reticule sat at her plate, looking oddly out of place. It clinked as she picked it up. A gold Napoleon clattered onto the burgundy tablecloth.

"Charles, what is all this?"

"Three thousand francs for you to spend in the city on whatever takes your fancy. There's more where that came from if you run out before we leave."

The monetary peace offering felt more like a bribe. A feeble excuse for the heart he had failed to give her—whether it was because he could not or would not, she had yet to determine.

"Charles, I will accept this on one condition. If you are giving this to me because you feel guilty, then I want no part of it. Or is it because you merely want me to enjoy myself?"

Charles's eyes narrowed at the accusation. He gritted his teeth as he reached for the bottle of champagne and screwed the corkscrew into the stopper with painful deliberation. The cork ricocheted off the window pane like a bullet. Josie flinched at the resounding pop. *Why didn't I just keep my mouth shut?*

Charles poured the sizzling bubbles into his wineglass. He sighed, raking a hand through his hair as he chose each word.

"Getting right to the heart of the matter seems to be a habit with you. The answer to your question is both yes and no. The money is a peace offering, that is true. I wanted to make the deficiencies of this miserable honeymoon up to you. However, it is also true that I want you to enjoy yourself in Paris. This is the trip of a lifetime. It's no secret that your father wasn't able to outfit you in the latest styles each season. I want you to soak up the feeling that you have money to burn for a change."

Tears welled up in Josie's eyes as she reached for his hand. She kissed it, pressing his knuckles against her cheek and marveling that she had never noticed his hands before. His fingers were sensitive and fine-boned, capable of infinite gentleness.

"You do care," she whispered, and when her voice caught, she didn't care that it betrayed her. She was tired of hiding.

"It's not as though I can't afford it," Charles scoffed. "I hope you can derive some pleasure from being rich, for it has never brought me anything but headache."

Josie refused to be put off. "Beneath your cold indifference, you hide a heart that cares deeply, but you are afraid to show it because you still carry the scar of betrayal. What woman betrayed you, Charles?"

Charles reached for his glass with his free hand, and it shook in his fingers as he drained it in one gulp. "Josephine—"

"I am not Josephine. I have never been and never will be Josephine. You called me Josie once when you dared to love me out of my fear. You called me Josie when you feared I had left you forever. Deep down I am Josie to you."

Charles did not deny it as he reached for the champagne again and then fisted his hand. "Why is it that I can never hide anything from you?"

Josie's thumb stroked his skin. "Because I care about you, darling. I want to be more than you are letting me be, but the key to your heart is yours alone to give. For now, I just need you to recognize that and understand that I have nothing but your best interests at heart."

"Don't cry," Charles said softly. "I'm not worth crying over."

His finger skimmed her cheek, and then he pulled his hand away. Josie sniffed and dabbed at her eyes with her serviette. "Didn't you hear anything I just said, Charles? I don't know what you are measuring your worth from, but don't listen to the lies the enemy of your soul wants you to believe!"

A knock sounded, and Charles shoved back his chair. Josie's eyes followed him across the room as he jerked the door open without ceremony. Two waiters in immaculate white dinner jackets carried in trays and set them at their places. They bowed stiffly and beat a hasty retreat as though sensing Charles's impatience.

"I hope you're hungry," he said.

Josie stared down at her rather overwhelming portion of filet mignon. She smiled and took a tentative bite. "My appetite has no complaints."

"I wish I could say the same. It seems mine is only for drink."

He poured himself a second glass. But Josie refused to cease probing the wound until she found its festering source.

"Talk to me, Charles. Tell me why you keep me a hundred thousand miles away from you. That bottle is closer to you than me."

He didn't meet her eyes. "What do you want, Mrs. Radcliffe?"

"I want the truth."

"If it's honesty you want, I will give it to you in its most brutal form."

Josie braced herself as he pinned her with a hard look. "When I was eight years old, I woke up one morning to discover that my mother had walked out of my world. At first I didn't realize it was permanent. For a while I convinced myself she had just gone on a long trip—or perhaps she was sick, as none of the grown-ups seemed to have any answers either. Then my father finally told me. My mother had run away with another man and abandoned both of us. She was never coming back to us. Not ever."

He hesitated until Josie doubted he would continue. But he did.

"I promised myself that I would never let another woman betray me. That I would never love another woman to the same degree again. I courted Delia against my better judgment and at my father's wishes, but in the end I was burned anyway when she proved to be just like my mother."

The missing piece slipped into place, and for the first time Josie understood his rejection. He could not give her what wasn't intact.

"If you felt this way, then why did you agree to marry me?"

Charles's face twisted as the blood drained away. The empty wineglass splintered between his clenched fingers. Josie gasped as his hand unfurled and shards fell from his bloodied palm. As she leaned toward him, he seized the tablecloth and swept its contents to the floor with a tinkling shatter. Josie froze as he sat breathing hard, eyes darkening with rage.

"Perhaps I no longer cared."

"You cared. You cared a great deal, for it is your nature, as much as you tried to freeze your heart against warmth or love. You married me for your father, just as I married you for mine. What I don't understand is the influence your father has on you. Your relationship doesn't strike me as close. Why is it so important to you that you never disappoint him?"

Charles stared out the window.

"To this day I don't know why she left . . . why she really left. What haunts me is that I wasn't worth staying for, despite how many differences she and Father might have had. She could have taken me with her, but she didn't."

"Oh Charles," Josie murmured and reached out for him. The coiled muscles in his frame jerked away, and he bolted to his feet. Stormy blue eyes collided with hers, their piercing force rippling in a rumble of warning. Her tears welled up as she lived his pain, raw and festering, and understood why she hadn't glimpsed his scarred heart until now. She had cornered him and forced it to surface. Now he watched her like a wounded animal, prepared to fight for the last shred of guardedness he maintained.

Josie took a deep breath and found she was willing to make the first move as she rose from her chair. She drew closer, and then he offered his palm. She accepted it like newborn life, recognizing the quickening of the feeling between them that had been dead for too long. His intense gaze rested on her face as she cradled his knuckles and picked the slivers of glass from his flesh. She dabbed at the cuts with her serviette and bound a fresh one around it. She kissed each of his fingertips as her tears flowed along with his blood, staining the snowy linen.

The words rumbled from his chest. "Now look what I've done. I've defiled your lovely eyes again."

He bent, and Josie shivered as he kissed her tears away. His lips rested against her eyelids, warm and tremulous. His arms pulled her closer, and she didn't dare to breathe lest the magical moment be shattered. She gasped for air as he pressed her against his heart, and his arms enfolded her until she thought she would be crushed. Then his embrace gentled, and she knew nothing but the bliss of strong arms that refused to let go. *He called my eyes lovely.* Her hands crept around him until they clung to the breadth of his shoulders.

"You were right, you know," he murmured as he rested his cheek on top of her head. "You are Josie to me, unlike any woman I have ever known. You have a beautiful soul with an abundance of compassion and love to give. I am a coward and a fool."

"No—"

"Yes, I'm afraid to love you, afraid to lose you, and above all afraid to be the husband you deserve. I want to protect you from . . . myself."

"That's not what I want."

"But I'll hurt you . . . I've already hurt you."

"I'm not a china doll. I won't break; I'm stronger than that. We are one flesh. When I vowed to marry you I also vowed to share your pain and your burdens. Let me, Charles."

Charles was silent for a long while.

"Old habits die hard. Is it possible for me to learn to trust a woman again?"

His voice was little more than a whisper. Josie's arms tightened around him, and his chest shuddered against her cheek.

"I'm not asking you to tear down the walls you have built around your heart to protect yourself. I'm asking you to give me the key and let me in so that we can face the pain and the lies together. I can't bear the thought of you living the rest of your life alone when I'm here to share it."

"It is not a question of what I want. It is a question of whether or not I am able."

Josie pulled away and seized his face between her hands. "You are, dearest Charles, I know you are! You don't want to hurt me, but nothing hurts me more than when you shut me out."

Her voice broke, and she buried her face against him.

"I don't deserve your love."

Josie fisted her hands against his chest. "Don't say that," she choked out. "Just because your mother abandoned you does not mean you deserved to be abandoned. It doesn't mean you aren't worthy of love. That's why you try so hard to please your father, isn't it? You're trying to prove to yourself that you are worthy of love."

He didn't try to deny it. Only clung to her like a drowning man as the shoulders beneath her palms heaved. Her heart was open to him, a vulnerable void, and even as it pleaded with him to fill it, it was a dangerous place to be. She had bared herself to be broken even as she clung to him with a tenacity that defied the imminent peril. Her love wouldn't be enough to quench his thirst. He needed the Great Physician to heal his brokenness. And the same was true for her. The knowledge lodged in the pit of her stomach. He was incapable of meeting her need for love. He could not give her what he had never known himself.

Charles gripped her shoulders, and Josie's heart shuddered.

"I am utterly unworthy of you and your love. If I keep you at a distance, it is because that is what is best for both of us."

Josie tore free of him. "No. You may think that is what is best for you—because if you consider me beyond your reach, you needn't try to be anything but a stranger to me. It hurts to try, doesn't it? To try is to open yourself to yet another rejection. Well, I refuse to give up on you, Mr. Radcliffe. I won't rest until I succeed in winning your trust, because I cannot bear to let both of our hearts freeze to death."

Charles's face twisted as he backed away and collapsed on the bed.

"My body will not deny you physical companionship, but I fear my heart is unable to provide you the warmth of intimacy."

"But I will deny you neither, for I am warm-blooded and prefer to remain that way. I pray to God you change your mind, for He alone can help you now."

Hot tears surged in her eyes and blurred the haunting depths of blue in his face. She sank to her knees, withered by the despair in his slumped shoulders.

"For the love of all that is sacred, Charles, don't exile me to a life of loneliness. I cannot bear it."

Charles leaned down and pressed his lips against her forehead. The tenderness in his voice was cruel. "I will not presume to ask for your forgiveness when I cannot forgive myself, but believe me when I tell you I am sorry it had to come to this. May your dreams be sweet, for I forbid nightmares to visit you."

"The only nightmare is the one I'm living. Chase it away from me, Charles."

Pain stood stark in his face. "Once I made you a promise to protect you from all harm. I'm sorry that I couldn't protect you from myself. When I pledged myself to you, I chained you with the same chain from which I have never been able to set myself free."

Charles rolled away as though unable to bear the sight of her. Josie rose and snuffed out the candle flames with her fingertips, for nothing could hurt her anymore. She had offered herself, and her husband had sacrificed her heart upon the coals of searing rejection. Pain lurked in the raw recesses of her heart, battling the encroaching numbness as she climbed into bed beside the man who might as well have been an ocean away.

Chapter Seventeen

*J*osie's heart-rending cries haunted him, and he wrestled the sheets that bound his thrashing limbs as he struggled in vain. *Chase it away, Charles, chase it away from me.* Then her voice began to fade in the darkness, and he panicked. He was losing her to that horrible unknown fate, and she was beyond his reach. Charles flailed in one last desperate effort to reach her and clutched something soft.

"Josie," he moaned.

"I'm here, Charles."

His eyes flew open to find her pillow clutched against his chest. He looked up and met her eyes in the mirror where she sat brushing her hair, distant as the stars—a stranger. His Josie had evaporated in the face of this woman's icy dignity. He clutched the pillow tighter, and pain stabbed his palm. It all came flooding back in more vivid detail than he cared to recall as he eyed the rusty stains lacing the serviette around his hand.

"You called me," he whispered.

The brittle gray depths of her gaze splintered like shards of ice floating on a swift current.

"No, Charles."

He sighed and buried his face in her pillow, absorbing the last of her warmth that still clung there.

"What I wouldn't give for a cup of good strong coffee," he groaned.

"That can be arranged. I hear it is excellent at the Palais Royale just down the street."

"I'm sure that is what every tourist and loyal Paris citizen has in mind at this very same moment."

"It is early yet. We can enjoy the gardens at our leisure if we hurry."

A knock sounded on the door. Josie rose to answer it, still dressed in her rumpled gown. Esther swept in with a bright smile that failed to chase away the gloom.

"Good morning," she chirped.

Charles staggered out of the bed. He didn't fail to catch Esther's raised brows at their choice of nightwear.

"I'll join you ladies shortly," he said, grasping the handle of his valise. He made his way to Thomas's room and pounded on the door.

"Wake up, lazybones, and repair your master's toilette with all haste," he thundered to the dismay of the more civilized guests emerging from their rooms.

Thomas opened the door and blinked at him. "Why the dashed hurry?" he grumbled.

"Just do as you are told for once in your life," Charles snapped and brushed past him. He wrenched his clothes off. The deep copper tub called, but a sponge bath would serve him just as well. While he washed, he glanced over at the clothes Thomas was laying out for him on the unmade bed.

"Not the brocade waistcoat. I have no wish to look the part of the dandified English fop."

Thomas grinned.

"What different ideas we have of Paris fashion. But then, you never were one to please the ladies."

Charles scowled as he pulled up a pair of fawn breeches.

"For a newly married man, you are dashed irritable."

"For a valet you are frightfully impertinent," Charles retorted as he donned a fresh linen shirt. Thomas shrugged as he held out a green waistcoat.

"Pardon my saying so, sir, but I couldn't help observing that matrimony does not appear to sit well with you. Miss Josephine is an attractive woman, though I daresay not the goddess type. Did you two have a little spat?"

"Egad, Thomas! You know nothing about such matters, and I'll kindly ask you to keep any and all of your future observations about my marriage to yourself."

Thomas's brown eyes looked pained, and Charles fell silent as his valet shaved off yesterday's stubble.

"Certainly I will respect your wishes, sir. I thought we were more than master and servant though, eh? Thought you might need a man to confide in."

Charles sighed and patted Thomas's thin shoulder.

"That we are, my friend. Forgive my pettishness. No doubt I'd have more to confide if I understood half of the mess I've made."

Thomas let that go. "What are your plans for today, sir? Sightseeing with the missus?"

Charles grimaced at the rather dismal prospect. "I suppose."

"I hear there are some frightfully exciting horse races in Paris."

Charles hesitated for only a handful of seconds before making his decision.

"I'll tell you what, Thomas. I'm taking Mrs. Radcliffe out for coffee at the Palais Royale shortly. She expressed interest in exploring the gardens for a bit. You could accompany Miss McAllister and dig up a good horse race while we're gone. No doubt the ladies will want to go shopping this afternoon."

Thomas whooped as he tossed Charles a towel. "Now you're talking sense," he exclaimed. "Let the ladies shop for their folderols and gewgaws while we place a few solid bets."

"I want no part of gambling, but I enjoy watching beautiful steppers fight it out neck to neck as much as the next man."

"Anything would be more thrilling than window shopping."

Charles shrugged into his coattails and chuckled as he eyed Thomas's nightshirt. "I trust you have something more suitable in mind to escort Miss McAllister."

"I'll be dressed in two shakes of a lamb's tail."

Thomas shadowed him like a puppy as Charles entered the lobby. He thought he had steeled himself against the sight of his wife, but his heart betrayed him as his gaze landed on Josie. She stood there perusing a fashion magazine with gloved fingertips, and he allowed himself to linger and study her profile beneath the brim of her plumed burgundy hat. Thomas had called her attractive, but that wasn't the word for his Josie. Goddess or not, to him she was the most beautiful woman God had ever made. Her lashes lifted, revealing raw gray-green depths that had lost their mesmerizing sparkle. Because of him. *Rogue! Villain! Selfish, vile brute!*

As she spotted him, the pooled hurt in her eyes congealed hard.

"I hope I didn't keep you waiting," he said.

A flicker of surprise filtered through her gaze as though she thought him incapable of consideration in its simplest form. Perhaps it was true, but for the first time he could remember, it bothered him.

"On the contrary," she murmured.

Her body was poker stiff as he took her arm.

"I'll go see what sort of amusement I can dig up for you, sir, accompanied by this lovely lady," Thomas said, grinning down at the ever-tolerant Esther. Charles glared at his valet, and Thomas beat a hasty retreat as he tugged Esther out the door.

A frown etched Josie's brow. "It is Englishmen like your valet who give our countrymen an uncouth reputation in the presence of real gentlemen."

Charles yawned. "I would hardly call these French flatterers gentlemen, Madame. Any beautiful woman, foreign or native, is a conquest to them and nothing more."

"I would prefer to be considered a conquest than invisible."

Charles quelled the retort that rose to his lips with an effort, and without a word, he ushered his wife outside.

The pink blush of dawn kissed the blond columns of the Palais Royale with ethereal light. Its mullioned windows were distant and haughty. Conceit was written in its every scrolled line, proclaiming that mere mortals were unworthy of such resplendence. Inside the Palais Royale, blinding filigree and cathedral ceilings encompassed them with a grandeur that threatened to overwhelm the senses.

A waiter in stark white escorted them to a table. The linen tablecloth scoffed at the mere notion of stains, and Charles yanked a chair out for Josie. She laid her serviette in her lap and studied the scrolled menu as though she belonged. Admiration shone in the waiter's dark, beady eyes. Charles clenched his fist as the lengthy seconds ticked by. It seemed to him the man was committing every feature to memory.

"May I take your order, Madame?"

"I'll have croissants, a pot of chocolate, and café au lait," Josie said in smooth French without batting an eyelash.

"Allow me to applaud your mastery of our language, Madame. For a foreigner it eez very good."

"Thank you, Monsieur. You are most kind."

Charles cleared his throat. The waiter diverted his gaze with a raised brow that expressed his disapproval for the British . . . with the exception of their women.

"Monsieur?"

"I'll have coffee and quiche."

Suaveness dripped from the waiter's words. "It will only be a moment."

The coffee arrived shortly before the quiche and croissants, brewed strong and dark. Charles drank his black, and its bracing bitterness matched his mood. The quiche didn't agree with him. Josie lingered over her unfinished chocolate and croissants.

"What do you say to a stroll in the garden?" Charles suggested. "I confess I find nature considerably more attractive than this artificial adaption."

Josie pinched the bridge of her nose.

"On a more positive note that was the best chocolate that has ever passed my lips. We should have left that ingenious beverage to the French. Back home I shall have to revolutionize our poor imitation," she said.

He reached out and gave her hand a gentle squeeze as his conscience nagged him. "I'm glad you enjoyed it," he said as they wandered out into the courtyard. "Father's chef is French. I'm sure he can replicate it to your satisfaction."

She squinted against the brightness of the sunlight, and he realized that chocolate was the farthest thing from her mind. Her heavy sigh made his own lungs ache.

"Charles, now that you have had your coffee, I hope you manage to do something equally pleasurable today."

"As a matter of fact, Thomas and I were thinking about taking in a horse race later."

Josie stared into the distance as though she were blind to the rare blooms around them. She seemed to look into the future—no doubt a future when she was finally free of him. They paused by a fountain as its water gushed with the rhythm of eternity. The silence grew heavy.

"And what did you plan for today?" Charles finally asked.

"Other than spending time with my husband?"

"Now what possible enjoyment could you derive from my company when you have three thousand francs burning a hole in your reticule?"

She didn't look at him. "There are some things money cannot buy."

He doubted she had intended the words as a barb, but it wounded him to recognize how low he lay in her estimation. "You speak as though I wasn't going to spend any time with you at all. I thought some time apart would do us both some good. You go buy yourself a dress that brings out the enchantment in your eyes, and I promise I'll take you out to dinner and the opera tonight. Only the best cuisine Paris has to offer will do."

Hope flared in her ever-shifting gaze, and his heart throbbed to meet it with a turbulent ache. "Just the two of us, Charles?"

He reached for her hand. It quivered beneath his touch like the bird with the broken wing he had once nursed back to health.

"I wouldn't have it any other way."

Josie gnawed at her bottom lip, leaving it red and swollen. The memory of her lips stirred in him, but their taste eluded him.

A shout from behind interrupted the moment. "Charles!"

The sound of his own name struggled to penetrate as Thomas darted toward them.

"I found a smashing race, but we've got to hurry, else we'll miss it."

"I'll see you tonight," Charles muttered.

Josie hardened as he walked away. A feathery touch landed on her arm. For the first time that she could remember, Esther's hand didn't bring healing.

"Come, luve," Esther murmured as she tugged on her elbow. "Let's go find that dress."

"So you heard?"

Esther's gaze held her steady. "I couldna help overhearing, luve."

"Then you know how it is between us."

"I ken yer angry, but yer not God, Josie. I ken ye better in some ways then ye ken yerself. Ye cannae bear for one soul in this world to be unloved, so ye've taken it upon yerself to love each and every one. Ye cannae mend every broken heart with yers, though ye long to, but ye must not feel guilt. There are some broken things we must bring to God to mend, like yer Charles."

Josie froze midstep as Esther nodded. A shadow of pain haunted her silvery eyes. "I've watched ye break yerself to fix him just like ye sacrificed yerself to fix Delia's life when she broke it. God's light shines through our brokenness, but I wish we didna have to break for Him to get through. The bitterness will only rot and poison ye if ye dinna forgive him."

"He has rejected my love. I cannot forgive him for betraying me body and soul."

"Yer a grown woman, Josie. I cannae treat ye like a bairn anymore, but I would start praying for him if ye can find it in yer heart to do so. In my own life it has been the only thing that has kept bitterness away. God can change that man's heart when nothing else does."

Josie sighed. "I suppose it was foolish of me to think I could do it on my own."

"I've walked this road, luve. I would have written your life's story differently if the pen was in my hand, but I'm not the Author of yer life. The Author is penning a far more beautiful story than I ever could, because He is also your Savior. Kenning He loves ye even more than I . . . that's what I cling to when I cannae see why. I just ken I can trust His heart."

"Don't you ever doubt, Esther?"

"Aye. Our flesh is weak, but God isn't limited by our limitations. Moses was a murderer, David was an adulterer, and Noah was a drunkard, but God used all of those people to show His power. His love wasn't defined by their deeds. It never dimmed or tarnished, and it is the same with us, Josie. Nothing can separate us from the love of Christ. He will always be enough for ye, Josie, if ye let Him. He will be yer best and dearest friend when everyone else forsakes ye. That is the beauty God brings from the ashes when our dreams go up in smoke. We find Him and ken Him because He is all we have left to cling to."

Josie couldn't find words as the shop windows called, regaling her with dresses of every description. A dress of Paris green fashioned with an empire waist caught her eye.

Resolve steeled her spine as she entered Madame Beauchene's. Charles would grovel at her feet tonight.

A dark Frenchwoman as tall as she was seductive approached with a frigid smile. "Welcome to my shop. I am Madame Beauchene."

"I am interested in the Paris green gown in your window."

Madame Beauchene's gaze swept her. "Ah, yes that eez most popular among the Engleesh. It lends height to the figure from the bodice down."

"Do you happen to have another? With it being such a popular style, I'm sure I could find it elsewhere."

The woman's cold blue eyes appraised her afresh. "Not at my quality and price," she retorted with grudging respect. "One moment, and I will bring it out for you."

The queen of dressmakers sailed into the back room, and Josie hefted her reticule. "Hoity-toity. If I wasn't confident in my French, I would have run out the door without so much as a good-bye to her highness."

"She does fine work," Esther said, fingering the material on a nearby mannequin. "She didna achieve this location without winning the respect of the local women first."

"Frenchwomen aren't the only ones who can do justice to such a dress."

Madame Beauchene emerged from the back room and pushed open the dressing room door with a flourish. "Be my guest. Are there any other colors or styles you are interested in trying on?"

Josie smiled at the monetary glint in her eyes. "I'll try on the blue serge, the gray poplin, and the rose silk."

"May I suggest that this red velvet would look delightful on you."

"You may indeed," Josie said, adding it to the load in Esther's arms. She shut the dressing room door in Madame's face and began wriggling out of her burgundy dress. Esther slipped the Paris green over her head. Josie held her breath as the vivid emerald enfolded her like a caress.

"Oh, Esther," Josie gasped.

Esther's lips curved in a tremulous smile as her eyes brimmed with pride.

Josie emerged from the dressing room and reveled in the widening of Madame Beauchene's eyes as she flung the dresses onto the counter. She had exacted her respect from society as Mrs. Charles Radcliffe for the first time.

"I'm not satisfied yet," she announced as they left.

Esther raised a dark eyebrow.

"We have yet to find you a gown. And don't protest, because I shan't listen to a word of it."

"Then I shan't."

Josie tightened her hold on the parcels as her eyes roved the shop windows. "There it is."

A lavender gown beckoned with silent dignity and grace from a mannequin's rigid form. The weathered plaque over the door creaked in the stiff breeze. *Mademoiselle Adeline's.*

"You've got to at least try it on." Josie mounted the steps, ignoring Esther's sigh. *You're long overdue for a new dress, Esther. You sacrificed enough through our season of want when it should have been within our power to reward you handsomely. I can never repay you, but I can pay off Father's final debt.*

An old woman with pins in her mouth and a lively sparkle in her dark eyes emerged from the fitting room. She removed the pins and beamed a gap-toothed smile at her new customers.

"Ah, welcome to Adeline's. How may I assist you?"

"I presume you are Mademoiselle Adeline?"

The old woman's dark brows rose beneath the crown of silvery hair. "You presume correctly, ma chere."

"We just came from Madame Beauchene's. If you'll permit my saying so, your warmth of manner does your countrywomen credit."

Adeline flung her hands up in the air. "Oui, Madame, merci. I always say that we must embrace equality for all mankind!" she declared. "Unfortunately, many of my countrywomen cannot get past the noblesse oblige and their blue-blooded airs. That aristo Madame Beauchene should thank her patron saint that her head wasn't kissed by Mamzelle Guillotine along with her husband's. Liberty, equality, and fraternity are a curse to her, but to every French citizen of humble roots they are salvation."

She squinted at them. "You are English, are you not?"

"Pray do not hold that against us."

"In spite of the differences between our countrymen, I am grateful for England's assistance in exiling the tyrant who dared to sacrifice France's noblest sons in his diabolical lust for power. Enough blood had already been shed amongst ourselves. Perhaps we will finally find peace now that we have escaped the scourge of that despicable despot's reign. The Blessed Virgin knows I would never be able to keep this shop open if it were not for English business. But enough of politics. What brings you to my shop?"

"That darling lavender dress in the window."

"Oui, that would look most charming on your lovely mother."

Josie blinked as Esther's soft gasp registered.

"My mother died when I was eight. Esther is my lady's maid."

Adeline's brows lifted. "I beg your pardon. It eez such a coincidence, eez it not? I just assumed that the two of you were related from looking—"

"If you mean to say our relationship is closer than most, you are right."

"Of course," Adeline murmured, but Josie breathed easier when the Frenchwoman redirected her piercing gaze to the window and busied herself removing the lavender dress. She draped it over her arm and handed it to Esther.

"Was there anything else you would like to try on, ma chere?" she offered.

Esther shook her head with vehemence as Adeline opened a door on the back wall.

"Do you have any Paris green?" Josie asked.

"I did once. It is quite the rage as they say, but I refuse to sell it."

Esther paused in the doorway.

"Why?" Josie asked.

The Frenchwoman wrung her hands. "People call me overly suspicious, but I fear it isn't safe. The green is most popular, yes, but dresses aren't the only item the dye is being used for. My daughter wallpapered my grandson's nursery in it. It is a damp old house, and I noticed an odd smell one night after a storm like a dead mouse. Then one morning my grandson was found dead in his crib. The doctor, he had read an article by a German chemist written several years ago, in which he warns of noxious fumes from such wallpaper. I have made some discreet inquiries. Among the dye's ingredients is our city's most popular form of rat poison. There are rumors circulating that the women known to wear it often are subject to fainting spells."

"I am very sorry about your grandson," Josie said.

"Luve—" Esther began.

"I'd rather beard a dragon in his den, Esther," Josie interrupted, knowing Esther wanted her to return the Paris green dress to that snobbish Madame Beauchene.

Esther frowned and shut the door with perhaps a little more force than was necessary.

"Do you have any hats?" Josie blurted. Adeline led her over to a shelf where a peacock chapeaux de paille caught her eye. She settled the jaunty bonnet on top of her twist and nodded. It lent her a bold air. Paired with the Paris green, it would dazzle Charles's senses.

"Could you please wrap it for me, Adeline?" she asked, shoving a wayward pin back into place.

The dressing room door swung open, and Esther drifted out. Josie was struck by the impression that she was graced by the presence of a goddess—but how unfamiliar her former governess appeared!

"Are ye satisfied, Josie? Can I go back to being myself now?"

"If you wish."

Esther's smile was forced, but she no doubt detected the disappointment in Josie's voice.

"'Tis good of ye, luve, but that season of life has passed me by."

The door clicked shut, and Josie's brow creased as she wondered why the dress had triggered Esther's strange reaction.

As soon as she'd paid for the chapeaux de paille, Josie went out and hailed a passing cab. The hat box well-nigh overwhelmed her stack of parcels as she waited. Esther came out empty-handed, and they passed the ride back to the Hotel Meurice in the most uncompanionable silence they had ever spent.

"I think I will go lie down," Esther said. "I feel a headache coming on. Should ye need anything, just send for me."

"Can I send for ice or anything for you, Esther?"

Esther waved her hand as she headed for the door. "Dinna bother, luve."

In her own room, Josie slumped onto the coverlet, wishing the featherbed would swallow her whole. Loneliness ached within her, and she willed her eyelids to shut out the sensation.

A large, hulking presence loomed over her body. She gasped, and Charles reeled away.

"It's just me."

Josie glared at him, and he raised his hands in mock surrender. "It wasn't my intention to startle you. Forgive me."

Josie groaned as she stretched her cramped limbs. "It wasn't my intention to fall asleep. What time is it?"

"It's only teatime or so. I can ring for tea if you like, but I doubt the French can brew a decent cup."

Josie stifled a yawn and shook her head. "Did you enjoy your little outing?"

"Until the rain came and turned the track to mud soup," Charles grumbled. "And to top that, I am now short one valet. Against my advice the young fool gambled away his paycheck. When he pressured me for an advance, I refused. He had the gall to tell me I had squelched his pleasure, and he found Paris to be so much more amusing than Cornwall that I could go on without him."

"It isn't your fault. If that's the way he feels, he wouldn't have remained with us for long."

Charles's gaze settled on the window as the raindrops chased one another down the glass. "I still feel somewhat responsible for his welfare. What's here in Paris for him but to get head over heels in debt or contract syphilis? If only I hadn't gone and lost my blasted temper."

Josie giggled. "I hear beards are coming into fashion."

Charles frowned. "I'll have you know I have no intention of growing one, with or without that young coxcomb."

"Good, because I wouldn't want to kiss you with one."

Charles regarded her with a rueful grin as he rubbed his jaw line, as though fearing he had sprouted whiskers in mere seconds. Josie flinched as a clap of thunder shattered the moment.

"Oh, couldn't it have waited until tomorrow?"

"I'll have you know that I have every intention of keeping my promise to you tonight, whether rain or shine. So wipe that glum look off your face."

She managed a smile. "I own I have been looking forward to it more than a little, and no doubt you know that."

"I gather you suffered no small amount of indecision on what to wear this evening," Charles said, gesturing toward the heap of dresses scattered all over his side of the bed.

"I assure you there will not be a better dressed woman in all of Cornwall when we return home. I took great pains with the money you so generously provided me."

"Quite frankly, I do not care if you wear silk or sackcloth so long as you are happy. You would look lovely in a flour sack."

"Why Charles I do believe you are flirting with your wife."

"On second thought, you would look even lovelier in nothing at all," Charles whispered as he leaned closer. Heat flushed her cheeks as she scrambled away with a squeal.

"Charles Radcliffe!"

A knock dulled the gleam she had hoped to fan into something more. Charles yanked the door open, and Esther gaped at him.

"Pardon me for the intrusion," she said as her eyes drifted past him to Josie.

Charles waved it off as though already thinking better of his playfulness. "No, not at all. I assume you have come to help my wife get ready, so I'll leave you two ladies to your toilette. Mrs. Radcliffe, I shall escort you to dinner at ten past five. I'll be waiting for you down in the lobby."

Charles bowed and pulled the door shut. Josie sighed for the hundredth time. Marriage was a stage, with both of them playing every part other than their own. She faced the mirror and began to shimmy out of her dress as Esther grabbed the Paris green.

"I dinna mean for ye to think I was ungrateful earlier."

"You don't have to explain anything to me, Esther. I understand."

Josie's eyes sought Esther's in the mirror. Inky fear dilated her irises as Esther averted her gaze in rejection of Josie's silent question. She was lost without her Esther, yet there was a place void of all that was safe and familiar that Esther retreated to on rare occasions. It had frightened Josie since childhood, because it meant that her angelic governess was a human mortal with something to hide.

"There are times from my past I have tried to forget," Esther explained as though she could read Josie's thoughts. "Memories I dinna dredge up if I can help it."

Josie nodded and tasted the pain touching Esther's mouth. The pain tasted of guilt . . . and the shadow of shame. Something whispered in the back of her mind—some whisper of truth, of illumination—but the roar of her pulse drowned it out.

Esther pressed a kiss against her temple. Josie exhaled with a dull ache in her chest.

"Dinna fret, luve. Jesus has redeemed my past as well as my future. There are just times when I forget and have to forgive myself again for mistakes I made in the past. Dinna borrow what ye could never hope to understand. Ye go and have a good time tonight with yer man."

Josie squared her emerald shoulders and set the peacock feather dancing as she nodded into the glass. "I've been cheated too many times to let that get away from me again."

Josie gripped the balustrade as she descended the grand staircase to the lobby, and she paused to let her head settle back onto her shoulders as a floating sensation threatened to carry it beyond the crystal chandelier. It wouldn't do for her to faint now and tumble the rest of the way down. She scanned the gentlemen below, and anxiety hitched her stride. She needed Charles's admiration more than the air she breathed in this moment.

Dread tied her stomach in knots and threatened to buckle her knees. Her gaze grazed the golden head atop broad shoulders, and she sucked in air as the world blurred. *God, please grant me some sign of hope from him.*

Her heart called his name, and Charles turned as though spellbound. Not a muscle twitched in his frame as their eyes met, but he followed her progress down every step as his topaz depths burned with desire. He reached out in awe as she reached him, as though she were an angel flown to earth. She took his hand.

"You are breathtaking," he whispered.

Tears surged into her eyes.

"You will never know how desperately I needed to hear you say that, Charles."

His lips kneaded the back of her hand, and a delicious shiver coursed down Josie's spine. She reveled in his strong warmth as he tucked her elbow into his with newfound tenderness.

"Shall we?"

She blinked, lost in the beauty of the gentle smile playing on his lips.

"I thought you'd never ask."

His laugh was tinged with the old bitterness, and it caused her heart to constrict. *Don't go tonight, Charles, please don't go there. I need you here with me to stay.*

Cold damp smothered her as they stepped outside. Rain dripped from the brim of Charles's top hat as he waved a cab down. Josie shivered as she darted inside it, and Charles bellowed an address before shutting out the rain.

He slid away from the damp leather by the door and pressed her into a dry corner.

"Dash it, you're dripping wet and cold to boot," he growled. She smiled as he took off his greatcoat and eased it around her shoulders. His warmth clung to the rough wool and seeped through her like a caress. She closed her eyes and snuggled up to him.

"You know what would warm me?" she asked.

"I pray you'll forgive me, Josephine. I was a mite hasty earlier, and it was uncalled for."

She scowled. "Mr. Radcliffe, I am under the direct impression that you consider your wife to be a prude. In the future, kindly remember that as your wife I welcome any flirtations you care to make, as they spare me having to wonder if you even know I exist."

"If you were a man, Madame, you would know that it is an impossibility in the presence of a woman such as yourself."

"Indeed, Monsieur, thank you for being so kind as to assure me in that regard."

"Think nothing of it," Charles muttered.

His tone stung, striking her shuddering heart with the same vengeance with which the rain drummed the roof of the cab. The warm fuzziness that had been there between them a moment ago froze into a hard knot that lodged in her chest and stole her appetite.

They arrived at their destination. Josie tensed in his arms as he swung her down from the cab, and she hid under the drooping folds of his greatcoat while he paid the cabby to wait. He laced his fingers through her cold ones as they dashed through the rain toward the pool of light spilling from the restaurant windows.

Charles scraped back a chair for Josie as she emerged from under his greatcoat. She was ravishing in a dress the hue of wind-tossed waves. The fabric shimmered in the candlelight, echoing the curious light playing in her eyes whenever his gaze strayed to hers.

Charles diverted his eyes to the menu. How he longed for the simplicity of a leg of mutton, but no doubt such a concept would be foreign to the French.

The waiter sauntered up to their table, relishing the sight of Josie. She ordered *les aiguillettes de canard a la bigarade* and the waiter turned a pair of conceited dark eyes his way. All Frenchmen were beginning to look the same to him.

"I'll have the same."

He struggled to define what shifted in the depths of Josie's gaze. He hadn't meant to bark at the man, but God alone knew how thin his patience was wearing at the wall between them. The wall he had fashioned with his own two hands.

Charles doused the nagging whisper that he was in the wrong with a gulp of wine. Her grief was palpable then as the shimmer of her eyes melted into the glisten of tears in her gray-ish-green pools. The wine burned down his throat. She was an appetite he could never quench. The very sight of her taunted him, as though his own demons were reflected in her innocent eyes. He shuddered at the thought.

Josie scrunched up the bridge of her nose. "I won't pretend to understand what men find so attractive about the vile drink. At times it surpasses even their desire for women."

Charles swirled his glass. "I pray you will never have to understand why."

Her breast heaved as she toyed with her serviette. The steaming dishes arrived with surprising speed, but Josie only picked at hers. Charles frowned as he polished off his last few bites and cursed the portion fit more for a child than a grown man. Her gaze landed on him as he scraped the last of the orange sauce from the bone china. She slid her plate forward.

"Please finish mine."

Charles speared a piece of the duck and raised his fork.

"Open your mouth," he commanded. Josie obeyed as he placed the tines between her lips. She held up a hand in protest as he selected another choice tidbit.

"I cannot eat another bite."

"If you keep eating like a bird, the wind will carry you away!" Charles exploded, and several heads turned in their direction. Josie blanched and leaned toward him.

"Don't shout, Charles. It's these stays . . . they're too tight," she mouthed in the barest of whispers.

Charles seized his serviette and flung it across the unfinished dish. With an effort he lowered his voice to match hers. "The moment we are alone, I will loosen them. I don't believe in women not being able to breathe all in the name of ridiculous fashion."

Josie's cheeks flushed, and Charles poured himself another glass with slow deliberation. He was desperate to avoid the pain in her eyes and the sharpness of his own existence, defined by every pang of expectation and failure. The last of the wine trickled out, and he blinked at the bottle.

"Do you have the time, Monsieur?" Josie inquired of the waiter in that adorable French accent of hers.

"It is ten past six, Madame," the waiter responded, no doubt mistaking her question for a flirtation. Josie turned toward Charles with wide eyes, oblivious to the way the waiter was leering at her.

"Charles, we must hurry if we don't want to miss the opera."

The waiter laid their cheque on the table. The rakish Frenchman didn't deserve a tip, but in the end Charles left the expected amount. He had already humiliated Josie enough for one evening. He pushed his chair back, and the world lurched with it as he stood. He wobbled around the table and clenched the back of Josie's chair. He gripped her hand tighter than he intended as she glared at him. She pulled him forward, steering him around the maze of tables. He was grateful for his former presence of mind when he glimpsed the waiting cab through the rain. He steadied the small of Josie's back as she sprang into it.

"Opera de Paris," he directed the cabby and fought against the wave of dizziness that engulfed him as he struggled to maintain his footing. He staggered in and collapsed on the seat, tasting her disgust. He closed his eyes, reflecting that the only good thing about the deluge was that it would protect her from the unsavory sights of Paris nightlife.

Josie's soft intake of breath interrupted the staccato of rain drilling the hood. He glanced out the window. Louis XIV's opera house glowed like a heavenly vision in the sodden night.

The cab pulled up to the glistening marble steps, and Josie flung the door open.

"Careful now, Josephine. Don't slip," Charles cautioned as his Cinderella floated up the steps, flinging a disdainful glance over her magnificent shoulder. She didn't pause, and he almost fell headlong as he scrambled after her.

She stood seething at the ticket desk, but her mouth curved with pleasure as he booked a booth.

"Oh Charles, I would have enjoyed it just as much from a seat and spared you the unnecessary expense," she said as they walked down the dim corridor lit by guttering wall sconces. The light was both fierce and fragile, just like the woman whose skirts rustled beside him.

"I think not. You shall enjoy the opera much more from a private booth, and I don't want to hear another word about unnecessary expense. That chapter of life is behind you."

Her impatience was palpable, as for once she had to slow down to match his stride.

"Oh, do hurry. I can hear the orchestra starting," she huffed and clutched his arm.

Everything swam with her as she fell. He dove for her as the motion overwhelmed his senses and landed on his knees beside her. As he struggled to focus his blurry vision, the candlelight failed to warm her chalky pallor.

He rolled her over and clawed at the buttons down her spine, fumbling with the knotted stays until he managed to loosen them. He breathed with her as the stays expanded and cursed the cruelty of fashion. But she did not revive.

"Josephine, Josie!" he shouted as he shook her, and she flopped in his grasp. He whisked her into his arms and staggered down the corridor. Fear gouged through his reeling senses, enough to bring a semblance of sobriety as he screamed for assistance.

A shadow appeared at his elbow as a man spouted rapid-fire French. The words bounced back at him through a haze as he screamed for a doctor. A calm British voice landed on his ear.

"Sir, you must get her back to your hotel before a doctor can be summoned. I will help you hail a cab, for there is an abundance at this hour. What is the name of your hotel?"

"The Hotel Meurice," Charles gasped out, and the middle-aged stranger hailed a cab at the door. His world was rimmed with a fuzziness he couldn't shake, clinging like the ominous tendrils of a spider's web.

"To the Hotel Meurice on the Rue St. Honore with all haste. Emergency," the man cried as Charles sprang into the cab.

"Godspeed," the stranger bade them, and Charles's thanks were drowned out by the clatter of hooves and wheels as the cab lurched forward. Josie's head rolled to the side on the seat as Charles gathered her up in his arms. Her lips were bluish in the occasional spurt of light as the streets of Paris shot by. He cradled her against his chest, frightened by the fierceness of his emotions. *Oh Josie, this is my fault. You're an angel of mercy that broke beneath the strain of trying to heal us. I cannot bear knowing I crushed your darling heart. I need your light in my darkness. Come back, oh please, come back to me! You promised you would never leave me unless I asked you to, and I'm asking you right now to stay.*

The cab grated to a halt, and Charles struggled to maintain his balance on the slippery seat as he curled his body over hers. The moment the world stopped whirling, he lunged for the door and stumbled out, pausing only to fling the fare at the astonished cabby. Josie's slight weight in his arms was cold and still as he dashed through the driving rain toward the halo of light emanating from the Meurice. *Please God, don't take her from me now. She makes me believe I can be a better man. I promise to try to deserve her.*

The bug-eyed clerk gaped at him from the front desk.

"Curse your dull wits, man. Send a doctor up to room 24A."

Charles's pounding footsteps on the stairs matched the erratic staccato of his heartbeat as the blood roared in his ears. "Esther," he panted as he ascended, but couldn't gulp air fast enough to yell. Apparently the sound of his flying feet had been an adequate summons, for she appeared on the landing. Every drop of blood drained from her face as she swayed and clutched the banister.

"What happened?"

"She fainted. The clerk is . . . sending for a doctor," he gasped out. He kicked the door open and deposited Josie on the bed. His arms refused to let go as he willed the warmth of his body into hers.

"Charles, give me yer penknife."

He stared into Esther's wild eyes, uncomprehending.

"Hurry," Esther snapped, and he dug into his pocket.

"What are you going to do? I already loosened her stays," he yelled as Esther sliced Josie's dress away from her body.

"It's just a suspicion," Esther explained as she worked. "After we bought this dress another dressmaker warned us that she believed the green dye possessed noxious fumes. Josie has never fainted once in her life, unlike some women who are given to fainting spells."

Charles swallowed as he tugged Josie's arms out of the sleeves, and Esther cut away the last of the gown. She tossed the tatters into the flames leaping in the hearth, but the last of them snagged on a brick. Horror clawed at Charles as the fabric became black as midnight but did not burn.

Esther rushed to open the window and strained against the stiff catch as her back arched in effort. Charles pried her away and slid it open with a grunt.

"Why in heaven's name didn't she return it if there was a risk of poison?"

"Because she wanted so terribly to look beautiful for ye."

Charles raked a hand through his hair and sighed. "Can you keep a secret?"

Esther nodded, and Charles looked back at Josie. "She couldn't be more beautiful to me than she already is. Her very soul is beautiful."

"She needs to hear ye say that," Esther murmured. "As a Radcliffe she feels she has to meet the expectations of society for yer sake. She needs to hear ye say she is beautiful without all the embellishment that smothers who she is inside. Ye and I both ken it, but Delia cast a tall shadow that Josie has never been able to live up to."

"I've tried many times, but the words just won't come."

He fought the rising panic. *Please God, give me another chance.*

Josie's dainty hand twitched against the coverlet, and an aching tenderness welled in his chest. The soul of his wife reached out to him even in her unconscious state to heal his pain in spite of her own. He cradled her fingers, stroking circles against the baby soft skin. Esther waved smelling salts under Josie's nostrils. Her thick lashes fluttered against ashen flesh.

The door swung open as a stranger charged through. "I am Doctor Fontaine. I understand the patient has fainted?"

Charles stifled the urge to bark at the man for trifling with formalities. His Josie mustn't be startled. Dr. Fontaine clasped her limp, lily-white wrist and took her pulse.

Charles glanced toward the charred remains of the dress, but Esther intercepted his gaze and shook her head in warning.

"Perhaps it was something she ate, *non?* In my experience Engleesh women have notoriously weak stomachs, especially when consuming foreign food. Her pulse is weak and irregular. I will bleed her now to drain her of any impurities that remain."

He dug around in his black bag and withdrew a basin and scalpel. Charles seized the doctor's wrist as he reached for Josie's arm.

"That won't be necessary, Doctor. I don't believe in bloodletting when a patient is already as weak as my wife. Name your fee and be gone. We won't take up any more of your valuable time."

"What an utterly preposterous notion. Unhand me at once," the doctor sputtered.

A light touch landed on Charles's shoulder and stilled his smoldering fury. He released the man.

Esther stepped in. "Pray name yer fee, Doctor, and consider yer duty done. Ye must allow a young husband his overprotective notions."

"We are all fools in love," the doctor conceded with a sigh. "Mind you my conscience is clear if he protects her right to death's door from everything but his own ignorance."

Charles bristled as the doctor gathered up his instruments.

"All I require is my cab fare," the doctor said.

Charles shoved a few coins into the man's hand. "Keep the change. Consider it payment to disregard our medical needs in the future."

"You can be sure I won't trouble myself with the likes of your countrymen again if I can help it."

Charles locked the door behind him. A soft touch lingered against his sleeve. "Calm yerself, Charles. It won't do for ye to be all worked up when she awakes."

Charles softened beneath the kindness of Esther's steady gray eyes and touch. Her thick accent was soothing, her presence a balm to his frazzled spirit. She was not unlike his Josie, but Esther's seasoned years provided a deeper wisdom.

"I can see why Josie loves you so," Charles said. "And you love her beyond what your station requires."

Esther's hand fell away—was she afraid? Perhaps she feared he deemed her affection inappropriate. The thought couldn't be further from his mind.

Before he could reassure Esther, Josie's eyes fluttered open. The movement was beauteous in its stubborn fragility.

"Charles?"

His heart jolted to hear his name spoken first. He captured her hand and drew it to his lips. "I'm here, darling."

At the endearment, her parchment cheeks regained a little color. The sluggish depths of her eyes brightened.

"What happened?" she mumbled.

"You fainted and gave us quite a fright. It was the dress. You were breathing noxious fumes from the green dye."

"Of course. How very stupid of me." Tears trembled on the corners of her wide, piteous eyes. "Are you very angry with me?"

Charles swallowed a lump in his throat. "How could I ever be angry with you when the blame lies entirely with myself for forcing you to go through such desperate measures to attain my attention? In my eyes, you are the most beautiful woman God ever made, Josephine Radcliffe. I'll be hanged if I ever let you forget it again. I feared I would never get the chance to tell you just how beautiful you are to me, but I hold you to your promise—I need you by my side. You calm my storms. I can only endeavor to try to deserve you with each breath I take."

Josie's doe-like eyes glistened as a teary wave washed over them and spilled down her cheek. "I love you, Charles Radcliffe."

Charles's chest ached, afraid to believe it. "How can you possibly love me?"

"Isn't it enough to know that I do?"

Charles buried his face against her chest. The door clicked shut as Esther left them.

"I've never known a love like yours."

"Just know you are loved and worthy of love," Josie whispered as she stroked his hair. "You had a lover long before me, Charles. The embodiment of Love itself was born, died, and rose again that you might know such love. It is a gift freely given, but you must accept it in your own heart and mind."

Unbidden, the sensations revisited him of soft warmth and feathery curls dusting his cheek. *Do you know how much I love you, my son?*

"My mother also claimed to love me."

Josie's nails dug into his shoulder. "Don't do it, Charles, don't go there. The more you allow her shadow to cut the love from your life, the more you let her win. It was she who was utterly unworthy of the son God gave her. Defeat her by refusing to let her betrayal define your worth. You are so much more. You are beloved in God's sight and in mine, so I implore you to bury her where she belongs."

Charles raised his head and captured Josie's sweet mouth beneath his own. He no longer wanted to think. He only wanted to feel the miracle of his Josie, who loved him and accepted him not for who he could be, but for who he was. His soul overflowed into hers as they kindled a desire for each other that refused to be silenced again.

Chapter Eighteen

Dearest Father,

We arrived in Venice yesterday after a fortnight of travel. This morning we toured St. Mark's Basilica, and it far exceeded my expectations. The paintings simply cannot do it adequate justice. I wish you could have been there, for I know you would have appreciated the light streaming through the stained glass. God feels very close here.

Paris felt like a dream. Charles provided me with a generous purse to go shopping, and I am up-to-date on the latest fashions now. I hardly recognize myself. Charles is eager to tell you of the horse races he attended, so I won't spoil it for him. We breakfasted at the Palais Royale, where the hot chocolate was decadent. I shall have to instruct Eliza upon my return on the proper technique, for I had no qualms in inquiring at our hotel. We toured the Louvre, and I shall have to give you the details in person. The Mona Lisa was exquisite. I was in a state of rapture, and my soul will carry the indelible imprint of beauty with me for the rest of my life. On the Sunday we were there, Charles took me to Notre Dame after the mass was over, and we just sat there and drank in the holy silence. One does not have to be Catholic to appreciate the beauty there.

*No doubt by the time you receive this letter we shall be on
our way back home to you. Esther is soaking up the sunlight on
the balcony, and I think I shall close to join her. I miss you terribly and send all my love.*

Your loving daughter,

Josie

Josie dusted the paper with sand and pushed back her chair
as she waited for the ink to dry.

"Would you allow me to escort you on your first gondola
ride?"

She glanced up to find her husband leaning against the door
frame.

"How long have you been standing there?"

Charles arched a dark blond brow. "How could I possibly
interrupt your concentration with that adorable little frown
scrunching your eyebrows?"

Josie smiled as she laid her quill to rest. "Say it again, and I'll
forgive you for spying, Mr. Radcliffe."

"Say what?"

"That you find your wife adorable."

"I do, but I think she already knows that."

"Then I wholeheartedly accept."

Esther stepped in from the balcony.

"Charles is taking me on my first gondola ride. Won't you
join us, Esther?"

Esther shook her head. "Three is a crowd, luve, and I'm a
mite weary. Enjoy yerself."

Charles looked anything but disappointed at being deprived
of Esther's company as Josie linked her arm through his.

"Dinna forget yer parasol, luve," Esther called after them. Josie sighed, but she grabbed it from where it rested against Charles's umbrella. The umbrella slumped as though she had deprived it of a mate.

"Something tells me you are not as concerned about your complexion as Esther is," Charles said as he pulled the door shut.

"Alas, a freckle is one of the unpardonable sins of polite society, and I am already blessed with too many of them," Josie grumbled.

"Hang polite society."

Josie's eyebrows lifted.

"I happen to like your freckles as they are without being heavily caked in powder. You mustn't ever let society change you, Josephine."

They stepped onto the blond stone street, and their gondola bobbed in the canal as though eager to carry them.

"Where is our gondolier?" Josie asked.

"You're looking at him, Madame."

"You? Charles, I cannot swim, and I have no intention of watching you flail about in the water if you fall from your lofty perch. You have no experience whatsoever—"

"Ah, but you are mistaken my dear. I engaged myself all morning in observing the gondoliers, and they were most helpful in instructing me as to the finer points of their craft. It comes down to whether or not you trust your husband even if you think him incapable."

"I didn't say that."

"You implied it clearly enough. Now do you want me to take you, just the two of us, or do you insist upon robbing us of that pleasure by making me hire a gondolier?"

"Of course, I want you to take me."

"You would think one's wife would appreciate his efforts to be romantic," Charles huffed under his breath.

Josie swatted him as he climbed into the gondola. It rocked under his weight, and she swallowed a stubborn lump of fear as he reached out for her. She clung to his strength as he swung her into the bowels of the gondola. Their bodies swayed together in rhythmic motion, and a thrilling shiver darted up Josie's spine.

"The seat is directly behind you. You can sit down, and never fear, I won't let you fall in," Charles murmured against her ear.

A jest sprang to her lips, but Josie found that her sober belief in him overrode it. She sank into the seat, and he climbed into the gondolier's perch above her.

Josie held her breath as he shoved off with pole in hand, but the gondola glided down the canal as though he had been doing it all his life. Josie surrendered to the magic of the moment as the water's shimmering highlights danced against the light stone buildings. The sun's warmth grew persistent, and she sprang her parasol with reluctance. Charles paused to strip down to his waistcoat, then drew a familiar volume out of his coat pocket before tossing the garment down beside her.

"Are you fond of poetry?" he asked. A fragile, elusive quality lurked in his eyes, but the blue depths were all the more beautiful to her for their transparency.

"I am immensely fond of poetry. How did you ever guess that Lord Byron is my favorite?"

The blue light stirred as his lips parted. He cracked the book open and managed to hold it steady with one hand while he nudged them forward with the other.

Josie reclined and let her hand trail in the water. She closed her eyes as his voice washed over her like a current, eddying in her heart and rippling through her mind.

"There is a mystic thread of life so dearly wreathed with mine alone that destiny's relentless knife at once must sever both or none.

There is a form on which these eyes have fondly gazed with such delight by day that form their joy supplies, and dreams restore it, through the night.

There is a voice whose tones inspire such softened feelings in my breast I would not hear a Seraph choir unless that voice could join the rest.

There is a face whose blushes tell affection's tale upon the cheek, but pallid at our fond farewell, proclaims more love than words can speak.

There is a lip, which mine has pressed, but none had ever pressed before; it vowed to make me sweetly blessed that mine alone should press it more.

There is a bosom all my own has pillowed oft this aching head, a mouth which smiles on me alone, an eye whose tears with mine are shed.

There are two hearts whose movements thrill, in unison so closely sweet, that pulse to pulse responsive still they both must heave, or cease to beat.

There are two souls whose equal flow in gentle stream so calmly run that when they part, they part? Ah no! They cannot part—those souls are one."

Josie smiled as she basked in the warmth of the sun's glow. She peeked up at her husband beneath her lowered lashes. His eyes caressed her as his lips moved—he was quoting from memory. Joy blossomed in her heart.

"I possess a copy of *Hours of Idleness* too, but I have never read that poem before."

"It wasn't published in the book. It was published in 1808 in volume 3 of the *Monthly Literary Recreations* magazine. I pasted it inside the front cover. It is entitled 'Stanzas to Jessy.'"

"I am glad I had never read it before . . . hearing you read it gave it a meaning that endears it to me forever."

"I see I married a bluestocking."

Josie was flummoxed at his derogatory reference to women whose literary pursuits were considered unfeminine, but the teasing light in his eyes was mild. "My dear sir, was it not Shakespeare that said: 'How well he's read, to reason against reading'?"

Appreciation flared in his. His lips parted to reply, but before he could, a shrill voice interrupted from the street.

"Stop, I pray you, sir!"

Josie gasped as the gondola heaved, and she began slipping over the edge. She bolted upright and seized the rim. Charles drew his pistol and leaned upon the pole.

"I mean you no harm. Do not be alarmed," the voice cried out. Josie turned and saw a little Italian man with his arms raised high, palette in one hand and brush in the other. Green paint dripped from the brush.

"What do you want?" Charles asked, lowering the pistol. The Italian's widened eyes swept over them with an imploring gaze.

"Please, Signor . . . I only want to finish painting you. The light, it eez perfect."

The Italian held up the canvas.

"Please Charles," Josie pleaded. A lump in her throat swelled at the tenderness of the scene captured in just a few swift strokes. It was beautiful. Charles glanced down at her, and his stormy blue eyes softened.

"All right," Charles conceded.

The Italian beamed with teeth that were blindingly white in his swarthy face, like the sun breaking free from the clouds.

"Please, Signora, pose as you were. Signor, continue as you were reading to your woman."

Charles scowled but cracked the book again. Josie dragged her fingers in the sluggish depths of the canal, capturing the moment in her heart as the artist's brush immortalized them. Her husband selected another poem, and his voice resumed its spellbinding depth as though the moment had never been broken.

"It is finished, Signor. A masterpiece."

Josie stifled the urge to splash him for interrupting them yet again. Charles angled the gondola until it bumped against the street. He leaped onto the stone and sent the boat lurching. The Italian swung his easel around. Josie's hand flew to her mouth. Pure genius had orchestrated the colors. The moment brimmed on canvas, echoing their love.

"We have to buy it, Charles."

Charles's eyes lit with a grudging approval. "Somehow you've done it," he told the painter.

"Signor?"

"Name your price. You have yet to honor me with a name, Signor."

"Signor Rossi, and my price is one hundred British pounds."

Charles raised an eyebrow. "That's highway robbery for disturbing our privacy and a souvenir I didn't commission. You play a clever game on unsuspecting tourists, but two can play at this game. Give it to me for fifty pounds, and I'll commission a portrait of my wife. I'm prepared to pay you well."

"You flatter me, Signor. For no brush, even that of Da Vinci himself, could do justice to such a madonna. I consider it a great honor."

"Would an appointment tomorrow morning suit?" Charles asked.

"Most certainly, for I am only a humble painter with few engagements."

"Then if you would be so good as to follow us, I will show you our lodgings."

"Very good, Signor."

Charles shoved off from the street as the artist collapsed the easel. Wind ruffled Charles's golden strands, muscles straining beneath his shirt. Warmth rushed through Josie's chest. *Oh my love, poetry gave your heart a voice. If I can only be patient a little longer, I know you will never shut me out again.*

Chapter Nineteen

Charles pursed his lips. Josie had not emerged from the bedchamber of their suite all morning, but she had already dismissed Esther. He rapped on the door.

"What is it?"

"Signor Rossi is due to arrive any moment. Are you quite ready, my dear?"

The pause stretched until Charles's jaw tightened.

"Would you please come in here, Charles?"

He shoved open the door. Josie stood in her chemise, arms clutched around herself as though she would fall apart. Dresses sprawled across the bed in a chaos of color.

She looked at him helplessly. "Tell me what to wear."

His jaw hugged her shoulder as he pulled her close and covered her fragile arms with his embrace. Her heart nudged his own as she melted against him.

"Does it matter when *you* are what makes each dress beautiful?"

Her shoulders heaved. He reached out and jerked a scarlet gown off the bed. Their gazes fused as he held it against her skin.

"It matters as I am mistress of Treathston Heights. Future generations will stare into this portrait and say, there is Josephine Radcliffe."

Charles cleared his throat. "This portrait is for us to look back when we're old and remember how young and beautiful you were when I married you. I'm proud of my little wife."

Josie draped the skirt against herself. "You like this?"

The crimson warmed her skin, and the cut would emphasize her tiny waist and generous bust. He did indeed like it.

"In my opinion, it is a crime for anyone else to see you in that dress. What did Esther think?"

Josie took the dress from him. "She wasn't herself this morning."

"Maybe it was that letter I picked up for her. But answer me this. Will you pose in this painting for me and no one else?"

"Yes," she said with doe-like eyes.

"Thank you."

He twirled her around and released the glossy curls from their hair combs, running his fingers through them.

"Charles, what in heaven's name—"

"Shhhh, I'm not done yet."

Josie whirled as the luscious waves of her hair rippled down her shoulders.

"Don't you shush me! I refuse to pose like this . . . I look like a slut."

Charles ignored her, reaching for the pot of rouge on her dressing table. She squirmed out of reach, but he seized her waist and kissed her hard. She went limp in his arms. Knocking reached their ears.

"Shhhh, shhhh," he hushed her as he swiped the cosmetic across her cheeks. Her mouth parted in protest, and he smeared her bottom lip.

"Oh, give me that." Her shining eyes betrayed her as she jerked the pot away from him.

Charles trotted to the door, and the artist flashed familiar white teeth as he opened to him.

"Forgive me, we were indisposed for a moment."

A virile gleam stirred in the Italian's dark eyes. "Ah, of course you were . . . married to a Madonna like that! If she were my woman, I would be sorely tempted not to ever answer the door at all."

"Please make yourself comfortable in the parlor and set up your easel. I will be right with you."

He poked his head through the door. While the rouge was not as dark on Josie's mouth as he had intended, at least it stayed within the natural lines of her lips.

She glared at him. "Now that you have parted my hair as crooked as a cow path and painted me like a doll, does my scandalous appearance meet with your approval?"

"Your appearance was too tame for such a portrait. Now you will be remembered for the hot-blooded woman you are."

"In that case, I forgive you," Josie consented.

His Josie possessed the patience of a martyr. Over the next two weeks, her beloved features materialized beneath the Italian's deft brush. Her soulful eyes assumed the third dimension, gripping Charles through the canvas as Signor Rossi played with light and shadow. At long last the artist flourished his brush.

"Magnifico, she is finished. This is the best work I have ever done, no? Signora Radcliffe, you have been a most gracious subject."

Josie stifled a yawn and stretched. "Thank you, Signor, but it is I who owe you a debt of gratitude."

The painter bowed and pressed a kiss against her hand. "Until we meet again in Cornwall, Signora. I have patrons in your country."

"You are welcome anytime, Signor Rossi."

Charles fought a smile. Grace characterized Josie's every word and deed. Queen Charlotte herself could not have done better.

"I'll see you out to your gondola and finish our business transaction," he cut in.

"Very good, Signor Radcliffe."

The shorter man followed Charles to the street and entrusted the tools of his trade to the keeping of the gondola. Charles pressed the wages into his bronzed fingers.

"It was a pleasure doing business with you, Signor Radcliffe. But I will confide to you the last detail that keeps me from being completely satisfied."

"What would that be?" Charles asked, wary of an attempt to coax more British pounds out of his pocket.

"I was pleased with the portrait, except for the matter of Signora Radcliffe's eyes."

"I was quite content on that score, so you may lay that concern to rest."

"I was not referring to their realism, Signor. There is a lingering shadow of sadness there, no? In her young heart it will either deepen with cruelty or fade with kindness, but I suspect that her fate rests with you, Signor Radcliffe. You must chase away the shadow now before it is too late. Believe me, I know, for the shadow of a beautiful woman's unhappiness haunts me even now because I did not change the course of our lives when I had the power to do so. Now I can but attempt to thwart the same fate for other young lovers."

Charles blinked, too stunned to be offended. "Thank you for your concern, Signor, and for your kind regard for my wife. I bid you good day."

The only nightmare is the one I'm living. Chase it away from me, Charles.

Charles darted up the steps, muscles tensing beneath Signor Rossi's lingering gaze. He was blinded by his scars. He wrenched the door open.

Josie's back was turned to him as she studied the portrait. His breath caught in pain as she glanced over her shoulder. The shadow was there, in her eyes, lurking like the gray light of dusk before night fell.

"A letter came for you, Charles."

He welcomed the distraction as he took it from her outstretched hand.

Dear Charles,

I hope this letter finds you and Josie well. I hate to be the bearer of evil tidings on your honeymoon, but I fear it cannot be helped. By the time this reaches you it will have been weeks, perhaps months, since the shipwreck of the Constance. The crew went down with the ship, and as you know our losses were, shall we say, considerable. The blow has hit the company hard, as I was counting on the profits to bring us to rights after settling Mr. Chadwick's debts. We are afloat yet, but I am having quite the difficulty managing without you, my boy. I confess I did not realize how invaluable your presence is to the company until I found it sorely lacking without you. I don't know how quickly this letter will reach you, but please hurry home with all due haste. We'll rally yet, for we always have, but I cannot do it without you, son.

Until then I will anxiously be awaiting your return. The very legacy I had hoped to give you and Josie could well depend on our recovery from this disaster. As I have always said, luck has but one hair on its head. Your fate depends on how swiftly you can seize it and how tightly you can hold onto it. I fear your marriage caused me to relax my hold on luck for a time, thinking we had made our own good fortune. Now we must seize it again or suffer the consequences, which could prove to be devastating indeed.

I remain your devoted father,

Sebastian Radcliffe

Charles crumpled the letter in his fist. Even across the channel, Father's grip was all powerful. There would never cease to be a limit on his demands—on Charles's responsibility to prove himself worthy as the only son and heir of Sebastian Radcliffe. If it were not for the unbearable prospect of proving himself less than worthy to his only remaining parent, he would have been tempted to turn his back on it all and live a life of his own choosing.

"Charles?"

Josie's tender touch surrounded his clenched fingers. Now his defeat was complete. He could not bring himself to meet her eyes.

"It is urgent business correspondence from Father. Our ship, the *Constance*, was shipwrecked, and with it all his hopes of profit for this annum. He said he needs me back home as soon as it can be arranged. Would you mind very terribly—"

She tilted his chin to face her, merging his gaze with limpid pools that bore no reproach for him.

"You do what you have to do, Charles. I understand."

"You do love me, don't you?"

"Do you doubt it?"

"No."

He let the letter fall to the floor as he leaned into her open arms of acceptance. Hers was the superior strength. Her eyelashes whispered against his cheek as he rested his forehead against hers.

"This is not how I wanted our honeymoon to end. I brought you all the way out here to escape it all, but even here the company's responsibilities have caught up with me. Now you are disappointed."

"An abrupt end cannot steal all of the wonderful times and memories of this trip. This is not the end, Charles, only the beginning of us. It won't hurt me to assume my responsibilities as mistress of Treathston Heights sooner than planned."

Yet the shadow deepened in her eyes at the grim prospect of navigating the tension between him and his father. Charles pulled her close to hide the anguish she was sure to detect, powerless to chase away the bleak prospects of the future that haunted them both.

Chapter Twenty

The rolling green of hillside and pasture flowed by the carriage window. The rippling blades of grass were not unlike the ocean waves whose crashing roar reached Josie's ears. Her lungs drew strength from the aromas of sun-warmed grass and tangy surf. *How I've missed Cornwall, but how I've dreaded living at Treathston. Charles's relationship with his father is sure to put strain on our own.*

Charles did not stir beside her, his heavy-lidded gaze lost in the expanse of sea. He had drifted away from her again—a sluggish pulse at her side rather than a throbbing presence too powerful to be denied.

The wheels crunched over the gravel drive of Treathston Heights, jarring her back to the present. Two men stood stark against the skyline of sea-hewn cliff as the wind rifled their hair and clothing. Her heartstrings sounded an ominous chord. Alongside Sebastian's sturdy form, Father's stooped figure appeared all the more frail and ravaged by time. In a twist of irony, the two mine owners represented the essences of their ores . . . Father was soft as tin and Sebastian as unyielding as copper, yet the two men remained inseparable, just as the two metals were found in the heart of the earth.

Oh, dearest Father! Randolph Chadwick's faded blue eyes were blighted with the echoes of what was and what might have been. Remorse seared Josie as she grappled with the latch, and her feet caressed Cornish soil.

"Forgive me for leaving you so long, dearest Father," she murmured as his weakened grasp enfolded her, pungent tobacco and briny sea spray vying to master her senses. His stubbled chin shifted against her brow, and his husky voice wandered through her heart like gentle fingertips. "There is nothing to forgive, my Josie. Oh, how I've missed you. Let me look at you, daughter."

A glimmer of the former mischief surfaced in his eyes. "Aye, I can see that marriage agrees with you."

"May I greet my daughter-in-law, Randolph?"

Josie turned as Sebastian embraced her. His burly bulk struck her as unfamiliar, accustomed as she was to the arms of her tall husband and her father. His muscular arms held her as though she were a kitten in the jaws of a cat, gentle in a grasp capable of crushing strength. She breathed easier when he let her go.

"Aye, Randolph, her complexion has always been pale, but Charles has put blooms in the apples of her cheeks."

"I'm sure she owes it to the mild climate and not to me," Charles protested.

Sebastian waved his hand. His grin was boyish, boasting fine teeth still white and sharp. "You always were too modest, my boy. Josie, you must divert us with your traveling adventures at dinner."

"We certainly enjoyed ourselves immensely. I discovered that your son was a man of many hidden talents, Sebastian."

"I'm sure you never experienced a dull moment. I am only sorry that your good times had to end on account of such unfortunate business."

"I am not sorry to be home, and I'm sure I speak for Charles as well."

A muscle ticked in Charles's jaw, and Josie's gut clenched. Navigating the choppy waters between Charles and Sebastian would require greater tact and patience than she had realized. Regardless of what the future held, she refused to let Sebastian come between her and Charles.

Throughout dinner, Josie failed to chase away the storm clouds gathering on Charles's brow. For the first time she found herself grateful for Father's friendship with Sebastian. They resumed a lively banter whenever she grew weary of recounting their travels.

Dessert came at last, and Josie dipped her spoon into the plumy concoction with relief. The custard was much too sweet for her liking, but she managed to polish it off. She would have to grow accustomed to such rich fare. The head of the Treathston kitchen was a French chef.

Charles's searching hand groped for the idle one that lay in her lap, and her eyes darted up to meet his as his familiar grasp closed around her fingers. His blue eyes were glazed with a pain the wine had failed to dull, and her heart winced to see it. Her thumb stroked reassurance into his hand as their souls plumbed the depths of each other. Remorse gripped her as she began to understand. She had been so preoccupied with making polite conversation with Sebastian that she had neglected to think about Charles leaving for London. They would be parted so soon.

His evident longing for her was precious to her, for there had been a time not far in the past when she had despaired to ever see it. Then his gaze and grasp ripped away, leaving a raw spot inside her as he drained another glass. A terrible air of resignation had mastered him from within, but she failed to detect the source as he pushed his chair back and flung down his serviette.

"I'll see to it that all of my luggage has been transferred to the hackney without mishap," he muttered. "I'd best be going now, Father."

"By all means, son. Best to get a head start," Sebastian agreed.

"Godspeed, Charles. No doubt the sooner you're gone the sooner you'll be back to your bride," Father chirped.

Charles dropped a hasty kiss on her forehead. "Good-bye."

Josie hesitated as his broad shoulders filled the door frame and faded from view. "Pray excuse me," she murmured to her dinner companions.

She was forced to trot to catch up with him in the hallway. He refused to break his long stride.

"Charles, darling, what is wrong? Tell me what is wrong."

"This is our life now, Josephine. You'll learn the hard way that nothing you do will ever please Father, and until the end of his days we'll both grow pettish and gray trying."

"It doesn't have to be that way."

"Well, that is Father's way, and as long as I can remember there have been no other rules by which to live."

"His rules don't have to affect us, Charles," Josie panted. "We can still be happy and start our own little family."

Josie gasped as Charles whirled and seized her shoulders. Darkness engulfed his eyes as twin storms burned through her.

"We will never be free from him, and don't speak to me of starting a family, woman. I refuse to let any child's youth be ruined the way mine was."

Josie trembled at the unbridled fury in his voice and touch. "Charles, please don't leave me like this."

"I'll be back within a week—or two, depending on how quickly the matter of shipments can be settled. Never fear on that account, Mrs. Radcliffe."

He lowered his head and kissed her. The hardness of his mouth softened against hers. He pulled away, breathing hard, and stormed for the door. Her heart cried his name, and he flung a final glance back at her. "At least now there is something for me to come home to."

Josie's lips parted, but the door slammed shut in her face.

I do love you so, Charles Radcliffe. I never understood how much a part of me you've become until now.

Deafening screams chilled the blood in Josie's veins. Fingers were wrapped around her throat. She rasped for breath as her chest tightened like a knotted fist. Her throat throbbed, and the knowledge dawned: the screams were her own.

Josie's eyes flew open to the smothering darkness. The only sound was the roar of blood in her ears as her heart thundered. She withdrew her fingers from where they had lodged in a struggle to fight off a rough wool embrace.

"Charles," her own unfamiliar voice croaked. She waited for the warm strength of his arms to surround her, but as her ears strained for rustling sheets or quickening breath, all she heard was the clicking of Byron's nails across wood. She lunged for Charles and clutched a cold pillow to her breast.

The coldness broke the denial she'd fought to maintain. Charles had gone and left her in a cold bed and an emptier silence to fulfill his duties as Sebastian's son. Fear and betrayal crashed over her in twin waves of mounting intensity. Somehow his presence all those nights, holding her fast against him, had possessed the power to chase away the nightmare. His arms were her safe haven, and whenever he held her, she never wanted him to let go. Yet he had let go—he had left her to satisfy Sebastian's desires. She had not yet secured first place in his heart because he did not love her.

Hot tears raked Josie's cheeks as she sat frozen stiff in the bed whose vastness threatened to swallow her. She couldn't bear to be alone tonight.

She scrambled for her dressing gown, ignoring Byron's whines. The darkness rendered her a little girl again as she ran for the comfort of Esther's arms. She shoved open Esther's bed-chamber door, but no form disturbed the rumpled covers. Josie fought the rising sense of abandonment. *Surely she has only gone to use the necessary.*

Josie crouched within the ring of firelight emanating from the hearth and waited. The door swung wider, but it was only Byron. Josie buried her fingers in his fur as the tentative seconds crept into agonizing minutes and still no Esther appeared. Above the hum of her tortured thoughts, a tender voice persisted.

I will never leave thee nor forsake thee, Josie. Yea, I have loved thee with an everlasting love: therefore with lovingkindness have I drawn thee. Refrain thy voice from weeping and thy eyes from tears: for thy work shall be rewarded, and there is hope in thine end, saith the Lord. Therefore my bowels are troubled for thee; I will surely have mercy upon thee, saith the Lord. Ah Lord God! behold, thou hast made the heaven and the earth by thy great power and stretched out arm, and there is nothing too hard for thee.

"I don't understand why I had to be the one to marry him, Lord! My heart is just as fragile as his!" Josie cried as she lit a candle and dragged Byron back to her bedchamber, deciding that canine company was better than none.

My daughter, I would not give you any work that would not make you run and ask for My assistance. My yoke is easy, and My burden is light. You wouldn't know Me if I did not give you the chance to see Me work by giving you a burden whose load the strength of your shoulders was not sufficient to carry.

"Forgive me, Lord. I know Your plans toward me are for good and not for evil, to prosper and not to harm me, to give me an expected end. Please help me to trust Your heart even when I cannot see Your hand or understand why You have given me a man whose scarred heart isn't capable of requiting my love with the words I long to hear."

Josie collapsed on the tangled sheets. Byron's eyes shimmered with mute entreaty in the candlelight, and she thumped the featherbed with a sigh. He leaped up beside her, and she drew a semblance of comfort from his furry warmth as she pulled him close.

"For being man's best friend, you certainly are the only friend who hasn't abandoned me," she whispered as his tongue lolled in bliss. She patted him until she grew drowsy, counting the strokes as her hand slid down his back. She got to one hundred and fifty-seven before sleep claimed her restless spirit at last.

Chapter Twenty-One

s Josie descended the stairwell, she reached the landing on the second floor and paused to massage a stubborn crick out of her neck. Hushed whispers drifted to her ears. She crouched low against the stout banister, and her straining ears caught a phrase here and there as secrets drifted by like dandelion fluff on the breeze.

"With God as my witness, I saw her with my own two eyes. 'Twas the ghost of Lady Chadwick she was. All ghostly and white she was—"

"Oooh, Helen, do stop. You're giving me gooseflesh, you are."

"Well, do you want me to tell you or don't you? She's risen from her grave to haunt the living, and she won't be satisfied until she has wreaked her vengeance on Chadwick blood once and for all. Her curse has not destroyed them yet, but mark my words: young Master Charles made a mistake marrying the new mistress, and he'll live to regret it. When the Chadwicks come crashing down, she'll take the Radcliffes with her."

Josie steeled her spine. *They have a lot of nerve spouting their superstitious ignorance behind my back.*

Throwing caution to the wind, Josie clattered down the stairs and sent the servants scurrying for cover like mice caught in the grain bin. She sailed into the dining room and tried to shrug it off. Servants always had a mind for gossiping, fueled by their voracious appetite for superstition. Cornwall had a reputation for breeding such tales, and she had heard more than one earful of Lady Chadwick's nightly escapades as a girl. Still, the steaming dishes on the sideboard failed to tempt her. Apparently, Lady Chadwick's curse hadn't died out with the older servants. Now the younger generation had resurrected her for their grisly amusement.

Her father-in-law was already at the table. "Did you sleep well, Josie?" Sebastian inquired as he helped himself to the clotted cream.

"I did, thank you, Sebastian."

"I'm sure you've observed my knack for not beating around the bush, so I'll get right to the point. You are mistress of Treathston Heights now, and I want you to assume the role just as capably as you ran Chadwick Park for your father. Do entirely what you deem fit and necessary with the servants and the housekeeping. Take whatever liberties you require, and don't hesitate to consult me on any matter, however trivial."

Josie tilted her head. "I am obliged to you, Sebastian, for your generosity. I shall indeed."

Sebastian did not attempt to hide his perusal of her, and she met his gaze of steel head-on. Her father-in-law was a proud man who made swift judgments and stuck by them whether they proved accurate or not. If Sebastian had wanted a timid, mousy daughter-in-law whom he could intimidate, he'd trifled with the wrong family, for Chadwick women were neither. Her love for Charles had already prejudiced her against him, and she foresaw his early attempt to rein her in just like he did his son. Let it reflect badly on him if she failed to live up to his expectations. His pride would not suffer for being taken down a couple pegs.

Josie helped herself to the popovers and preserves. *I daresay he will find me a bit more of a challenge to control.*

"Ah, you take your coffee black."

Josie's eyebrows lifted at him over the rim of her cup. "Yes, I prefer bitterness to sickening sweetness."

Sebastian's laughter boomed like an overcharged cannon. "I think I am going to like you, Josie, for a daughter-in-law. You aren't afraid to tell it like it is because you've got spirit. Charles needed that in a wife."

Josie grimaced as she set her coffee down. "If you like people to get right to the point, I'll tell you how it is, Sebastian. I love your son and respect him. I have no intention of taking advantage of his good graces with a woman's wiles, whether I am spirited or not."

Sebastian smiled, sincerity glimmering in his eyes like dappled sunlight. The warmth lent a marvelous softness to them she had not heretofore witnessed.

"I fear you have mistaken me, my dear. I did not take you for a woman who would prey on my son to get at his pocketbook. No doubt, it was out of the goodness of your own heart you were willing to risk a match to a man you barely knew."

Josie's guard slid a bit as his warmth thawed her reserve.

"Pray forgive me if I mistook what I deem now to be a fine compliment."

Sebastian stretched like a lazy tomcat content to sun himself after prowling the night away. "Now that we understand one another, Josie, I believe I had best be off to attend to affairs sadly neglected in Charles's absence."

"Charles was vague regarding how long he would be gone. Have you any notion?"

"It is hard to say, but I'm sure he will cut his usual gallivanting entirely to get back to you, my dear. Barring any unexpected emergencies, I expect him to be back within the week. You miss him already, do you?"

"I don't mind telling you that nights are lonely without him," Josie admitted.

Sebastian regarded her with unexpected thoughtfulness. "You do care a great deal more than I'd anticipated considering the hastiness of your attachment. I am glad to hear it. The boy deserves . . . happiness."

The conversation was not at all what she had expected, and Josie let her guard down for a moment. "Has he always been distant? I find it difficult to approach him most times."

"Ever since his mother left us. She saw fit to destroy him young, but don't take it to heart, my dear. I have not seen him with that light in his eyes for quite some time. It's possible you are the sunshine his life has been lacking. I credit your sex with that ability. God knows this house has been empty of it for far too long."

On that parting word, Sebastian scraped back his chair and left before she could ask him any further questions. For now, it was enough. Their relationship had been grounded upon a foundation of blunt honesty. At least it was a language they could mutually share without fear of misunderstanding one another.

Josie wandered into the library. She could always tell a lot about a man from his books. She scanned the impressive floor-to-ceiling shelves holding a wealth of titles. Naval histories, encyclopedias, atlases, world history, military strategy, economics and astronomy . . . they reflected the practical, business-like Sebastian.

A lonely bookshelf near the window caught her eye, and as she perused the spines she caught herself smiling. Though Charles's personal library did not boast nearly as many titles as his father's, every volume of poetry and classic literature was creased and dog-eared. She traced the worn spines of Weatherby's *An Introduction to a General Stud Book* and *General Stud Book Volume I*, reflecting that Charles's knowledge of thoroughbred bloodlines and pedigrees must be extensive indeed.

"Och, there ye are, Josie!"

Esther's breathless voice sounded a note of alarm as Josie whirled around.

"Whatever is the matter?" she gasped at the sight of Esther's eyes luminous with tears.

"It's Suzanne. Ye better come now if ye want to see her one last time."

"Esther, is that where you were last night?"

"I didna want to worry ye, luve."

Josie followed Esther out the side door where Father's gelding, Roundhead, stood waiting. After Esther mounted, Josie swung up behind her. Roundhead broke into a canter under Esther's prodding.

Suzanne had lived through so much and retained such a zest for life that it was hard to imagine living without her. Deep inside, Josie knew Suzanne's sparkle would always reside in her heart and in all the art she would leave behind. But the emotion Esther had shown surprised Josie. She hadn't realized that Esther and Suzanne were that close.

The cottage already looked bereft as Josie slid out of the saddle.

"I'll forewarn ye, luve, her mind might already be gone. Even if she cannae recognize ye, yer presence will be a comfort to her."

Josie nodded as they approached the doorway. The fire had gone out in Suzanne's hearth as though in a prelude to death, and the damp air settled clammy against Josie's skin. In the dim light, she glimpsed the old woman's body stretched out upon a lumpy, straw-tick mattress. Blankets swallowed her frail form, and the only sound in the stillness was the rasp of her breathing.

"Suzanne, I brought yer Josie to visit ye," Esther explained as she leaned over the older woman, but there was no response. Josie swallowed the lump forming in her throat, but she almost choked on it as she watched Suzanne's sunken chest shuddering in the struggle to rise and fall once more. She seized hold of her cool, bony hand and pressed a kiss against her swollen knuckles. Her body swept low across the old woman's like a hovering angel, and Suzanne's expression was peaceful and void of pain.

"I'll see you on the other side, Suzanne. This is not good-bye, merely farewell," Josie whispered into the cocked ear. Somehow she knew Suzanne was listening.

Esther embraced the old woman's tired body and watered Suzanne's heart with her tears. Her aged muscles shuddered once, and then her body stilled.

Josie turned to the doorway as Esther pulled the blanket over Suzanne's face, straining for that fleeting glimpse of eternity in the fragments of blue and cloud that made up the sky.

"She's in a better place now," Esther whispered in the quiet of the room, but Josie found she couldn't break the vulnerable holiness of the moment just yet. *Precious in the sight of the Lord is the death of his saints.*

Josie's restless eyes probed every corner of the humble room, and she found she could smile when her gaze found the painting of the mama doe and fawn. She fingered the pale-washed blue of the sky, remembering the deft strokes of Suzanne's brush. Father had called her "doe-eyes" as a little girl, and Suzanne had said she moved like a deer.

Esther's sharp intake of breath broke the silence. Josie glanced up as Esther darted in front of a canvas on another easel as though shielding Josie from something evil with her body.

"It's still wet," Esther stammered as an unspoken question rose to Josie's lips.

Esther's foot inched to the side, but Josie guessed what her next movement would be. As her foot knocked the easel's support out from under it, Josie caught the canvas before the paint could bite the dirt.

"Josie," Esther pleaded, but Josie had to see what had possessed the power to shake Esther's calm. She flipped the canvas over. Staring up at her was a grotesque portrait of a man's face split down the middle . . . one half held Father's features, and the other depicted Sebastian's leering eye, curled lip, and straggly hair.

Josie's eyes fused with Esther's. Her own horror was mirrored back at her.

Chapter Twenty-Two

*C*harles ignored his tailbone's indignant jab as he leaned forward in the carriage seat, scanning the grounds for the first sight of her. Would she fly out to him with billowing skirts or canter alongside him on horseback like a windswept spirit?

The carriage lurched, and Charles clutched his pounding temples as he expelled the last of his breath in a haggard sigh. Something always possessed the horses to find the worst of the potholes and rocks strewn across the Cornish roads.

His body slumped back of its own accord as the endless motion ceased at last, and the full extent of his exhaustion stole over him. The scuff of a trunk raking the roof above him sounded as the footman unloaded his luggage, but in the end it was only his longing for Josie that pushed him from the seat. He followed the footman up the drive, searching every window and bush to no avail. Even Byron had failed to greet him with his usual enthusiasm.

He sensed a burning pair of eyes fixed on his back and whirled to meet a rider's ruthless gaze—a man was seated atop an unfamiliar horse on the rise that divided their estate from Chadwick land. Charles recognized the hate-filled glare from his wedding day. Those soulless brown eyes had haunted his dreams. The man, whose plain clothes put him in mind of a hunter, disappeared over the rise onto Chadwick land. *He certainly has a talent for preying on my nerves at the most inopportune times. Maybe Josie can name the sinister character for me.*

No one but Craven greeted him at the door. This was what he deserved for entertaining fantasies of Josie flying to his side.

"Where is everyone?" he asked.

"Master Radcliffe has gone hunting, and Mistress Josephine has gone to a funeral, sir."

Charles nodded, his conscience twinging for attributing her absence to avoidance. "Was I acquainted with the deceased?"

"I believe it was Suzanne Glynn. I confess I was surprised at the mistress's desire to attend a tenant's funeral."

"Upon better acquaintance with your new mistress, I trust you will find Mrs. Radcliffe to be a woman of uncommon kindness. When she returns, inform her of my arrival. I will be in my bedchamber resting."

Craven gave him his signature peremptory nod. Charles stalked up the stairs. The empty silence mocked him. Once he had craved the stillness, but now it was a void without his Josie. He sank into the comforting familiarity of his featherbed.

He didn't know how long he had lain there when a soft gaze settled over him like a blanket. The sensation glided closer as the peace of her presence returned to him.

Josie's silky lips grazed his forehead as a strand of her hair tickled his throat. He opened his eyes, drowning himself in the tender depths of her gaze. He reached up and pulled her down against him. For once, Byron's whines failed to rouse his sympathy.

"Oh, Charles."

A shiver coursed through him. His lips sought hers, and she melted in his arms as she poured out her heart and soul. The taste of her quickened his blood and stirred the feeling in him again. His Josie was breaking the chains that bound him.

"Oh, how I've missed you, Charles," she gasped, fighting for breath.

"I've missed you too."

"It's as though you knew I needed you back today."

He brushed a rebel strand of hair out of the corner of her eye as tenderness welled within him. "And why's that?"

"Suzanne's funeral was today. She's been like a grandmother to me since I was a little girl."

"I'm sorry to hear it. She was a spirited old lady, wasn't she?"

Josie half-smiled, but then her mouth wobbled as she buried her face against his chest. He rubbed her shoulders as she wept, the warmth of her tears soaking his chest.

Byron's silky head sprang up beside her, and the setter's shaggy ears shook with indignation as he perched his paws on the white coverlet. He barked, and Josie swiped away tears as she reached out to pet him. Charles couldn't suppress a grin.

"I see Byron has won your undivided attention."

"He has been a companion for me when I was lonely for you."

"Craven liberally expressed his astonishment that you cared to attend a tenant's funeral. I informed him my wife was uncommonly kind. You'd have to be to miss my company, dry as it is."

Josie shook her head at his jest, shifting until the light from the window hit him full in the face. He rested his forearm over his eyes as his temples throbbed.

"You poor darling. You look completely worn out, and this cravat is well nigh to choking you I'm sure."

He half-smiled as she fumbled with his cravat until she managed to untie it and loosen his collar.

"Much better. Who was that man I saw skulking about when I got back? A glowering fellow with dark, curly hair, and piercing brown eyes?"

She scrambled out of his reach before he could protest. Byron's tongue peeled across his idle fingers.

"I believe that was Mr. Chatham, my father's steward. Now you go back to resting as you were before I had the gall to wake you up, my love. I'm going to get these unpacked for you."

"Let the servants do that."

"I'm not leaving you, darling, for I've grown fond of your dry company. I might as well make myself useful."

The nearness of her presence and Bryon's silky head beneath his fingers relaxed him to the point where he was on the verge of falling asleep. The silence grew awkward. He cracked an eye open. She was holding the gilt frame he kept so carefully hidden among his things.

His heart jolted him out of the bed with a sharp pang. Byron yelped and sprang out of the way. He snatched the frame out of her hand and slammed the drawer shut.

Josie's knowing gaze filtered through his hurt. "I can see the resemblance."

"Is it any wonder Father sent me away to school as a boy and sends me on long business trips as a man?"

"I'm not a stranger to rejection. My mother distanced herself from me while she doted on Delia."

"At least she wasn't an adulteress."

"There's nothing I can say or do to make it better, Charles. God knows I've tried."

She pecked his cheek and retreated. To add insult to injury, Byron followed Josie out into the hall. Charles snorted in the emptiness of the room and stormed through Josie's adjoining door. He pounded down the stairs to the decanter of port in the library that called his name. His hands shook as he poured himself one glass and then another. The door shut behind him with a click of bitter finality.

"Arguing already, are we?" Father drawled. "My, but it doesn't take you long to lose your temper and drown yourself in demon drinks."

Charles glared into his father's eyes of stone.

"I have made a decision, son. Your business engagements concerning the plantation and shipping have taken you away from your home and family long enough. It is time for you to settle down with your pretty little wife and start raising a family. All that I have done, all of your efforts to strengthen our business ventures, have been to this end. You must seize the time when it is ripe to produce an heir to the fortune we have striven to attain. Thus I have hired a business manager who will replace you in your travels and manage other similar details so that you can invest your time in worthier pursuits."

Bitterness rose like bile in Charles's throat, threatening to choke him. "How kind of you to consult my wishes on this matter, Father, before informing me of your decision. Clearly our financial state is not as precarious as you made out when you called me home from my honeymoon and sent me away from my wife within minutes of our arrival. There will come a day when everything we have built is reduced to ashes, ripped down by the very incompetent hands you set in motion just because mine were not satisfactory."

"Those hands will not make one move we do not approve. This manager will be a puppet pulled by our strings to do our bidding."

"Ah, in the end that is all I am to you too, Father. Your favorite puppet perhaps, but I am tired of my strings being pulled. I resent the implication that I have been avoiding my own wife. That is none of your concern. Everything I have done is for Josie's future prosperity."

"What you are doing right now—burning the candle at both ends and failing to be everywhere at once—is what I did. I refuse to send you on another business matter for the sugar plantation. You can manage the copper mine's affairs and stay closer to home. Looking back at my younger self, I see that is how I lost your mother. I was so busy looking out for her welfare that I failed to look out for her heart. A woman must be nurtured and cared for like a tender plant or she will go to someone who can."

"Don't placate me with the copper mine. This isn't really about business management or Josephine, is it, Father? It is about your ambition as always, and right now you want an heir to further your cursed ambition. Well for once, this puppet's strings are out of your reach. I don't believe in two people bringing a child into the world who will inevitably be scarred by circumstances beyond its control."

Charles punctuated his rant by slamming the library door shut. He needed to escape. Father had crossed the line by tethering him to the estate like his favorite stud horse and expecting him to produce an heir. Josie was no broodmare either. He had been born in this cage, but he didn't know how much longer she would be able to stand it before she flew the coop without him. He refused to be manipulated into allowing his father to make another child motherless.

Chapter Twenty-Three

*J*osie's hand stilled on Byron's head, and this mournful brown eyes pleaded with her. The garden had lost its peace, and all her plans for its betterment had lost their meaning. She had heard every word that passed between her husband and father-in-law. *Why did I have to choose this bench so close to the open window?*

A door slammed to her left, and she peered around the hedge to see Charles stalking toward the stables. Some whispering instinct held her fast where she sat, and only her eyes moved as they followed the thundering horseman astride Stalwart. The stallion's hooves devoured the ground in the direction of Portreath—and the Red Lion Tavern. Josie's heart plunged into the hollow void within as Byron bounded after his fleeing master.

Another set of hoofbeats descended on her numbness, and Josie turned to the approaching rider. The sight of Bertram curdled her stomach.

"What are you doing here?" she demanded, blinking back tears.

Bertram's direct gaze cooled several degrees. "I came for an audience with the senior Mr. Radcliffe, but his charming daughter-in-law will do nicely."

He dismounted as Josie's lips parted in protest. "You know business matters are none of my affair."

Bertram seated himself beside her with a maddening grin. "Rather abrupt with an old friend, aren't you?"

"You really are incorrigible. To what excuse do you presume to owe the nature of this visit?"

"Poachers. I trailed them to your woods."

"If you really want my opinion on the matter, I say let them poach. Last summer, if you could call such frigid months a summer, there was no harvest. I don't blame them for trying to feed their families' hungry mouths. Pilchards don't go very far."

"Dear Josie. You always were too kindhearted for your own good. I would blame you for jilting me, but then that was only in the interest of being loyal to your father, was it not?"

"You forget yourself, sir. I am a married woman."

"I won't ask your forgiveness for observing that you are a very unhappily married woman. Don't try to deny it. There were tears in your eyes just now."

"I refuse to be subjected to your impertinence one moment longer," Josie snapped. She bolted to her feet, every vein rushing hot as molten lead. Bertram's wiry arm shot out quicker than she could retreat, fingers locking around her wrist.

"Unhand me at once," Josie hissed, trembling.

"I grow weary of waiting, Josie. Weary of both of us suffering while you remain blind to the cure. What will it take to convince you that we were born for each other?"

Josie reeled back and slapped him for all she was worth. She wrenched away as his eyes glittered with a cruel, sharpened light. A flush suffused his skin further than where her palm had left a red mark.

"Your resistance is admirable, but my patience is not without limits. I will not be denied."

"And I will not hesitate to have you arrested for trespassing if you dare to set foot on this property again. I could have you discharged from my father's employ, but I bear you no ill will, Bertram. All I ask is that you keep your distance."

Bertram rose and mounted his horse. He nodded, but the hooded shadows cast by his deep-set eyes were scornful. Josie clenched her fists as he receded into the distance and stomped her foot. *Such impudence. How dare he mock me.*

By dinnertime Charles still had not appeared. Sebastian cleared his throat as Josie's spoon swam halfheartedly through her cold chowder.

"My dear, we simply cannot have this at all. You must eat something and attempt to familiarize yourself with these moods of Charles's. Believe me, he has always been moody even as a child. His tempers fade in time, but starving yourself will not help matters any."

"You forget I have lived with him for over four months now."

"Apparently you have yet to learn the art of indifference."

Temper flared in her heart. "I beg to differ, Sebastian. I have found that indifference breeds contempt. God knows the start of our marriage has been difficult enough as it is. Pray excuse me before I ruin your appetite along with my own."

Sebastian's incredulous snort did not escape her ears as she mounted the stairs and stifled the urge to scream. These walls creaked under the oppressive strain that Sebastian bred. She hoped she was a worthy match to combat the lurking shadows.

Josie yanked out her hairpins one by one and seized her hairbrush. The familiar rhythm absorbed her as she counted the strokes.

A door slammed in Charles's adjoining bedchamber. Josie flung her brush down, straining for footfalls. All she detected was the disheartening clink of a decanter. Cold resolve propelled her forward. He did not even notice her as he stood there gulping down a glass of merlot.

"Charles?"

He turned and grimaced at the sight of her. "What do you want?" he slurred.

"I want you to stop."

He slammed the glass onto the dresser. Josie steeled her spine as he staggered toward her with his eyes frozen over.

"Have you visited your sister?" he demanded.

"Not yet."

"I absolutely forbid you to do so. Do you hear me? I absolutely forbid you to ever visit that whore."

"What are you talking about?"

"She is at the Red Lion, serving ale and other delights that can be had for a price."

The air whooshed from Josie's lungs. "Oh, Lord, have mercy."

"Even the Lord judges sinners like her, Josephine."

"But what of her husband? He is a decent man. I cannot imagine him condoning such behavior!"

"Wheal Mary was forced to shut down due to lack of funds to operate the pump. I have reason to believe my father may have called in the debt Mr. Ladd owed him. He'll sniff out the copper in that old mine if there is any to be had. Even love wouldn't feed Delia's belly for long. They'll do whatever it takes to eat."

"And the baby?"

Charles's eyes narrowed. "I neither know nor care what happened to the baby. I imagine some miner's wife takes care of the brat while its mother warms some stranger's bed."

"Oh," Josie sobbed, her vision blurring.

Charles's face contorted with rage as he seized her shoulders and shook her.

"Don't cry for her, woman! She deserves whatever she gets."

Josie tried to twist away from his tight grip. "My only consolation is that perhaps she will keep you from that hellhole if your wife cannot!"

"There are other taverns to be had," he shot back. The fumes on his breath overwhelmed her.

"She is my sister, Charles. I cannot hate my sister."

"Apparently love is like a disease with you. She of all people deserves your hate. It wasn't enough for her to drag herself through the gutter. She had to go and muddy up her sister's name along with it so that no other man would have you but me . . . a despicable drunk not worthy of you."

Josie writhed in his grip as he screamed, "Look at me! Deny it. I can read the loathing written all over your face! Do you think I would make a suitable father for your child? Because apparently marrying you wasn't enough for Father. I have to give him an heir too. Well, we'll give him one . . . we'll make him relive my childhood all over again."

"Don't do this, Charles," Josie shrieked. "Don't let the fear of your father's wrath control you. No child deserves to be conceived in anger."

The stinging blow sent her reeling. Josie blinked in shock. He had struck her with the full strength of his arm. The same arm that had held her, the same fingers that had caressed her face. He shoved her onto his bed, but in his inebriated state he misjudged the distance and stumbled. Josie seized her chance and bounded for the door like a wounded doe. He latched onto her skirt, and the ripping of fabric resounded as she tore away, echoing the rending of her innermost soul. She slammed the door shut with shaking fingers, securing the latch just as he crashed against it. The panels shuddered at the blow.

Gut-wrenching sobs threatened to sever Josie from within as she collapsed on her floor with the warm saltiness of blood on her tongue. His fists hammered the door. Glass shattered on the other side with a splintering crash. A heavy thud shook the floorboards beneath her, and the heaviest silence Josie had ever known followed. Against every instinct, she unlatched the door and peered through.

Charles lay like a fallen tree in a twisted heap of limbs and shards of glass. Merlot dripped like blood from the shattered remains of the dressing table mirror, staining the rug where the fragments of the decanter had fallen. Her ears strained to detect any approaching footsteps, but these ancient walls were thick. Charles didn't stir as she took a step forward and gazed down at him in pity. This was not the man she knew. Alcohol had warped him into the monster whose hand had struck her tonight and instilled fear.

Love gave Josie the strength to drag him away from the glass. Love possessed her to cradle his body against her, willing healing into the temple of his broken heart and wounded soul. She placed a pillow under his head and tucked the coverlet around him before she fled back to her bedchamber with a strangled sob. The bolted door didn't give her a shred of security. He had robbed her of that and mangled her trust along with the dressing table mirror.

There are some broken things we must bring to God to mend, like Charles.

Josie drew a painful breath as Esther's words filtered through her despair. The Spirit breathed conviction in her heart. She knelt on the cold floorboards and rested her elbows on the bed.

You always manage to get my attention, Lord, even when I'm running away. I'm angry, Lord. Charles failed to be the fulfillment of my expectations. I wanted him to embody the unconditional love I crave. All my life I've sought love from sources that proved to be shallow and conditional. In the moments when I was starving, I shielded myself with perfection instead of running into Your arms. I thought through perfecting myself that I would become worthy of love. I let their failures define my worth, when You say I am Beloved just as I am. I'm a stubborn girl. I had to watch my control dissolve into chaos before I turned to You. Perhaps all along I have substituted Esther's faith for my own. Please forgive me, Lord. Forgive me for my pride in thinking my love would be enough to heal Charles's heart, and forgive me for running from You when things didn't go my way. I forgive Charles. You have called me to love him, but You alone have the power to heal his brokenness. Jesus, You are my Warrior. I ask You now to fight this battle, because I cannot go on. I give Charles to You, and I let go. You love him even more than I. You are my Redeemer. I know You will restore my marriage. I know You will move the mountain of Charles's alcoholism. I trust You to set him free from this addiction!

Josie's fists unclenched as her soul took a breath, free from drowning beneath the flood of her own will. The red volume she had spirited out of Charles's suitcase peeped up at her. The soft leather caressed her palm as she pulled it from underneath her pillow.

The magazine clipping entitled "Stanzas to Jessy" was pasted inside the front cover. However, Charles had crossed out "Jessy" and replaced it with "Josie." The canal in Venice had not been a dream. She continued to leaf through the book. Words, phrases, and sometimes entire paragraphs had been underlined throughout in silent tribute to her. Doubts plagued her, but she refused to give them root.

Chapter Twenty-Four

Charles clutched his skull as agony's claws raked him and exacted the bitter price of drink. The irony did not escape him. Always he chose to dull the heartache for a moment and endure the physical pain for hours. The relentless truth remained that any pain paled before the suffering of the heart.

The muscles in Charles's back complained, but the rope springs of his bed failed to protest as he shifted. Where was he? He sat up on the floor, covered by his bedspread. The room swam into focus. He squinted up into the dressing table mirror and gasped at the distortion in the broken glass. One eye blinked back at him, his face disfigured beyond recognition as the remains of his nose and jaw flashed across the fragments of glass still hanging in the frame. With a shudder he rose to his feet and waited for the whirl of dizzying to set him back down. It wasn't the first time he had awoken to something he had destroyed in the height of his cups, but remorse stirred as he surveyed the damage. The shards reflected the jumbled pieces of his mind. There were vital pieces of information missing in his recollections of the night before. His mind leaped from one crevice to another, scene upon scene flashing by, as he spanned the gaps by leaps and bounds. His Josie was the recurring theme he recognized, her face standing out sharp and white in a sea of blur. Anger colored everything else. Father's shadow loomed, elusive in the recesses of his memory.

Charles moved toward Josie's door, fear and hope mingling in a nauseating blend. The knob offered him dead resistance. A barrage of sensations came flooding back with jarring force. The crashing slam of her door, the grating metal as the bolt slid across, and the crushing impact of flesh and bone against wood as he tried to batter his way inside.

"Oh, Josie," he moaned. He rushed into the hallway, praying she had forgotten to lock the other door. The breath hitched in his lungs as the door swung open.

Josie was kneeling at her bedside, head lolling to the side at an unnatural angle. Her hands were still clasped as though in prayer. He frowned, reaching out and brushing her shoulder lightly as though she were a page that might crumble into dust. A whimper sounded in her throat. Her lashes lifted, and in her stupor he witnessed her initial response unveiled by pretense. Her eyes were onyx twins, pupils swollen as though reflecting the blackness of his former wrath. She flinched away, but a shadow lingered as the soft morning light touched her jaw. Dread roiled within him as he cupped her face. The bruise was undeniable as her downcast eyes avoided his gaze. Horror blurred his vision. Her raw gaze sought his, and he read the broken trust pooling there.

"Charles," she began, and he stifled a sob behind his hand.

"Dear God, what have I done?"

Emotion swelled her breast as the sheen of compassion touched her eyes. "It wasn't you, Charles. That demon drink possessed you."

He shook his head. "You are the light of my life. Many men can hold their liquor without beating up their wives. Why don't you leave me, Josephine?"

Tears glistened in her darling eyes. "You know why, Mr. Radcliffe."

"It's beyond me, Mrs. Radcliffe."

She took a step toward him, but he backed away. "Don't touch me."

He held her gaze with all the tenderness with which he longed to hold her. "Darling, I beg your forgiveness. I don't deserve your love, but if you will stay I promise to stop drinking. Old habits die hard, but I need you by my side more than I've ever needed anything."

"Oh, Charles," she cried and flung her arms around him. "You are forgiven. I could no longer leave the man I love than I could stop breathing."

He kissed her jaw, drew her wrists to his mouth, and kissed her bruises one by one.

She continued, her voice soft but strong. "You cannot give me what you have never known, and I have relied on you to fulfill me when only Jesus can. I cannot fill the void in your heart crying out for Him. I believe in you, my love, but this rage that drives you to drink is bigger than you. Jesus is the only one with the power to set you free. The Bible says: 'There is no fear in love; but perfect love casteth out fear: because fear hath torment. He that feareth is not made perfect in love.' Jesus alone can free you from that torment with His perfect love."

"Jesus and I haven't been on the best of terms."

"We can be as close to Him, or as far away, as we choose to be. But if we are bought with His blood, our heavenly Father never leaves us nor ceases to chase us down when we stray."

Her words struck a chord of sense, but he didn't know if he would ever get to the place of faith where she was. For now, her simple belief in him was enough.

He held her a little tighter. "All I know is that because of you I have the desire to change, and I'm not so blind that I can't see God gave you to me for a reason. As for my father pushing us to give him an heir, we will give him one when we are good and ready and not a moment before, do you hear me?"

She shook a little, but he couldn't tell if it was from suppressed laughter or tears. When she looked up, he could see all the way into her beautiful soul.

"Just to set the record straight now that you are sober enough to listen, I think you will make a more than suitable father when the time comes. Once you give yourself the freedom to love, parenting our offspring will come naturally to you."

"Yes, Mrs. Radcliffe," he said and sealed the understanding between them with a kiss.

Chapter Twenty-Five

*J*osie swung Ebony's head toward the sea. Her responsibilities as mistress of Treathston Heights had lost their intimidation these past few months. Life had settled into a steady albeit monotonous rhythm as Josie turned the page of her eighteenth year. Now Christmas was approaching faster than ever. In spite of the mutual understanding they had reached as a couple, to Josie's bitter disappointment Charles had only increased the distance between them. The closed door between their bedchambers spoke volumes every night. Charles had never *said* he loved her. Perhaps in her naivete, she had been desperate enough to assume the impossible. He cared for her only as a possession, because she belonged to him. She might as well have been a doll sitting on his shelf . . . a beautifully dressed, rosy cheeked, yet woefully neglected doll.

Stalwart, ever the gallant gentleman, had learned to curb his reckless stride to match Ebony's. Charles's reins slackened beside her as he gave Stalwart his head. Josie couldn't even remember when the ritual of taking an evening ride together had begun. It just had one evening when Charles found her watching the sun sinking beneath the rose-gold waves from the cliff's edge. She had asked him if theirs was a rising or a setting sun. His cryptic response, "Try to live in the moment," had haunted her ever since—and perhaps him as well. She often caught a glimpse of his embedded pain under the glow of the Cornish sunset. In a way, they had been brought closer by the shared acknowledgment of their marital frailty. Sometimes they shared poignant silence; other times light conversation, but always raw soul-searching.

The groaning leather of Charles's saddle distracted her as he shifted his weight as though her silence unnerved him. She glanced up at him, and he ran a hand over his mouth as if trying to wipe away the telling sag there.

"I was just thinking. This will probably be the last of our evening rides for a while."

Josie gnawed her lip as he leaned forward and gestured to the brilliance of the sunset, rendered deeper by the clouds smearing the horizon. She drew a lungful of sea air and nodded. Its clean sharpness hinted of snow. Thus far only a playful dusting had reached them, but the ominous brewing clouds prophesied Old Man Winter's unbridled fury.

"The prospect disappoints you."

"Yes. What other time do we find to be alone together?"

"I surmise that if I found the time, it would alleviate your disappointment."

"Finding the time wouldn't be difficult for you if you truly desired to spend time with your wife." Josie spoke into the sea, half-hoping the wind would snatch her words away. There was no end to this friction between them, only brief reprieves.

He laid a hand on her shoulder, forcing her to meet his eyes. The steely blue there skewered her as he bit out the words. "Why else do you think I have followed you out here every evening for these past few months? You called me, and I had to answer. Sometimes I think you discredit the hold you have on me, Mrs. Radcliffe."

"Then why do you still feel so very far away?"

"That is answering a question with a question."

"A question we both refuse to answer. I hardly have to guess the reason for that."

Josie wheeled Ebony around with more carelessness than she was wont now that several inches of snow coated the ground. Words—always pretty, meaningless words that rang hollow as the heart in her chest. Ebony broke into a trot as Josie's frustration reached her.

"Josephine, wait," Charles called, but she had no intention of doing so. Let him catch up. Perhaps it would wake him a little from his infernal callousness.

Josie lurched in the saddle as Ebony's hooves skidded on ice. She clung to the pommel. If she hadn't had the sense to ride astride, she would have been thrown. A spasm ran the length of Ebony's neck, and Josie shuddered along with her.

"Whoa, whoa," she murmured and slid down. Dread seized her as the mare stumbled forward with a pronounced limp. Josie dropped to her knees and seizing Ebony's black foreleg.

"Josephine, stop."

Ebony shied as Charles seized her reins and knelt beside her. She surrendered her grasp to his practiced fingers. Charles nudged Josie. "Get up out of the snow, woman, before you catch your death of cold."

Josie stood, and he brushed the snow from her skirt with his free hand whilst his frown deepened. "It is a slight sprain, but at her age she won't recover like she used to."

"It's all my fault. I should have had better sense than to bring her out here when it's icy."

"If it had been Stalwart, I would have done the same thing. It doesn't come easy, retiring a beloved horse. You ride Stalwart home now. I'll be along in a bit."

The unexpected compassion and patience in his tone thawed her heart's frost. "No, I'll accompany you. It is much too cold."

Charles gave a dismissive shrug, but he did not protest as she walked Stalwart along beside him. He hunched his broad shoulders against the biting wind as he led poor Ebony. The sunset was fading to hues of dim lavender gray that mirrored her despondence. Treathston loomed dark as they neared the stables.

The life and warmth of light spilled onto the snow as Sebastian's broad frame filled the doorway. "Ah, there you are, you two," he hollered above the moaning wind. "I was about to come looking. Come in quickly out of this frightful cold."

Movement caught the corner of Josie's eye as Alfie took the reins from Charles and listened to his instructions. The boy was unable to disguise the shiver wracking his thin body. She would ensure he received warmer clothing this Christmas.

The head stableman approached, and Josie handed him Stalwart's reins. A footman appeared at the entrance of the stables to take Stalwart. Charles turned and reached up to assist her. She slid into his arms, but he did not immediately release her. One arm surrounded her shoulders and took the brunt of the wind until they reached the doorway. Then it fell away as though Sebastian's presence had in some way burned it off her body.

"I just invited your father for Christmas Eve dinner following the candlelight service at church," her father-in-law said. "He said he was expecting cousins of yours, Josie, and of course they are most welcome. I gather an Aurelius Haverhill and his daughter?"

Josie pasted a smile onto her face. "I trust he accepted?"

"He said he had no better place to be. I'm sure you especially will enjoy it, Josie. It will be just like old times for you. I told him they might as well also join our fox hunt on Boxing Day as I understand Aurelius is an avid sportsman."

"He most certainly is, and he will be most appreciative of your hospitality."

"Well, what good is it to possess grounds like these if I can't have a smashing hunting party every now and then?"

"In other words, you are most eager to show off your estate and marksmanship, Father."

"I expect the same from you son, man to man. Now bring Josie in by the roaring fire. She looks half-frozen."

They seated themselves on the settee by the crackling flames, and Sebastian resumed his pipe in the wingback chair close to them.

Charles leaned close enough that his breath fanned her cheek. "I've never seen you so delighted."

She whispered back. "There has never been any love lost between Aurelia and me. I'm sure this year will prove no different, other than the fact that Delia will not be here to humor her."

A tinge of regret crept into his expression. She hadn't mentioned Delia since that night, but apparently guilt had hounded his every sober moment since. "I should never have broken it to you in that way. Dashed insensitive of me."

Josie reached for his hand and gripped it. "Don't go back there now."

Something wistful and tender played at the corners of his mouth, as elusive and fragile as a reflection upon water.

It wasn't enough to distract Josie from her thoughts. The shivering flames took on Aurelia's willowy shape, and Josie could see her clinging to her husband all over again, whirling together as they had the night of their betrothal ball. She recalled the mocking curve of Aurelia's mouth as she laughed and the knowing gleam in her topaz eyes.

"She always thought me frightfully dull. I'm sure she will change her tune at the sight of you."

"Now don't go and dredge that all up again."

The mere pretense of sitting with him in front of the hearth like the lovers they weren't became unbearable. Josie rose and glided toward the door.

"Where are you going?"

She wrinkled her nose at him. "To find something festive to wear for tomorrow night, my sweet."

Sebastian chuckled, but Josie doubted that he had caught the full purport of their exchange as she mounted the stairs. She would certainly best Aurelia on one score. Her cousin would not be wearing anything from Paris. Her feet grew wings as they carried her up the staircase.

"Esther?" Josie called, peering around the edge of Esther's bedchamber door.

"I'm right here, luve, ye needn't shout," Esther responded, so close to the door that Josie jumped. A shaky laugh bubbled from her throat.

"Oh Esther, you gave me a fright. I need you to help me decide which dress from Paris to wear this Christmas Eve."

Esther gave Josie's retreating behind a swat. "I assure ye all yer dresses are still hanging just as ye left them."

Josie pawed through her dresses and heard the door click in Esther's wake. She found the crimson Paris gown she had worn in the portrait and held it up.

"Should I wear red or green?"

"I am guessing yer indecision involves cousin Aurelia," Esther observed with a knowing smile. "Ye are unsure whether to be yerself in the subtle green velvet or to become the brazen red vixen in an attempt to command Charles's gaze all evening."

Josie's arm sagged. "It all sounds very foolish of me when you put it that way."

"Charles wanted the brazen red vixen in the portrait," Esther said with a shrug of her slim shoulders. "I only want ye to be true to yerself, regardless of what yer wearing. I cannae help it, luve. Sometimes he grieves me nigh to death. Ye deserve to be sure of his love just as ye are. A worthier woman never breathed air."

Josie blinked back the threatening moisture in her eyes, but her brave smile quickly melted into a sliding tear. Esther's thumb caught it as she reached out to take the dress.

"One never kens until she tries it on."

Esther fumbled with Josie's buttons, and her dress pooled at her feet. She stepped out of it as Esther pulled the billowing skirt of crimson over her head. The bright folds around her shoulders gave her the heady impression of a butterfly breaking free from its cocoon. Esther tugged and fussed, but Josie's freedom was short-lived as the once perfect fit became a constrictive struggle.

Esther stepped back with a frown.

"Have I really put on that much weight, Esther?"

"Hardly, at the rate ye've been eating of late."

"Cinch me up then."

Josie heard Esther's drawn-out sigh as she seized her stays, as though the slow scream of Josie's insides pained her.

"Ye could be with child, luve."

Fear hitched Josie's breath further.

"Don't be absurd, Esther. My monthlies never come regular," she managed between clenched teeth as Esther fastened the back of the dress. She hefted her skirts and pranced over to the full-length mirror. She smiled with satisfaction. Breath came at a cost, but that was the lesser of two evils.

"Absurd?" Esther echoed.

Josie's mirrored eyes froze over as her lips formed the bitter words. "As rarely as he's been with me? Yes."

Chapter Twenty-Six

*J*osie twisted a strand of garnets around her fingers until they were as knotted as her stomach. What had she forgotten? *Francois is preparing the syllabub and assured me the mince pies are cooling. The yule log is cut, and the wassail is ready for the carolers. I'm ready to hang the Christmas bunch—*

Josie jumped in the hallway as someone pounded on the front door. A blast of cold air whipped the blood into her cheeks as Craven opened it and maintained his unruffled decorum. A white-cloaked figure scurried in and secured the heavy oak door behind her.

"Och, but it is going to be a cold Christmas, luve," Esther exclaimed, reaching up to yank off her hood.

Josie shivered by way of a nod and rubbed some warmth into her arms. Esther held out a basket filled with brown paper shaped logs.

"Esther, how many times do I have to tell you that you are not a servant? I told Helen to go to the chandler's."

"Aye, but I met her on the way, and her sister's bairn will be born this night. I took the liberty of telling her to go see to her and brought these to ye. 'Twas no trouble."

Esther dug through the packages and pulled out the largest. She unwrapped the brown paper, revealing smooth beeswax. "The chandler says happy Christmas to ye."

Josie accepted the basket. "A yule candle . . . it is kind of him indeed."

Esther chucked Josie's chin and succeeded in spreading her own smile to Josie's mouth.

"Dinna fret yerself so, luve. We shall have plenty of cheer this year. God kens last Christmas 'twas hard with that debt hanging over our heads, but the past is behind us now. I doubt yer husband will allow ye to ken another cheerless Christmas such as that."

"I have so much to be grateful for. I just want everything to be perfect for Charles, and Sebastian has so many expectations."

Esther snorted and placed a hand on her hip. "Och, that man struts around just like he pleases, and no one hardly dares breathe without his permission. Ye are the mistress of this house, and what does a man ken about homemaking? If he doesna let ye do just as ye please, he will have me to reckon with. As for Charles, he only wants ye to be happy, Josie. Naught else but that matters to him. Have a care to remember that, luve."

Josie willed her smile to remain, but beneath it the cruel tremor lingered. Her innermost soul cringed and shivered like a naked branch shuddering in the winter wind. The time when she would have believed Esther had come and gone where Charles was concerned. The wound was raw, but she refused to cry another tear or bleed another drop. Fantasies were pleasant only until reality left you numb.

A brisk step sounded as Craven reappeared, bearing the punch bowl of wassail. He set it on the entryway table and began the process of arranging the glasses in his meticulous manner.

"Craven?"

"Yes, Mistress?" His hands stilled beside the mulled cider with an air of smothered impatience.

"We have an odd number at dinner this Christmas Eve, which would be unlucky. Would you be so kind as to join us and make us an even eight?"

His hooded eyes blinked at her. "I am honored indeed, Mistress, to accept your gracious invitation."

"Excellent. Dinner will be served at six o'clock."

Craven gave a curt nod before resuming his preparations.

Josie turned back to Esther. "I must see to the hanging of the Christmas bunch. The guests will be arriving shortly."

Esther nodded with a gleam of understanding and pride shining in her eyes. "Aye, fetch Charles to help ye, luve. I shall be in the library if ye need me."

Josie gave Esther's arm a squeeze of thanks and swept through the door into the drawing room. She neglected to mention that she had no intention of enlisting Charles's aid. She refused to suffer the mortification of standing beneath the bunch of greenery, forcing him to pay her a kiss. She sighed as she dragged a chair over and eyed the chandelier, knowing she would be skirting it all night long. The Christmas bunch sat there awaiting her approval on the table—a festive bundle of mistletoe, apples, and holly suspended within three wooden hoops. She set the basket of candles down and grasped the loop of scarlet ribbon. With a firm grip on the back of the chair, she mounted it and hung the bunch from the center of the chandelier. She remembered the lonely sprigs of mistletoe that had graced the chandeliers in London. The Christmas bunch was a Cornish tradition, and it wouldn't do for such a charming tradition to be broken in spite of her misgivings.

Josie raised the yule candle to her nostrils and breathed in the sweet purity of the beeswax as she carried the basket into the dining room. The lazy maid was setting the table with a clatter, a task that should have been completed hours ago. Josie's chest grew tight at the thought of the guests arriving to an unset table.

"Ah, there you are, Genevieve. Here are the candles I ordered. After you are finished, please see to the sconces in the hallway and refill the candelabra in the drawing room."

"Yes, Mistress," the redhead responded without an ounce of hustle.

Josie left the basket on the buffet and set the yule candle on the polished silver candlestick. She rearranged the sprigs of holly with pursed lips. Harsh laughter floated to her like a pungent scent. Cousin Aurelia had arrived to test her patience this Christmas Eve.

"Hurry and scurry, Genevieve," Josie admonished as she jerked at her apron strings and tossed the garment to the maid. Aurelia would leap at the chance to insinuate that her hostess's preparations were lacking. Josie steeled herself as she swept into the parlor and jerked the dining room door shut behind her. *Please, Lord, grant me patience and grace this evening.*

"Josephine, darling," Aurelia cooed through the expressive red pout that Josie remembered all too well.

"How good of you to come, Aurelia. Mr. Haverhill, how do you fare this Christmas Eve?"

"Marvelously, Josephine. I must say that you are looking exceptionally well."

"Thank you. You are too kind. Permit me to return the sentiment."

Out of the corner of Josie's eye, she glimpsed Charles striding toward them with Sebastian close at his heels. Sebastian and Aurelius greeted one another with enthusiasm. Meanwhile, Aurelia batted her eyelashes at Charles. Josie bristled until her father diverted her attention.

"Happy Christmas, daughter," Father murmured. Josie kissed his cheek as the arms of her childhood enfolded her.

"I trust you have taken the time to enjoy the season apart from all this decorating, dress fitting, and menu planning."

"You know I'm a married woman now, Father. I haven't the time for daydreaming anymore."

"Always take time to enjoy being young, my dear. Fretting over such nonsense is how you get wrinkles like mine," he said with a loving squeeze.

Josie's heart filled with warmth. "I can do both, dearest Father, as you know full well. Come into the drawing room by the fire and enjoy the fruits of my labors. Francois is preparing all of your favorite treats as we speak."

"I have no doubt of that," he chuckled. "Eliza has already seen fit to test the integrity of my buttons. You may prove to be their demise."

Josie laughed. "I have a way with a needle should the need arise," she teased.

"Josephine's needlework is lovely indeed. Why she should want to waste her talents on buttonholes I can scarcely fathom," Aurelia exclaimed.

Josie turned, annoyed to find her cousin eavesdropping. "Did you finish that exquisite sampler you were working on last spring, Aurelia?"

"Very nearly. My fingers have difficulty concentrating on stitches when they would much rather be dancing across the pianoforte."

"Aurelia is very accomplished in music. If she were a man, she would be composing music at the university," Aurelius bragged.

"Poor Father," Aurelia said. "He can never forgive me for not being a son. No doubt he will change his tune once I snag myself a wealthy husband."

"You know you are most welcome to avail yourself of our pianoforte whenever you like."

"Why Josephine, of course, I shall be most delighted to entertain your guests! You never were very fond of music, were you? This Christmas I shan't have much competition for the instrument, seeing how poor Delia couldn't join us."

"Aurelia," Josie's uncle warned.

"Some of us must finish our samplers, dearest cousin," Josie responded. She caught Charles's eye, and the insufferable man had the gall to be amused. Josie snatched the tinderbox down from the mantle.

"I do believe the sun is setting. Charles, will you come and light the yule candle?"

"Yes, dear," he responded. So he wanted to play the part of the long-suffering husband in front of her beautiful cousin, did he?

Josie sailed into the dining room with Charles and shut the door. She didn't trust herself to speak, so she slid the candle toward him and slammed the tinderbox down beside it.

Charles raised his eyebrows as he began fumbling with the flint and steel. Sparks showered down onto the muslin as he lit a spunk from the catching flame.

"No love lost between you indeed. You and Aurelia are worse than two cats with their tails tied in a knot," Charles muttered as he held the match to the virgin wick. He stole a glance at her, and his hand shook with suppressed laughter.

"Have a care, sir, before you snuff the flame. I don't believe in such superstitions, but I don't want the servants all in a dither my first Christmas Eve as mistress of this house."

Charles's lips parted to speak, but at that moment a timid voice ventured:

"Mistress?"

Josie turned toward the kitchen maid with raised brows.

"Francois told me to tell you everything was ready."

"Thank you, Bridget. You may bring it in."

Josie took a deep breath and kneaded her pounding temples. It would be a miracle if the night progressed without further mishap. "Did you make a wish, Charles?"

Warm breath rushed against her ear as he kissed her hair. "I found I had nothing to wish for when I already have everything I could possibly want in you."

Josie's insides melted like butter, but she wasn't letting him off the hook that easily.

"Are you proud of your wife's homemaking efforts?"

Charles smiled, but it was the fondness written there that her heart thrilled to see. She had always known she pleased him as a woman should, but she longed to know if she held the key to his heart.

"I have never seen such festive decor, such decadent sweetmeats, or such a beautiful hostess at Christmastime."

"Good. Then I shall endeavor not to care what Aurelia or anyone else says."

Josie opened the door and announced, "Dinner is served."

As everyone found their seats, Josie surveyed the table with satisfaction as the steaming dishes were brought out. She could find no fault with the dinner. However, she had yet to taste a mouthful.

Charles pulled back a chair for her, and Josie seated herself with a rustle of crimson satin. Aurelia paused beside Charles's chair. He pulled a chair out for her and brushed behind Josie to a new seat, placing her between them. Josie hid a smile behind her water goblet as she raised it to her lips. Her husband was not unaware of Aurelia's flirtatious intentions.

Craven appeared, his collar starched even more than usual though Josie wouldn't have thought it possible. As he seated himself across from Aurelia, she had the lack of good breeding to give him an aghast glance.

"Charles, I think it would be a capital idea if you said the blessing this Christmas Eve," Sebastian proposed.

Josie's poor husband looked anything but blessed as they all bowed their heads and clasped hands. Aurelia's flesh was as cold as the blood that flowed through her veins.

"Father, we thank You for all that You have so bountifully bestowed upon us. I thank You for my wife and all of her preparations, which have made this season cheerier than past Christmases for me. Please bless this food and the hands that have prepared it. Thank You for sending Your Son Jesus to earth so that we might receive Your salvation. In Jesus's name, Amen."

"Amen," Josie murmured as her heart smote her. She had not always been thankful for all the little ways Charles strove to show her kindness. She clung to his hand, and his fingers curled around hers with a comforting squeeze. Warmth rippled through her chest long after their skin ceased to touch.

Josie focused her attention on the mince pie with difficulty and placed a steaming wedge on her plate. She turned to Aurelia. "Pie, dear?"

"Since when did eating in mixed company become one of your holiday traditions?" Aurelia hissed as Esther slid into her seat beside Craven. Josie stifled the urge to dump the pie in her cousin's satin lap.

"It was a question of eating in mixed company or breaking tradition by having an odd number of guests at our holiday table. I must say it is a pity if such a trifle spoils your appetite."

Aurelia slid the proffered piece onto her plate with her fork and speared a stray currant with unmitigated wrath. Josie sawed through the pie and distributed it amongst the eagerly proffered plates. Sebastian's plate was loaded last, and all eyes watched him take a bite of pie before diving in. Josie took a tentative bite and found it to be tender and flavorful. Her lips curved to return Charles's smile around the bite of food.

"My compliments to the chef," Aurelius declared. "I want to propose a toast to the health of the Radcliffe and Chadwick households. May the new year bring you joy and bounty."

"Likewise to the Haverhill household," Sebastian declared as glasses clinked all around. The yule candle cast its glowing pool of blessing, and Josie stole another look at Charles over the rim of her glass as she remembered another candlelit dinner that seemed an eternity ago. Marriage had changed him for the better. His face was fuller, lending a softness to his harsh lines. He appeared content in their settled pattern, but where was the passionate abandon of a lover? Perhaps it would never again be that way between them. Perhaps she should settle for the faithful, however passive, version of the man beside her.

Do you long for something more too, Charles? Mistresses have provided zest for other monotonous marriages. I pray it will never come to that between us, even if we continue to drift along on this sluggish current. I cannot believe you are content, for I have glimpsed the wild side of you, and there are many women far more beautiful than I who desire you.

Sebastian interrupted her thoughts. "Why don't we retire to the drawing room? There is a yule log ready and waiting to be lit." Chairs scraped back as a chorus of agreement rose.

"I'd best take my leave now, luve," Esther murmured.

"Nonsense, Esther," Sebastian protested as he offered his arm. "You needn't deprive us of your charming company."

Esther forced a smile as she took it. Josie frowned. She wasn't sure she liked Sebastian's admiration for Esther's beauty.

Charles followed suit as he escorted her into the drawing room. The replenished candles blazed with light, creating a magical setting as the muted shadows of the dancing flames in the hearth twined with the sharper warmth of candlelight. The gleaming punchbowl of syllabub resided on the table hemmed in by sparkling crystal glasses like a resplendent gem in a setting of diamonds. Charles released her to fetch the yule log.

"Syllabub, anyone?"

"Don't mind if I do, Josie," Father responded. "Eliza already scolded me for skulking around the kitchen this morning. She knew I would have my fill of your syllabub tonight, so she is saving her batch for the morrow."

"I dearly hope it can compare to Eliza's, Father," Josie admitted as she poured the golden liquid and passed it to him. After serving a hearty portion of the bowl, she took a sip herself and sighed. Having a French chef was trying at times, especially at Christmastime when he was unaccustomed to preparing traditional Cornish recipes. Eliza's syllabub was airier. Francois's froth left something to be desired, and he had been a little too generous with the nutmeg. But it would have to suffice, for she wouldn't run the risk of offending Sebastian over such a trifle. Father didn't seem to notice the deficit, indulging in two glasses before Charles appeared with the stout log braced over one shoulder. He knelt and laid it on the rug with a grunt.

"Darling, the chalk and the yule splinters from last Christmas Eve are on the mantle," Josie said.

As Charles turned to reach them, Aurelia perched herself on the log so that her blossoming bust was set to best advantage in the firelight. The moment Charles's gaze landed on her, she said in a husky tone Josie would have thought her too young to master: "Charles?"

Charles just gaped at her, as though she had cast some kind of spell upon him.

"Aren't you going to wish me good luck in the New Year?"

Charles bent and drew the stick man onto the other end of the log, signifying the death of 1817 and the birth of the New Year. "All one needs to avail themselves of good luck is to sit upon the log, cousin Aurelia."

Aurelia's breast heaved as she whispered, "Still, I would like to hear you say it just the same."

"I wish you good luck," Charles said, extending his hand. Aurelia took it, and as she rose to her feet, she leaned in closer than was necessary as her ripe lips parted.

"Thank you," she breathed with fluttering lashes. Charles stared like a man turned to stone. A log popped in the fireplace, but Josie could have sworn it was the undeniable chemistry leaping between the tall blond man and willowy blond woman.

Aurelia's dusky lashes lowered in false modesty as she drifted away and stood just beneath the Christmas bunch. Josie gasped for breath. Her cousin's audacity captured the air in her lungs, whilst Charles's blue eyes seemed to drown in twin tidal pools that threatened to pull him under. After some moments, he appeared to awake from his entrancement, and he touched the splinters of lit wood to the yule log, shoving it into the blazing flames.

"Come now, we must have a game of snapdragon," Sebastian declared. Josie gritted her teeth as she seized the silver dish of raisins from the mantle and poured half a decanter of brandy over them. It was just like Sebastian to suggest a game that placed Aurelia in close proximity to her husband. She set the raisins in the middle of the flagstones before the fireplace, and Charles dropped a lit match. The bowl burst into cheerful blue flames, and Aurelia, Charles, Josie, Esther, and Sebastian all knelt in a circle around it.

"Come now, Papa," Aurelia coaxed, but Aurelius shook his head.

"Three is a crowd, and there are already five of you! My fingers aren't as nimble as they once were. I know when I'm licked."

"I've no doubt I will be highly entertained just watching," Father echoed.

"What shall we have for a forfeit?" Aurelia asked.

"A kiss," Sebastian insisted like a mischievous schoolboy. Josie's gut clenched with dread. She might have known. They all poised a hand over the blue flames.

"On your marks, get set . . . go," Sebastian called out.

Five wrists shot out as twenty-five fingers attempted to snatch the burning raisins from the flames. The sweet stench of the fumes threatened to suffocate Josie as her fingers darted around the edges of the bowl. She had been good at this game once, but Aurelia's fingers appeared to be possessed as they flew in and out of the flames. Charles paused now and then to blow on a finger while Sebastian's forehead scrunched in concentration. Esther kept getting elbowed out of the way by Aurelia.

At long last, Josie succeeded in snatching the last raisin, but her heart sank. Her pile was a molehill compared to Aurelia's mountain. They counted them amidst the blowing of fingertips, and Aurelia had won by twenty-three raisins.

As though through a haze, Josie watched her red lips form the words. "I require a forfeit from you, Charles."

Aurelia sailed over and stood beneath the Christmas bunch. Charles followed her, and time stood still as he bent his head and pecked her lips. However, the blonde vixen wasn't satisfied. She encircled his head with her arms and kneaded him full on the mouth. Their lips broke apart with a soft smack as Charles pried her arms off his neck.

"I think you have had your forfeit and then some."

Aurelia beamed up at him with a triumphant curve to her swollen lips. The stunned silence in the room was interrupted by a sharp rap on the door. Carolers, surely. Josie flew into the entryway, welcoming any chance of escape. Craven opened the door, and a chorus of voices assailed her.

"Happy Christmas, Mrs. Radcliffe!"

Josie bared her teeth in a poor attempt at a smile at the poor carolers, struggling not to choke on the hot bile that had risen in her throat. Their rustling skirts and footsteps flanked her as the carolers serenaded her guests with a round of "Auld Lang Syne."

Josie sucked in the cold air to chill her boiling blood. "Thank you, ladies and gentlemen. Would you care for a cup of wassail?" she heard herself say in a strained voice.

"Aye!"

Josie stepped aside to let Craven do the honors. Soon the empty cups were passed back again.

"Happy Christmas to you all," Charles belted out.

Echoing shouts of the same were heard as the half-frozen souls piled back into their sleigh and snuggled under their lap robes. Josie's breath blew white as she shut the door with a shudder.

"We can scarcely let the night pass without more music. The pianoforte is just begging to be played," Aurelia declared as they all trooped back to the warmth of the drawing room. She seated herself as though the bench were her throne before launching into a brisk rendition of "God Rest Ye Merry Gentlemen."

Josie told herself listening wouldn't hurt as she endured every tinny note, sitting on the edge of the settee as though the cushions threatened to spring up and bite her. The candlelight shimmered off Aurelia's hair like strands of spun gold. Charles's eyes lingered with rapt attention as she trilled the notes in a resounding climax, but Josie should have known that commanding the entire room's attention wouldn't be enough drama for her insufferable cousin. Aurelia began to sing an operetta, and her piercing shrieks threatened to send the chandelier toppling from the ceiling. Josie sprang from her seat and announced above the din that she was fetching chestnuts to roast.

She tore down the servants' stairs until Aurelia's voice was muffled to a receding echo and slammed shut the door behind her that cordoned the servants' quarters off from the rest of the house. "Why did I have the pianoforte tuned?" she groaned.

Francois's voice drifted to her. "And the ghost of Lady Chadwick—"

"Francois, I need the chestnuts," she called as she approached the kitchen.

"What eez dying up there, Mrs. Radcliffe? It eez worse than two tomcats fighting," Francois observed as he brought her the bag.

"Nothing has died . . . yet."

As she began to walk back down the servants' hallway toward the staircase, she collided with a broad chest, and chestnuts rat-a-tatted to the floor.

"What are you doing down here, Charles?" she sputtered as she dropped to her knees and began picking the chestnuts up as though her life depended on it.

"The same thing you are. Trying to escape that infernal racket upstairs."

Charles knelt down beside her and began dropping chestnuts into the burlap sack. "Josephine, we need to talk."

"Yes, well, this is neither the time nor the place, Mr. Radcliffe. I highly doubt that you want to hear anything I have to say. So you just go back up to your charming company, and if you want some peace and quiet, tell your adoring Miss Aurelia that you have a smashing headache. I'm sure she would be happy to oblige you with cold cloths and caresses aplenty."

Josie let out an outraged cry as Charles scooped her into his arms as though she weighed no more than a child. He carried her to the doorway as she clawed at him. "Put me down, you insufferable ingrate. You abominable ape. You wretched winebibber. Have you taken leave of your senses, you belligerent blockhead? If you don't put me down right now, you obstinate ox, I swear I'll—"

Her next words were smothered by the taste of his mouth. She arched her back and writhed, helpless in those powerful arms. Warm lips kneaded hers with a tender passion she had never known before. Every muscle went limp. She was unable to breathe, yet she wanted to drown in the heady sensation that mastered her. She seized his head in her hands as she poured her innermost soul into his. Heat thawed every frozen place inside. Warmth trickled down her fingers from the corners of his eyes.

Oh Charles, your heart has been bleeding all this time, starving for me.

After what seemed like hours, their lips broke apart.

"Charles you have never—kissed me—like that before," Josie panted.

"No one has ever called me an ingrate, an ape, a winebibber, a blockhead, and an ox all in one breath before either, but I must say I deserve all five and more that should never cross a lady's lips."

"Charles—"

He brushed a finger across her lips.

"Hush now, sweetheart, and come with me. There's something I want to show you that can't wait until tomorrow."

Josie looked back over his shoulder and saw the sprig of mistletoe hanging in the doorway, forever redeeming the white berries in her eyes from the part they had played in Aurelia's stolen kiss.

As he carried her out the back way, Charles grabbed a couple of lap robes and flung them over her. A blast of biting wind hit them in the face as he opened the door.

"It is beastly cold this eve," he grumbled.

"Where are you taking me?"

Secretive delight played over his features. "Wait and see."

Just when it appeared that they were heading in the direction of the stables, Charles covered her eyes with his hand. The howling wind snatched his words away, but Josie was content in his arms. Snow stung her lips until the howling ceased. Sweet, moist warmth underlined by subtle pungency told her they were inside the stable before he lifted his hand from her face and set her down. The familiar sounds of the horses stole over her with their comforting cadence, draining the tension from her neck and shoulders. With every passing second, her curiosity stirred.

"Just one moment," Charles said as though sensing her growing impatience. "Let me light a lantern."

He pulled a tinderbox from his pocket and fumbled with the flint and steel. The flame flared to life, scattering the shadows.

Stalwart snorted as Charles bypassed him and tugged her to the opposite end of the stable.

"Happy Christmas, sweetheart," he said as a chiseled dark head thrust itself over the bar. He pulled a carrot out of his pocket, and the thoroughbred's velvet nostrils flared as Charles held it just out of reach.

"She's all yours. An accomplished horsewoman such as you deserves a mount who can keep up with Stalwart. I'm sure Ebony will understand."

"Ohhhhh," Josie breathed as she took the carrot from her husband and offered it to the bay beauty. Moisture blurred the lines of the stable as tears pricked her eyelids. *Surely Charles, you wouldn't give me such a gift unless somewhere deep down in the recesses of your guarded heart you have found a semblance of affection for me.*

The proud carriage and curvature of the mare's head proclaimed her pure blood. Josie took a deep, shuddering breath. "Oh, Charles I—"

Her voice broke. She flung her arms around his neck, lungs bursting with suppressed yearning. Her shoulders heaved with the ache as his arms enfolded her, but the three words she wanted to say didn't leave her lips. She couldn't bear it if he didn't return them again. Charles's voice rumbled tenderly against her ear.

"You are most welcome. I see I have succeeded in making you quite speechless. I don't know if I have ever told you. This is the beginning of my dream for our own stud farm. Just think of the foals Stalwart will sire with her."

Josie's lips curved with joy as she glanced back at the thoroughbred. The mare's regal bearing reminded her of King Arthur's dark-haired queen.

"Her name is Guinevere," she said.

"I wholeheartedly approve. We shall name the stud farm Camelot in honor of its first dame."

"Thank you for sharing your dream with me."

A gleam of adoration entered the shadowed depths of Charles's eyes. "And you alone are the only woman I shall ever share it with, for you are the queen of my heart, Mrs. Radcliffe," he breathed with reverence. Josie didn't dare to breathe as her gaze held her beloved's, lest the worship she read there would vanish.

Charles's eyes swept her face, and her surging doubts clouded his blue depths. His voice grew desperate. "Aurelia is jealous of you because you have that beauty and purity of heart that she never will."

He bent and snatched an apple from the feed bin. He held the shiny red surface to the light.

"Seductive women are flawless on the outside," he said, but then he turned the apple to reveal its rotten, worm-riddled core. "But on the inside their shallow core is rotten, and time reveals it to those fools first entranced by their beauty as their skin withers. My mother was one of those women. I am ashamed to confess I once thought the same of you, but God in His grace has opened my eyes to your true beauty. Pray tell me it isn't too late for you to trust me with your precious heart."

"You have had my heart all this time, Charles, regardless of trust, because I love you. You have wounded me many times, but your heart has the power to heal as well as to hurt."

Tears shimmered in his eyes then. "Then you forgive me? I haven't lost you in spite of my cruel stupidity?"

"No," Josie began, but then his mouth covered hers.

Chapter Twenty-Seven

crash jolted her awake. Josie groaned as she rolled over and pulled the covers around her chin. No doubt one of their guests was trying to find the necessary and knocking things over as they navigated unfamiliar territory. She had the blizzard to thank for that—they'd all been forced to stay the night.

A low growl rumbled at the foot of the bed and stilled Josie's thoughts. Byron pawed at the door and whined. Charles didn't stir, and for once she wished he didn't sleep like the dead. Father had always said dogs could taste evil on the air.

Josie flung the covers back and decided to get some warm milk. If Aurelia was snooping, it wouldn't hurt to catch her in the act. The coldness of the floor seeped through her stocking feet as she groped for her dressing gown. She managed to light a candle from the dying coals in the hearth.

"Byron, come here," she whispered, seizing his collar as he obeyed. She pushed the door ajar and ventured into the dark hallway. The clicking of Byron's nails matched the thump of her heart in the stillness. Esther's door was ajar. Josie cupped the flame with her fingers as she nudged the door wider.

"Esther, did you hear a noise?"

Her hissed whisper fell on deaf ears. She drew closer to the bed, but even the shadows could not hide the fact that no form nestled within the thrown-back covers. A quickening of relief eased the tightness of Josie's chest. No doubt Esther had woken her as she passed Josie's door on her way to the necessary.

Byron whined, straining for the door, and Josie obliged him. He lunged for the hallway, but she dragged him down another stairwell into the kitchen instead. Craven would throw an unholy fit if Byron relieved himself on the front lawn. Josie unbolted the deadlock, but Byron showed no interest in going outside. She slid the bolt back with a shrug. He followed her into the kitchen as she fetched a mug. A growl rumbled from his throat, and Josie seized his collar afresh with trembling fingers. Something lurked in the shadows skirting the candlelight, and she could no longer deny that an ominous presence lingered in her house.

Josie froze as floorboards creaked above her head. Her appetite for warm milk deserted her as she considered how long it would take her to fetch milk from the larder and heat it through. All she wanted was to get back to the safety of her own bed.

Byron snarled and lunged for the door, nearly wrenching her arm from its socket. The tin cup clattered to the floor as the collar ripped free of her fingers, and Byron bounded out of reach. Josie snatched up her candle and charged after him. The setter made a beeline for the dining room. Josie paused against the wall. Blood roared in her ears. Byron had found whoever it was, but he did not bark. She approached the doorway, obeying an impulse that commanded her to blow out the candle. She peered around the door frame, and her spine prickled.

Byron stood beside a white-cloaked figure whose back was turned to her as the figure reached toward the yule candle . . .

and killed the flame. Her breath caught in her throat as the room was plunged into darkness. The white cloak stood out as it glided toward her. Icy terror knifed at Josie's chest as she braced herself against the wall. Who would want to snuff the flame when tradition declared that death or misfortune would visit the family in the coming year whose yule candle went out in the night?

The ghost-like figure glided past her, and Byron trotted after it. There was a whisper of annoyance, and Byron obediently turned to go back upstairs. To her surprise, the person followed him. *Lady Chadwick's ghost doesn't whisper.* So someone wanted to investigate how Byron had gotten out of Charles's room.

Josie hurried the other direction and dashed up the servants' stairs, biting back a yelp as she stubbed her toe. Through her mind's eye, she trotted down the hallway in the dark, remembering to leave her door ajar before bounding into bed. She tensed, fearing Charles would demand to know where she had been, but his breathing didn't quicken. She willed her own to slow as she cracked her eyelids just enough to discover the identity of the spectral phantom.

Byron trotted into the room and lay down in his usual position at the foot of her bed as though prowling around in the middle of the night was a normal occurrence. An ominous shadow appeared on the wall. The white form waited in the doorway, peering toward their bed. Josie willed the stranger to come closer into the firelight, but she—or he— remained where the cloak shadowed the ghostly face.

At long last the stranger faded from view. Josie did not have the courage to follow the figure back into the darkness as she waited a while before tiptoeing to the door and dead-bolting it.

She laid her head on Charles's chest, and only the steady thump of his heart soothed her enough to fall back asleep.

Josie's remembrance of the flitting form ravaged the morning's stillness like troubled ripples on a glassy surface. The phantom had robbed her of joy this Christmas. Someone harbored the desire to wreak fear and havoc within her home. Charles still slept with that contented half-smile on his lips that she wanted to remain fixed in place forever. Last night was the first in a long while that he had fallen asleep in her bed.

Josie kneaded the small of her aching back as she pondered whether or not to tell him about her encounter. He couldn't downplay the ghost as a practical joke, knowing how the Cornish respected all superstition and folklore. Someone wanted to wield fear over this household for a sinister reason she could not fathom.

A scream froze the blood in Josie's veins. Charles bolted upright in their tangled sheets as she flung her arms around his neck.

"What in heaven's name?" he sputtered, but he left the question hanging as their ears strained in unison for any further sound. Running feet pounded along the hallway in a panicked staccato, and somewhere a door slammed like a punctuation mark. Their door shuddered with blows.

"Master, Mistress!" a voice screeched.

Josie surrendered her hold on Charles and commanded her legs to carry her across the room. Her fingers trembled as she struggled to unfasten the deadbolt. At last she cracked the door and peeked through the sliver of light.

"Oh, Mistress, something simply dreadful has happened," Helen burst out with a sniffle. The maid's dilated pupils stood out in sharp contrast to her ashen skin.

"Come in here, quickly," Josie ordered, grasping for any semblance of control.

Charles was up behind her, glaring. "Pull yourself together, woman. Whatever has caused you such tremendous agitation had better be worth waking me from the soundest sleep I've had in months."

"'Twas the ghost of Lady Chadwick, Master. She's done come back again, she has. I saw her floating down the hallway in the servants' quarters, knocking on all the doors. Then this morning when I went in, the yule candle was burnt out. Mark my words, Master Radcliffe. There'll be a death in this family before the New Year is out."

"Helen, if I hear one more word about the ghost of Lady Chadwick I'll have you dismissed. Is that understood?"

Helen blanched even paler until her skin appeared translucent. "Yes, Master Radcliffe," she said, fidgeting with the edge of her apron.

"You may go," Charles said in a softer tone. The girl wobbled a curtsy and flitted through the door as though she were a wraith herself. As the heavy oak door clicked shut, Charles squinted toward Josie.

"Why, may I ask, did you have the door dead-bolted? Are the ghost stories getting to you now as well?"

Josie gnawed at her bottom lip. At her hesitation Charles demanded, "Surely you didn't think that with Aurelia in the house I would—"

"No, of course not. Someone was moving around in the night downstairs. I know we have guests, but when Byron growled I was worried."

"Did you investigate?"

"Yes . . . I didn't see who it was."

"But you saw someone snooping perhaps?"

"I did."

Charles snorted. "I daresay it was your cousin, but I haven't the slightest notion why you would dead-bolt the door on account of her unless you thought she would lose her way in a negligee."

The suspicion in his tone pricked Josie, but she needed more evidence before telling him exactly what she had seen. He would chalk the ghost up to her fear of the dark and leave it at that. "It would seem as though someone is getting a devilish amount of enjoyment out of resurrecting your poor grandmother," Charles growled. "I for one am getting unearthly tired of all this super-stition. Would you be so kind as to enlighten me to the ghoulish tale?"

Josie took a deep breath as she lowered herself onto the bed. She had never believed the story herself, but it wouldn't hurt to familiarize Charles with it.

"My grandmother, Violet Chadwick, was my grandfather's second wife. She was young and beautiful—in other words, everything his first wife was not. He had married her for her inheritance. After his first wife died, he fell madly in love with Violet, and his fondness for her only deepened with the birth of my father, Randolph. My grandfather, Reginald, was a rak-ish man who gambled and drank. On the other hand, every-one in Cornwall loved Violet. Many folks said Reginald didn't deserve her sweet purity of heart. This proved to be true one stormy night when they were on their way home from a soirée in an open carriage. My grandfather was drunk, and in his haste he drove them to their death over the cliff's edge. A fisherman found their broken bodies on the rocks the next day. Violet had been carrying a child, which only added to the outrage against

Reginald. The ghost story was the Cornish way of giving my grandmother justice, I think. Folks said they had seen her ghost wandering the cliff's edge seeking revenge for her unborn baby. They said she had placed a curse on Chadwick Park and would haunt it until judgment day."

"Such a tragedy should be cause to let a poor soul rest in peace and not keep digging her up out of the grave. It is an ungodly pity, that."

"All ghosts die sooner or later, even in Cornwall."

Charles's scowl only deepened as his bare feet hit the floor-boards. "Why does it have to be so beastly cold?" he grumbled.

Just as she had predicted, Christmas Day was spoiled for Josie, though her preparations were carried out to the fullest. The plum pudding was the best she had ever had, but it became sawdust in her mouth when Aurelia fished the good-luck wish-bone out of hers and smirked for Josie's benefit. Sebastian had added a great many guests by way of private invitation that he had neglected to mention to her. The servants' doomsday prophecies only deepened her headache. By the time Charles was ready to whirl her out onto the dance floor that evening it only made her headache worse, and Aurelia was more than happy to be her substitute for the one dance chivalry forced Charles to allow.

And all evening long, every white cloak and gown made Josie all the more determined to find the culprit.

Chapter Twenty-Eight

*A*urelia wrinkled her aquiline nose in disgust as they tromped through the snow back to the sleigh, puffing white breath like a dragon. Josie gritted her teeth at the sneer on Aurelia's face as they climbed back into the sleigh, and the longsuffering footman urged the horses forward. She doubted her wisdom in permitting her cousin to accompany her on her merciful errand of giving alms to the poor on Boxing Day.

"I cannot understand what permits them to live in such squalor."

"Many are not as fortunate as we, Aurelia."

"Hoity-toity, dear cousin. You would think one would be more grateful for my assistance during a wretched duty such as this."

"Perhaps I would be more grateful if it was considered more of a privilege."

"Well, I certainly know when I am not wanted. I shall avail myself of more appreciative company at the nearest opportunity."

"With the preference being male, I assume?"

"But of course. Women can be such frightfully dull creatures at times, don't you agree?"

"In my experience, I find most women to be not so much dull as they are deliberately provoking."

Aurelia fell silent, though Josie could not tell if it were for lack of a fitting retort or because she was stirring a pot of grudges. Josie flung off her lap robe and scrambled out of the sleigh. *Thank God this is our last tenant.* Aurelia did not bother to follow her out of the warm sleigh, and Josie was glad as she floundered her way through yet another drift of snow the wind had blown across the doorstep. She rapped against panels that threatened to give way at any moment. The miserable excuse for a door creaked open, revealing a haggard face.

Josie's heart stopped. The glazed depths of the young woman's once beautiful eyes widened in horror. She slammed the door shut in Josie's face, but Josie pried it open with a strength that overrode the bony wrists on the other side.

"Delia, for the love of heaven, what has happened to you? Charles told me you had left Cornwall!"

A bitter laugh escaped Delia's cracked lips, but then she doubled over as a gut-wrenching cough seized her. She held a handkerchief to her lips, but when she lowered it the cotton was spotted with drops of crimson.

"I daresay he would have liked to evict us after that night at the Red Lion, but even he didn't have the heart to throw us out when winter came. I think Esther must have twisted his arm."

"Esther?"

"Yes, she visits on occasion and brings us some victuals to keep the breath in us a little longer. The only reason I let her is because it really isn't charity coming from her. She really . . . cares for us."

Another fit of coughing left Delia wheezing for breath. "You shouldn't be here, Josie. I could never live with myself if—"

Delia's voice trailed away. Grief etched premature lines in her skin.

Josie's heart was breaking, but she kept her tone calm, beseeching. "Tell me, Delie."

At the endearment, Delia's face crumpled, and the hardness slid down her face in a scalding tear.

"If my sickness took you along with my baby. As it stands, I will never forgive myself for killing Rose. Her innocent blood has stained my hands for eternity. I came home one morning, if you can call this wretched hovel a home, and she was gone. Her little body was all stiff and blue."

The edges of Delia's shattered soul pierced Josie's heart. She reached out with healing in her arms.

"Don't touch me," Delia shrieked and flung up stick-like arms blotched with purple bruises. "I am unclean. Go home, Josephine. Go back to your fairy tale and leave me be."

Josie shook her head slowly at the sight of the bruises, trying and failing to process all she saw. "So James is hitting you now? I can't leave you here, Delia. Not like this . . . sick and abused in body, mind, and spirit. Come home with me, I beg you, before it is too late and this disease wastes you away."

"He only hits me when the drink takes him away from me for a time. I'm all he has, and not for long. Can't you understand, sister? I want the consumption to take me away from this wretched world so I can be with Rosie again."

"How can you say that?" Josie cried as she set the box on the rickety table against the wall.

"Be gone then, if you can't stomach the truth. We've still got our pride, my James and I. The day you take me back to Chadwick Park is the day you bury me . . . if the graveyard would even have me. A sinner amongst the saints."

"Oh," Josie gasped and stepped back. The taint of death had overtaken the hut, polluting the very air she breathed.

"And you can take your charity with you," Delia screeched as she flung the box of alms into the snow. A fit of coughing interrupted her curses as the door slammed shut on rusty hinges.

"I see you've finally had your fill of wretchedness," Aurelia observed as Josie scrambled into the sleigh. Without waiting for an answer, Aurelia barked, "Driver, take us back with all haste!"

Josie didn't dare to speak. Her gloved palms tingled. She clasped them in her lap, heart thundering an outraged cadence as blood surged to her cheeks. All those she had been foolish enough to trust had betrayed her. Charles had lied to her about Delia's whereabouts, and Esther had confirmed the lie. Even Delia's promises that she would be happy with James had been a lie. She, gullible Josie, had believed them all. Love had blinded her to the truth, and the price of her naiveté had cost her everything. Now her beloved sister was dying. Josie had sacrificed for her once, but in the end nothing could save Delia from herself. If something was not done, they would lose Delia to a fate worse than death. Her very soul was suspended in the balance. She had no hope in this world or the next.

Absorbed in her anger, Josie was startled when the motion around her ceased. The footman came around to assist Aurelia first, and Josie alighted with a toss of her head. She didn't have time to waste on formalities when every ounce of her depleted patience must be reserved for Charles.

As if on cue, his tall, squared form bounded around the corner. "Ah, there you are. I was beginning to wonder where you had gone off to when there is a foxhunt about to commence. On behalf of Guinevere and myself, I beseech you to accompany us."

Josie opened her mouth to refuse, but Aurelia beat her to a reply.

"Oh, I dearly love a rousing foxhunt. How good of you to ask the ladies, Charles. I most heartily accept. My Velveteen has been a little restless, and a hunt is just what she needs to spend her liveliness."

Josie was aware of Charles's silent plea as his long-suffering blue eyes pierced her.

"I scarcely see how I can refuse," she said with a calmness smeared over her fury. Perhaps a spirited ride would diffuse her anger enough to restore rational thought. "I'll go change into my riding habit."

Charles bent low until the words tickled her ears. "Before I let you come along, please promise me that you are as skilled riding sidesaddle as you are astride?"

"I assure you, sir, that I can hold my own."

"Don't misinterpret my concern. You've yet to even ride Guinevere."

"Don't forget why you asked me along either."

Charles's expression of bewilderment satisfied her as she marched up the steps and nodded to Craven. As she attacked the staircase, her resolve grew with each step. *It will do him good to reflect upon his actions and choices leading up to this point. Did he think me so stupid that I would never find out about my sister?*

Josie whipped the forest green riding habit out of her armoire, grateful Esther had insisted upon her purchasing it in Paris. Now she could hold her own against the blonde vixen, who was every bit as cunning as their quarry. She stabbed a hatpin through her hat and chignon.

As she descended the stairs, the shimmer of approval in Charles's gaze mollified her a fraction. He wasn't hard on the eyes either, with his long legs encased in fawn breechclouts and the breadth of his shoulders hugged by a forest green jacket. But Josie hardened her heart.

"On second thought," Charles said with a smile, "maybe I shouldn't take you with me. You and Guinevere may prove to be too much feminine charm and serve as a distraction."

"Flattery will only take you so far, Mr. Radcliffe."

"Implying that I have done something for which flattery cannot atone, I presume?"

"This is neither the time nor the place to discuss it."

He had the decency to look bewildered. "It seems we had a very similar conversation just last night, as I recall. How quickly I fall from your good graces, Mrs. Radcliffe."

"'Tis indeed a pity. Some things have been swept under the rug for far too long."

Aurelia emerged in a scarlet ensemble that fit her like a glove. Josie hid a smile, envisioning buttons popping off the overripe figure as she mounted her horse.

"My, my don't you two make a fetching couple in matching habits," Aurelia sang out. The mocking curve of her mouth intimated that it would take more than color to make them compatible. Josie bristled as Charles tucked her arm into his.

"Are we in readiness, ladies?" Charles queried, steering Josie toward the door before she could take the bait. Josie tasted blood as she bit her lip. She couldn't take much more from her incorrigible cousin.

Outside, she flung her sidesaddle across Guinevere's back with vehemence. She had saddled her own horses since the day in her youth when she'd been thrown. If it had been any horse other than Ebony, she would have been dragged to her death that day. Ever since, she had never trusted anyone else to make a horse ready for her.

Guinevere stood two hands higher than Ebony. Josie frowned as she cinched the girth tight. Most big horses were deficient in brain and made up for it in brawn. She hoped Guinevere possessed some sense behind her chiseled features.

She stroked the mare's velvety neck. Muscles shuddered beneath Guinevere's skin, sending a thrill through Josie. As though beseeching her trust, the mare's onyx eyes sought hers. Josie read the wisdom carved in their soulful depths and knew Guinevere sensed her pain and apprehension. The mare's breath came in soft blows as Josie surrendered to the voice her heart heard calling and rested her head against the horse's broad forelock. A bond was forged between them in that magical moment, knitting their hearts together for as long as they would hover between earth and sky with the wind as their song. Josie clung to the peace Guinevere offered like a gift as she struggled to mount.

From behind her, strong arms lifted her up like an eagle's wings. Charles's eyes were a blue shade of tenderness, like the sky after the rain, as their fingers twined.

"You're my woman," he said as he looked up at her. "You show the world that now. You show them your beautiful, brave sweetness of spirit that has called to me from the moment I met you. No one else could ever take your place in my heart."

Tears threatened to fall from her eyes, dousing her anger.

"I will," Josie whispered, not trusting herself to say more. Her thumb stroked the strength of his hand before he released her fingers with a sigh. He tugged at her gaze, striding to Stalwart's stall where the stomping stallion stood saddled. Out of nowhere, Byron bounded through the stable doors and danced around Stalwart's feet as Charles swung up. A rare laugh parted Charles's lips as he prodded Stalwart alongside her.

"Byron has never been content to merely be a bird dog since he discovered he can be a foxhound as well. Hunting is in his blood."

Josie's grudging smile answered his laughter as she nudged Guinevere forward, but the mare needed no coaxing. A bracing wind nipped her cheeks as they set off. The hunting party awaited them in the drive, and Aurelia waited in her place beside her father for a change.

Father prepared to open the kennel gate for Sebastian as he ensured the foxhounds' collars were secure. His dogs were the finest—but that was no surprise. Since when had her father-in-law possessed anything but the best his money could buy?

Josie sensed a gaze landing on her, and her eyes strayed to the mullioned windows. Disapproval hardened Esther's expression as the curtain fell. Josie recalled her suspicions of pregnancy with a frown. She still refused to believe it. She and Charles weren't ready for a child yet, and if Esther expected Josie to stay behind and let Aurelia ride off with her husband all for the sake of an unconfirmed suspicion, she could think again.

Sebastian motioned to Father, who swung the gate open. The hounds burst free and circled around the horses, quivering with enthusiasm as they waited for their master to give the signal. Their dark nostrils flared with the scent of their quarry on the wind. Every heart pounded, every muscle grew taut, and every eye fastened on Sebastian as he mounted his horse and raised his pistol. The shot cracked with a leaping tongue of flame, and the hounds lunged into a frenzy of motion as they ran into the pasture.

Guinevere shot forward at Josie's command with a thrust of power she had never experienced from a horse before. Her redingote tugged at her throat as the world washed away in a blur of colors and sounds. Josie's fingers tightened around the pommel as she shifted in the saddle to maintain her balance. There was no sense in begging the mare to pace herself. Guinevere's heart would push her until she had spent the last of her strength, and Josie would not insult the mare's spirit by asking her to do anything less.

Stalwart's head charged into her line of vision. Charles leaned across the stallion's neck with flapping coattails. His broad, breathless grin filled her with wonder. She was doing him proud. Her heart soared to heights of dizzying bliss as she surrendered to the pull of the sky. She was flying beyond the touch of pain and disappointment as the wind pulled her hair free from its pins. She never wanted this taste of freedom to end—she never wanted to lose touch with this dreamlike reality where she drank the wind. Tears seeped from the corners of her eyes as she released her grasp on the world.

Let Me carry you, My Beloved. Trust Me enough to carry you and all you hold dear. Let everything except the sight of Me fade away and rest. Peace, be still . . .

Time had never slipped by Josie with such ease. Then the hounds lost the scent in the blank canvas of open field. They panted and whined as though their canine hearts were broken, scouring every inch of snow for even a whiff. A howl of victory tore free from one throat, sending a thrill skittering down Josie's spine. The echoing bay was carried by every hound as they dashed into the forest.

Josie forced Guinevere to take it slow as they picked their way through the trees. The mare trembled as she brought up the rear, but she obeyed in spite of the insult to every vein of her blue blood. Human voices joined the hounds' resounding chorus, and Josie drew rein in a sharp slice of motion. The fox had given them a good chase. She couldn't bear to see the cunning creature slain.

Josie swung Guinevere's head around and patted her neck in reassurance. She would give the mare her head again once they were beyond the tree line.

Grim clouds hid the sun, brimming with the fresh threat of snow as Josie emerged from the trees' shadows. Guinevere's trotting stride reeked of impatience as Josie guided her to the top of the hill. The main road from Portreath was outlined in the snow like a smudged, leaden line across paper. Josie decided to take a shortcut through the forest to reach the road. She gave Guinevere her head, and they cantered as one through the sparse trees. Tremors traveled from her tailbone to her neck as Guinevere's shuddering muscles echoed the ominous gunshot. The mare tossed her head as a hush descended on the forest with the death of one of its denizens.

A moment later, a splitting crack sent Josie's heart plunging as Guinevere stumbled and backed away. Snow caved in where the mare had stood, sending chunks of ice sailing into slushy depths. Black, crackling fractures reached for them like skeletal fingers. Josie clutched the pommel as Guinevere lunged for the pond's edge in a surge of power. Her back hooves broke through with a gurgle, but the mare's forelegs churned for a stronger footing on the bank. She staggered over the mound of earth and then lunged into a full gallop, running with all her might from the threat behind them. Josie drew rein to no avail as Guinevere's possessed pace picked up speed.

A log glared in their path, but Guinevere refused to be steered as Josie sawed the reins. Her spooked muscles gathered beneath her like coiled springs as Josie's lips formed a protest. She seized the mare's tousled black mane between gloved fingers as Guinevere grew wings. The sidesaddle pitched to the side as they glided through thin air. Josie scrambled to right it, but gravity was stronger, and she crashed to earth.

Pain exploded across the base of Josie's skull, licking at the edge of her consciousness like an encroaching wildfire. Darkness stole over her. The caustic taste of fear landed on her tongue as she battled the shadow taking her away from the man who needed her. She recalled the way tender blue depths of his gaze had searched her soul with infinite longing. A plea was her answer to the silent cry of his heart. *Charles, don't let me go far . . .*

Chapter Twenty-Nine

An undignified whoop of triumph sprang from Charles's lungs as he watched the fox collapse. It had been a clean, merciful shot. Wind ruffled the prime red fur as he dismounted to examine his prize. The bullet had entered the base of the skull without damaging the rest of the pelt.

Feminine eyes fastened on him. His gut clenched when he met Aurelia's possessive gaze. The huntress's full lips curved, but the warmth of her smile did not reach her crystalline eyes. He tugged his hunting knife out of his boot and slit the fox's throat. Aurelia averted her head as Charles stepped back before the spreading warmth of blood could stain his breeches. His eyes roamed over the group. His nurturing Josie hated to witness any life taken, but she was not even lingering on the outskirts as he had expected. Anxiety welled in his chest.

"Has anyone seen Mrs. Radcliffe?"

The men's heads swiveled around. Aurelia's husky voice was swift with her response. "I fear she is too squeamish for such things. I saw her ride back."

"Why didn't you accompany your cousin, Aurelia?" Aurelius demanded. "It isn't seemly for an unmarried woman to accompany a whole hunting party of men!"

"I have no such qualms, Father."

Charles clenched his jaw at her insolence. A strong hand grasped his shoulder. "Stop fretting, son. Our Josie is a capable horsewoman, as you well know, but I'm sure she proved to be too tenderhearted for such a sport. No doubt she is waiting now with hot apple toddies prepared for us like any good hostess."

Mr. Chadwick nudged Roundhead closer. "Aye, you'll find my daughter waiting home for you, as I have on every hunt we ever contrived to take together."

"No doubt," Charles echoed, but their assurances did little to allay his apprehension.

Stalwart couldn't gallop through the windblown drifts fast enough for Charles. The party faded in his wake as their weary mounts enjoyed a leisurely pace. However spent, Charles knew Stalwart would exert the last of his strength for Josie.

Reaching the house, he dismounted, seizing the fox in his hands, and hammered up the front steps in the echo of his racing heart. He wrenched the door open.

"Craven, is Mrs. Radcliffe within?"

"No, Master Radcliffe. I was informed that she was with you."

"Are you absolutely certain she hasn't returned?"

"Mr. Radcliffe, I assure you I have never left my post," the head butler sputtered.

"I fear something has befallen her."

Craven's expression of surprise deepened to horror as Charles forced the limp body of the fox into his gloved hands.

"Now don't drop him, Craven. There's a prime pelt on him."

"Yes, sir."

The butler's weak tone snagged Charles's ear as he dashed down the steps. Byron awaited him at the bottom. The setter's sides heaved, and Charles winced as he took in the animal's ice-caked paws.

"Master Charles!"

The shrill young cry cocked all of Charles's reflexes as Alfie ran toward him.

"What is it, lad?"

"It's the mistress's horse," Alfie panted. "Guinevere just galloped into the stables as though the devil himself were at her heels. Something must have spooked her. She was all lathered up, and the mistress's sidesaddle hung from her belly."

"Thank you, Alfie." Heart pounding with dread, Charles knelt in the snow and ruffled Byron's feathery ears. He dug into his coat pocket and withdrew one of the embroidered handkerchiefs that Josie had given him for Christmas.

"I need you to find Josie for me, Byron. Find Josie."

Byron's ears perked in recognition, and he snuffled the cambric square as his molasses-brown eyes narrowed. Charles hoped he detected confidence in the setter's gaze. He swung into his saddle as Byron shifted his frozen paws in the cutting wind.

"Sorry, Stalwart, old fellow. We must find Josie with all haste."

Charles's heart leaped to his throat as Byron bent his head against the wind, resolve hardening the dog's narrow, fringed shoulders. He broke into a loping bound in the hunting party's track-riddled wake. Stalwart needed no coaxing as he followed Byron's lead. Charles doubted he had ever done enough for these animals to merit their sacrifice. But they made no complaint.

The temperature dropped until Charles's breath blew white. The first flakes of snow began to fall faster than the ticking seconds as a storm blew in from the sea. Charles grimaced at the remembrance of the fashionable yet impractical riding habit

Josie had worn. The redingote that had billowed around her with such filmy elegance had been unsuited to keeping the chill from biting through her bones. He tugged his greatcoat closer and hunched his shoulders.

The passing minutes felt like hours as Byron made feeble progress. In the blowing snow, their surroundings became unfamiliar as Charles squinted at the seemingly endless tree line. Each tree was as fathomless as the next as they stood in silent rows, guarding their elusive secrets.

"Josie!" Charles screamed.

The wind flung her name back at him with a mocking howl—but then he spotted the pockmarked snow of their entry into the forest. As he hesitated, Byron barked and continued to follow the tree line. Stalwart lunged forward of his own accord, and Charles repressed a shudder as the dread gnawed his gut. Byron stumbled into the forest, and Charles followed him as he realized with a sinking heart that had the dog not been leading him, he would have passed by the imperceptible tracks.

Byron located a set of hoof prints that branched away from the rest. The tracks led them across the meadow and back into the bowels of the wood as Byron picked up his pace.

"No, Byron," Charles cried as Byron set foot on a frozen pond. The setter's piteous whine prickled the hairs on the back of his neck as he studied the snow-covered ice with a dark patch of water in the middle. He stifled the urge to fling himself into the water and probe the murky bottom. If Josie had fallen in, she couldn't have survived more than a couple of minutes.

Byron's sharp bark drew Charles's fixated gaze away from the jagged edges of the break in the ice. He swung Stalwart's head around. The setter pressed his paws against crumpled green fabric in the snow.

Charles's lungs constricted until he struggled to breathe, strangling the cry that rose to his lips. He leaped from the saddle and rushed to her side. Her limp, twisted body looked so frail against the barren snow. He seized one of her hands in his own, praying for warmth, and the chilled stiffness of her gloved fingers struck terror into his heart like the knell of death.

"No, no, no," Charles choked out as his breath came in heaving gulps. He couldn't feel a pulse in her wrist nor hear it against the pounding of his own heart. The flimsy redingote had fallen over her face and gathered an inch of snow. He whipped it away from her beloved features, and the blue veins in her temples were a sharp contrast to her cheeks, which were as bloodless as the snow.

"Oh, dear God, no," Charles prayed as he reached for her mouth. His heart skipped a beat, waiting to feel a puff of life against his fingertips.

It was there. There was warmth in her lips as her moist breath blew, fragile as the flutter of a bird's heart against his flesh. Her brows were dark slashes above the lashed crescents of her closed eyes as her head tilted at an unnatural angle. He prayed she hadn't broken her neck in the fall, but he had to risk moving her. Charles unbuttoned his greatcoat at his throat and wrapped her in it as best he could. With infinite tenderness he cradled her in his arms and lifted her. The crimson splash against the snow sickened him, but he steeled himself with an effort and whistled for Stalwart. The stallion trotted over to him. The cold seeping through his shirtsleeves brought a sharp wave of consciousness.

"Down, Stalwart," Charles commanded with a quaver in his voice. Stalwart knelt, allowing Charles to crawl into the saddle with his precious burden.

"Up, Stalwart," Charles called, his legs gripping Stalwart's broad sides with all he was worth. The stallion stumbled to his feet, and Charles willed his tense muscles to slacken and flow with the stallion's movements.

"Home, Stalwart," Charles yelled above the mournful wind chilling the marrow in his bones. Byron lay in the impression of Josie's body, gazing up at him with wise eyes as shivers wracked his body.

"Home, Byron," Charles pleaded, and a pathetic whimper proceeded from the back of Byron's throat.

"I can't carry you too," Charles protested. He kneed Stalwart forward, but his heart winced at the thought of losing Byron. If the sight of his beloved master and mistress fading from sight into the trees wasn't enough to rouse the loyal setter, nothing would be.

Stalwart wound through the trees, but Charles couldn't bring himself to look back. Josie had to come back to him. He couldn't live without her, faced with the knowledge that he had so often rejected the love she offered him. He couldn't bury her knowing he had broken her precious heart. Even when he had feared losing her heart on Christmas Eve, he had not been able to bring himself to tell her that he loved her. Fear imprisoned the words inside him.

Guilt hounded him, clinging to him like a silent companion all the way back to Treathston.

Chapter Thirty

harles ran a hand over his gritty eyelids and smothered a yawn. His sleeping beauty had still not awakened. Faithful Byron had managed to limp home and join him in his lonely vigil at her bedside. Caring for the setter's frostbitten paws had been Charles's only reprieve. He glanced over at the hands of the clock. It was now midafternoon, but ever since last night, he hadn't dared to catch a wink for fear that the fragile rising and falling of her chest would cease altogether. The doctor said she had suffered a grave concussion.

Her Bible lay open on the nightstand. As though his eyes were captured by it, he leaned over to study it. The words gripped his heart with a holy squeeze of conviction.

> *For I am persuaded, that neither death, nor life, nor angels, nor principalities, nor powers, nor things present, nor things to come, nor height, nor depth, nor any other creature, shall be able to separate us from the love of God, which is in Christ Jesus our Lord.*

His name was written beside it in Josie's flowery hand. His grasp tightened around the fine bones and cool flesh of her hand, begging her not to leave him now. For once, Byron's pleading whine failed to move him as his eyes caressed her alabaster features. Through it all, she had loved him in spite of his being a selfish, cold-hearted wretch. Through it all she had pointed him to the God he had forsaken. Because of her, Charles could no longer swallow the lie that God had forsaken him. His heavenly Father had been a convenient scapegoat, a childish ideal of a fairy-like God upon whom he could heap blame.

As a man, he could not deny that the Almighty had been generous with His gift of free will. The choices men made did not reflect upon their God's goodness, nor did sin define God's nature. God had provided every means of deliverance from sin, but even when man's sinful choices hurt God's heart, He didn't turn His back. He pursued humanity with arms of love spread wide and provided ways for men to see His love.

The thought of it ached in Charles's heart now. For all these years God had seen his twisted brokenness, his perception of his heavenly Father mangled by the rejection of earthly parents. He had in turn rejected the One he thought should magically erase all of his wounds and right all his wrongs with a pinch of fairy dust, but the Lord's ways were higher and mightier than his own. He chose to heal through circumstances that pointed to the Healer. He chose to redeem His beloved's scars through the mercy of a woman's love until Charles understood that her love only reflected a Higher Love that nothing could separate him from. He hadn't run far without being forced to acknowledge the relentless presence of the God who refused to let him go.

Tears lapped the corners of Charles's eyes as the gracious goodness and provision of his God overwhelmed him.

Father, forgive me for running. Forgive me, Father, for my rejection of You when You already bore the ultimate rejection for me. Thank You for the priceless gift of my Josie. When You gave her to me, I am ashamed to admit I underestimated her worth, but she is a loyal daughter of Yours. She never let me look at her once without reflecting You. I couldn't bear to lose her now, Father. Please give me another chance to love her back. Please give me a second chance to love You, Father, for You are worthy of all I can give. I praise You and thank You for not giving up on me. Your mercy and Your love toward me, while undeserved, have known no end. Please redeem my broken life, precious Father, for I am Yours. In Jesus's name, Amen.

The peace that had eluded him for as long as he could remember flooded his being and rippled into the farthest corners of his mind. The Redeemer of his past, present, and future had forgiven him.

Charles gasped as, in those holy, fleeting seconds, her fingers tightened around his own. His heavenly Father had restored the broken and made all things new.

Josie cracked her eyes open, but the light turned into spearing pinpoints that jabbed up beneath her eyelids. A low moan escaped her as she scrunched them shut. Someone had taken an ax to the back of her head but failed to put her out of her misery.

"Doctor, Doctor, she's awake!"

The excited voice drifted to her, and she frowned as she tried to place it. It was a woman's voice.

Another tender murmur brought a sense of belonging with it. "Oh my dearest, have you come back to me at last? Please squeeze my hand if you can. Tell me I have not lost you forever, darling."

Josie concentrated and recognized a warm grasp surrounding hers. She squeezed back with an effort. "Charles, my Charles, I came back to you. I heard you calling me, love."

"Thank you, Father," he sobbed.

She tasted warm lips, salty with tears, and returned his kiss with all of her heart.

"Oh, I was so afraid I had lost you," he groaned.

"Permit me to examine your wife again, Charles, now that she has regained consciousness," a masculine voice said. "Mrs. Radcliffe, can you open your eyes for me?"

"The light hurts my eyes," Josie responded, squinting up at the vague form above her. Someone whisked the shades closed, enabling Josie to open her eyes the rest of the way. She recognized Dr. Lee's kind face as he held a candle close. Josie winced as her head seemed to split wide open, and the flickering tongue of fire threatened to gouge her eyeballs from their sockets.

"The pain will only last another moment," he murmured. He sat back at last and set the candle on the bureau. "When you fell, you suffered a concussion, Mrs. Radcliffe. Your left pupil is still dilated. I advise you to keep the lights dim until it returns to normal. I prescribe plenty of bed rest, at least until that goose egg on the back of your head shrinks, and light fare only. Nothing too rich or heavy. You may be a little nauseous from time to time. Mr. Radcliffe, I advise you to let her sleep now. When she awakes she will be much more rested."

"Certainly, Doctor. Thank you for everything. I'll show you out."

"I'll follow you out in just a moment," Dr. Lee responded. "I need a moment alone with the patient."

Charles blew her kisses, and Josie smiled back as he reached for the doorknob. Esther hesitated beside the door.

"Esther, please stay," Josie said weakly.

"I'll be back later, darling. You rest now," Charles ordered as he pulled the door shut.

Dr. Lee turned to Josie. "Might I have a private word with you, Mrs. Radcliffe?"

"Certainly," Josie consented. "Anything you have to say to me can be said in front of Esther." A frisson of unease stirred within her.

"I know this news could have come at a more opportune time, but I trust it will be happy news nevertheless. In my examination of you to ensure there were no internal injuries, I discovered that you are with child," Dr. Lee said with a twinkle in his brown eyes.

Alarm deepened the throbbing pound in her skull. Josie clutched her stomach, hating the quaver in her voice. "Is the baby all right?"

"Everything seems to be just fine. I would estimate that you are about three months along."

Josie's heart thrummed a breathless dance of ecstasy. How ironic that this little life was already inside her in that awful moment when she had overheard Charles and Sebastian arguing about the heir. Esther had known it all along, even as Josie had maintained that her frequent weariness was due to Christmas preparations.

"Thank God," Josie breathed as she returned Esther's broad smile. "You have not told anyone yet, I hope?"

"Certainly not. I hold that the wisest course is for the mother to do the telling. After all, she is the one doing all the work to bring a new life into the world."

Josie's joy dimmed a bit. Would Charles be pleased?

I don't believe in two people purposefully bringing a child into the world who will inevitably be scarred by events that began before the child's birth.

Josie swallowed her sense of disappointment. She couldn't tell him about the baby just yet. It was still too soon. She didn't want Charles to try to love her just because she was carrying his child.

"I know of an excellent midwife in Illogan. I could contact her for you if you like, though I shall also be in attendance if you should need me before the birth. You can rely on me to act with the utmost discretion."

"That would be most kind. I am most grateful to you for everything, Doctor."

"Thank me by making a full recovery, Mrs. Radcliffe. I want to see you back to your usual, smiling self."

"I will," she responded, smiling back.

"Well, I'll let your good husband show me out so you can follow my orders and get some rest."

The door clicked shut behind him, and Josie reached for Esther's hand.

"You knew it all along, but I was too stubborn to listen."

"All that matters is that ye and yer bairn are safe, luve," Esther murmured as she pressed a kiss to Josie's brow. "I'm so happy for ye and Charles."

"Please don't tell Charles yet, Esther. Not just yet."

"It's for ye and ye alone to do the telling, luve," Esther answered as she tucked Josie's hand beneath the covers and pulled them up to her chin. "Now ye must obey the doctor's orders. Yer resting for two now."

Josie's dragging lids didn't need coaxing as her eyes slid shut. She cupped her womb with a smile just before sleep claimed her.

Charles closed his eyes, but he could find no peace in the void of the night, rendered darker without the light of his Josie's presence. He could not continue on with his former pattern of indifference. All he wanted was to hold her tonight.

Byron echoed his sentiments by scratching at the door of her bedchamber with a mutant whine. Charles shushed him and snapped his fingers. Josie needed her sleep.

He didn't know how long he had lain there, filled with the ache of missing her. But just as he began to fade, a scream jolted him awake. It was his Josie. His heart raced as he sprang toward the adjoining door. The thick darkness smote him as he wrenched her door open. Not even a coal glimmered in her hearth. He could taste her terror in the deafening silence as she tried to make herself invisible to the predator that stalked her in the night.

Charles retreated to light a candle for her. With that offering of light he dared to approach, and as its flicker caressed her form, she drew up with a sharp cry against the headboard. It tore at his heart. How had he neglected to ensure she had light while she slept?

"Darling, it's only me, Charles," he said. One slim hand clutched the sheets in a tangled knot at her throat. Her knees pressed against her chest as her fisted hand shook. Trapped. Josie's eyes gouged his own, rendering her a stranger as fear honed her soft features. Cruel shadows lurked in the hollows and sockets of her face, emphasizing her delicate bones.

Charles swallowed hard, tasting her wretchedness, and set the candle on her nightstand as he waited for a glimmer of recognition. Did he dare to reach out and touch her if she were still asleep? Reason told him to be cautious. But his arms did not obey. Softness born of the tenderness in his heart bled through his strained voice as he pulled her into his arms.

"Josie."

The bed creaked beneath his weight. Her tortured eyes absorbed him as she flinched, but she did not resist as his arms enfolded her. She melted into his chest with a soft sigh as her arms locked around him. Her lungs shuddered with every breath as her hammering heart threatened to bruise itself against her ribs. This was no ordinary fear possessing her. Charles's every sinew tensed with the fierceness of his need to protect her.

"It was worse tonight, Charles."

Her voice wobbled as his grip tightened around the fleeting softness of her form.

"Tell me," he whispered.

"The woman's voice was not that of a refined lady, like I've always thought it was—it was roughened by tears, or perhaps an accent. The tune of the lullaby was familiar, but I can't remember the words."

She was not describing the contorted reality of a dream, but an event she had lived. A memory so terrible her conscious mind couldn't bear to reproduce it. Charles frowned as she continued, "The man's greatcoat reeked of pipe tobacco. He wrapped me in it, and I felt trapped. It was so cold. Icy flakes of snow stung my cheeks until he pressed me against him, and I thought I would suffocate. It always ends that way . . . suffocating as I try to get free."

Her shudder resonated in his chest. The dream was a jagged shard that did not fit into any period of her former life as she had known it. His jaw clenched. The only possible cause was a dark secret buried somewhere in her past. The unknown birthed a resolve in him.

"I fear I cannot make light of it for you, but I promise with every fiber of my being that from this night forward, I shall endeavor to chase it away from you forever."

She let out a soft gasp as he slid an arm under her legs and lifted her into his arms. He slid off the bed, blowing out the candle as he went. Her fingers traveled along his shoulder, arm brushing against his neck as she clung to him.

"Remember that night in Paris?" he asked as she rested her head against his shoulder—a gesture of trust that threatened to steal his breath away. He licked his dry lips. "You told me you had not had another nightmare since sleeping with me every night. So help me, you'll not spend another night alone."

Charles nudged the door open wider with his foot and opened his heart along with it. The firelight gleamed a welcome as he bent and deposited her in his bed. The broad expanse of sheets and pillows seemed to swallow her petite form . . . and the curves that were made for loving. His throat closed at the sight, and he tore his gaze away to light up her world. He laid another log on the fire and lit all the candles he could find until the room was ablaze with light. He found her watching him, and the candlelight illuminated the sheen of tears in her bewitching eyes. The sight sent him flying to her side.

"I'm here, my love, I'm right here," he reassured her as his fingers cupped her face. His thumb caught a tear as it slipped from her lashes.

"That's why I'm crying. You're all here, Charles. I know I have all of you right here, for the first time."

His heart smote him as he nodded, knowing it was true. Oh, the world of pain that could be found in the simple truth. "I know it, Josie."

His voice caught with the confession. He was powerless to hold the tears back. He blinked as she leaned closer and kissed them away. He turned his head, and their lips met as they tasted each other as if for the first time. He buried his fingers in the mane of soft waves flowing down her back as she wrapped her arms around his neck. A low moan sounded in her throat as he deepened the kiss. She went limp in his arms as they fell into the featherbed.

"Say it again," she gasped between kisses.

He paused in surprise. "Say what again?"

"My name."

The fragments of memory stirred and fell together. He had never called her Josie, with the exception of that time in Paris when he feared he had lost her. The realization had never penetrated that she was Josie to him only in his thoughts. He hadn't been prepared to give her that place of intimacy in his heart. Now he knew he could never call her anything else. She had been right in what she said several months ago. Josephine simply did not fit the woman he loved.

"Josie," he murmured, nuzzling the sloping curve of her neck. "My own dear, sweet, beloved Josie."

She shivered, but he knew she wasn't cold. It was a shiver of desire, echoing the same desire that coursed through his veins. His lips fastened upon the hollow of her throat where her pulse throbbed with it.

"Stanzas to Josie," she whispered.

Charles's lips broke away from her skin.

"How the devil did you know about that?" he growled with mock wrath.

Her lips curved with playful warmth, and the teasing gleam in her eyes sent his heart galloping. "My husband is very poor at hiding what he doesn't want found . . . his poems and his heart."

"His wife is blasted determined for a woman. A trait I find insufferably adorable."

"How do you find me?" Josie asked, her gold-flecked eyes serious. Remorse nagged like hunger pangs at the sight of her insecurity.

"Delicious," he teased and grunted when Josie shoved him away. She squealed as he caught her by the waist, halfheartedly resisting his caresses.

"I find that I love you more with each passing day, Josie, and the day I thought I would have to live without you was the day I realized I had brought it upon myself by not returning your love."

Josie went very still in his arms, and fresh tears stung his eyes as he released her. He crawled to the edge of the bed and knelt on the cold floorboards. Their eyes fused with mutual tears.

"I bow before you now as the man whose heart is your throne, but we both remember a time in the not too distant past when my heart was cold and denied you the devotion and love you deserve. I find that unforgivable, but I believe God has forgiven me. I clasped your hand at your bedside and begged God not to let my innocent wife suffer because of my selfishness. God and I haven't been close for many years, but that was because of my own bitterness. Can you, Josie, find it in your heart to forgive me?"

Josie blinked away tears. "I confess I bore bitterness in my heart toward you a long while, Charles. Then God grasped my heart with conviction. It wasn't my job to fix you. He called me to love you as He Himself loves you, as His child. I forgave you then, and I forgive you now, Charles. I also forgive you for lying to me about Delia. Now you need to find it in your heart to forgive yourself."

Charles frowned at the fresh accusation. "I don't know what you are referring to . . . I've never lied to you about Delia. Esther told me they had left Cornwall."

"Oh Charles, it was all a dreadful misunderstanding, and I'm sure Esther was only trying to protect me. The Bible says that charity thinketh no evil, but as your wife I have always been quick to assume the worst of you. Please forgive me."

Charles read guilt and sorrow in her features. Fresh tenderness welled in his chest.

"Beloved, there is no need to ask my forgiveness when I was the one who gave you cause to doubt countless times. I know Delia's dire straits have wounded my bride's soft heart. What can I do to alleviate your suffering?"

"You do understand me, don't you?"

The wonder in her voice sent his heart tripping. "Believe me when I tell you that I want to with all that I am."

She brushed the hair away from his forehead as their eyes held. "It's just that I did everything in my power to free her from the obligations that would ruin her life. I sacrificed everything to make her happy . . ."

"And she chose the path of destruction," Charles finished.

Josie nodded with glistening eyes, and Charles wiped moisture from the corner of her lashes.

"Let me send them where her husband can make a decent living at something other than mining. Our sugar plantation is in need of British management. Maybe the warmer climate will cure her lungs. All we can give her is a second chance and leave the rest in God's hands."

Rivulets streamed down her face in liquid relief. "I take it back," she whispered. "I didn't sacrifice everything. I risked my heart in a step of faith when I had everything to lose . . . only to gain the heart of the man God knew would complete me."

"How did I win your heart? How did you love me through all of those cold, lonely nights knowing I was drinking?"

"Love is sacrifice, darling. God is love, and Love became the ultimate sacrifice for us. How could you have known what Love was if I had not loved you with the same Love with which I have been loved?"

Charles could only sit there and drink in the beauty of this miracle that had happened to him.

"Would you get off that cold floor, Mr. Radcliffe?" Josie burst out. "The night is young, and we've got a lot of loving to make up for."

"Oh Josie," Charles whispered. "I really do love you."

Her brows lifted at him as he drew close. "And I really do love you, Charles, even if you sorely try my patience at times."

He chuckled then, but the chuckle died in his throat as she leaned forward and grazed his lips with a tenderness more addicting than any wine.

"Now Aurelia never kissed you like that, did she?"

Charles groaned. "Don't go and remind me of that she-cat!" he complained. "My lips were bruised for a week!"

"If she is a cat, then what am I?" Josie demanded.

Charles grinned as he took her in his arms once more. "You, my love, bear no resemblance whatsoever to any mortal creature. You are an angel flown to earth."

Chapter Thirty-One

Josie stirred, drinking in the warmth of Charles's arms as the budding petals of their love unfurled. She wanted to halt these blossoming moments in time when the sacred birth of his love for her was tender and new. They were so absorbed in their relationship that time had slipped by like an afterthought as she recovered from her injury.

His chest rose and fell against her back as he drew deep, rhythmic breaths. A shiver of content coursed through her as she remembered her hands splayed against delineated muscle. *Thank you, Father, for giving me Charles's heart.*

A tender smile curved Josie's mouth as the groping fingers of dawn caressed her skin. Charles held his child as well as his bride. In his arms, sheltered and cherished, the edges of reality blurred. A blissful sigh escaped her.

Charles's breathing quickened against her hair. He arched with a yawn. Moist lips fastened against her temple.

"Oh, Charles, I wish you could hold me like this forever," Josie murmured.

"In my heart I always will, beloved," he whispered.

She half-turned, and he brushed the hair away from her forehead. His mouth pressed against hers. Josie buried her fingers in his hair as she drank in the warm adoration of his lips.

"I love, love, love you," he mumbled with a drowsy huskiness that she found delicious.

"Oh, darling, waking up beside you all these winter mornings has been so lovely. Why am I still afraid?"

"Are you afraid of losing me all over again?" Charles groaned. The unvoiced ache in his heart haunted her.

"I'm afraid that this happiness is too good to last. It's been several weeks since that night, and ever since I've felt your love was a cocoon, sheltering me from the harsh reality of life. Someday I'm afraid I'm going to emerge into the blinding sunlight and find it's all been a dream."

"Just remember that I've got you," he said as he pressed a hand over her heart. "I won't ever let go, Josie. I promise. Together we have wings to fly through whatever life brings."

Josie covered his hand with hers, absorbing the promise as his palm resounded with her heartbeat. "I believe you, beloved."

His sigh of relief fanned her cheek as her stomach rumbled in the stillness. Charles chuckled.

"I'll bring you up a breakfast tray this morning."

"Why can't the servants bring it up?"

"And deprive me of the pleasure of selecting your favorites?"

Charles planted one more kiss on her forehead, and Josie melted in his arms. He released her, but she basked in his worship as he tugged his clothes on as though unable to tear his eyes away.

"I'm not going anywhere, my love," he promised.

His boyish grin caused the blood to rush to her cheeks as he pulled the door shut. Her husband's eyes had never been so blue. She wanted to kindle that youthful light in their topaz depths again and again until that smile was a fixed expression on his face.

Her fingers splayed across her abdomen as a tremor gripped her. She'd lost count of the times the news had tingled on her lips, but she still didn't think it wise to tell him about the baby so soon. A sense of unease clung to her like the cloying perfume had clung to the woman's gown in her nightmare.

Who are you? Why can't you just leave me be? Will this sense of loss and abandonment haunt me forever? What secret holds such power over me still?

The tendrils of mother-love wafted and curled around Josie's heart, the feeling toward her unborn child almost over-powering. A vow rose fierce in her breast. Her child would never suffer such doubts. Her child would always know it was beloved.

Charles nudged open the door, interrupting her musings. Josie stifled a laugh at the sight of the groaning tray in his hands.

"I hope you don't expect me to polish all of that off by myself."

The crystalline blue of Charles's eyes sparkled like sunlight bouncing off ocean waves. "Rest assured that I will finish what-ever crumbs remain."

A knock rapped at the door. An unnamed dread writhed in the pit of Josie's gut as Charles called for whoever it was to enter.

"Forgive the disturbance, sir, but Mr. Haverhill's done called. He's waiting on you in the drawing room."

"Thank you, Genevieve."

"Must you go?"

Josie winced at her own tone. She sounded like a petulant child. His smile was patient as he turned to her.

"Just rest, my love, and you'll hardly miss me."

A sigh escaped her. "I grow weary of resting. I shall go mad with boredom."

Charles darted to his bureau and retrieved a familiar red volume. "This should amuse you. Byron took the words right out of my mouth . . . however, they are more aptly poetic than if I had penned them."

"I doubt that."

He returned her smile, and then he was gone. The worn leather caressed her palms as she cracked its pages open. Her restlessness mounted with each passing minute, robbing her of focus. She wished she would have thought to ask him to fetch her Bible. She could use the peace it would afford.

As the minutes stretched into hours, her restlessness increased to alarm. Her eyes strayed to the bell pull. She knew better, but a body could only take so much suspense before it cracked under the strain. Patience never had been her greatest virtue.

Josie whipped back the covers and planted both feet on the floor. Her legs trembled as she took a determined step forward and then another. A wave of inertia blurred her vision as she seized the tasseled cord and yanked. Her lips tightened into a firm line. She refused to faint.

"Sakes alive, Mistress. One would think the world had gone deaf from the way that bell carries on!"

"Where is my lady's maid?"

Sadie pursed her lips. "I'm not saying 'twas her, mind you," she began with a quaver in her voice. "But when I done passed, a woman was crying her eyes out in the vicinity of her room."

A whisper of trepidation fluttered in Josie's chest as she recalled her fears that such happiness was too good to last. Esther had never been wont to show such displays of emotion… something would have to be very wrong indeed.

"Then where is my husband? Has Mr. Haverhill taken his leave yet?"

Again, the scullery maid hesitated. Josie sank back onto the edge of the bed and clutched her throbbing temples.

"I believe so, Mistress. I can try to fetch Master Charles for you. Would you like me to help you change into a fresh night-shirt first?"

"That would be most kind of you, Sadie. I fear I have been most trying of late. Do forgive me."

"Oh no, Mistress," Sadie burst out. "You are an angel. If you don't mind me saying so, Master Charles was in one of his tempers, and I was afeared to speak to him."

Josie closed her eyes to shut out the whirling room.

"Mistress?"

The voice sounded miles away. A soft touch of tangible reality landed on her shoulder and gave her something to hold on to.

"I'm all right, Sadie."

"You shouldn't have gotten out of bed, Mistress. You're still too weak to stand with your poor legs shaking like a newborn lamb."

"I confess he has a frightful temper betimes," Josie admitted, ignoring Sadie's concern. "But what is amiss with this house-hold, I wonder?"

A tremor traveled through the hand on her shoulder as the maid shuddered. "Ever since that yule candle gone out, it's as though the house is holding its breath . . . waiting for something dreadful to happen."

A denial rose to Josie's lips, but she found she couldn't give voice to it. Her hand itched to cover her womb, but she sup-pressed the urge.

"Josie."

Josie's eyes flew open as Charles stalked in. Everything about him screamed defeat, from his sunken shoulders to the strain pinching his lips. Every nerve inside her leaped with a sharp thrill.

"You had a spell, didn't you?" he demanded.

Sadie shrank from him as his gaze bored through her.

"What did you tell her?" he barked.

Josie grasped the icy cold hand as the scullery maid jumped. She forced calmness into her voice. "Don't frighten her, Charles. I grew restless and rang the bell. She has done nothing wrong."

"Your face is as pale as parchment," he said with a frown. "Thank God the doctor called and can take a look at you."

Josie had failed to notice Dr. Lee standing there. As she caught his eye he smiled, but grim shadows grazed his features. An elusive entity lurked in haggard lines around his eyes and mouth, and his smile failed to chase it away.

"How do you fare this morning, Mrs. Radcliffe?"

"I'll not try to pretend, unlike the rest of you, that I am not experiencing anxiety."

The doctor's bewildered expression matched the creasing of Charles's features as they exchanged a worried glance.

"I am not blind, gentlemen," Josie burst out. "I beg you to cease all of this nonverbal nonsense and get right to the point. Charles should know me well enough to understand that trying to hide anything from me is a futile effort. Darling, what were you afraid Sadie had told me?"

"We're trying to protect you, Josie. In your condition you mustn't suffer any excitement," Charles huffed.

For a moment Josie feared Dr. Lee had told him about the baby before realizing he spoke of her injury.

"Allow me to examine you," the doctor said. Josie's mind raced in frantic rhythm with her heart as she surrendered to his gentle ministrations. When he finished, she seized his hand before he could pull away.

"I know you're impatient, Mrs. Radcliffe, but you are recovering nicely. These things take time."

"You just came from Chadwick Park, didn't you?"

His eyes found her coverlet fascinating, giving Josie her answer. Tears burned as her heart sensed the truth. The silence mocked her, halting between life as she had always known it and a shattering whose fragments would pierce her innermost soul.

The doctor patted her hand and took back his own as her grip slackened.

"I advise you to tell her, Charles, before she hears it from a less discreet source. Your wife is strong, and it will be easiest coming from you. Perhaps you can cushion the shock."

Charles sighed as Dr. Lee retrieved his bag.

"If you should need me for any reason, you know where to find me. I dare not risk giving her a sedative when she is recovering from a head injury."

The door clicked shut as Sadie followed the doctor out. Josie struggled to breathe as Charles sank onto the bed. His strong arms surrounded her, pulling her into the warmth of his solid chest. Josie buried her face against him, clenching her fists.

"No, no, no," she groaned, her voice muffled by his waistcoat.

"How does one find the words, knowing they will cause the love of his life such pain?"

Josie tensed, awaiting the blow. The blood roared in her ears.

"Last night your father's heart stopped beating."

The words rumbled through her, shattering the blissful dream they had awakened to only that morning. Her heart squeezed with pain, bleeding in trickling drops that rained down her cheeks. And nothing, not even Charles's love, could staunch the mortal flow.

Chapter Thirty-Two

*J*osie shuddered as the ominous folds of cloth encompassed her, dark as midnight. The seamstress gathered the black bombazine in her hand and adjusted it with a critical eye. She removed a pin from her lips.

"Please turn, Mrs. Radcliffe," she mumbled.

Josie obliged, swallowing her sigh. It was not Mrs. Burnett's fault that black was the color of mourning. God knew she had postponed her fittings as long as she dared. Her injury had been the perfect excuse, and she had even borrowed a black dress from Esther for the funeral rather than be fitted with her own. Unfortunately, she was no longer a little girl. She could no longer hide in her bedchamber until the storm passed—though the prospect of drowning in her cauldron of grief was tempting. Charles had been so wonderful throughout the ordeal and funeral details. The most she had really done was to attend, but she could no longer neglect her own duties, including ordering her mourning garb.

A long day loomed ahead of her in all of its unpleasantness. Father's solicitors had contacted her, requesting certain papers before they could proceed with the legalities of reading the will. Josie dreaded going through Father's desk and sorting through all of his personal effects after the long ride back from Mrs. Burnett's dress shop in Truro.

"There. Now is there anything else you would be wanting?" Mrs. Burnett asked as she finished all of her measurements and removed the pins. The material fell away from her like unshackled chains.

"No, dear, that will be all."

"Everything should be ready to be picked up within two weeks."

Josie winced. That was what she got for dawdling, but the high-waisted style would be forgiving of her swelling belly.

"How much do I owe you?"

"Oh, you needn't pay me until you pick them up."

"Allow me to pay you now. I know business is slow this time of year."

The widow blinked her surprise. "Certainly, Mrs. Radcliffe. It comes to seven pounds and a shilling."

Josie fumbled for her reticule and held out a ten-pound note. Mrs. Burnett stared.

"I'm sorry, but I fear I haven't the change for you at the moment."

Josie reached for the elderly woman's veined hand and pressed the note into her palm. "Keep the change as a tip for your excellent services," she urged.

Mrs. Burnett's smile wobbled as though it were rusty from disuse. "I'm most grateful. Please accept my condolences, Mrs. Radcliffe. Your father was a good soul."

Josie contrived to smile, but grief had dimmed her spirit. "Thank you, Mrs. Burnett. He was indeed."

Josie emerged into the weak February sunlight and squinted. The shadows of the Radcliffe coach afforded a little comfort, hiding her from the prying eyes of the town. Ever since Father's death, the harsh edges of reality had cut into her soul. She had no kinship with the sunshine since grief had clouded her happiness. Storms held the pull of empathy for her. Fresh tears stung her eyes at the remembrance of the budding child growing within her. Her father would never get to hold his grandchild. She had never even gotten to watch joy brightening the depths of his eyes at the news. Death had robbed her of him, denying her even a good-bye. These days, that wounded her most.

The endless blues and greens of the sea flew by the coach window, bringing a semblance of peace. The restlessness of the waves mirrored her soul, whispering the endless passage of time. Life always had and would continue to go on amidst loss.

The lull of motion ceased with a lurch in the drive of Chadwick Park, startling her. Her thoughts had gobbled up the miles faster than the horse's hooves. The footman's seat creaked, followed by the crunch of his boots biting the frozen gravel.

Josie took a deep breath as he opened the side door, shedding a path of light across her lap. She gripped his proffered hand in case of ice as she alighted.

The front door swung open as though of its own accord as she approached, and Graham broke with his traditional stoicism to smile a broad welcome. "This old house has surely missed you, Miss Josie," he said with gentle warmth. Josie stroked the solid oak of the doorway as she entered.

"I miss it and my childhood," she whispered. He nodded in sympathy, and she patted his shoulder in passing. A lump formed in her throat as the library door loomed. Her footsteps rang hollow in the hall. She steeled herself as she swung the door open.

The heady onslaught of leather and tobacco assailed her with memories. Her father's presence clung to the very air she breathed, but the library was cold for the first time in Josie's eighteen years. She gulped back a sob as she paused by his chair. His spectacles lay on top of an overturned book alongside his pipe and decanter. The glass was still half-full, and he had been reading Virgil. Her fingers caressed the worn spine and traveled to rest on the arm of the chair. She could almost feel his hand beneath hers.

Blinking away the tears, Josie turned toward his desk with dread. Every step she took was an intrusion, every disturbance of the way he had left things a sacrilege to his memory.

She retrieved the key to his roll-top desk from the urn over the mantel and inserted it into the lock. The magnificent walnut panels slid back, revealing ink stains and unorganized cubby holes. Josie scraped back the chair and sat down with heaviness weighing on her chest. The words of the letter echoed through her memory.

Due to unresolved financial discrepancies, we would be most grateful if you would be so kind as to send us your father's ledger to review.

Josie doubted the ledger would be difficult to locate. She began pawing through the sheaves of papers and correspondence, but her shoulders slumped as she only unearthed more mess with each drawer.

A bundle of letters tied with an ink-stained yellow ribbon caught her eye. Her hand stilled on the edge of the drawer as she recognized the sweeping flow of the handwriting with a sharp thrill of disappointment. Against her will, Josie's fingers stretched out and closed over the paper, worn and creased from the lingering touch of time. She pulled the loop of ribbon free, torn between fear of knowledge and letting the unknown sleep undisturbed.

Within the first few words, her world crumbled further into dust and ashes.

"Esther, how could you?" Josie whispered. She forced herself to unfold the letter further and willed the words to stop swimming before her eyes.

My Dear Randolph,

I miss ye madly. I ken I sound like a petulant child, but I am so lonely. Please come to me, my own love, and make me forget the imperfect world we live in. I only want to feel yer arms around me once more. My love for ye cannae recognize the boundaries that part us. I beg ye to tear these walls down. I have tried in vain to be content apart from ye.

Yer Highland Chridhe

Numbness enfolded Josie as she folded the paper and tossed the sheaf into the drawer. What *chridhe* meant she neither knew nor cared. Father had lied about Esther, and Esther's very presence in and of itself had been a lie.

The smug ledger resided in the following drawer. She seized it, catching a glimpse of penciled sums before a torn book page fell out. It was crumpled as though Father had wanted to throw it away and thought better of it. Josie frowned as she bent and picked it up. Father would never mutilate one of his beloved books. She smoothed the paper over her knee and flipped it over. A skull leered up at her, and Josie's heart beat faster as she studied the cavernous eye sockets. It was an anatomical drawing torn from a medical book. She squinted in an attempt to decipher the smudged scrawl in the corner.

RIP Randolph Chadwick . . . You won't live to see 1819!—H.C.

Josie leaped to her feet, knocking over the chair. Her eyes followed the fluttering page's descent to the floor with horrified fascination. She pressed a hand to her stomach and gulped for air. When she closed her eyes, she saw the ghost's filmy arm reaching out to extinguish the candle.

Ever since that yule candle gone out, it's as though the house is holding its breath . . . waiting for something dreadful to happen. Mark my words, Master Radcliffe. There'll be a death in this family before the New Year is out.

Josie snatched up the ledger and slammed the roll-top shut. The avalanche of papers could wait. She stabbed the key into the lock and tossed it back into the urn. A shudder possessed her as she bent and picked up the page with two fingers as though it were the tail of a dead rat. A lone thought punctuated her existence like an ugly blot of evil as she stuffed the letter into her reticule . . . had Father been murdered? Did *H.C.* stand for Highland Chridhe, or for someone else?

"Miss Josie, you look as though you've seen a ghost," Graham said as she clipped her way toward the door.

"Graham, I want you to lock up the library. On no condition whatsoever is anyone allowed in there. I don't want anything of my father's disturbed. Is that understood?"

"Of course, Mistress," Graham said with widened eyes, no doubt attributing her outlandish actions to the madness of grief.

The footman scrambled down to escort her down the icy walkway, but Josie had already reached the coach.

"Mrs. Radcliffe, you are shaking like a leaf. Are you quite well?"

"No, I doubt very much that I will ever be well again."

The footman's lips were a thin white line of shock as she stepped into the coach. "I, I'm sorry," he stammered. "Am I taking you home now then, Mistress?"

"No, you're taking me to Dr. Lee as fast as you can manage."

"Yes, Mistress, right away."

The horses thundered down the drive, but Josie preferred the rattling of her bones to the torment of her thoughts. She wouldn't rest until she heard from Dr. Lee's own lips that Father had died of natural causes.

The doctor's humble cottage appeared, tucked into the snowy Cornish countryside. The thought thundered over and over in her mind. *Murder. My father was murdered.*

Please, God, no. I don't know how much more suffering I can take.

Josie did not allow the footman time to assist her, seizing the handle and wrenching the door open. She darted up the brick steps and pounded on the door. When Dr. Lee opened it, Josie suspected that nothing ever disrupted that mask of calm.

"Oh, thank God you're home, Doctor!" she burst out.

"Mrs. Radcliffe, you look unwell," he stated, taking her elbow. Josie resented him for stating the obvious.

"Please have a seat and take a deep breath to calm yourself," he said as he waved at the shabby furniture. For the first time in her life, Josie didn't care to follow the doctor's orders. She dug into her reticule and thrust the sinister page in the doctor's face.

"What I need to know from you is whether or not my father was murdered."

Blood drained from the middle-aged man's cheeks as he studied the cryptic note. "Sometimes I fear you can read my mind, Mrs. Radcliffe. You must stop it, for you are too feminine for such grisly details."

"The fact that I am a female has nothing to do with it."

"I meant no insult, Mrs. Radcliffe. My conscience has not been clear since the funeral, but I haven't known how to tell you of my suspicions, especially since you just suffered a serious head injury."

Josie wrung her fingers. "You think murder is a strong possibility, then?"

"As you know, your father suffered from a weak heart for a good number of years. However, he had seemed to be doing better of late. He was found dead in his chair in the library the morning I was summoned, and by the time I got there, rigor mortis had already set in. It impeded some of my observations, but not enough to allay all suspicion. It did appear to me at first that he had died from heart failure, but his pupils were fully dilated. That struck me as odd, and I remembered reading that heart failure induced by digitalis results in dilated pupils. His attitude was not that of a man whose heart had simply given out, but that of a man who had experienced cardiac distress before breathing his last. I took the liberty of obtaining a sample of liquor from the glass by his chair for testing. I just got the results back from London this morning. It tested positive for digitalis, I'm afraid."

Josie's hand flew to her mouth as the air whooshed from her lungs. The doctor paused to take her hand, but his warmth was foreign to the ice in her veins.

"Whoever wanted to see your father dead, Mrs. Radcliffe, wanted it to appear as though he had died from natural causes related to his heart condition and was nearly clever enough to get away with it."

Horror twisted Josie's insides like the poison that had killed him. Who could have wanted Father dead?

Chapter Thirty-Three

*J*osie's tailbone screamed in the straight-backed chair. The swinging pendulum of the barrister's clock counted the agonizing seconds as she questioned her wisdom in not contacting the authorities. The will would be read, and no one else knew what she and the doctor knew—that her father's death had been unnatural, premeditated murder. For all she knew, the murderer sat inwardly gloating in this very room. It struck her as odd that Father's barrister was reading the will instead of his solicitors. Perhaps Father had feared the will's contents would be contested, but for what reason?

Charles reached for her hand, stroking comforting circles of warmth into her skin. Guilt wracked her heart at his touch, but she justified hiding the truth from him by recalling the heat of his temper. She couldn't risk having her cover blown when it was her only chance to discover the identity of Father's killer. Sebastian and Aurelius shifted beside him as though they also found the mounting suspense unbearable. Josie prayed the will would give her some answers. She gnawed at her lower lip as her gaze strayed to Aurelius. Father's cousin had always seemed the typical country squire, shallow and self-conceited, but otherwise harmless—or so she had always thought. Now she wondered if anyone was who they seemed deep down. She gripped Charles's fingers tighter, marveling at their feverish, thawing heat.

The barrister rose from his desk and paused to straighten the tumbling, powder-white curls of his wig. Peering through pince-nez, he intoned in a voice worthy of gravel:

"This is the last will and testament of the late Randolph Chadwick Esquire concerning his estate, Chadwick Park. I, Randolph William Chadwick, being of sound mind and health on the 23rd of July, 1817, do hereby bequeath my estate and all that I possess to my cousin, Aurelius Haverhill—"

The words slammed hoof-like into Josie's gut. She fought for breath as Sebastian leaped to his feet. "There must be some mistake!" Sebastian roared, quivering from head to toe.

The barrister's withering glance skewered him. "Kindly sit down, Mr. Radcliffe, and do not interrupt these proceedings until the will has been read in its entirety."

The mottled rage of Sebastian's cheeks deepened to purple at the barrister's patronizing tone, but he perched himself on the edge of his chair. The room whirled as Josie's head swam in shock.

The barrister cleared his throat as he squinted through the pince-nez at the parchment document.

"To my illegitimate daughter, Josephine Chadwick Radcliffe, I bequeath an annual annuity of £100 to be granted at the time of my death. In the case of her untimely death, it will revert to Aurelius Haverhill's estate. Her relations are not permitted to exercise it upon her behalf."

Illegitimate. The word plunged sharp through Josie's heart, severing her identity from her existence. The rest of the barrister's words were muted by the sheer volume of the cry within her. Her entire life had been a lie.

Warm strength surrounded her shoulders as she turned to meet Charles's gaze. As his fingers gripped her shoulder, the message in his expression was clear. He would never let go of her, no matter what the cost. Eyes of Copenhagen blue shone with a love that touched and held her trembling being.

The droning of the barrister's voice ceased, and Sebastian exploded with a gale's fury. His vehemence sent a cold chill spiraling down Josie's spine.

"I demand an explanation of this."

"My dear sir, you are not in a position to demand anything."

A volley of sailor-worthy epithets streamed from Sebastian's mouth.

"Father, I beg you to control yourself in the presence of a lady," Charles protested.

Josie shrank away as Sebastian shook his finger in her face with an expression of venomous disgust. "Josephine Chadwick is no lady. She is the illegitimate bastard wench of a whore. I hope you are satisfied now that you have wormed your way into the Radcliffe name and legacy, you little snit!"

Something in Josie snapped as she looked into the icy blue eyes, piercing through her like cruel slivers of glass. She would not be abused in this way. Before she could form a word, Charles shot to his feet, his eyes crackling with electric sparks. Josie touched his arm in warning and answered Sebastian herself.

"So you have reaped what you sowed, Sebastian. To satisfy your greed, you connived to snag what you thought to be the Chadwick heiress nearly at the price of your son's eternal happiness. I am as shocked by these revelations as you are, but I feel no pity for you. I refuse to stand for your insults and disparaging remarks. You have made your bed, and now you can lie in it."

Charles stepped in front of her, interpreting the motive behind Sebastian's twitching fingertips before she did. Josie fled as the room erupted. She slammed the door, muffling the battle within as she sagged against the wall. She no longer had the strength to hold back the blinding tears as they rained down her cheeks.

The knob twisted, and Charles's blurred form crossed the threshold. His eyes flashed through her tears.

"We are going home, Josie. Let the dogs fight over their bones."

"Where is home, Charles?"

"With me."

His grimness frightened her, but the tenderness of his fingers belied his tone as he skimmed the wetness from her cheeks. She fell into step beside him, thrusting each foot into a future she could no longer trust.

Once within the temporary haven of the coach, Josie crumpled in a ball of hurt.

"Shhhhh, don't cry. Don't cry now, my own love," Charles murmured, pulling her into his arms. "I promise you it will be all right, Josie. I'll fix it, just like I sent Delia and James on their way this morning."

Anger flared deep inside her. He didn't understand—he was brushing away her pain and betrayal as if she were a little child with a sore finger. She pulled away with a sharp breath. It hurt even to breathe.

"You can't make me legitimate, Charles. Nor can you tell me who my mother is or why my father died so suddenly."

Charles pulled a letter out of his waistcoat pocket and offered it to her with brimming pain in his eyes.

"Maybe this has the answers, Josie. God knows, all I want is to spare you further suffering, but I feel as though my hands are tied. Your father gave it to me on our wedding day for safekeeping."

Josie recognized her father's penmanship. Fear and hope struggled for supremacy as she took the letter and broke the wax seal.

My Beloved Josie,

I write this to you now not knowing when the time will come for you to read it, but I know the day will come when you must learn the circumstances of your birth. For reasons I will leave unmentioned, I believe that might be sooner than any of us expect. Now that I am an old man I see the suffering my sins have caused you. Forgive me, dearest child, for I love you very, very dearly. You must always know that, even when my own selfish choices may have indicated otherwise.

You are the daughter of the woman I loved in my youth, and she is the only woman I have ever loved. You are the daughter of my heart. I fear it would be unwise to reveal her name to you now. It would only cause you further pain, so I will err on the side of caution. She was a good woman of humble birth with a heart of gold. She remains the most beautiful creature I have ever laid eyes on. You remind me of her so much, Josie. I am grateful that you inherited her kind, gentle spirit. Her nurturing instincts will be of good stead to you one day when you bear children of your own.

Rose was the woman I married for status and wealth. She married me for my name. We were not very happy, two selfish creatures coexisting together. I thought it best for you to think that you were Rose's daughter. The doctors told us that Rose could not have another child after Delia, thus I took you from your mother, whom I still visited quite frequently in a love nest of ours. She gave you up unwillingly, but I knew it was best for you to be raised in a home that could provide you with everything you deserved. I lost her shortly thereafter, and it was my own doing. May God forgive me. I find that I still cannot forgive myself for the suffering I caused her, the love of my life, and you, the perfect culmination of the sweet love we shared. I used her sorely and ill.

When you read this I will be gone, but oh, do not grieve, dearest child, for I am not worth grieving over as you now know. I know it was unfair of me to convince Sebastian you were the heiress, but I fooled the fox at his own game. At least you are married to a good man and Chadwick Park will not crumble away. Should anything ever happen to Charles, the trust I have laid aside for you should provide for you comfortably into your old age.

I'm sure there are many things you would have liked to ask me, but it is best this way.

Your father,

Randolph Chadwick Esq.

No doubt her birth mother had died of a broken heart. Josie frowned, crumpling the letter in her hands. *Best for you maybe, Father, but then you never did place my comfort above your own.* Now the hand of death had also robbed her of memories of her real mother. As always, he had taken the easiest way out for himself, leaving her to pick up all the mangled pieces.

Fragments of her nightmare floated into place. The event had been seared into her innocent subconscious forever as she was taken from the mother who loved her—by her own father. At least now she knew the coldhearted woman of her childhood never had been any relation to her.

The phrase throbbed in Josie's mind like a sluggish pulse.

For reasons I will leave unmentioned, I believe it might be sooner than any of us expect . . .

The letter had been dated July 23, 1817. Josie sighed at the implications. There had been threats made long before the one she had discovered in the library. She shuddered at the thought of digging more notes from the bowels of Father's desk, but they were her only link to the murderer. Her gut told her the mysterious tunnel played some part in this nightmare. She hated to think that the killer was someone Father had known and trusted, and it was possible a stranger had known about and utilized the tunnel in order to gain entrance into the house since there had been no sign of a forced entry. The vague fear that had haunted her entire life was no longer in the past but in her present. Josie would have no future until she laid it to rest once and for all.

A grim resolve was born in her. The murderer would escape justice only over her own corpse.

Warmth enfolded her clenched fingers as Charles's touch numbed the sting. The depths of his eyes glistened with compassion. Of course, he understood. His heart still bore the scars his own parents had inflicted. She slid up against him, and there was no need for words as his arms drew her close. He would always be there, standing between her and the pangs throbbing through her world. Fresh tears stabbed her eyes as the question hovered. Could she allow herself to trust him with all her secrets now?

Chapter Thirty-Four

*J*osie raised the lantern in the west wing of Chadwick Park, frowning as she remembered how thick the wreath of cobwebs had been around the tapestry the last time she passed by. Not a thread of them remained. She lifted the tapestry, and fresh apprehension rolled over her as the panel stared back. If she slipped and injured herself inside, no one would ever find her . . . except perhaps a murderer masquerading as a ghost. Her thirst for justice doused the barrage of fears as the darkness gaped.

Lord, You are the Just One. Give me the wisdom and strength to perceive what I should do. Give my father justice, please. He was a sinner, but I always knew he loved me. He never missed a Sunday, but I pray he made things right with You before the end. In Jesus's name, Amen.

Josie entered the bowels of the tunnel. The chill failed to penetrate her numbness. She reached the fork and studied the left path with prickling awareness. Footprints were carved into the mud. Instinct screamed at her to turn back as she stepped into the killer's trail. The walls closed in all around her as she continued. She caught a glimpse of smaller footprints here and there. Josie's breath quickened as she recognized the footprints of a man and a woman. Did the murderer have a female accomplice?

The tunnel wound on for quite a distance and continued to narrow until at one point she had to step sideways to scrape through. Desperation drove her forward even as she prayed for a glimpse of daylight. Brine landed on her tongue as the tunnel swerved to the right. The muffled roar of waves echoed off the walls as her footprints blended with dozens of others interspersing the damp sand. Curiosity dulled her fear as Josie passed cavern-like rooms piled high with crates and sacks. Daring to peer over the edge of one crate, her stomach flopped as she viewed imported bottles of rum. She had stumbled upon a smuggler's cache. Josie quickened her steps. The smuggler mustn't find her snooping. She knew the revenue agents had been casting a wide net for smugglers on their coast, but she had never dreamed the illegal operation occurred so close to home. No doubt this enterprise had existed for quite some time, passed down through the generations, as the smugglers' pockets were padded during wartime and famine while other families in Cornwall suffered. Tariffs were still high on imported goods of any kind.

Josie squinted as she stepped into daylight. Her shoes sank into wet sand. The crashing roar of the incoming surf filled her ears, but apparently the sliver of beach broadened at low tide enough for the ship to anchor and unload under the cover of darkness without being noticed by revenue agents as evidenced by the overturned rowboats whose oars lay idle. She shaded her eyes, trying to get a sense of the beach's location. Recognition sparked as she glimpsed spray rising from the sea's depths as the incoming tide surged over a dangerous sandbar that the local fishermen and sailors knew to avoid. This beach, or treath as it was called in old Cornish, was the namesake of her husband's estate, Treathston Heights. Shock cushioned her reeling senses . . . her father-in-law was a smuggler.

The smuggling did fit Sebastian's refined tastes. His wine cellar was stocked with imported liquor, and he possessed a prime location that had accelerated his rise to wealth. She refused to believe Charles was a participant, and the pieces fell into place as she recalled the many times that Sebastian had spirited Charles off on an urgent business trip just to hide his illegal activity when the ships were due to unload their cargo. Yet, even if Sebastian was capable of smuggling, it didn't mean he was a murderer. He had never shown Father anything but goodwill, and the initials H.C. didn't match.

An object on the beach caught the sunlight with a fierce glint. Josie stooped to pick it up, and her frown deepened as she brushed grains of sand from the sapphire-encrusted surface. It was her mother's—no, Rose's—brooch. The one father had given to Esther in payment for her services as governess when finances became such a complicated affair. Or had the brooch been a gift for other services rendered?

"I always wanted to know your secrets, Esther. Now I wish to God I had never read that letter," Josie huffed as she mounted the rough stone steps embedded in the cliff's face. Each lungful of air she sucked in was a stab of pain, a prayer cried from the innermost tenderness of her being.

Oh, dear God, please don't let the killer be my Esther. I could forgive her any sin but that.

Josie's heart thundered in cadence with the crashing waves as she watched the white form ahead of her glide through the stillness of the night. As she drew closer in the moonlight, she couldn't deny that Esther's white cloak bore a remarkable resemblance to the unidentified ghost that had snuffed out the yule candle. She still could not believe she was following Esther in the night like a criminal. She was beginning to doubt her judgment of character. Every person near and dear to her on earth was proving her conceptions of them to be false.

Esther flung a frightened glance over her shoulder, and Josie paused in the shadow of the garden hedge. Her governess had always embodied a silent strength, but now her every movement betrayed tremendous agitation as she headed straight for the cliff steps.

Josie's fingers tightened around the brooch in her pocket. Esther was afraid. The knowledge reduced her to the little girl who had refused to wear black taffeta to Rose's funeral.

A tall, shadowed form darted toward her. A scream rose in her throat until the moonlight fell upon the profile of Charles's face.

"Could you not sleep?" he asked.

Out of the corner of her eye Josie saw the flitting white disappear over the cliff's edge. She swallowed hard as bile climbed into her throat.

"No."

Charles drew closer, forcing her to look up at him. Her hand slipped from where it had traveled to her abdomen.

"I couldn't sleep either. You are shivering. It is much too cold for you to be out here at this hour." Her husband shrugged out of his greatcoat and pulled it over her pelisse. His warmth settled around her like a bubble of protection as he rubbed heat into her upper arms.

"You're frightened. You jumped like you had been shot when I came out. Is it my father?"

"There are many things that are not as they should be."

"Care to tell me? You've been quiet ever since you read the letter this afternoon. You spent so much time at Chadwick Park that it worried me, but then I couldn't find a trace of you. Now I find you wandering out here alone in the dark. What is wrong, Josie?"

"I used to know who I was and where I belonged. I don't believe any of it anymore."

"There's something else you're not telling me. Come inside by the fire, and we'll talk."

For the first time, Josie dared to search his eyes where fresh, glistening pain had surfaced. He laced his fingers through hers, leading her indoors. Their breath blew white in the night. Josie admitted she hadn't been thinking when the creak of Esther's padding feet woke her. She'd followed her into the melting snow with flimsy satin slippers. She had her answer as to where Esther disappeared at night, or at least part of it, but it was far from comforting.

Josie collapsed on the parlor settee as Charles settled a log onto the coals and coaxed it into flames. He eased himself down beside her, and she crawled into the warm haven of his lap. His words reverberated through the hollowness inside.

"I know I betrayed your trust many times, Josie, but when you forgave me I didn't expect you to keep the wall between us. How can I love you if you won't let me in?"

"Oh, Charles." Josie gripped his greatcoat tighter as the flitting shadows threatened to swallow her whole. "I don't know how to trust anymore when everyone I've ever loved has lied to me. My parents, my sister, my governess—"

"And your husband, but I'm not lying to you now, Josie. I only want to be there for you, but first you have to let me, darling. Love and trust go hand in hand. Why else do you think I couldn't love you for the longest time? You earned my trust, Josie. Don't shut me out just when I'm trying to earn yours."

Josie drew a shuddering breath. "I never meant to shut you out, but I know I have. I'm sorry, my love. Silence doesn't always mean that I don't trust you with my thoughts. I just don't even know what to think anymore, Charles. I'm all tangled up inside. I don't even know which knot to untangle first. Sometimes it is hard to put thoughts into words."

"There's one knot I know I can help you untangle."

Josie flinched as Charles's palm cupped her womb.

"How long have you known?" she blurted.

"I suspected it the night after the accident, but then I knew it was true when you nearly ceased eating altogether and started taking naps. I thought you were waiting for the right time to tell me, but then the days stretched into weeks without a word."

"I promise I was going to tell you—"

Josie covered her mouth to drown out the sobs as the scalding tears fell like rain. The rough wool of his greatcoat scratched her cheek as he pulled her closer to his heart.

"I—I overheard you say that you didn't believe in two people bringing a child into the world to be scarred by events that began before their birth. I wanted to be sure of your love for me before I told you. I didn't want you to try to love me only to spare your child the wounds your parents inflicted. Forgive me."

Charles's fingers cradled her jaw as they sat cheek to cheek and heart to heart. His voice was a tender thread knitting their souls together.

"You said you didn't know who you were or where you belonged anymore. You belong to me, beloved. You are Josie Chadwick Radcliffe, the woman who has been lover, mother, and friend to me. I love you just as you are, but the baby makes my joy overflow, because it is the fruit of my love for you."

"I do love you, Charles. So much that it frightens me sometimes. I promise to trust you from now on."

"Nothing could ever change the depths of my love for you, Josie."

Josie tucked the comfort of his adoration into her bruised, aching heart. She would believe in their love if nothing else.

An indignant creak overhead roused them, and Charles groaned against her ear. "Father has ears like a cat."

Josie refrained from telling him that Sebastian's ears weren't his only attribute that reminded her of the predatory felines.

"Charles? Josephine?"

"We're in the parlor, Father."

Sebastian appeared with a pistol stuck in the waistband of his dressing gown. He raised grizzled brows at the blazing fire.

"Are both fireplaces in your suite suddenly insufficient?"

"You might as well know, Father. Josie is with child, and she hasn't been sleeping well of late."

Sebastian snorted. "For someone who doesn't believe in having children, you certainly wasted no time. I wish you had adhered to your former convictions on the matter."

"We just needed a little time, and now you'd better adjust to the prospect of being a grandfather."

"So Josephine," Sebastian growled, and a shiver traversed Josie's spine as the narrowed slits of his eyes rested on her. "Not only have you succeeded in getting your bastard hands on my son's inheritance, but now you have corrupted the Radcliffe line with your illegitimate blood."

Nausea swirled in Josie's stomach as Charles gathered her up in his arms and leaped to his feet as though he could prevent Sebastian's poison from seeping through her veins.

"If you dare to address my wife that way again, I won't hesitate to get a house for her elsewhere until she feels welcome in her own home."

"I won't pretend to be happy at the prospect of welcoming an heir into the family who no doubt will inherit his father's weakness and his mother's deceit!"

"I'd rather have my child endowed with some of the sensitivity you regard as weakness than to inherit his grandfather's heartless, cold-blooded will of iron. And as for his saint of a mother—"

"Charles, take me upstairs. Don't give this beetle-browed tyrant the satisfaction of making you angry one moment longer," Josie interrupted.

Charles glared at his father. "We'll settle this later."

"You do that, son," Sebastian muttered, and Josie shuddered at the hard glitter in his gaze. She expected a forked tongue to flick out between his thin lips as Charles carried her upstairs.

Chapter Thirty-Five

osie flinched at the blunt knock and sat up with a sigh. The baby had been restless, waking her with fluttering taps in the wee hours of the morning. Charles never grew tired of feeling their child nudge his splayed fingers, but Josie was beginning to miss those hours of sleep. Even as she tried to catch up, someone always managed to interrupt her naps.

"Come in."

Esther slipped through the door and tugged her plaid shawl into place. Josie's heart softened in spite of herself at the sight of Esther's haggard features. She hadn't been the same since Father's death.

Their eyes met, searching, and a tear dripped down Esther's cheek. There was no guilt written in her luminous eyes, only a rawness that made every muscle in Josie's body tense.

"Did I wake ye?"

"You are more important to me than sleep," Josie said. She patted the coverlet, inviting Esther to join her.

"I—I cannae stay I'm afraid, luve. It's breaking my heart, but I have no choice. Sebastian just dismissed me. I have to be off the premises within the hour."

"No."

The word was wrenched from Josie's lips, and she watched every drop of blood drain from Esther's cheeks.

"I've already lost Father, Esther. I cannot lose you too, and I absolutely refuse. Sebastian had no right to dismiss you, so as of this very moment, you are reinstated. If he will not listen to me, I will demand that Charles speak to him."

Esther's strong arms surrounded Josie as her embrace held her and the pieces of her broken heart together.

"Nothing ye or anyone else says can make any difference now, luve. There are reasons ye cannae ken, but just believe me when I tell ye that for yer safety and for mine, it is best if I leave now without a fight."

"Secrets," Josie bawled into Esther's shawl. "Always the stupid secrets that are tearing my family apart! I've got to put an end to this."

Esther pulled away and gripped her shoulders. Josie stared back into the wise, heather-gray gaze she had always loved. Esther's eyes swept over her face as though committing every line to memory.

"Now ye listen to me right now, Josie Marie. One day ye will ken all the whys and wherefores of this life, but nothing, not even the truth, is worth yer health and happiness. Ye take care to remember that. I won't go far, and ye ken I will always love ye more dearly than ye can ever imagine. Ye will see me again."

"I love you," Josie echoed through the blur of her tears. "My baby still needs a godmother. Promise you won't leave me forever."

"Nothing could ever induce me to do that."

Esther's shawl slid down as she reached out to wipe away Josie's tears. Josie gasped. Esther's blouse was torn from shoulder to collarbone.

Josie frowned as she studied the jagged edge. There were blue marks on the snowy flesh of Esther's upper arm.

"He manhandled you."

Esther's eyes flicked away at the statement. "He wanted me for services beyond that of a lady's maid, and when I refused him like any moral Christian woman would, he told me I was no longer wanted here."

Rage simmered in Josie's veins. She swallowed bile and sat up straighter on the bed, clenching her fists. "He will pay for daring to touch you with his filthy hands and dirtier mind, even if it is on the other side of eternity. I know you must go, so take the ten-pound note from my reticule, and I will come find you."

Esther's lips brushed her cheek with tremulous warmth.

"God is just, Josie," she said gently. "He is fighting our battles even as we speak. Dinna be afraid, for I believe we will have our justice yet. Ye must be wise as a serpent but harmless as a dove."

Josie's nod hid a heart cold and hard as stone. As the door clicked shut, she sprang out of bed. Resolve settled flint-hard in her chest as she seized the knob. Charles would listen to her. He knew her love for Esther.

As her heels tapped an indignant staccato down the hallway, Sebastian almost collided with her. He grunted with displeasure as she glared at him.

"Have you seen my husband?" she demanded.

"He is in the stables, but it is no use complaining to him about your maid. I am still the man of this house."

Josie's palm tingled to slap him, but she held herself back with effort.

"And I am his woman. I wonder who holds more sway over him, Sebastian? You or me?"

"You've got spunk, I'll grant you that. And you are going to need it, wench, because no one crosses me and gets away with it."

Josie arched a brown brow and sailed beyond Sebastian's reach. She gulped the fresh March air the moment she was outside.

A quick scan of the stable's interior revealed no one present except . . . Bertram? His face lit up at the sight of her, and Josie gritted her teeth.

"My dear Josie. I knew you would come once you read my letter."

"What letter, Bertram?" Josie demanded.

"Oh, don't play innocent with me now," he teased as he grasped her hands. "I knew you weren't happy. We were meant to be together, dear heart, and now I will make you the happiest woman on earth."

"Bertram, stop this nonsense immediately," Josie insisted, squirming out of his grip. "I never received a letter from you."

"I have never given up on you," he groaned as his eyes devoured her face. "I have loved you since we were children, and I have waited all these long, lonely years until you could be mine."

Josie blinked at him. There was a crazed, hungry look in his eyes. He wasn't hearing a word she said.

"Bertram, I know you have always cared for me deeply. But I assure you I am truly very happy with Charles. I love him, and he loves me. Really, I—"

Anger honed his features. "Is that what you came out here to tell me?"

"No, but I need you to know that—"

"Oh, my darling. I understand now. You are afraid to leave him, but don't lie to me, Josie. You never loved him, and you never will. I've seen you crying your pretty little eyes out, and it is time for you to free yourself from him. I can give you myself, and that is more than he ever gave you. Am I right?"

Josie backed away, but his arm snaked around her back with groping fingers. She reeled back and slapped him hard. Shock glazed his eyes, and she broke into a run. Before she was midway to the door he caught her by the waist and hauled her up in his arms. It was as though she weighed no more than a sack of oats as she flailed and kicked. She had misjudged his wiry strength.

"I like a woman with spirit, just like good horseflesh," he grunted. "I see I shall have to tame you, my sweet. I shall have to convince you how beautifully we complement each other. By the time I'm done with you, Josie girl, you'll never want to be in any other man's arms again but mine."

"Bertram, stop it. Let me go," Josie pleaded, but he only laughed. A shiver coursed through her as he entered an empty stall.

"Are you cold, beautiful? Let me warm you . . ."

His breath rushed hot against her face as his mouth pressed down hard against hers. He was like a leech, trying to drain the life and breath from her. Josie clawed at him, and he dropped her into the hay with a yelp of pain. He swiped at his chin with a ragged sleeve and stared down at the stain of blood. Something hardened in his face when he looked down at her, revealing the cruel side of his nature she had always suspected was lurking just beneath the surface.

"You shouldn't have done that, Josie," he sneered. "Because I can play just as rough as you."

Josie leaped for the stall door, but her full weight slammed against the unyielding surface. He must have reached through the bars and managed to slide the bolt shut from the outside with his superior height. She crashed onto the floor, panting on the cold stone as she tried to suck some wind back into her stunned lungs. He seized her arm and dragged her back until her shoulder screamed. Just when she feared he would wrench it from her arm socket, he let go. Her heart tripped in her chest as his weight pinned her down. She whimpered, praying harder than she had ever prayed in her life. A glimpse of humanity appeared in his crazed expression.

"I don't want to hurt you, Josie," he said, brushing a wayward strand out of her face. Fascinated, his fingers explored the nape of her neck and tugged out her hairpins one by one. He ran his fingers through her tumbling hair.

"Don't be afraid of me," he murmured as he seized her jaw in his strong fingers and kissed her again, kneading her mouth as though he wanted to milk her life's blood. His other hand explored the base of her throat, fumbling with her buttons. Josie cried out, and he broke away.

"My arm . . . it hurts."

He glanced at it, taking his eyes off her face for the fraction of a second she needed. She whipped her arm back, but her elbow glanced off the side of his head as he dodged the blow. Josie kicked him away and darted to her feet. She knew exactly where the lock was on the other side of the stall, if she could only reach it. She stood on her tiptoes, straining, and groped desperately for the cold metal. There . . . she began to slide the bolt back, but she wasn't quick enough.

A rough hand grasped the back of her neck, but Josie writhed out of his grip as she held onto the metal bars of the stall and lashed out. Fabric tore as he ripped the back off her dress and took her with it. He pounced on her like an animal, his cruel hands groping and fumbling. Josie opened her mouth to scream, but his calloused fingers clamped down over her mouth.

Charles couldn't quite believe what he was seeing as he looked down at the two bodies entangled in the hay. He hoped against hope the woman wasn't Josie as he gripped the back of the man's collar and hauled him off her. As he flung the scum into the wall he could see that it was.

She looked up at him and froze. Mussed hair spilled down over her open bodice, revealing a bosom heaving beneath her stays in a picture of guilt. His eyes studied her swollen lips as they mouthed his name. One hand fumbled at an undone row of buttons as the other tugged her skirt down over her exposed chemise and drawers.

He couldn't draw the air to speak as the seconds ticked by. He knew only the pain of a gaping wound where his heart had once been. Tears leaked down her cheeks in a confirmation of her betrayal.

"Thank God you came," she sobbed. "I—"

"Hold your breath, Josephine," he said through gritted teeth. "I don't want to hear anything you have to say."

She blinked as though in pain. The man pulled himself up, panting, and Charles saw the blow coming. He ducked and drove his fist into the man's midsection with the full force of his hurt. It was the same creep whose daggered gaze had watched him on their wedding day.

The steward crumpled like a felled tree. Josie's anguished cry broke through the haze of shock.

"Charles, he forced me. He—"

"Father showed me the letter. He told me you had come out to meet him and agreed to leave me."

"It's a lie," Josie insisted as the tears streamed down her face. She knelt at his feet, dress slipping from bared shoulders as she clung to his legs. He scowled as she choked out, "Your father wants to get rid of me. Don't believe him, Charles. It is all a trick to turn you against me. I love you."

"Don't you dare say that to me again when the baby isn't even mine!" Charles roared. He hauled her up by the throat, and only when she made a strangled sound did he realize the tightness of his hold. He loosened his grip as he stared into her beautiful eyes. All he could see was his mother and Delia there. To think he had trusted her never to hurt him. Now, through the guise of love, she had plunged the fatal dagger into his chest.

"I hope you're satisfied," he said as his voice broke in an echo of his heart. "Your little scheme to get my name and your father's wealth failed miserably, and I caught you just as you were trying to run off with your true love. Well, now I am rid of you, and I wash my hands of your sin. Now go and leave me be."

"Oh, dear God," Josie gasped, her words vibrating through his fingers.

"One day you will live to regret the brokenness you have caused, and I will not spare you that pleasure."

She fell back and collapsed as though her legs had no strength to support her weight. He took one last look at her, at the wife who had cut out his heart, and severed her memory from his mind as he fled.

Chapter Thirty-Six

*A*ll Josie could see was the frigid relentlessness of Charles's eyes as she choked on her sobs. She stuffed clothes into her valise as a plan born out of sheer desperation formed in her mind. She would go to her cousin Mabel's in Devon and throw herself upon her stingy mercy. It would have to do until Charles came to his senses. He had played right into Sebastian's hands.

A chill stole over her as though the thought had summoned her father-in-law's vile presence—and then he was there. Rough hands gripped her throat from behind. A rush of ominous breath fanned her cheek like the hiss of a serpent's tongue. Josie recoiled from the evil gleam in Sebastian's eyes as he leaned over her shoulder. She watched his lips form the words as his fingers cut off her air.

"You won't need that where you are going."

The hatred in his expression twisted his familiar features until he was a stranger. The blots of darkness before her eyes spread, shutting out the hideousness of the world.

When Josie awoke, she was tied to the chair she was sitting in, though her hands had been left free. A gag was clamped between her lips with a tightness that made her eyes water. Only a feeble candle illuminated the cavern, whose wavering light was a fragile comfort. Josie flinched as something moist nudged her palm. She turned and glimpsed Byron's faithful gaze shimmering with devotion in the candlelight as he thrust his nose into her fingers again. Josie ran her fingers through his fur, envious of his canine innocence. The irony of the setter's presence didn't escape her . . . the dog's heart was more loyal than his master's.

Sebastian dragged the setter away by his collar and forced a quill and piece of paper into her hands. When Josie poised it on her knee, he thumped the overturned crate in front of her.

"On a flat surface, woman. I can't have your pretty penmanship so messy that it's illegible."

Josie glared at him, and his eyes narrowed to predatory slits.

"Now you will write down every word I dictate exactly as I say it upon the pain of death. 'My beloved Charles, I cannot live without you. I have buried my heart in the depths of the sea . . .'"

Josie snorted in disgust and shook her head. She didn't want to live without Charles, and she would rather die a thousand deaths than tell him she had killed herself.

Sebastian smirked at her. "I know you have no qualms about suffering yourself, but what if I told you that Esther's life depended on your cooperation?"

Josie's nostrils flared above the gag. What she wouldn't give to dig her nails into his fat, jowled throat. The quill scratched across the paper in a rough echo of her fury as she scrawled: *I demand proof!* She underlined it with three harsh lines for good measure.

Sebastian glanced down at the indignant sentence, and his bushy brows rose. "I am impressed, but you always were too clever for your own good. Does this convince you?"

He withdrew a long mane of curly black hair lined with silver and bound with a ribbon from his pocket. Josie gaped at the horrifying sight of Esther's locks dangling from the very fingers of the monster who had hacked the tendrils from her head. Her father-in-law would show no mercy to either of them. He had given her no other choice but to obey.

Sebastian crushed her final act of defiance in his fist and produced a fresh sheet of folded paper from his waistcoat pocket to her dismay. He resumed his dictation, word by horrifying word, and she wrote the letter with growing revulsion. Her trembling fingers dropped the quill as the flow of words ceased. Bile burned her throat as her stomach churned in revulsion. She willed her eyes to stop leaking. She would suffocate if her nose clogged up.

Sebastian snatched up the paper and scanned it with a grunt. "I am glad you have learned the merits of obeying orders," he muttered as he folded the abominable missive and tucked it into his pocket. He stared at her for a moment. Her pathetic appearance must have roused a shred of whatever humanity still lingered in his calloused soul. The candlelight reflected a sheen of pity as it surfaced in his eyes.

"I regret that it had to turn out this way, Josie, I truly do. In heart and spirit, you are everything I ever wanted for my son."

Sebastian hesitated, but then he sighed as he ran a hand along his leathery jaw.

"I suppose it doesn't hurt to tell you the rest. You deserve that much. First off, meet your uncle. I am your father's older half-brother, Horatio Chadwick. I changed my name to achieve my desired revenge."

Josie managed an outraged croak. A cruel smile played on the edges of his blade-thin mouth, echoing the gleam in his eyes.

"Yes, I killed him."

Liquor had numbed the pain for a time, but now the ache had doubled as it rimmed his heart and skull with splitting agony. Charles groaned as he lifted his head from the table littered with shards of broken bottles. The light of dawn was harsh, commencing the beginning of a day he didn't want to live.

A sheet of paper, penned with familiar, slanting curves, caught his eye.

My Beloved Charles,

>   *I cannot live without you. I have buried my heart in the depths of the sea. Perhaps there I will find peace at last. When the waves crash and the winds blow do try to remember me fondly. I have caused you enough suffering, and now perhaps you can start afresh knowing I am gone from you forever.*

Farewell my love,

Josie

Charles blinked to refocus his blurred vision. His hands began to tremble. If she were dead, would not his heart believe it? He found himself in utter denial. It just didn't sound like Josie. Surely Father had taken her to Devon yesterday to live with her cousin Mabel, as she had declared to be her plan.

"Oh God, no, no, please no," he groaned. "I cannot bear this."

He sank to his knees as gut-wrenching sobs ripped him from within . . . and prayed for a miracle.

Charles didn't know how long he had knelt there as the room's shadows shortened and sunlight gushed through the windows. His father's brisk step stirred him out of his grief, and as he turned, his neck screamed a sharp complaint.

"It isn't true, Father. Tell me it isn't true."

"I'll take you there and let your eyes discern for yourself, son."

Charles probed the frosty blue eyes so like his. As usual, Sebastian's gaze remained unintelligible.

"If I must."

The walk took only minutes. Charles forced himself to put one foot in front of the other as Sebastian led him to the cliff's edge. The horror of what he was about to behold crept with a numbing chill into his veins. He tried not to think or feel as shock cushioned his senses.

There, snagged on a gorse bush twenty feet below, a flash of color caught his eye. The torn blue dress was unmistakable as its tatters fluttered in the wind. His eyes followed the cliff face the rest of the way down with horrified fascination until they fastened on the cruel rocks pounded by the foaming surf. His heart stopped with the knowledge that she could never have survived the fall.

"Josie!" he screamed, and his cry of grief blended with the waves' roar. Sebastian caught his arm as he tried to take a crazed step forward. Charles shook him off, causing the older man to fall to one knee. His outstretched fingers trembled as he reached out for her one last time, curling them into a tight ball as he realized the futility of it. He shook his fist at Death. When his father touched his shoulder, he whirled and shook it in his face.

"No!" he roared with all his breath and watched Sebastian's cheeks grow ashen. "I loved her, Father. I loved her, but my own words shoved her off this cliff. Now she will never know just how dearly I loved her."

Charles collapsed and wailed as his tears mingled with the dirt. He was nothing except an empty shell with a dead heart. His soul wandered with hers somewhere beyond death. He wanted his body to be buried here beside her so she would never be lonely again. Perhaps her soul would visit him when the sea grew too cold. He strained to hear her voice above the moaning wind. He could be the solid place for her to find rest.

His voice rose in an ancient rhythm akin to a funeral dirge.

"'Tis long since I beheld that eye
which gave me bliss or misery;
and I have striven, but in vain,
never to think of it again:
for though I fly from Albion,
I still can only love but one.

As some lone bird, without a mate,
my weary heart is desolate;
I look around, and cannot trace
one friendly smile or welcome face,
and ev'n in crowds am still alone,
because I cannot love but one.

And I will cross the whitening foam,
and I will seek a foreign home;
till I forget a false fair face,
I ne'er shall find a resting-place;
my own dark thoughts I cannot shun,
but ever love, and love but one."

Chapter Thirty-Seven

Sebastian's dogged step landed on Charles's senses. He swore as he thumped the decanter down on the bureau. It seemed solitude was too much to expect nowadays.

"Do I have to stop breathing to get a moment's peace?" he demanded as his father opened the door. He watched the grimace twist the corners of Sebastian's thin lips.

"I had hoped you to be in a more pleasant mood for this discussion. I realize the suitable mourning period has not elapsed since your wife's death, but one mustn't let grief or convention get the best of sound judgment. There is a business proposition you must consider."

"What scheme have you concocted now, Father?" Charles asked, setting down his glass.

"Our new neighbor has refused to sell for any price. That leaves us with only one other way to get at Chadwick Park. It is Aurelia Haverhill's dowry—"

"No!" Charles roared.

"You will hear me out on this, Charles Radcliffe!"

Charles's hands curled into fists at his sides. "Don't you dare speak to me as though I were still a child."

"Then stop playing the part of an unreasonable spoiled brat and use the brain I passed down to you. The marriage will be a private affair once we obtain a common license, and it is not illegal for a widower to marry so swiftly. Upon its consummation, you can go on a long business trip if you need to get away for a while, but Aurelia will also be the means of fulfilling your duty in providing a Radcliffe heir. You must confess the prospect of marrying her is not unpleasant."

Charles snatched up his glass and threw it into the hearth. It shattered against the bricks, and the dripping spirits made a whoosh of flame. "No. I do not love her, Father."

"Love," Sebastian scoffed. "Open your eyes, son. I loved your mother and look where it left me. Don't let Josie become your undoing."

"If you find Aurelia such a bewitching creature then marry her yourself."

"Don't be absurd. She would never consent to marrying me when she has eyes only for my son."

"She is only a woman. Surely her father could be made to see the reasonableness of such an arrangement," Charles retorted.

"Don't make me regret calling you my son!" Sebastian hissed. "I want to see you established and carrying on the Radcliffe line before I die. If you fail me in this—"

"You'll what? Disown me?"

Charles laughed as Sebastian's face flushed varying shades of purple.

"You're frightfully drunk. I won't waste my breath."

"Go ahead. Disown me," Charles flung at his retreating back. "See if I care one whit. Perhaps now I can finally be freed from your tyranny."

Sebastian turned and leveled his gaze with the calmness Charles despised.

"Are you going to let the wench who betrayed your trust destroy you, or are you going to fight back like a man and triumph over her worthless life? Son, you deserve to be happy. I would be most disappointed in the man I raised if he saw fit to allowing a woman who wasn't worth her salt to ruin his future. Consider yourself well rid of her. All women are the same. We men must stick together, or women will rule the earth. Avail yourself of the pleasure they afford, but don't give them your heart. Mull that over for a while in your thick skull before you give me your final answer on the matter."

The door groaned shut, and Charles stared into the hypnotic flames.

"But I was happy," he whispered.

A creak roused him, and Charles glanced up. "Alfie."

The stableboy flinched at the sound of his name as though fearing Charles would strike him for intruding. "Please, Master Charles, don't get me in trouble! That pretty lady with the Bible name asked me to give this to you."

Charles forced his mental capacities to sharpen as his vision snapped into focus. He accepted the folded sheet of paper, and Alfie dashed out.

Dear Charles,

I need to speak to ye urgently. It concerns yer wife, and it is a matter of life and death. Please come and meet me at Chadwick Park as soon as ye receive this message. Graham will show ye where I am. I look forward to alleviating yer worst fears.

Yer humble servant,

Esther

Charles frowned as he tossed the paper into the hearth and watched as the words were eaten up one by one. He doubted the woman could resurrect Josie, but the letter intrigued him nonetheless. He sighed, reaching for his greatcoat. It certainly could not get any blacker than this.

He strode through the sludge that remained of the snow, not feeling the chill, as it matched the numbness in his soul. Josie's former governess had better not be blackmailing him, or she would pay.

The night had a dreamy vagueness to it as the stars glittered above him like diamonds in velvet. His feet knew the way in the darkness. Dash it, Josie's presence was all around him.

The door fell open with a sudden burst of light as though the old butler had been expecting him. The shadowed outline of Graham's stooped form beckoned him in with a flustered gesture.

"Please come quickly, Mr. Radcliffe," Graham urged as he snatched up a candle. The old butler glided down the hall with more dexterity than Charles would have given him credit for. He had to trot to keep up as the candle flung long shadows.

Graham rapped briskly at the library door.

"It's Graham," he called out, and Esther's muffled voice bade them enter.

Charles absorbed the sight of the lady's maid in disbelief. The woman's beauty was sharpened by the atrocity of her black hair being shorn short as a man's. Her eyes gleamed with a strange light as she endured his scrutiny.

"What in tarnation—"

"Please sit down, Charles. Some of this may come as a shock to ye," Esther interrupted.

He lowered himself into the chair across from her, further unnerved by the realization that this was the chair in which Randolph Chadwick had been found dead.

"In many ways this is a trial, Charles. I am about to present a case to ye, but before I proceed with the evidence, ye may question how I came by such knowledge. My answer to that is that while ye have kenned me simply as Esther, yer wife's former governess and lady's maid, I am also the recently widowed Mrs. Randolph Chadwick."

Charles blinked. "Proceed, Mrs. Chadwick."

"I hardly ken where to begin. Ye cannae reveal my married name to anyone. We were secretly married seven years ago when I refused to live in sin with him, but there were complications with Josie's birth mother that made it a necessity for us to keep it hidden from the outside world."

"Josie never permitted me to read Randolph's letter on the subject."

"Probably because she thought exactly what I did. It was a lot of sentimental, rambling nonsense that evaded the truth and left her with more questions than answers when it was supposed to serve as an explanation. Randolph was an evasive man in many respects, refusing to take responsibility for his actions and subjecting his daughters to a world of grief for his own selfish ends. I loved him in spite of his faults, but in the end they cost him dear indeed."

Esther's voice broke, shoulders heaving as though it took all her strength just to hold body and soul together.

"My husband didna die of heart failure. He was murdered."

Charles couldn't take any more pain in himself or another. He reached for the woman's hand. It was cold as the grave.

"What makes you say that?"

"Dr. Lee suspected that his heart had not failed of natural causes and sent a sample of the whiskey in his decanter to London. It tested positive for digitalis, a poison which causes the heart to fail."

Charles sucked in a sharp breath of shock. "Why? I thought Mr. Chadwick hadn't an enemy in the world."

Esther raised wise, powerful eyes to his, and her form emanated a force of will that moved him. A vague emotion he could not name flickered in her eyes.

"Oh, he had an enemy . . . an enemy of blood."

Charles understood her hesitation. Instinct curled with a nameless dread in the pit of his gut, like a snake waiting to strike. She did not want to darken his world with the horror that had darkened hers, and yet it concerned Josie somehow.

He licked some moisture into his lips. "Tell me."

"Randolph had a half-brother, Horatio Chadwick, the son of the first Mrs. Chadwick. She died very young, and he was sent off to boarding school as soon as he was old enough. It was as though his father was eager to forget there had ever been a first Mrs. Chadwick. After the tragic death of Randolph's parents, everyone assumed Horatio would inherit as the eldest son. But the will came to light, and everyone was shocked to find that Horatio had been disowned and Randolph had been named heir of the estate. That act spawned the birth of a monster."

Esther's voice trailed off, and her fingers trembled within his own. Her grief struck a chord of resonance within his crushed spirit. He reached for her other hand, and she seized his fingers in a grip that was oddly comforting as they both struggled not to drown in the same sea of pain.

"Mr. Chadwick had left such deep debt behind that his solicitors could barely keep the estate from going to his creditors.

When his solicitors made arrangements for Horatio to stay with his mother's relatives, the school sent word that the boy had run away. He was never located, and Randolph never even kenned of his existence. Randolph began to receive threats several years back, but we assumed they were from his creditors, who had been hounding him for quite some time. The last threat my husband received was signed: H.C. Horatio Chadwick came back for revenge on his family, and the only way he could do that was by changing his name to Sebastian Radcliffe."

Charles fought for breath. Horror flooded his soul at the implications.

"He connived to get ye to marry the Chadwick heiress so that he could get his hands on the estate and inheritance that should have been his. Upon discovering that Josie was not the Chadwick heiress, yer father was enraged—to put it mildly. All of his carefully laid plans had been thwarted in one blow as Chadwick Park slipped out of his hands. He couldna take the chance that Josie carried yer legal heir. Thus he took drastic measures. He kenned ye had always carried a deep feeling of rejection from yer mother, and he contrived to make ye think Josie had betrayed ye with another man."

Guilt wracked the depths of his wretchedness. "Oh, merciful God forgive me," he panted, squeezing his eyes shut to block out the memory of Josie's tear-streaked face. "The babe was mine. Now their blood is on my hands!"

"Charles!"

The sharpness of her tone knifed him as she seized his face, forcing him to meet her intense gaze.

"Josie is alive!"

Wonder filled him, piercing through his despair with such power that moisture leaked from the corners of his eyes as though his body could no longer contain such joy. *Oh Father, have You given me a second chance in Your divine mercy?*

Esther smoothed the hair away from his brow as Josie had been wont to do in so many tender moments. "Please, continue," he managed, and she resumed her seat.

"He succeeded in his deception when he forged Josie's handwriting and sent the incriminating letter to Bertram that he later showed ye. All he had to do was fail to deliver Bertram's reply and orchestrate it so that Josie unwittingly met Bertram in the stables. The outcome was inevitable, and he staged it so that ye arrived on cue."

"How the devil did father know of Bertram's infatuation with my Josie?"

"He overheard them arguing and manipulated the situation to his advantage. Later that day, Sebastian cornered me and informed me of his intention to make me his mistress. When I resisted like any righteous woman would, he dismissed me from Josie's employ. I spoke with her briefly, and then I left. Sebastian followed me on the path to Portreath and struck me from behind. The blow knocked me unconscious for several hours. When I came to, I was imprisoned within the west wing's tower at Chadwick Park, sheared short as a sheep in spring. Fortunately, Sebastian didna realize that I kenned about the tunnel, and I escaped."

"What tunnel? Do you mean to tell me that there is a secret tunnel that you, my father, and Josie all knew about? I assumed Josie freed Delia by borrowing her father's key."

"Aye. The tunnel connects Chadwick Park to the beach for which Treathston is named, and it has existed since the Dark Ages. It was once used to hide Catholic priests from Queen

Elizabeth's persecution. In more recent years, it has been utilized by a smuggling ring that yer father operates. But I digress."

Charles didn't know if he could bear any further revelations. He was still reeling from the knowledge that his father was a murderer, a smuggler, an abductor, and a Chadwick.

"With both of us out of the way, our beloved Josie was left vulnerable to Horatio Chadwick's evil plot. He told ye he was taking her to Cousin Mabel's in Devon and abducted her. As soon as I escaped, I enlisted the aid of yer setter Byron. He found Josie before, and he found her again. I followed him to a Roman dungeon in the cliffside about a mile up the coast. Josie had endured similar rough treatment, with the exception of a haircut. Sebastian had to wait until she regained consciousness, which enabled me to overhear their conversation. Fortunately, Sebastian wasn't suspicious of Byron's appearance, kenning his attachment to Josie. He forced her to write the suicide note, insisting he would kill me if she failed to cooperate. When she demanded proof that I was in his power, he produced my hair. After the note was in his possession, he proceeded to answer all of Josie's questions. Josie is still alive only because she is the pawn in his last desperate attempt to grasp Chadwick Park. He tried to make ye think Josie was dead, but if he cannae persuade ye to marry Aurelia for her dowry, then he will force ye to by threatening to kill Josie."

Every word was a bullet, riddling Charles's existence until the gaping holes threatened to swallow him whole. Esther's delicate features blurred and swam as shock glazed his vision. He swallowed hard, and the lump in his throat refused to budge. He was the spawn of deception, and he had swallowed every one of Horatio Chadwick's lies. A tear spilled from the caustic cauldron of grief and guilt within him.

"Och, now Charles," Esther's sweet voice murmured.

"He already proposed that to me," Charles choked.

"And I trust ye refused?"

"Yes, but he considered me too drunk to be taken seriously."

"Ye must accept his proposition in earnest after we rescue Josie, for ye mustn't raise suspicion. We both ken he will kill Josie regardless. He cannae take the risk that the child she carries is yer male heir. We'll set the stage to expose his evil deeds at yer wedding to Aurelia by revealing that yer wife still lives."

Charles covered his face with his hands as the cruel truth broke through, hammering through his conscious brain with devastating blows. His father had forsaken him along with all of the paternal affection he should have borne. He had forsaken his beloved wife, leaving her alone to face certain death.

The tenderness of a woman's arms cupped his head and pulled him against an even softer warmth as her breast muffled his sobs. It was as though Josie was holding him again, and the pain stabbed sharp.

"Josie loves ye, ye ken. And yer heavenly Father has not forsaken ye."

Could the woman read his mind?

"But Esther, I abandoned her when I should have protected her. I believed all of the lies instead of her dear heart."

"Love covers a multitude of sins. She will not hold it against ye. Have faith, son."

"If he harms one hair of her head, he will pay a higher price than he bargained for," Charles vowed as he stood. He bent and kissed Esther's cheek. "Thank you. I don't know how I can ever repay you."

"Just help me bring Josie back safe and sound. Vengeance is the Lord's. He will repay."

As Charles made his way toward the door, Esther burst out, "We must be careful, Charles. Yer father is a gambler, and gamblers always have another card up their sleeve."

"His luck has turned, Esther. The Lord is fighting this battle for us, and He will win."

Charles heard the smile in Esther's voice.

"Aye, that He will indeed."

Chapter Thirty-Eight

oldness licked at the edge of her consciousness, and every muscle tensed in protest. Josie curled herself tighter on the hard ground, willing the chill away, but then the frigid wetness pricked her face like needles. She moaned as she tried to crawl away from it.

A deafening roar filled the chamber. The waves were angry this morning. She forced her eyes open, and the cramped stiffness of her limbs evaporated in the face of shock. Josie sprang to her feet as lapping water invaded the chamber, and her eyes adjusted to the dim light. This was not the room that had been her prison cell for the past several days. It was narrower, and the door had no peephole. A familiar tightness constricted her throat as she told herself in vain not to panic. Her gruel must have contained a drug, and Sebastian had transferred her to this drowning chamber while she was dead to the world. Now she would be forced to watch the seawater grope its way toward her until it climbed over her head. Her nails dug into her palms as she clenched her fists. Sebastian thought he had won.

Her eyes fastened upon the foamy surf as it gushed from multiple crevices in the rock wall, trickled out of the chamber, and then rushed back in with fresh vigor. The encroaching hiss of the water matched her sharp intake of breath as she backed away until her palms met the moist stone of a dead end. Josie's eyes clawed every inch of the chamber for a method of escape.

She spotted a rusty, iron hook embedded in the stone ceiling. No doubt prisoners had been cuffed to it in times of old, but perhaps if she clung to it, the water wouldn't reach her nostrils. The chamber plunged into murky darkness as the rising seawater drowned the daylight.

Oh, Father, why didn't you teach me how to swim?

No doubt the crashing force of the waves would bash her skull against the rocks, but Josie had to try. She splashed through the freezing knee-high water and locked her fingers around the hook in a death grip. Her heart sank at the realization of how low the ceiling was. How many of the Romans' victims had met an ignominious death in this wretched cell where humans drowned like rats? The sea had always been one of her closest comforts, but its waves were about to snuff her life's breath in one fickle act.

Josie's teeth began to chatter.

God, I have chosen to believe all this time that You are just and faithful. Don't let me die like this. I can't let Sebastian get away. Deliver me.

Rivulets of warm salt mixed with the cold on Josie's cheeks as the rushing sea rose to her hips and then her waist. Her raised arms shook, weakened by hunger.

Oh, Charles, I love you still even if you betrayed my trust. I cannot bear to leave you like this . . . knowing you will never know the truth.

Josie groaned as the pain bit into her soul. She had lost her husband's heart, and now she had failed to bring her child into the world, though she would have given her life for her offspring. She had failed as a wife and a mother. The oppressive darkness loomed, settling onto her shoulders with the agony of defeat. Water lapped at her throat like a beast's tongue, tasting her before finishing her off. Her fingers were slipping . . .

A splash echoed off stone. The shadowed outline of a human head popped up in front of her. Josie opened her mouth to scream, but a wave caught her full in the mouth. She spat out the salty water. The sound of Charles's voice filled her with wonder.

"Josie, my love."

The familiar strength of his arms surrounded her. Her fingers slid from the rough iron onto his shoulders.

"Don't be afraid, beloved. I know you can't swim, but I need you to take the deepest breath you can and hold on to my waist. Don't let go no matter what. I love you."

Josie opened her mouth to tell him to loosen her stays, but he faced the thunderous roar. He would never hear her now. She sucked wind into restricted lungs, locking knuckles around his waist. He tensed, timing his action until the precise moment when the sea would be suctioned out.

The icy water rushed over her head, and the shock threatened to steal the breath she needed to live. Josie scrunched her eyes shut against the burn of surging brine. Muscle hardened against her fingers as Charles shot forward with a thrust of power. *Spare us, Lord. Please spare us.*

A furious swarm of bubbles whooshed in her face. Charles's strength conceded to the powerful current as it sucked their bodies under a shelf of rock. The sea's frigid grip numbed Josie's every sensation until her shin collided with a sharp rock. Her knee exploded in a fireball of pain, telling her she would have a livid bruise if she survived to see it. The dull ache in her chest deepened to a burning scream for air. Josie squeezed Charles's writhing abdomen, demanding oxygen. Gray light cut the darkness, but she didn't dare to open her eyes. Her head broke the surface. Josie sucked in a lungful of air before going under again.

Charles's body went limp in her arms. Fear shredded her courage as his dead weight sunk them both, but she would drown with him before she let go. Josie writhed, feet flailing as panic clawed her chest. Their sharp descent continued as the current sucked them deeper. The crushing pressure increased until Josie's ribcage threatened to burst beneath her stays. Her bruised lungs fluttered, but she denied the instinct to take a breath.

No. I refuse to let us die when we have a lifetime of love ahead of us.

Her foot bounced off a rock. Josie gritted her teeth against the crushing pain as she strained for a hold. The wave's force abated just long enough for her legs to gather strength beneath her like a coiled spring. Her other toe brushed the rock's rough surface, and Josie thrust them both away. They surged upward as Josie prayed them to open air.

Her head broke the surface. Air had never tasted so good as she gulped it in. A wave crashed over her. The shove tumbled her forward, threatening to drag Charles out of her grip. Her toes dug into sand. She clawed for a foothold and jerked Charles's head above water. Blood streamed from his temple.

"Help us!" she screamed. She no longer cared if Sebastian heard. His son's life was on the line. Each wave weakened her hold on Charles.

A splash seized her attention, and she turned her head to see a familiar—and welcome—form. Esther's eyes bulged with fear as she churned toward them. Josie surrendered Charles to

Esther's strong hands and clung to her skirt as she dragged them to shore.

Cool sand grazed her cheek as Josie gasped for air. She caught a glimpse of Esther pumping Charles's chest. Warm seawater roiled in her throat. She retched onto the sand and shivered until her teeth chattered. *Oh gracious God, please be merciful. I love him so.*

Charles's lips were turning blue. Josie lunged forward and slapped him with the last of her strength. The apple in his throat bobbed in a violent motion. His chest heaved, and Esther rolled him onto his side as water gushed from his mouth. He drew a ragged breath. A fit of coughing seized him until Josie feared it would tear him in two.

"Speak to me, Charles," Josie urged.

Charles groaned in reply as he collapsed on his back and wheezed for breath. Josie tore a piece of cotton from her chemise and held it against his wound. Her hand was trembling too much to be gentle. He winced and reached up to grab it.

"Ow," he complained.

Sobs wracked her as Josie gathered him into her arms. Esther patted her heaving back. "Thank Ye, God," Esther sniffed. "Thank Ye."

"How did you find me?" Josie blurted, looking up into Esther's brimming eyes.

"I kenned Sebastian was up to no good. I escaped, and Byron led me to him that night after he took ye. I overheard every word. Charles kens all of his father's wicked deeds now, luve."

"Josie?" Charles rasped.

"I'm all right, my love. You saved me."

Josie's fingers refused to stop shaking as she brushed the damp blond hair away from the gash. Esther clucked like a mother hen. "Just look at the both of ye, shivering nigh to death."

Charles's blue eyes glazed with pain as a shawl settled around Josie's shoulders.

"Can you ever forgive me for betraying your heart?"

"Yes, Charles."

"I never stopped loving you. When I thought you had jumped off that cliff, my heart died inside me."

"I know. You resurrected my heart from a watery grave."

His face twisted, and Josie read the destructive power of self-hatred.

"Now that I have forgiven you, you must forgive yourself, Charles. I don't believe your father would have taken such drastic measures if I hadn't carried an heir to run all his plans."

"Don't make any excuses for him, Josie," Charles said with a grimace. "He deserves to have the book thrown at him, and that is exactly what he is going to get."

"All right, come, come now," Esther urged. "Charles has a meeting with Vicar Nance at ten o'clock, and we must spirit ye away, Josie, before Sebastian comes investigating."

"The vicar?" Josie echoed with a frown.

"Now dinna get yer hackles raised, luve. We have a plan to expose Sebastian, and it was the only way to save ye."

Josie looked askance at her husband, guessing the plan without much trouble. "Just as long as you don't go through with it."

"We'll need your cooperation," Charles said.

"Has that seawater pickled your brain, Mr. Radcliffe?" Josie demanded.

A grin tugged at his pale lips. "It's Chadwick now, though I know that will take some getting used to."

"You simply cannot expect me to call you Mr. Chadwick. That was what people called my father, but Charles Chadwick has a pleasant sound."

"You are the solid evidence we need to bring Horatio Chadwick to justice. Without your presence his word is just as good as ours, my love."

"All right," Josie conceded with a sigh at her husband's insistence. "If that is what it takes." But she didn't know if she possessed the strength to face her would-be killer again.

Chapter Thirty-Nine

harles's fingers shook as he struggled with his waist-coat's pewter buttons. He needed a drink, but he had promised Josie on a night not long ago that he would stop. He aimed to keep his promise. She deserved better than a drunkard for a husband, and their child deserved a better father. Softness stirred in his being as he recalled the ripe curvature of her womb. He prayed her health wouldn't suffer from the ordeal she had just endured.

He eyed the clock with dread. The fated hour was approaching faster than he liked. He tugged his gloves on and fetched his top hat. *Dear God, help me to win this battle.*

The carriage ride was over all too soon as the church appeared. Every sinew in Charles's body protested as the carriage lurched to a halt. It had taken all the force of his will just to propose to Aurelia Haverhill. His brain replayed the scenes like a magic lantern show, flashing through his mind. Her cold, calculating gaze, as faceted as crystal in the moonlight; the shadows that had revealed only that which she wanted displayed; and the exaggerated shiver she had enacted to perfection as she gave him an invitation to warm her that no man could have refused.

A smile tugged at the corners of his lips as he remembered the contented sigh that had escaped her in his arms. He had fooled her into losing at her own game. Her touch had drained him as he longed for Josie's caresses, which always left more than they took. He was nothing more than a conquest to Aurelia, a temporary thrill that would fade if he grew familiar. Hers was a shallow soul, absorbed and governed by Self until she had nothing left to offer another.

Charles mounted the church steps, drawing strength from his wife's heart. To think he had almost missed seeing its beauty, distracted by his own pain. His heartbeat quickened. His life without her would have been a study in selfishness, and he shuddered to think what would have happened if he had met Aurelia first. Josie's love had made him a better man, redeeming him from his own self-destruction. *Dear God, help me never to take her for granted again. I promise to spend each and every day I have with her as though it were my last. I want to find a new way to love her with the dawning of every sunrise.*

The air reeked of moral decay. Charles submerged his grimace beneath a grin at the sight of a triumphant Aurelia decked in white. He would take acute pleasure in watching Jezebel fall. Her eyes sought to possess him with bewitching mastery, and he assumed a dog-like devotion as he walked to her side.

The barrister appraised him from the pew as though measuring his nerve. Charles returned his gaze, hoping the middle-aged man's nerves were fashioned from the same steel.

Sebastian gave him a broad grin of approval, and Charles exulted as he severed the heartstrings between them with a stroke. He couldn't wait to see the puppeteer's face when he jerked only to discover his son a freed man. The approaching exposé gave him no pain. There had never been any love lost between them, and now justice would be meted out.

Charles prayed he could rejoice in his freedom without the bitter aftertaste of the past. God knew he had suffered enough to deserve that much. He probed the depths of his heart for pity, struggling to milk enough for his parent. If only his father had been content to rise above his circumstances without exacting revenge on the innocent.

Staring at his sire, Charles couldn't muster forgiveness. The seething blackness of hate bubbled within him like a toxic plague. Not only had his father robbed him of a childhood, he had robbed him of the father who might have been. That was Horatio Chadwick's most unforgivable crime of all.

The vicar's gaze pierced him with sharp rebuke. Charles knew he deserved the condemnation. He himself was far from innocent. One right did not make up the crushing load of wrong his poor Josie had endured being yoked to him.

Aurelia stole a shrewd glance at him through heavy lashes, and the lie his own lips had uttered hung heavy between them. Charles shuddered as the words echoed through his mind. *Ever since the night we danced I've wanted you, dearest Aurelia, and fate played a cruel trick on me when I pledged myself to Josephine. Now I'm free to love you and make you my own as it was always meant to be . . .*

The vicar cleared his throat as though steeling himself to commit sacrilege. Charles pitied his moral dilemma. Such scruples would not benefit him when his stipend depended on Sebastian's coffers.

"Dearly beloved, we are gathered together here in the sight of God . . ."

Charles tensed as the irrevocable question approached. He hoped the constable had not fallen asleep where he was posted in the baptistery stairwell, but if Father got past him, the revenue agent was waiting outside.

"Is there any reason for which these two may not be lawfully joined together in matrimony? Please speak now or forever hold your peace."

The barrister rose with impressive dignity, unruffled by the intensity of Sebastian's glare. "I protest, your honor, and assert that this marriage cannot continue."

A glimmer of interest stirred in the vicar's hooded gaze. "What is the reason for your contestation of these proceedings?"

"I assert from evidence procured by my profession that Mr. Charles Radcliffe is legally bound to another living wife, a Mrs. Josephine Radcliffe."

A tremor passed through Aurelia's cool fingers up his arm. Her nails dug into the flesh of his bicep.

Sebastian rose from the pew. Charles alone knew the barrel-chested man well enough to spot the tensing jaw as he planted his feet wide apart. Sebastian's gruff voice remained smooth and confident, but his was the tone of a man who had everything to lose. *Your cockiness loosened your grip on luck, Father, and the one-haired man has slipped away. Don't make this any harder than it needs to be.*

"Mrs. Radcliffe committed suicide. If you assert that she still lives, as a relative of the groom, I demand proof."

"I can do better than mere evidence. I can procure the woman herself. Bring forth Mrs. Radcliffe," the barrister announced.

Josie and the constable appeared in the doorway. Charles's heart pounded a drum roll at the sight of Josie's face blanched as white as the corpse she would have become. Sebastian's start was almost imperceptible as the cords bulged in his throat. Josie seemed to draw strength from the silent encouragement in Charles's gaze as she rallied before him.

"As you can see for your own eyes, I am alive and well in spite of an evil plot to bury me in a watery grave, thanks be to Almighty God. I implore every eyewitness present here today who may have to testify upon what they have seen and heard in a court of law on my behalf . . . do justice and love mercy. As for the man who abducted me and made an attempt to take my life and the life of my unborn child, all I will say is this: may God have mercy on your soul, Horatio Chadwick."

The constable leveled his pistol as Esther appeared and led Josie outside to the safety of the waiting carriage.

The vicar's fleshy lips parted, gaping like a fish, but Aurelia snatched the words from his mouth as she wrenched her arm out of Charles's. The back of her hand caught him in a stinging blow across the mouth, snapping his head sideways. He tasted the warm saltiness of blood seeping over his tongue.

"How dare you," she hissed between bared teeth. "I am not a pawn to do with as you please."

"It was a matter of life or death, Aurelia."

Aurelia's swift retort was interrupted by the constable's sober voice: "Horatio Chadwick, I hereby place you under arrest on the heinous charges of murder, smuggling, abduction, and attempted murder."

"Come, dear," Aurelius Haverhill said as he took his daughter's arm and steered her out. "I know your pride is sorely wounded, but it is expendable, whereas your cousin's life was not. Be grateful you were saved from participating in the destruction of innocent life."

Shock set Sebastian's features hard and impenetrable as stone. "What murder am I being accused of?"

"The murder of your half-brother, Randolph Chadwick Esquire of Chadwick Park," the constable barked.

"You've got the wrong man, Constable," Sebastian continued as he held up his hands in a motion that struck Charles as unnatural. "I'll prove it to you."

"We've got all the proof we need of your guilt. I would not be so swift to call two witnesses insufficient if I were you."

The constable unhooked the handcuffs from his belt and approached Sebastian. Charles detected a gleam that flashed in his father's eyes. A warning parted his lips, but it never escaped as his father delivered a sharp chop to the constable's upper forearm. Sebastian snatched the falling gun midair, but Charles's reflexes were quicker. He sprang forward, knocking his father off balance, and their fingers scrambled for mastery of the weapon. Charles's fist connected with Sebastian's gut, but he collapsed with a hiss of pain as his father's foot drove sharply into his ribs. The constable received a clean uppercut to the jaw from his burlier adversary, followed by the crashing thud of his unconscious demise.

Father brandished a wicked-looking dagger and held it to the unconscious constable's throat as his gaze collided with Charles's in a clash of wills. As Charles watched in horror, his father reached out and retrieved the pistol. A door creaked behind them, and Sebastian's head whipped around just in time to see the vicar and barrister making good their escape. Charles leaped for Sebastian's wrist, but he froze as the blade pressed against the constable's throat. Sebastian's lip curled as he seized the handcuffs and motioned toward the railing hemming the pulpit steps.

"Sit down with your back against the bars."

Charles obeyed for the constable's sake as Sebastian slid the dagger back into his boot and kept the pistol trained on the man's prone body. He winced as Sebastian forced his forearms through the narrow openings and cool metal clamped around his wrists with a click. Father sneered down at him.

"You stupid fool. You'll live to regret the day that trollop birthed you."

"Go to the devil."

Charles tensed as Sebastian's arm flew back. Pain exploded at the first stinging blow, and his vision blurred with the second as his head snapped to the left.

"She can't hide from me, son. Remember that. I will find her."

"You're no father of mine!" Charles yelled after him as the door slammed shut. He let out a growl of frustration. His ribs ached as he tested the integrity of the railing. The wood groaned as he strained against it, but it didn't give way.

"Halt!" the revenue agent shouted outside. A gunshot ripped the air. Charles's eyes darted to the window as Sebastian appeared and blew the smoke from the pistol barrel with a sardonic grin.

"The gallows are too good for you!" Charles shouted as his father faded from view. He prayed the diversion had given Esther enough time to spirit Josie away to Aurelius's estate as he waited for the vicar to return and free him.

Chapter Forty

*J*osie gritted her teeth as she bounced on the leather seat. Every bone in her body threatened to rattle loose. The carriage springs groaned as Esther pushed the horses to their limits. They would both breathe easier once they reached Haverhill Hall and received word of Sebastian's capture. The agonizing minutes ticked by into hours, but no shout of alarm sent her bow-string nerves whizzing into frenzied action.

Lights gleamed murkily through the dimness of the falling dusk. Josie hadn't been to Aurelius's estate since she was a little girl, and she strained to remember the last time. Ah yes, when she had been invited to Aurelia's tenth birthday tea. Curiosity piqued inside her. Had Haverhill Hall changed since she had viewed it through the eyes of a twelve-year-old?

As the carriage drew alongside the Grecian pillars thronging the door, Josie understood why Aurelius had always coveted Chadwick Park. Haverhill Hall was a poor attempt at imitation. The replica paled in comparison to the seasoning only age could provide.

"Get out and hurry inside, luve, while I hide the carriage. They are in readiness for ye," Esther bellowed, and Josie's lips curved in spite of herself. She had never heard Esther raise her voice in her entire life. Resentment steeped inside her as she reached for the handle. She wanted to breathe the clean, open air without thought of how she planned to steal it. Freedom came at a cost now that Sebastian had placed a price upon breathing and robbed her of living.

Mahogany-paneled doors swung open like a welcoming embrace. A swarm of concerned servants whisked her inside in less than two shakes of a lamb's tail. A buxom woman in a housekeeper's tidy apron and cap bustled toward her, assailing her nostrils with the scent of lemons.

"Welcome to Haverhill Hall, dearie. I'm the head house-keeper, Bertha Mae Higgins."

"Thank you. How do you do, Mrs. Higgins?"

"Just fine. Now don't you fret, dearie," Bertha Mae crooned in a syrupy sweet voice as kind as her molasses-brown eyes. Her grip was warm as she took Josie by the hand.

"Land sakes, yer whiter than a bedsheet, and cold to boot. We'll warm you right up and put roses in yer cheeks afore long."

The head housekeeper bustled up the stairs, sweeping Josie along. Josie's lips quirked as she wondered if Esther had met her mothering match in Bertha Mae Higgins.

"The master gave me strict orders that I wasn't to let any-one disturb you," Bertha Mae fussed as she opened one of the thick oak doors flanking the corridor. An enormous feather bed looked decadent in the pale blue room, a frothy mound of snowy white lace and fluffed pillows. Josie was convinced it was a cloud that would dissipate the moment she sank into it.

The head housekeeper turned down the sheets and thumped more volume into a fluffed pillow. *Drift*, the room seemed to say, caressing her frazzled senses like a gentle breeze. Was it pos-sible that she could finally let her guard down, or was this all a trap—a false peace luring her into unawareness?

As if reading her thoughts, Bertha Mae selected a key from the jangling ring that identified her as head housekeeper and inserted it in the lock. The faint click was a sweet sound. Bertha Mae turned and held an arthritic knuckle to her lips.

"Rest now, dearie, and take a respite from yer troubles. Yer safe now."

Josie knew Esther would join her when she could. As her bruised body slid beneath the cool sheets, she seemed to be resting in a slice of heaven. The softness embraced her as it conformed to her limbs, and sleep stole over her as her cheek kissed the pillow. She let herself drift into oblivion. Her last thought was a longing for the comfort of her Charles's arms.

Muted voices fell on Josie's ear, blending with the soft shades of light and shadow like a pencil sketch. Her lashes fluttered open, and a shiver of joy quickened in her chest at the sight of Charles sitting by her side. His expression was fraught with tenderness as he leaned over her, but she sensed a ripple coursing bittersweet just beneath the surface as her arms surrounded his neck. She breathed in the essence of him, earthy and strong. Tears sprang into her eyes as his touch conveyed something desperate. The moisture pricking her lids was mirrored in his pools of purest blue as he touched his forehead to hers.

"Beloved, you must go with Esther to your place of refuge, where I pray to God you will remain hidden. I must leave you in Esther's care while I lead the predator onto a false trail as far from you as I can."

A moan bubbled from Josie's lips as her heart clenched with pain. Sebastian had managed to elude the authorities.

"How long must we be parted? My heart aches with missing you."

Charles took her hand and pressed it to his chest. His heartbeat echoed within, resonating in the hollow loneliness.

"Nothing shall ever truly separate us, Josie. Feel the rhythm of this heart that loves you more than life and always remember that it will protect you from all harm because it has pledged itself to you alone as long as it beats."

Josie nodded, blinking away tears as the sensation of his heartbeat thudding through her fingers carried her back to the night when it had all begun with his promise to be faithful and true no matter what the circumstances of their union.

"Beloved, promise you'll come back to me."

He smiled. "Together we are stronger than the storm. Believe in us, darling. Believe in a future I have dreamed of where we shall never be separated again."

"I believe, Charles Chadwick."

The words staunched the pain of parting like a dressing on a wound.

He lowered his head and kissed her. His gentle strength seeped through her veins, numbing her fears.

He pulled away with a grin. "As they say in Paris, *Au revoir*."

"Until we meet again," Josie echoed with a brave smile that wobbled at the corners. He reached out and caught the tears rimming her lashes before they could spill onto her cheeks. His hand cupped her face.

"That's my Josie," he whispered with pride and love shimmering in his eyes. He backed toward the door with a half-hearted wave and rapped it once. The knob turned as the door swung open, revealing Esther's patient form waiting in the hall.

"Thank you, Esther, for everything," he said in a husky voice as she stepped into the bedchamber.

"Ye needn't thank me. Have a care, Charles."

He nodded with a visible air of hesitation. "Am I making a mistake leaving the two of you?"

He looked so lost standing there. Josie's fingers curled into fists against the sheets. She was powerless to help him. A potent anger found its voice as it raged hot inside her, stoked by her helplessness. She was not accustomed to the feeling. Always she had made a way for those she loved, but now there was not a blessed thing she could do.

The taste of defeat was caustic on her tongue. For a moment she basked in hatred for Sebastian as its unholy glow quickened her blood like a glowing coal in her bosom. She knew she should drop it before it burned her, but something wouldn't let her as she witnessed the doubt swimming in her strong husband's eyes. Even if she could find it in herself to forgive Sebastian for what he had done to her, she would never be able to forgive him for how he had hurt her Charles. If Sebastian had been at her mercy in this moment, she would have choked the breath from his lungs with delight.

Esther spoke at last, as though she too had been weighing the evils in her mind. "Luve, the Lord alone kens what is best. Ask Him for wisdom and make the choice He gives ye peace about."

"He hasn't given me peace about staying. I know Horatio Chadwick too well, Esther."

"Our prayers go with ye then."

Charles's grim eyes lingered on Josie's face one last time as though he needed her consent to leave. Josie nodded, though he would never know what the wordless exchange cost her. There was a frightful air of finality when the door closed behind him.

Esther approached the bed and sank onto the edge with a sigh. "Och, I shouldna have sat down."

Her lips curved as she reached out and cupped Josie's face, thumb stroking across her cheek. "Ye looked so peaceful sleeping. We hated to wake ye, luve."

Esther's eyes were huge in her pale face, pupils dilated in their dusky depths.

"I forgive you," Josie teased, but her tone failed to rouse one of Esther's chuckles.

Esther seized her hands, and her grasp was cool as she bowed her head. "Father, we come to Ye confessing we dinna ken where to turn. Yer the only One that possesses the power to protect our Josie from the evil Horatio represents. We ken we fight not against flesh and blood, Father. The enemy wants to ravage and destroy, but Josie is Yer child whom Ye hold in Yer hand. Cover us beneath the shadow of Yer wings, Father, and please grant us Yer protection and victory. In Jesus's name, Amen."

Peace descended and rippled through Josie's being, ironing out every crease of fear and doubt. Her conscience pricked her for forgetting that the Almighty was still in control.

"And please help me, Father," Josie added, "to find it in my heart to forgive Horatio Chadwick. In Jesus's name, Amen."

A key grated in the lock, and Josie bolted upright. Esther scrambled off the bed and produced a pistol faster than Josie could blink.

Aurelius peered through the cracked door. Esther flushed red as she deposited the gun on the nightstand.

"That's quite all right," Aurelius said as Esther's lips parted in breathless apology. "One cannot take a killer too seriously.

Everything is in readiness. The moon is a little brighter tonight than I'd like, but it cannot be helped."

His gaze shifted toward Josie with a kindly crease around his eyes. "My dear, I trust you are well rested for the journey?"

"Yes, thanks to your gracious hospitality," Josie said with a smile. She glanced at Esther with the question hovering on her lips. Just how far were they actually taking her?

Aurelius handed Esther a bundle of some kind. He dropped a kiss on Josie's cheek. "Godspeed, my dear. Once this dreadful affair has been settled, I look forward to being neighbors."

"I'm hoping it will be settled sooner than we expect."

"Aye, 'tis unfortunate that this kettle of fish could not be avoided. As for around here, I highly doubt things will settle back to normal anytime soon, but that is what one gets for toying with another woman's husband. I hope you can find it in your heart to forgive Aurelia one of these days, Josie."

"It is strange how death gives you a fresh perspective on life. That seems trifling in comparison now."

"I'm glad you see it that way. You're a dear girl. Good night."

"Good night," Josie echoed.

Esther had already loosened the bundle's knot. It appeared to be a muslin sack such as a laundress would use. Josie's eyes widened as Esther pulled out a man's tricorn hat, a white linen shirt, a serviceable green waistcoat and matching jacket, brown breeches, stockings, and gold-buckle shoes.

With a wry twist of her mouth, Esther held the masculine articles out to her. "Forgive us, luve, but 'twas the only way we could ensure Horatio doesna recognize ye if he is watching this house."

"And what dashing gentleman, pray tell, am I supposed to be?" Josie asked.

"George Smith," Esther rattled off. "He is staying here overnight. If Horatio Chadwick sees the same visitor leave that he saw arrive, he will think nothing of it. If it is any comfort to ye," Esther added as she fished around in the bowels of the sack and withdrew a footman's uniform, "I too shall be donning the garments of a gentleman."

Josie accepted the outfit with a sigh, but as Esther released her stays, she suspected that the switch from fashion to comfort might not be unwelcome in her delicate condition.

The man's shirt enveloped her in a billowing cloud of linen, but she struggled to fasten the last two buttons of the waistcoat as her belly strained against the fabric. Josie willed the buttons to hold as she shoved an arm into the jacket. The breeches slid on without difficulty. Esther assisted her with the stockings and shoes as Josie planted the tricorn on her head. She approached the mirror with gravity, but at the sight she dissolved into giggles. The rather potbellied gentleman before her sported a jacket whose drooping shoulders boasted an excess of fabric, whereas the seat of his breeches was filled in without a wrinkle to spare.

"With no disrespect intended, I hope Mr. Smith is not slim in the midsection," Josie groaned. She couldn't prevent a snort from escaping her as a buxom footman sidled up beside her in the glass. Esther frowned back at the reflection.

"Other details are not so minute, but all one can do is hope that my cloak provides ample protection from exposure," she said with a shrug. Josie tried to smother her laughter as they stepped out into the hallway. She sensed Esther's scrutiny.

"Ye would do well to put a bit of swagger behind that gait. Just march along as though ye own the world like any man, Josie."

Again, Josie bit her lip, but her chest heaved with silent laughter as they began to descend the stairs. Tears squeezed from the corners of her eyes as she scolded herself for laughing—she feared popping every last button off the waistcoat.

The butler avoided their eyes as he opened the door. Josie's cheeks flamed as they passed by him. She attempted to stride toward the waiting carriage, mimicking Charles's long-legged gait in her mind's eye. She began to pause once she reached the carriage, but then she remembered that she was a man. No one held the doors open anymore. She seized the handle and mounted the step, catching herself from reaching down to drag her skirt out of harm's way.

Josie had never been so relieved to sit on a rigid carriage seat. The moonlight spilled into her breeches-clad lap, and she clenched her hands together. *Breathe in, breathe out . . .*

Josie almost jumped out of her skin at the crack of a whip. Cool night air rushed against her blushing flesh through the open window. She prayed that Esther could control the team and find her way in the dark.

The world floated by, dreamlike in outlines of moonlight silhouetted by the shadows. Weariness stole over her again, capturing the tension in her neck and shoulders as Josie's eyelids grew heavier by the minute. The knowledge penetrated that she was still ignorant of their destination. Exhaustion claimed her as she slumped in the seat. Her last sensation was that of rough leather sliding against her cheek.

Chapter Forty-One

*T*he rocking motion of the carriage ceased to be, and Josie's body lurched forward at the lull. She scrambled to right herself and blinked at the sight of her legs encased in breeches. Remembrance swept over her in a sharp wave. Dim gray light filtered through the window of yet another day she doubted she had the strength to face.

Josie leaned out the carriage window and studied her surroundings with renewed interest. A white clapboard cottage sat within a weathered picket fence. On its sloping, snow-covered lawn, an oak groped the swollen lead of the sky. It was a quaint setting, though the peeling paint and shuttered windows of the cottage evidenced that no one had been home for quite some time.

The box seat creaked, and Esther's boots sucked through the mud as she approached the door. Esther's bloodshot gray eyes sought Josie's above the sill.

"Welcome to Lilac Cottage, luve."

The latch gave an obliging click, and Josie alighted.

"You needn't have gotten the door for me, kind sir," she teased and received a brisk swat to her sore behind.

"I dinna ken what's gotten into ye," Esther groaned.

"Sleep, for one thing," Josie returned, studying the bruised crescents under the older woman's eyes that betrayed her exhaustion. Was something else troubling her? Esther turned away as though resenting the scrutiny and climbed back into the box seat.

"Where are you going?" Josie demanded.

"Luve, I'm hiding this in the barn across the way. A fine carriage is too conspicuous for such a lowly place."

Esther fished around her neck and withdrew a beribboned key. Josie bent low to catch it as it arced toward her with a sweep of peach satin. Esther coaxed the lathered horses forward, and Josie stepped away from the carriage wheels as they tossed globs of mud her direction.

She fingered the worn, frayed edge of the ribbon as she stepped toward the gate. As the key swayed like a pendulum, it clinked against another object. Josie glanced down and spotted the dull gleam of gold rubbing against the key's age-darkened patina. It was a wedding band, held by the same ribbon. Questions flooded her, but she pushed them aside.

No, I can't afford any distractions just yet.

She shoved the gate open with a faint squeak. A chilling wind tore strands of hair from beneath her tricorn. The cottage emanated a lonesome presence as her shadow darkened the threshold, but Josie doubted she was the one it missed. The cottage's charm, however distressed, had been nourished by the touch of someone in bygone years.

Her fingers shook as they reached for the key. Instinct stirred within, warning her that something awaited her on the other side of the front door. She wasn't afraid—*expectant* was the word she would have used. She felt the quickening of a knowledge that she was supposed to be here. Somehow she belonged, and the cottage conveyed a warm welcome.

Josie blamed her fanciful notions on wanting to make her dreams a reality. All she wanted was to feel safe again. A refuge, Charles had called this place. She turned the word over in her mind like a sweet morsel as she inserted the key in the well-worn lock. She liked the thought that he had selected this place just for her with the intention of keeping her safe. Perhaps he had known that this place would have this strange, welcoming effect on her.

Josie gave the weathered wood a gentle push, and it groaned open on arthritic hinges. The impression smacked her in the face like a pungent odor. She had been here before. A shiver skittered down her spine as the dim interior beckoned with relentless power. She took a fateful step, and the fragile semblance of peace evaporated as Josie fought for breath.

"No," she whispered. "No."

The whisper of memory deepened to a shriek as Josie whirled, the undeniable details of the yellow room punching her in the gut—the painting of puppies romping with children, the worn books arranged on the shelf, the blue wedding-ring quilt on the bed. This was the room that had haunted her dreams for eighteen years.

The quilt's blue circlets brought a fresh wave of recall. The wedding band presented an array of sinister possibilities as Josie considered that Esther had worn it around her neck all these years. Suspicious scenes flashed through Josie's mind as she remembered brooches in the sand, ghosts in the night, and a musty stack of love letters. The gold circlet was cool against her clammy palm, content to retain its secrets—as cold and void as Sebastian's composure had been as he plotted her end. The question rocked her world. Was Esther in league with Sebastian?

It was a preposterous notion to even consider, but reason abandoned her as the nightmare sprang to life. Oh, how she wished she could wake up and hear Charles's soft snores. Esther had helped Charles to rescue her, but did her former governess have an ominous motive for bringing her here?

Josie backed into the blunt corner of a table, and glass shattered, echoing the fragments of her life scattering right before her eyes. The overpowering scent of lavender filled her senses. Her head swam, remembering the feathery brush of curls against her cheek as she inhaled the nightmare's scent. The room began to whirl, but the staccato of running feet snapped her back to a state of high alert.

"Josie, are ye all right?"

Esther burst through the door. Fear flowed wild in her eyes.

"Who are you?" Josie flung out. Her tone was sharper than she had intended.

"Luve," Esther began, but Josie backed away as she came closer. Pain surfaced in Esther's eyes like scars long hidden.

"No," Josie blurted. "You tell me first exactly who you are."

A tear slid down Esther's cheek as her curved mouth trembled.

"I'm yer mother, Josie."

Josie's legs buckled underneath her, but her back met the wall as she clawed for a handhold. She slid to the floor, gaze fused to Esther's as though seeing her for the first time. Neither of them moved a muscle, as though if a word were spoken, their hearts would break. Josie gulped for air as her pulse gushed in her ears—but the knowledge brought the softness of a caress to her heart. Everything made sense to her now . . . the tender glances Father had exchanged with Esther, the fierceness of the maternal love Esther had always shown, the mysterious pain

Esther had always tried to hide from her. Josie thought her heart would burst with joy as the beauty of the truth painted her soul every color of the sunset.

"Oh, Mama, dearest Mama!"

Esther's face twisted in a reflection of Josie's own as she rushed toward her, rivulets streaming down her cheeks. Esther's arms pulled her close, and as Josie clung to her softness, she found herself unwilling to let go ever again.

"My bairn," Esther managed through the downpour as their tears mixed. The world of joyous awe in her tone healed a broken place inside Josie. For the first time, she knew what it was to be whole.

"How can I have been so blind?" Josie sobbed.

"Forgive me, bairn. Please forgive me," Esther wept as her back heaved so hard Josie feared she would fracture right there in her arms. "I—I didna want ye to live a lie, but yer father made me promise."

"I love you, Mama. I have always loved you."

For a long while they just clung to each other, rocking back and forth as they watered their hearts with the tears that held the power to heal their scars.

Chapter Forty-Two

The tavern's lit windows blinked at Charles through the falling dusk, their lazy, hooded depths promising victuals and possibly a place to bed down. No doubt the sleazy establishment boasted other less than desirable qualities, but Charles was too exhausted to continue on his journey.

Stalwart quickened his plodding step for the first time in miles as his pricked ears detected the neighs of four-hoofed brethren. Charles dismounted with a groan, fearing he would be condemned to walk bow-legged the rest of his life. For over a week now he had led Sebastian on a merry chase around the countryside. He was willing to bet he had landed in every rat's nest for miles around, but thus far he had not been robbed. No doubt thieves could smell his itchy trigger finger, and all but the cockiest among them always vouched for easier prey.

A scrawny shadow approached him. His heart went out to the waifish stableboy, but he knew better than to tip him. It would only risk his well-being as well as Charles's own. He laid a hand on the bony shoulder, and the boy flinched. His huge, puppy brown eyes reminded Charles of Alfie.

"I'll have a hot meal sent out to you, lad, for your trouble."

The broad grin that flashed through the grime on the lad's face gave him a pang. "I'm much obliged to you, sir."

"You earned it," Charles muttered as he pressed the reins into the boy's grubby fingers. As he approached the tavern, he could make out the splintering crashes and drunken yells of a brawl. Only his quick reflexes allowed him to avoid colliding with the chief culprit as a broad body that reeked of gin hurtled past him and splashed into the mud.

Charles sighed as he pushed through the door. The familiar clouds of tobacco and splashes of cheap liquor assailed his senses. He leaned against the splintered wooden bar.

"What'll ye have?" the round bartender barked.

"What have you got for fodder?"

"Salt pork and beans," the man mumbled and spat a brown stream of tobacco into the spittoon beside the counter.

Charles clinked a shilling down. "Oh, and have a hot plate of the same sent out to the stableboy," he added. The bartender gave him an odd glance, but he nodded and bellowed the order over his shoulder.

Charles grimaced as he climbed onto a stool, and the aching muscles in his legs protested. His arrival had not gone unnoticed by the seasoned barmaid, who sauntered toward him.

"Buy me a drink, blue eyes?" she crooned, linking an arm through his. Charles was tempted to slap her hand away, but then the shimmer of compassion in his Josie's gaze arose in his mind's eye. Beneath the heavy layers of makeup, the older woman's eyes were haggard and worn. He had been there. Living every moment for the next drop and draining every bottle in search of answers.

"It appears to me you've had more than enough already," Charles said. After taking a moment to study her as a fellow human being, he truly pitied the woman. She gave him a hearty slap on the back and cackled.

"That, my good fellow, is for me to decide."

Charles shook his head as he watched her sidle off in search of less sober victims. Josie had certainly changed him for the better. The very thought of her made his heart ache. His head began to nod, and he rested his forehead across his forearms.

Charles jumped as someone roughly shook him by the shoulder. He must have fallen asleep.

"Mister, yer snores will scare away the sober ones. If it's a bed you be wanting, it's two shillings a night," the bartender growled as he thrust a steaming plate of food under Charles's nose.

Charles smothered a yawn, and the bartender glanced at him askance as he flung the coins down without protest. The price was exorbitant, but one couldn't place a value on sleep, and unlike the rest, Charles could afford it. He could also afford to be particular, as the bartender would have been blind not to notice.

"Do you have a room with a good view of the road?" he asked.

The bartender grunted and tossed him a key. "Up the stairs, third room on yer right."

"Much obliged," Charles said, stifling another yawn. He took a bite, but the warmth of the hot food sliding down his gullet only made him drowsier. A few bites later, the beans settled like sawdust on his tongue as weariness rolled over him in waves. He forced them down and slid the empty plate forward before his feet hit the floor.

A blonde vixen who could have been Aurelia's twin sashayed into his path as he headed toward the staircase. With a flutter of kohl-enhanced lashes, she said in a sultry voice, "You look lonely, handsome."

"I've always been a loner," Charles muttered as he side-stepped her.

"Suit yourself," the dame sulked with a pettish shrug of her slim shoulders, but he didn't miss her cat-like green eyes flaring in outrage at his indifference. She was like Aurelia in more ways than one. Charles was too weary to be amused as he mounted the stairs. He nudged open the door to find the room swept and dusted, and fresh sheets on the bed. At such a steep cost, no doubt the shrewd proprietor had established a reputation for providing pleasure more than sleep.

As the night wore on, there was still no sign of Sebastian in the ill-lit yard. Dread pooled in Charles's gut. He should have known that he could not outsmart the fox for long. He had led the hunter on a merry chase away from his quarry, and now Sebastian was wise to him. The moon wasn't out tonight, and no man could find his way in the pitch dark. At first light, he would begin backtracking. He collapsed on the straw-tick mattress. He prayed Sebastian would run smack into the arms of the authorities as his gritty eyelids surrendered to the pull of gravity.

The impatient sputter of the teakettle interrupted Josie, and Esther rose to get it. A pensive smile curved Josie's lips as her mother poured the steaming liquid from the old-fashioned copper spout into the mismatched china. In so many ways, she would not have traded the past several weeks for anything in the world. The baring of their souls had birthed a bond between them that Josie cherished for the gift that it was. Living in the quaint little cottage had breathed new life into her weary spirit as she turned a fresh page in life. She would never have believed that hanging laundry as it flapped in the April breeze and drinking tea from chipped china could hold such pleasure. Sometimes it was the simplicity of life that made the living of it beautiful. Josie laced her fingers across her belly in utter contentment.

"Ye look as though ye ken a secret, daughter," Esther murmured as she carried the teacups to the table.

Josie gave a little shudder. "No, no more secrets."

"Och, not all secrets are bad ones, luve," Esther crooned as she gave Josie's fingers a warm squeeze. Her eyes smiled at her over the rim of her teacup.

"Go on then," Josie teased and gestured to the lavender dress she had found hanging in the closet.

Esther's eyebrows rose as her teacup clinked against the saucer. "I can still take ye across my knee, Miss Impertinence," she said in a poor attempt at sternness.

"The love nest?" Josie prodded.

"Aye," Esther murmured with a far-away look in her eyes. "That's what we called this place. My Randolph brought me here to avoid a scandal after I told him I was with child. He and Rose had been married for two years, and Delia was thirteen months old. Their marriage was unhappy from the start. He told me he had only married Rose because she was a socialite with a tempting dowry, and he was in serious debt, having gambled away the mine's profits as fast as they came in. None of that mattered to my broken heart, for I had loved him long before Rose ever came along. I kenned I should never have accepted his advances, but I was young and foolish. I was too flattered by the fact that the master would look upon me, the Scottish maid, with favor that I didna think of the consequences until it was too late. I considered running away to an unwed mothers' asylum, but I kenned Randolph would find me there. I had nowhere else to run."

She smiled sadly, looking into the hazy past as she spoke. "He carried me over the threshold like the bride I wasn't and looped the key around my neck while he kissed me. This will be our love nest, my Highland cridhe, for our love child, he promised. He kept it and visited me often on so-called business trips. As the last month of my pregnancy arrived, he sent Suzanne to stay with me. Ye were born on a stormy night in September. It was a difficult labor for me, but I fought because ye were the only thing I lived for. When I laid eyes on ye, Josie, I kenned I would love ye with my every breath till the end of time. My love for Randolph after that seemed so shallow, but I didna regret ye, Josie. I still loved yer father in spite of his betrayal of my heart. I loved him for giving me ye."

A lump formed in Josie's throat as Esther squeezed her hand. "Ye were a perfect bairn. Suzanne was an angel, and to this day I dinna ken how I could have made it through those weeks without her. In many ways I was like a bairn myself, needing to be fed, have my dressings changed for I had lost a lot of blood, and assisted in tasks as simple as using the necessary and dressing myself. She nursed me through as tenderly as though I had been her own daughter and confessed to me she had lost her own little girl. In nursing me back to health she felt she had fought death all over again and won. I think caring for ye helped her grieving heart to heal, Josie, when I was too weak to care for ye properly myself. Randolph wanted to pay her and send her on her way after that, but I wouldna hear of it. That was one battle I won, and she was faithful to the end."

Esther's hand shook a little as she brought her teacup to her lips. Tears stung Josie's eyes as she grasped the sacrifices that comprised the foundations of her very existence.

"Randolph deeded me this cottage to ensure the two of us would always have a roof over our heads, and he provided for us financially," Esther continued. "I found it in my heart to believe him when he told me I was the only woman he would ever love. Yer father wanted a son terribly, but shortly after yer first birthday he discovered that Rose would never bear another child. He was most disappointed in Rose. It seemed to me that history was repeating itself, for Suzanne had told me of all the Chadwick hardships concerning yer grandfather's two wives. The hardest night of my life came shortly thereafter, when Rose became quite ill. The doctor prescribed a warmer climate for her recovery, and Randolph came by to tell me that he was taking her to Europe for a year and perhaps longer."

Esther's voice trailed off, and as her eyes grew moist, Josie already knew what had happened on that night.

"He took me that night, didn't he, Mama?" she whispered.

"Aye," Esther sniffed as she dabbed at her eyes with the corner of her apron. "He was convinced he could give ye a better life than what I could give ye. Rose wanted another child desperately, but he couldna persuade me that she would love ye as much as I. We both loved ye, I think, more than we loved each other. He knew I couldna forgive him for marrying Rose. At first, amidst our passionate farewell, I thought he had forgotten the notion. Then in the middle of the night while I slept, I heard ye screaming through the open window. I raced outside just in time to hear receding hoofbeats as he took ye from me."

Josie wrapped her arms around her mother's heaving shoulders, marveling at the miracle that they had found each other at last in spite of such odds. In the name of love, her darling mother had endured such suffering on her behalf. Esther's ragged breathing slowed at last, and Josie released her so that she could close that chapter of their lives once and for all.

"On his pillow there was a letter with enough pound notes enclosed to keep me eating for a while, but not for a lifetime. For several weeks I hunted for a means to support myself, desperate to escape this cottage and the memories. When I lost ye I lost my world, and I had to find myself again. There are no words to describe the blackness of my grief. I sought solace in the only other friend I had in the world, Suzanne. If she had not led me to the only true source of joy, I fear I might have perished, for I had no desire to live without ye. She was a strong Methodist, and she introduced me to the Lover of my soul that night. Not only did she aid me in finding eternal life, but she told me of a home run by the Methodists that prepared unwed mothers for respectable paid positions, such as teachers, governesses, ladies' companions, and ladies' maids. I went, and they took me under their wing. For two years I was educated there in the genteel arts and graduated from the program early. I wasn't sure if the reference they provided me had any substance to it or not, but I responded to an advertisement for a position as lady's maid to the heiress of an affluent family. I am convinced that it was only by the Lord's grace that they gave me the position. My mistress, Catherine, was a dear girl with a kind heart. The Lord had endowed her with beauty, goodness, and riches. I contrived to please her, and she confided in me more than her own mother at times, I think. After Catherine married, her mother Mrs. Hollingsworth kept me as her companion, saddened by the loss of her only child, who had inherited the fortune of her late husband. Two years later an advertisement caught my eye as I was reading her the paper. A widower was looking for a governess for his two motherless girls . . ."

Josie's gasp halted Esther's narrative, but her mother's answering smile was patient.

"Aye, daughter. The Lord united us again all those years ago. My heart nearly stopped beating when I read the address given of Chadwick Park, Portreath, Cornwall. Mrs. Hollingsworth gave me permission to visit a relative in Cornwall on urgent family business. I feared yer father would drop dead of shock when I applied for the position. Strangely enough, he was not angry, and he immediately gave it to me. I think only then did he truly understand the depth of a mother's love, for he believed what he did was best for ye at the time. Time had proven him to be sorely wrong as he told me of yer night terrors. He was sincerely penitent for taking ye, and the Lord helped me to forgive him."

"I don't think he ever forgave himself though, Mama. That burden of guilt aged him beyond his years. Did you read the letter he gave to Charles on our wedding day?"

"Aye, that it did, luve. I begged him to tell ye the truth, but he took that secret with him to his grave. Yer father's confession of abiding love went a long way in softening my heart toward him again. It grieved me to leave Mrs. Hollingsworth, but my heart gave me no choice in the matter. I returned just long enough to pack my bags, but Mrs. Hollingsworth understood when I told her I had found my daughter. It was difficult seeing ye again, Josie, and kenning I'd missed all the years of yer childhood growth. At first I wondered if perhaps I had made a mistake, not kenning if I could bear being in a relationship with ye where ye didna even ken yer own mother. However, I fell in love with ye all over again. Mere weeks went by before I realized to my deep chagrin that yer father was determined to resume our intimate relations with each other. When I expressed my desire to leave that life behind because the Lord had made me a different woman, he wouldna hear of it. He argued that in the sight of God we were already man and wife. I couldna bear to lose ye all over again, so I agreed, God forgive me, upon the contingency that he secretly marry me. He proposed, rather gladly as though he thought that would redeem the sum of his past mistakes, and we were married in a secret ceremony. He was no longer ashamed of my lowly status, but he could not afford to announce our marriage publicly because it would expose his deception regarding ye. Everyone believed Rose's lie that she had miraculously conceived and given birth to ye in Europe, never dreaming that ye were a stolen love child. At first I married him solely for yer sake, Josie, but in time my love for him was rekindled. Yer father had many weaknesses, but I can assure ye with all my heart that I loved him until the day he died." Esther finished with a brave smile.

Josie's tongue clung to the roof of her mouth, and she swallowed the last of her tepid tea. "I always knew Rose didn't love me the way she loved Delia. She didn't even like me. Father always favored me, the daughter of the woman he loved, over her daughter."

"She was a cold creature," Esther said in a brittle voice. "I suppose one shouldna bear ill will toward the dead, but I think I always have, deep down, when I think of how she punished ye for yer Father's sins."

"I found Rose's brooch in the sand outside of the tunnel when I tried to investigate Father's death. Forgive me, Mama, for doubting you. I followed you one night, believing you were masquerading as the ghost for some sinister purpose. After I found your love letters to Father I didn't know what to think. What does *chridhe* mean in Gaelic?"

"Heart. I was his Highland heart," Esther explained as her eyes grew moist. "That white cloak became a legend in itself after ye married Charles. I couldna assuage the rumors, because it would have revealed my late-night rendezvouses with yer father as his wife. I can understand why ye were afeared, luve. But how did ye ken that was Rose's brooch?"

"I used to amuse myself with her jewelry box when I was bored."

"I think every time I wore that, it was in secret triumph over Rose, as proof that she was dead and buried to his heart. It truly was as though she had never existed between us after I became yer governess."

"It must have been very hard on him when I took you with me on my honeymoon. I never guessed what you really were to each other."

"It was him that implemented the secrecy that bound us the rest of our married life, Josie. Ye cannae be blamed."

"The servants used to gossip something fierce about you and Father. I remember telling Father what I had overheard, but he evaded the truth. In my childish innocence I believed him, of course, but he sent those maids packing in a hurry. How did you know about the tunnel, Mama? I found it when I disobeyed Father as a girl and played in the west wing."

"Suzanne kenned it was there afore Sebastian's smuggling operation began and told me of it hoping I would nail the panel shut. She was always afraid someone would use it to sneak into the house at night. If only I had listened . . . her fears were not unfounded."

Josie reached out and squeezed her mother's hand.

"Mama, there is no way you could have known. When you spoke to Charles about his father, how did he react?"

Esther's mouth pursed as though in deep thought. Her eyes were a cloudy gray after reliving the storms of her life as she stared past Josie out the window. "Shocked, horrified, yet strangely . . . freed," she said after a moment.

When she spoke again her voice was raspy, as though the revelations had wrung her dry. "Mercy, it is getting dreary in here. I'll light a lantern so we'll have light to cook by. No doubt poor Edward is getting hungry."

Josie laughed aloud at her mention of the crusty curmudgeon they had hired as a guard, causing Esther to break into a wide smile as her arms opened in a wider embrace.

"He is just grateful he doesn't have to eat his own cooking," Josie observed.

"There were times I didna think I would hear that laugh again, luve," Esther whispered as she pressed Josie's head against her bosom. "Och, thank Ye for giving me my daughter back, precious Lord Jesus."

The door crashed open with a bang. A shudder traveled through Esther's arms as they slipped from Josie's shoulders. The sight of Sebastian's leering face froze Josie's feet to the floor.

"My, my what a cozy little scene. Mind if I join you?" he asked with a mocking sneer.

"How did ye find us?" Esther demanded. She stood and angled herself in front of Josie.

"Charles thought he could lead me off the trail, but I saw through his little ruse. I promised him I would find you sooner or later. I remembered reading some old love letters where Randolph mentioned a cottage in Redruth where he kept his mistress. I searched for the carriage, but in the end it was the matching Bays in the pasture that betrayed your hiding place."

With a cruel gleam in his eyes, he approached Esther until he had backed her against the wall.

"Now I have a question for you, my elusive little creature. Just who do you think you are?" he asked, running the pistol barrel along her cheek until it cupped her chin. Esther's calm gray eyes never wavered, clear as the glassy surface of a lake.

"I'm Josie's mother and Randolph's wife."

"I knew I should have gotten rid of you while I had the chance," Sebastian snarled. "To think I had Randolph's wife beneath my roof this whole time! I could have made you my own little Highland cridhe . . ."

Josie flung herself at Sebastian's feet as she found her voice. "Please, take me if you must, but don't hurt my mother."

Sebastian glanced down at her with indifference boring his features. "It is indeed a pity, Josie, that this Scottish blood had to flow in your veins and taint your soul. Your father always was a weakling, and now I must purge you before the name of Chadwick is polluted by the son you carry."

Esther hauled Josie upright, and Josie's voice was hushed by horror. "Why are you doing this?"

"I was the eldest son, rightful heir to the Chadwick name and fortune, and as such entitled to all the privileges thereof. What robbed me of this life I could have led, where everything was handed to me on a golden platter? A beautiful woman, who gave birth to Randolph. What sin had I committed for being so unjustly punished for my existence? My mother had been unlovable in my father's eyes. Even her death, all while trying to please him in giving him an heir, failed to redeem me from the taint of their union. He shipped me off to boarding school the moment I was old enough to be out of his sight, and I only came home on holidays. Meanwhile he met your grandmother

Violet, whom he loved madly, and when she gave birth to a son, it sealed my fate. When my father in a drunken fit of rage drove himself and Violet off the edge of the cliff, all of his debts came to light. Rumors of the Chadwick ghost have haunted this family's name ever since . . ."

"Which you purposefully fueled even further! Why did you snuff the yule candle in that white cloak?" Josie interrupted.

"It was a message to your father that his doom was coming. Now I have a question for you, daughter-in-law! Who was Lady Chadwick's ghost of flesh and blood?"

"Esther in her white cloak sneaking over to Chadwick Park to visit her husband."

Sebastian's laughter rang out, reminding Josie of a blade being unsheathed from its scabbard.

"For a clever wench, I hood-winked you along with everyone else. No one dared to investigate the beach at Treathston Heights for smugglers with Lady Chadwick's ghost flitting about in the dead of night, and the servants spread the rumors very well. I am her ghost, and the legendary curse of the hussy that robbed me of everything proved to be a blessing in disguise!"

Sebastian smirked at his own pun. "I was only eleven years of age when I was informed that my father had disowned me in favor of my younger half-brother, I ran away from the school. I vowed that one day I would have revenge on the man who fathered me but refused to carry any paternal recognition or duty toward me. I swore I didn't need my father's inheritance to make my way in the world. I was going to do more than just exist; I was going to thrive and be more successful than he ever was. If he thought me unworthy, I was going to prove him mistaken, but I wasn't going to let him or Randolph cheat me out of what was rightfully mine."

Josie blinked at the irony of it all. The true Chadwick curse was a plague of rejection. Both she and Charles had inherited their sense of unworthiness from the plague, and the roots of the Chadwick family tree were a twisted tangle of guilt and bitterness. What rotten fruit the seeds had borne. Sebastian's vile gloating continued until she wanted to cover her ears.

"I became a powder monkey in Her Majesty's Royal Navy and gradually worked my way up. During the war I was given the commission of captain and captured several ships. I invested the considerable reward money I'd gained in a sugar plantation, which turned a tidy profit every annum. Ready to abandon the bachelor lifestyle, I managed to snag with my good name and fortune a beautiful heiress named Adelaide Corbyn. Charles was born, but then we lost her. Freed from all obligations, I knew it was time to come back to my roots and begin taking back everything that was mine. I changed our names to Radcliffe and purchased a copper mine, Treathston Heights, and as much land as I could get my hands on surrounding Chadwick Park. Soon I found out that the only way I could get at Chadwick Park itself was by Charles's marriage to Delia. There was a time when I would have let you live, but now it is too late. There is the risk that the child you carry is a boy. I cannot allow the Chadwick heir to come from your womb."

"If you pull that trigger, you will lose a son," Josie cried. "Is that what you want? To kill your relationship with Charles?"

"He may turn his back on me, but he is the last of the Chadwicks. He cannot turn his back on his name. Charles is still young. Another woman will come into his life and help him to forget you. Then our glorious bloodline can continue uncorrupted as it always has been."

Sebastian raised the leveled pistol barrels, taking aim as he cocked the hammers back. A second faint click echoed it, and Sebastian sidestepped like greased lightning.

Josie's breath caught at the sight of Charles, but the moment was cut short when Sebastian pressed one pistol to her temple and the other against Esther's.

"I knew you couldn't shoot your own father in the back, son. Now drop the barking iron, or I'll blow both of their brains out."

"You taught me all you know with a gun. I wouldn't have to shoot to kill to make you wish you'd never laid eyes on this cottage."

"I also taught you that it would be foolhardy to shoot at a target this close to other persons. Aye, I taught you well."

Sebastian laughed, causing the cold ring of metal to shudder against Josie's skull with the imminent promise of death. Josie willed her teeth not to chatter and invite the bullet, but ice flowed through her veins.

The blood drained from Charles's face as he bent and laid his pistol on the floorboards. Sebastian circled them again, waving Charles against the wall as he took several steps back. Josie willed him to meet her eyes one last time, and their gazes fused. The hard, blue depths of her beloved's eyes did not soften. She read his message loud and clear. This was not good-bye.

"No, son," Sebastian chuckled, "Don't go a step further unless you want to be spattered in blood."

"For the love of all that is sacred, Father," Charles burst out. "If you pull that trigger I will never forgive you!"

Sebastian's lip curled. "Josie is the death of all I have lived for. I must try to resurrect my dream from the ashes of all you have destroyed. Nothing has ever stood in my way, and a woman certainly isn't going to stop me now. Women have always been the ruin of this family. My father and Randolph both were ruined by women they loved when their hearts became ruled by them. I will not allow you, son, to make the same mistake. Women are useful for many things. They bring wealth, status, children, and pleasure, but the mistake comes when men surrender their hearts in a blind worship called Love and their once sound judgment is colored like sentimental, lovesick fools. I will not allow you to throw everything away for a woman, Charles. If I were to let her live now, her child, the fruit of love, would triumph over the fruit of duty."

Josie watched Charles's slender hands clench and saw what he meant to do. There was a rush of motion. Her heart screamed as spurts of flame belched from the pistols, and Charles fell. Her brain registered a rushing whine of wind beside her ear followed by splintering wood as a second bullet missed her by a hair's breadth. An awful silence fell, her eardrums still throbbing as Esther rushed in front of her. She waited for the sounds of a scuffle. A man's gut-wrenching sob ripped the air.

"No, Mama," Josie hissed as Esther's body pressed against her, cutting off her view. She strained to see over Esther's shoulder as the hair prickled on the back of her neck. She heard a metallic thud as another pistol hit the floorboards. She twisted, wrenching her body at an unnatural angle, and caught a glimpse of Sebastian raising her Charles with his free arm. A crimson tide drenched Charles's shirt, and Josie's knees turned to jelly.

"No!" she screamed. Esther's arm shot out and yanked her back as she fought to get to him. Josie's strength drained as the life bled out of her husband, drop by agonizing drop.

"Curse you, Charles," Sebastian spat. "You always get in my way."

Sebastian dropped his second pistol and tore off his shirt, pressing the balled fabric against Charles's wound. Desperation lit the father's eyes as Charles's lips moved, but Josie could detect no sound. One brawny arm held Charles upright as Sebastian's other hand snaked toward the pistol.

Esther's shoulder struck Josie's as her mother lunged for the twin to Charles's pistol lying on the floor. Time stopped as Josie watched Sebastian's fingers close around the pistol. Resolve steadied Esther's fingers as she raised the gun and squeezed the trigger in the span of a heartbeat. The deafening shot mingled with the roar of Josie's thundering pulse.

A bloody hole riddled the center of Sebastian's chest, reddening his salt and pepper hair. Shock and pain registered in his fierce eyes before they glazed over. The final curtain had fallen for Horatio Chadwick, but with characteristic stubborn will, he rasped out his final words through blood-frothed lips.

"You're weak, just like your mother. She almost ruined my plans by landing in the Bethlem asylum, but now you've succeeded in destroying everything I've worked for."

Sebastian slumped over Charles's body. A spasm wracked him, but then at last he was still.

Esther flung the gun away with a whimper and rushed toward Charles. Josie followed close at her heels, but a stitching pain gripped her abdomen. She crumpled to her knees with a moan as the sensation of something warm and ripe splitting open gripped her. *No, baby, don't come yet.* She couldn't draw a full breath, but she managed to crawl forward to her beloved. He was unconscious, and her scalding tears burned as they welled up in her eyes.

"How bad is it, Mama?" she panted.

Esther's brow creased as she applied pressure to Charles's wound. "It's a clean wound just beside the shoulder. The bullet went straight through, but he's losing a lot of blood. I hope it didna puncture a lung."

Josie pulled his head into her lap, studying the beloved features to forget her own pain. His chalky lips accentuated the ashen pallor of his face. He hadn't been taking care of himself. The hollows of his cheeks were gaunt, there was several days' worth of stubble on his jaw, and the bruises beneath his eyes betrayed too many sleepless nights.

"Luve, take a few deep breaths and calm yerself. Yer Charles is strong. He'll fight through this. Sebastian can't take him from ye now after all he's done to be with ye."

A drop pelted Charles's nose like rain, and Josie brushed it away.

Remember . . . together we are stronger than the storm. Believe in us, darling. Believe in a future I have dreamed of where we shall never be separated again.

Josie clung to the scrap of comfort she derived from the recollection, but then her pain refused to be ignored any longer. She doubled over him as Esther gripped her shoulder. Fear honed an edge in her mother's voice.

"Josie, what's wrong?"

"Baby," Josie gasped out.

"Oh, Lord have mercy," Esther groaned.

A man's familiar voice intruded. "Ladies, are you all right?"

Edward creaked in, holding a kerchief to the back of his head.

"He hit ye, Edward?"

"I'm sorry, Miss Esther. I heard him coming, but he was too fast for me. When I came to, a goose had laid a powerful-sized egg on the back of my head. Land sakes, Missy, it looks like a gale hit this room. Is he dead?"

"Aye, he cannae hurt anyone again, but he left plenty of damage behind. He shot Josie's husband Charles, and now her bairn is on the way."

"I'd hitch the horses to the carriage, Missy, but that poor feller looks too far gone to be rattled and bounced about. I'll ride for the doc, and don't you fret now. 'Taint far at all."

"Thank ye, Edward. Ye are a godsend," Esther called after him.

Neither of them blamed him for failing to protect them. Even a younger man wouldn't have stood much of a chance against Horatio Chadwick. Josie prayed that Edward would muster all the haste his old, tired bones could hurry with.

Chapter Forty-Three

oncerned voices drifted to Charles as though he were lost in a London fog. They descended through the haze as beams of pain radiated through him with every breath, cutting a sharp path of awareness. Wincing, Charles made an effort to pry open his eyelids. The light overwhelmed his screaming senses. His lips formed Josie's name, but his mouth was dry as sandpaper. He tried again, and a graceful shadow slanted over him. A gentle hand smoothed damp hair away from his forehead, and he tasted the rim of a cup. He bent forward, ignoring the searing pain, and sucked the water down. It sloshed and dribbled down his neck in a trail of cool relief. He squinted at the woman hovering over him, and disappointment swelled in him as he made out her features.

"Esther," he grimaced, but she was gracious enough to smile at him. Behind her, he recognized the cottage.

"Yer wife is rather indisposed at the moment."

Frustration blossomed through him. What could possibly be more important to Josie than him? He swallowed the urge to whine as a moan sounded beside him. Craning his neck, his heart leaped at the sight of Josie on the neighboring pillow. Her features were pained, and tendrils of her hair clung to perspiring skin.

"Josie, you've been shot!" he exclaimed, bolting from the pillows. A hiss escaped his gritted teeth as the pain stabbed without mercy.

Her eyes widened in alarm. "No, darling, you mustn't move, or you'll start bleeding again," she said, reaching for his hand.

"But you're in pain," he insisted as their fingers laced together.

"Someone wise told me on my honeymoon that I didn't always have to know everything."

Her smile reassured him somewhat. Then she grimaced again. She gripped his hand for all she was worth and held her belly. Awareness crashed down on him. Her time had come . . . too soon.

"You don't have to protect me, love," he murmured. "I may be a man, but I would have to be blind not to notice what's happening."

"Just please stay calm, Charles. The baby's coming before its time because I was so afraid."

"I won't make any promises. It's hard watching you suffer," he muttered.

"Just listening to the sound of your voice and feeling your hand in mine is a great comfort. Now don't do anything foolish."

"I'm going to have to take our child out from under your wing every so often, or you'll smother him to death," Charles teased.

"What a scoundrel I'm married to," she sighed, but then she stiffened again. His gut clenched in synchrony with hers.

A movement stirred out of the corner of Charles's eye. He glanced up as a man exuding professionalism approached from the shadows.

"I'm Dr. Inglewood. How do you feel?"

"Me or her?"

The doctor chuckled with wry amusement.

"Why you, of course. You're the man that's been shot. She'll feel better, I expect, within the next hour or two."

"That soon?" Charles demanded.

"You still haven't answered my question. Something tells me you are going to be a difficult patient."

Josie purred her agreement, and Charles frowned. "It throbs, but when a bullet goes clean through you that's what happens," he snapped.

"I know the little wife is listening to every word you say, but I can't help you if you are a typical husband with bloated pain tolerance. Is the pain manageable?"

"Barely," Charles growled, and the doctor nodded.

"That's better, young man. I'll give you some laudanum."

Charles held up a hand in protest as the doctor dug through his bag. "If that's going to make me half-sprung, it can wait. She needs me here with her."

The corners of the doctor's mouth lifted as he returned the bottle to the bag's bowels.

"You've got a good husband there."

The light of Josie's smile dimmed his pain as she leaned over him. Her swollen belly seized against his side, causing her to catch her breath.

"The dearest, bravest, and most loving husband in the whole world," she pronounced after a moment, though her voice shook. When their lips met, salty from perspiration and tears, Charles knew it was the sweetest kiss they had ever shared.

"And he's going to make just as good a father," she added, stroking his hair. A sharp cry escaped her as terror darkened her eyes. Esther and the doctor sprang forward, lifting the hem of her nightshirt. Charles's insides trembled for her as tears rolled down her cheeks.

"Oh God have mercy," Josie sobbed as she crushed his fingers in a vise grip. "I'm scared, Charles. The baby wasn't supposed to come until the end of May."

Esther gripped her other hand, blinking back tears.

"Miss, your baby is crowning. You must remain calm and push right now," the doctor instructed.

Josie's features twisted as she bore down. Charles leaned close, gritting his teeth as he clutched his throbbing shoulder.

"Our baby will be just fine, beloved," he gasped out, "because it has a strong, brave mother. I trust you, Josie, and I trust God."

Her pain-glazed eyes brightened at his pronouncement of belief. She was such a little thing, heaving with all her strength to push their child into the world. Every vein bulged as she strained and then collapsed against the pillow.

"Yer doing fine, luve," Esther praised. "Breathe deeply and just give us several more strong ones. Ye'll get to hold yer bairn any moment now."

Charles didn't know how much longer he could bear to watch her strain. Just as he feared she would break, a second mewling cry blended with hers.

Josie sank back, beaming in triumph as joy split her face like the sun breaking free from the clouds. Charles's heart pounded against his ribs as the doctor lifted the tiny, squalling infant. A boy. A son. Bloodied buttocks twitched, and pink feet thrashed as Esther dried him off and wrapped him in blankets she had warmed on the spirit lamp in the corner of the room. His lusty cries belied his delicate, premature size. Their son was a fighter. Charles's breath hitched in his chest as Esther turned the bundle, revealing the scrunched, red features of the miraculous new life their love had created. *Thank You, Lord, for the lives of my wife and child.*

"Charles and Josie, ye have a son," Esther rejoiced.

Josie flung her arms around Charles's neck, and he winced as she jolted the bed.

"You did it, Josie," he choked, stroking her back. "You did it!"

"No, we did it together, Charles," she whispered as the wetness of her tears soaked his cheek.

She released him, and he propped the pillows behind her back as Esther carried their son over to be adored. Charles marveled at the taut umbilical cord trailing from the edges of the blanket.

Josie's eyes kindled with the fierce glow of mother-love as she took their son into her arms. Charles feasted on the sight. His Josie had never looked so beautiful. She angled toward him so that he could see their son's face. Charles beamed as his eyes caressed the child's bald head, feathery lashes, and tiny nails. He was everything their son should be. A rush of pride warmed his chest.

"Charles Randolph Chadwick?" Josie suggested.

"Randolph Charles Chadwick," Charles corrected. "One Charles is enough for this family."

Josie giggled, causing her dimple to flash.

"Oh Charles," she remonstrated, and he grinned back.

"Mrs. Chadwick, the afterbirth should come within the hour. Your son's lungs sound as strong as can be expected for over a month early, but it is critical to his survival that you keep him warm and feed him as often as he will eat. He may only be strong enough to suckle for short periods of time, which makes frequent feedings a necessity. As for you, Mr. Chadwick, this laudanum should help you sleep. I'll be back to check in on you all in the morning. Miss Esther will certainly have her hands full with the three of you, but I have another birth to attend tonight."

Charles opened his mouth to receive his dose and grimaced at the galling taste as he swallowed.

"Thank you for everything, Dr. Inglewood. We are most grateful."

"The pleasure was all mine. You've got a fine family there, Mr. Chadwick. Good night now."

Esther trotted after the doctor to snag the last of his instructions. She returned a moment later, fussing with the coverlet and kissing her grandson.

Charles fought the sense of grogginess as Esther cut the cord and tended to the afterbirth.

"Both of ye have one job, and that is rest," Esther admonished them as she patted her hands dry.

Gratitude overwhelmed him for Esther—the mother of his Josie, he remembered with a rush of warmth as he recalled the conversation he had overheard when his own flesh and blood threatened to rob him of his true family. In such a short time, the nurturing woman had become a mother to him as well.

"I don't know what we would have done without you, Esther."

"Now dinna thank me, Charles. I owe ye my life and the lives of my daughter and grandson. Randolph would be most proud. Somehow I ken he is watching us, relishing his justice and the sight of his namesake. Good night, my luves."

The door creaked shut. Charles slid an arm around Josie, fascinated by the milk stains spreading through her nightshirt as their son nuzzled her breasts. Josie fumbled with the buttons and guided her son's mouth. After much patience, she succeeded in feeding him.

"Ouch," Josie complained. "He is his father's son, eating everything in sight."

"Pardon me?" Charles asked with mock offense.

"If he grows up to be as tall, strong, and handsome as his father, I don't mind," Josie murmured with a tender smile playing on her lips.

Charles yawned. "Now don't you tell me I look tired," he warned as Josie's lips parted. "Because you are certainly more exhausted than me. Moreover, I can afford to stay up a little longer until my son finishes his first meal."

"Yes sir," Josie quipped, but Charles's lids grew heavier by the moment until she blew out the candle.

"You don't need the light, my love?"

"No, Charles. You are my light."

Her smile warmed him in the darkness. The sheets rustled as she groped for his hand and their fingers entwined.

"Come here," he commanded.

"Oh darling, I don't want to hurt you."

"Nonsense. I've slept without you in my arms for far too long."

Josie pressed herself against him. His son's downy head grazed his bare chest as he wrapped his arms around their softness.

"I've missed you too," she whispered.

Charles pressed a kiss against Josie's brow, drinking in the silkiness of her hair against his cheek and the milky, newborn scent as he listened to his son's soft breathing.

"We aren't going to lose him, are we, Charles?"

"I'm not God, Josie, but after all we've been through, I doubt it very much. If our son is anything like his father, he'll thrive. I too was born before my time."

"You always know how to reassure me," Josie murmured. Charles faded, but her next question jarred him awake. "How long were you conscious?"

"Long enough to grasp Horatio Chadwick's final confession."

"I'm ever so sorry, darling. I wanted to break it to you gently."

"My sweet Josie, you've given me far better reason to concern myself with the present rather than the past."

Her soft sigh lulled him to sleep.

A woman's voice shrieked his name. Her horror-stricken blue eyes implored him through the barred window. Chains rattled from bony wrists as Charles hesitated. He didn't know this woman, and yet those eyes belonged to his mother. He took a step forward, and her shriveled lips parted in a maniacal laugh. A chill swept over him as she pointed a claw-like finger at something behind him. Charles whirled as his father pressed the muzzle of a gun to Josie's temple. Screams deafened him as Sebastian grinned and pulled the trigger. Blood gushed from Josie's eyes.

His foot met something solid. The air pulsed with screams to match the throbbing pain spreading through his chest.

"Charles."

His eyes flew open in the darkness. The screams continued, piercing his eardrums, but his mouth was closed. Who . . . ?

"You woke the baby."

Josie wriggled out of his grasp to light the candle. Its dim glow fell upon his howling son. Charles's fingers curled around a flailing fist as Josie gathered the child into her arms.

"Forgive me, son," he gasped.

The baby's lusty wails ebbed into greedy suckling. Josie collapsed against the pillow as she fixed her husband with a concerned glance.

"Poor darling, you're hurting."

Charles rubbed a hand over his eyes. His fingers came away wet. "I know better than to lie to you."

"You kept calling for your mother," Josie prompted. "Then you screamed my name. All the time you squeezed me harder until your son decided he had been smothered long enough."

Charles's eyes caressed her dear, haggard features as sweet relief engulfed him. "Oh Josie," he choked. "We almost died tonight."

Her eyes glistened back at him as she leaned closer and pressed her cheek into the hollow of his jaw. Silence fell as he lay there, vulnerable and comforted in the shadow of her heart.

"But we didn't die, Charles."

"I was so angry with her. So hateful and bitter and ashamed of her all those years, Josie. And she was the victim all the while."

"Anyone would have felt the same, darling. You were betrayed regardless. Let the wound bleed out, my love," she whispered, touching the wetness of his cheek. "And then I pray you will find it in yourself to let the scar heal."

"How does one bury the past? We can never forget. Every time you call our son's name, won't it hurt you?"

"It will at first, but the pain will dull with time. Randolph is the beginning of my healing, Charles. He is the living triumph over the evil that took Father from me."

"The shadows of the past will always haunt us like ghosts. I've made a decision, Josie."

She propped herself up on one elbow, her eyes luminous in the candlelight, as she waited for him to continue.

"We're not going back to Treathston Heights. It will always be stained with blood. We're going to get a fresh start for ourselves and begin a new life together. I already know the estate I want. Seabrooke. Before I knew you, Josie, I would pause there, on my way back to Treathston, and dream of a better life where home actually meant something good. I made inquiries this past week while I was leading the fox astray and learned that it recently came up for sale. You will love it, Josie. Acres upon acres of lush pasture that kisses the ocean's edge. The charming Elizabethan manor house is named after the brook that flows through the property into the sea. We'll build big stables and yards of white picket fence that Stalwart and Guinevere can roam to their hearts' content. Their foal will be the first of the finest bloodline of thoroughbreds England has ever seen."

"It sounds enchanting. I have only one condition."

"What's that, angel?"

"That our suite will consist of one large bedchamber, not adjoining rooms. That way we have to make up if we fight, and we can't shut each other out ever again."

"I wholeheartedly agree," he said, but as he leaned toward her, she placed a restraining finger on his nose.

"On second thought I have one more condition."

"Yes?" Charles drawled impatiently as he nibbled her finger.

"That Esther comes along and lives with us."

"Madame, that is an even more ingenious condition than the first. May I compliment you upon the fact that within that beautiful head resides a highly intelligent brain?"

"You may indeed. Thank you, Charles Chadwick," Josie mumbled before their lips met. As the kiss broke, Josie demanded, "When can we go see Seabrooke, Charles?"

A thrill ignited in his chest as her excitement waved the spark of a dream into the blazing flames of reality. He reached out and touched her cheek. "As soon as young Randolph is strong enough to withstand the travel. I daresay he will be by our anniversary."

Her ears never failed to catch the subtle change in his voice. "What is it, darling?" she whispered.

A lump formed in his throat, and Charles swallowed hard as he prayed she would understand. "A whole year has flown by, Josie, and I wasted so much of it. I wish I could do it over again."

"Now don't call one step of the journey we've made together a waste, Charles Chadwick. I wouldn't trade the healing we've found in each other for anything."

"It will no longer be just the two of us. Now that you've had the baby, promise me you won't forget you were my baby first."

Love shimmered in her luscious eyes, and she kissed him again. "I promise, but don't forget to remind me every so often, especially when I feel fat, ugly, and unlovable after each of our future children are born."

"That's a promise," he said with a grin. "Because my baby will only become more loveable to me every day I get to be with her."

Chapter Forty-Four

harles's breast heaved as he sucked in the tang of rain-washed air. The cleansing water gushed into his eyes and mingled with the tears of his soul as he knelt on the mossy heart of his mother's grave. The words there blurred with the dripping moisture as his fingers caressed the rough lines cut in granite: *Adelaide Corbyn Chadwick. Born 1749— Died 1790.*

Charles clung to the harsh edges of the tombstone as the weight of his guilt-ridden heart threatened to sink beneath the mud. He willed the deluge of pounding rain to wipe away the memory of Bethlem and its roar to drown out the horror no wall of stone could ever hope to muffle.

"Dearest Mama, forgive me," he cried out. "I lost all faith in you, but in my heart the love I bore toward you has refused to die all these years."

The grief congealed hard in his throat, choking back the words, and he pressed his lips against the cold stone. *The care you gave the soul entrusted to you was not in vain, Mama. God in His mercy has exposed the lies, and I know in eternity you have received your just reward.*

Charles rested his head against the stone and caught his breath as her sweet voice echoed through his memory more clearly than he had heard it in years. *I love you, my son . . .*

"Thank You, God," Charles gasped. The knowledge of her forgiveness rippled through his being with the softness of a healing touch, as though his mother had reached down from heaven. She understood that God in His grace had released him from the chains with which Sebastian had bound him. The guilt within him died, and as Charles rose, he knew he had been liberated from his past.

He turned and walked into his future, sensing the pressing weight of Josie's gaze from the carriage. He fought back a grin at the sight of her face squashed against the glass, breath fogging up the pane. She didn't speak when he opened the door, but her eyes swept over him with a tenderness he couldn't have described with a thousand words. He reached for her hand, and as their fingers gripped one another as tightly as their heartstrings, he found the sum of his thoughts.

"The truth set me free, Josie."

"And what is that, beloved?"

"God has redeemed my past as well as my future. And you are the angel Mother asked God to send into my life and free me from myself."

The silence swelled with an emotion too deep for words as Josie laid her head on his shoulder. The coach lurched forward, and the baby's eyes widened with pleasure as he rocked in the crook of his mother's arm.

The motion lulled Josie and the baby to sleep as the minutes lapsed into hours. Charles leaned back with a sigh of satisfaction. All of the past weeks of preparation were complete. He had found a willing buyer for Treathston Heights in Aurelius Haverhill after Aurelia's betrothal to her childhood sweetheart. Charles knew Josie had been disappointed that Chadwick Park should bear a new name as Aurelia's dowry, but she agreed with him that it was all for the best. No doubt Josie was relieved to pass the Chadwick ghost into her cousin's hands.

By the time the rocking ceased, Charles's own head was beginning to nod. His heart bounded in anticipation. His wife and child were home. He tipped Josie's slumped chin to meet his own and kissed her until she stirred.

"We're home, my love."

The twin tidepools of gold-flecked sea sparkled with excitement in her face. Charles scrambled out of the coach, and when she laid a hand on his shoulder, he caught her up into his arms. The baby's deep breathing didn't quicken as he strode up the drive. Josie's soft gasp made every minute of planning well worth it.

"Oh Charles, it's more beautiful than I dreamed," Josie breathed.

"Can you see it, Josie?" Charles exclaimed, sweeping his fingers across the sloping emerald lawn and blue horizon as they approached the brick Elizabethan manor house.

Josie nodded as her lips formed the vision. "Thoroughbreds grazing in the pasture, children playing in the yard, and us walking in the rose garden."

"I'll have a swing built on the stout limb of that oak for Randolph," Charles promised. "Seabrooke is your canvas, angel, and you are my inspiration."

Her smile sent his soul dancing. The white trim and mullioned windows gleamed in the evening light's soft glow as he mounted the steps and knocked.

The new butler swung open the door with a broad grin of welcome. "Welcome to Seabrooke, Mr. and Mrs. Chadwick. I trust you had a pleasant journey."

"We did indeed. Thank you, Blackwell," Josie exclaimed as Charles carried her across the threshold. He knelt down and Josie slid from his lap.

"Charles."

Charles turned at the sound of a voice husky with emotion and met Esther's brimming eyes.

"I dinna suppose I can tell ye just what it means to me to have a place to call my own after all these years, but my heart is so grateful to ye for the chance to have a fresh chapter in life. The cottage is lovely, but most of all it's mine to make new memories in with all my loved ones close by."

On an impulse, Charles cupped the older woman's stunning face in his hands. "Esther, you are the mother of my bride, and there is nothing too great that I can do to honor all the sacrifices your heart has made. So please accept it as gift of gratitude from Josie and me."

Esther blinked back tears as her lips curved in that broad smile characteristic of her. She nodded, and Charles pressed a kiss to her cheek before releasing her.

Josie's eyes were moist as she deposited their son in Esther's open arms and embraced them both. "Oh Mama, God has been so good to us."

"Aye, He is a rewarder of them that diligently seek Him, luve."

"I know you're eager to tour the house, Josie, but I have a surprise for you first," Charles explained.

Her dimple teased the corner of her lips as she laughed. "All right, my love, I'm coming."

He took her hand and led her by the sweeping staircase. Josie's breath tickled his ear. "I heartily approve of our person-able new butler."

Charles chuckled. "He is an improvement on old Craven, is he not?"

They reached the stairwell, and he absorbed Josie's wide-eyed silence as she gaped at the paintings hemming it. She smiled fondly as she gazed up at Suzanne's doe painting nestled among a dozen other finely executed works. "Mr. Pembrooke died, and the executor of his estate was kind enough to sell his art collection with Seabrooke."

"And you were so thoughtful to include Suzanne in it for me. Did you know she painted it the day I told her of our betrothal? Thank you, darling."

"You just wait, Mrs. Chadwick. Your husband is full of surprises."

Charles led Josie down the hallway as the evening light caught the rich, burnished glow of paneled cherry. He gripped the doorknob, and soft light flooded the parlor in a blessing all its own. Josie's eyes sparkled as she took in the warm wine walls, velvet settees, and twin Queen Anne wingback chairs flanking the fireplace, but it was the portrait that hung above the mantle in a gold gilt frame that commanded the gaze of all who entered the room. It was the portrait of Josie, painted during those magical days in Venice. Three-dimensional sea-hued eyes echoed the warmth in the curve of her rosebud lips. The Chadwick heirloom rubies sparkled at her ears and throat, accentuating her milky white skin above a cherry red gown.

Josie cupped his jaw and kissed him until they were both breathless. "It's perfect," she panted.

Charles cradled her face in his hands as his gaze caressed her beloved features. Her eyes were glossy with happiness, her skin glowed rosy with health, and her expression brimmed with the openness of her heart.

His voice was husky when he spoke. "It's gone."

Josie cocked her head at him.

"Signor Rossi told me his brush had captured the shadow of sadness in your eyes. I alone could banish it, he said, and it appears I have succeeded by God's grace."

Tenderness softened the depths of her eyes. "Will she haunt you?"

"No. Every time I gaze into the eyes of the original, I'm reminded just how far we've come, and I know we can never go back after all we've gone through to be together."

Charles pulled her closer as they studied the portrait of the mistress of Seabrooke. He was grateful for the testament to the power of Christ's love . . . a love that redeemed, restored, and never relented. "Never fear, I'm not sorry we commissioned it. Her presence will never let me forget I once took you for granted, but you're not that woman anymore, my angel. The windows of your soul now reflect the openness our hearts share."

"We were both broken. God knew it takes two broken hearts to make a whole."

"You were a reflection of His relentless love for me when I couldn't see that He had never forsaken me. When we were wed, He began knitting the edges of our broken hearts together again until we found healing as one. He atoned for all the dreams that went up in smoke by bringing us beauty for ashes. Sweet Josie, you are the beauty atoning for my ashes."

"Esther has always told me that He is a rewarder of those who diligently seek Him. You are my reward, dearest Charles."

"When I felt worthless, you reminded me that Jesus Christ sacrificed His life to save mine. He calls me Beloved and calls me to love you in an illustration of how He loved the church and gave Himself for it. You are the woman who sacrificed her dream of marrying for love. I am the man who felt unworthy of love from the rejection in my past. In finding each other, we found the Lover of our souls, and because of Jesus Christ we have a united future in His love. For the first time in my life I look forward to what our future holds. I love you with every fiber of my being, every day for the rest of my life and beyond."

"And I you, Charles," Josie murmured. "I am eternally yours."

Warm lips merged as their hearts beat as one, throbbing with the sweetness of shared dreams and desires. Charles drank in the wonder of it all and willed this joy never to fade away.

The End

Contact the Author

I love to hear from my readers! Connect with me on social media to keep up with my latest exploits!

Official Website: http://kaitlincovel.com/
Email: kaitlin@kaitlincovel.com
Facebook: @AuthorKaitlinCovel
Twitter: @kaitlin_covel
Instagram: @kaitlin_covel
Pinterest: @Kait356
Goodreads: Kaitlin Covel